T0354896

Better Days Ahead

Leonard Fiske

Order this book online at www.trafford.com
or email orders@trafford.com

Most Trafford titles are also available at major online book retailers.

Printed in Victoria, BC, Canada.

ISBN: 9781-4251-8597-8

*We at Trafford believe that it is the responsibility of us all, as both individuals
and corporations, to make choices that are environmentally and socially sound.
You, in turn, are supporting this responsible conduct each time you purchase a
Trafford book, or make use of our publishing services. To find out how you are
helping, please visit www.trafford.com/responsiblepublishing.html*

*Our mission is to efficiently provide the world's finest, most comprehensive
book publishing service, enabling every author to experience success.
To find out how to publish your book, your way, and have it available
worldwide, visit us online at www.trafford.com*

Trafford rev. 01/18/2010

 www.trafford.com

North America & international
toll-free: 1 888 232 4444 (USA & Canada)
phone: 250 383 6864 ♦ fax: 812 355 4082 ♦ email: info@trafford.com

I Want to dedicate this book to my Son
Charles Leonard Fiske
He passed away with a massive heart attack.
He was only 64 years old.

CREDITS FOR ALL OF THE PEOPLE THAT GAVE ME THE
COURAGE TO CONTINUE
My wife Winnifred Fiske, Sharon Konkol, all of my family and
friends that would ask, when is the other book coming out.

The first book, "Homestead Days in Montana" was for the period of 1910 to 1963. It took me a long time to do the first section, but I hope this part will go a little faster and maybe a little easier. I have wanted to do this for many years. Being a poor writer with a pencil, I started on the typewriter. This turned out to be such a mess, so when the computers came out it was the answer to my dilemma. Now that I have learned this monster, it makes me feel good about doing this writing. After I got my first computer, I had people tell me that anyone **more than** 40 years old could not learn one of these new fan-dangled things. Now that I am 92 years old, I feel like a kid with a new toy. This portion of the story will be from my days working at the best job one could have to who knows when. There is a power greater then ours that makes these decisions. I don't think that I would like to be making or calling the end. I had a full life for the first 92 years and plan on the next 92 to be just about as full only a little slower at times. Maybe someone else would have to finish it for me.

Just a little review as to where I came from when I wrote the first book, "MONTANA HOMESTEAD DAYS." As I continue, I will not be in Seattle but in Centralia, Washington where I am now. After World War II broke-out I had been working for the Boeing Aircraft Company for three months but I tried to get in the service. I went to the Seabees, a branch of the Navy, because they had jobs like building airports and bridges and they use a lot of heavy equipment but they sent me back to the Boeing Company. They said that I had been with them too long for me to change and they were correct. Boeing got furloughs for me months in advance. That is where I stayed until the War ended.

This was the day to remember as the defense plants were all shut down until farther notice. Working for four years with hardly any time off I took advantage of this and the whole family, my wife, Zelda and our son Charles, packed up the tent and went to a park at Mt. Rainier. We were gone a week and when we got back, I had this call from the

Boeing Company that the government had given them the go ahead on all the planes that were on the assembly lines so they wanted me back to work. As I was someone that knew something about the wing line, they had been trying to get me for several days. They wanted me to come to work the next day on the day shift, I told them I would be there at 8:00 am. Upon arriving, I had the biggest shock of my life. I had been use to going in the plant when it was running 24 hours a day. Today when I walked into the plant, it was dark in most places and there wasn't any noise, it was like walking into a morgue. When I got to my old shop there wasn't anything going on, hardly any lights on. I was met by a foreman that I had seen around there but he was a general foreman at that time now he was a floor foreman. When I started to get my tools out to go to work, he said not to get in a hurry as he would get me some help. After about one half hour, the foreman came with two men, then he said you can get acquainted and I will find someone else to help you with this job.

While the boss was gone, we were standing around talking about where we had worked before and some of that was very interesting. One of these men was a floor foreman in one of the other shops. And the other was from another shop where he had a good job. Each of these men had 15 and 20 years service with the company. It was then that I thought to myself that there is no way I could come out of this without getting bumped out of a job as I had only 4 years service. I had known how the Union works, those with the seniority would get the job and I would be out on the street. When the foreman got back, it was a hard thing to do but I had to tell him that I wanted my leave slip and I told him just why I had to do it. He was very nice about it and gave me a checkout slip. He did say he was sorry that I had felt like that but did understand. I left the plant that day taking all my tools with me and never went back. There is a little more to this story. I ran into this foreman in a store some months later and he told me that he couldn't tell me at the time but I was scheduled to be a floor foreman in a short time.

Now I was unemployed for the first time in four years. It didn't bother me much because I was use to being in this situation many times in the past. The next morning I went looking for a job, nothing the first day. The next day by noon, I had a job with a trucking company that wanted someone that knew some thing about mechanics. This company was going to take several older trucks and make a road truck, by taking the best parts from the broken down ones and making a good unit. That's the kind of work I was looking for but conditions were terrible, outdoors in the mud, that part didn't appeal to me but it was a job. It was about two weeks later that I went to work for the Game Department. I had wanted to get a State job as I had been working for the State of Montana when that job ended and then I came out to Seattle to work for the Boeing Company. I liked the State jobs, not for the salary but for the perks, (it was non-union and a better chance of not getting laid off the job). When working for Boeing I had a carload of passengers and one of them was Mrs. Margaret Condon. Her husband was the business manager for the Game department. As a result of this association, I went to his house one evening and spent about an hour talking with Mr. Condon. The next day I went to their office and made an application for a job. It wasn't the application that got me the job. It was the interview that I had with Mr. Condon and the way I answered his questions. I was honest and truthful about what I could do and what I wanted from the agency, not what the agency could do for me.

It was in the fall of 1945 that I went to work for the greatest agency in State government. This agency was like a large family. It was a self-supporting agency, which didn't receive any tax moneys. It operated on the sale of hunting and fishing licenses. My first job was driving a truck. It was very difficult to get jobs right after the War was over, so many men laid off from the defense plants. This agency wasn't a political one, where you had to donate a sum of money to get a job and to hold it. When I got my job, I was to deliver supplies to the installations in the State. These were the game farms, fish hatcheries, game ranges or moving the State personnel, from one place to the other. Also, moving the Game Warden when they transferred to a different location.

Back to the story telling. It so happened that the Department was very small at that time as many of their employees had been in the War and their jobs would be there when they returned from the service. They

3

had only one hauling truck so that meant that I was there to do the hauling of everything that had to be hauled. It was left up to me to do the best I could. I enjoyed my job so well that I would put in many hours more then was asked of me. I am sure that it was hard on the family that I was gone so much of the time. I took this job and the pay was a monthly paycheck of $97.00 plus $3.00 a day for meals and lodging while on the road. If you don't think it wasn't a let down as I had been taking in about $800.00 a month working for Boeing, in addition to the overtime that I got, and then I worked out at some side jobs whenever I could get them. It wasn't only a month at the starting pay they gave me a raise to $125.00 and then after six months I got another raise to $ 175.00 and they raised the meals and lodging to $5.00 so that helped a lot. On this job there wasn't any overtime paid but you could take off time in place of pay. There were times that I would take off several days at a time when there wasn't any hauling scheduled.

It was about one year and a half that I drove the truck. In that period of time I had several things that happened to me, some were humorous, others were scary and some were just part of the job. The first was when I hadn't been on the job more then a month and I got a note that I was to move one of the personnel from one of the fish hatcheries on the west side of the State to the furthest hatchery in the eastern part of the State. This was part of my job and I had been told about it. This truck was a general hauling vehicle and the cargo box was a standard flat bed sometimes called a stock hauling rack type with ventilation sides. This person was being made a superintendent of this other station. After getting there and starting to load the truck, I was doing the packing the way it should be packed so that the furniture wouldn't get damaged during the move. We had put on about six items when he said to me that you don't know anything about packing furniture. You know, I said that you pack it your way, which he did. After getting it all on the truck, I roped it all down and covered it with a trampoline. The distance that we had to travel was about 350 miles to where we had to unload. We made it and when they started to unload there was mess of broken items and a chair leg had put a hole in the davenport. I felt real bad about his loss but I was told to get down from the truck and he would do the packing. After unloading I had another small load to pickup and then back to Seattle, that took a couple of days. When I got back, the boss called me into the office and wanted to know what had happened, as this superintendent had written to the Department director a letter stating all these things that had been damaged. He also told the Director that I should be fired for this damage and the State should pay him for this damage. I explained to my boss just what took place. Then the next thing I knew was that my boss had written a letter stating that the damage that was done was of his own judgment when he ordered the driver to get off of the truck. This didn't make him one of my friends. We would clash again and again during the next several years.

This next episode was a bad one. I had hauled a load of fish food to one of the hatcheries on the east side of the mountains. As I was getting ready to head home to Seattle there was a call came for me, that I was to go to the Yakima area and haul some live wild elk. So being a good guy I went there and found the person that would know about this hauling job. He informed me that they hadn't trapped the Elk yet but would have them in the morning. This kind of thing was the same for a couple of days and then I thought I had better call my boss and let him know what was going on. When I got him on the phone, it took him about 10 minutes to inform me that he gave the orders and know one else. What was said isn't fit for print; I will leave it at that. You can bet I got the message as to who was the boss. I think it made me think a lot more of my boss for his action. I sure knew where I stood.

It wasn't, but two weeks later that I did get to haul these Elk to a new location. I never did know where that order came from to go now and haul these animals. After I got back to Seattle and found out all the details it meant that I had to have the truck bed reinforced and the box had to have a dark area sides and top so they wouldn't try to jump out. The carpenters fixed the truck, which took a couple of days for that. It was then that I got the hauling slip to go to Yakima and haul them, then bring them over to the west side of the mountains. Every thing was set up with the news writers and a lot of sportsmen that were to go to the site where they were to be unloaded. On the way, I stopped at the Game Wardens home and took him with me up in the mountains where it had been approved for the planting of Elk. This place did at one time have a very large herd of these animals several years back. That is what I had heard and that was maybe twenty years back. It was said that the loggers had killed them all off when there had been large logging operations in that area. There must have been one of those same poachers still living in the area. In a couple of days I had returned with some more Elk and I saw where some one had killed one of the first load already.

When I first started to work driving truck, the boss gave me an order to take some supplies to setup a Game check station just east of Cle Elum, Washington. It was a place in the road divided into two roads one going to the East and the other to the north. I had picked up the tent and everything that went with it from the Warehouse. When I got there, the first thing was that there wasn't a hammer in the kit to drive stakes, so I had to go to town about two miles back to Cle Elum and get a hammer. I was to meet some one there to help put the tent up but as yet, there wasn't any one so I worked there in the wind trying to get this 12 x 12 wall tent to stand up in the wind, what a chore. Soon after I did get it to stand the help did arrive. He wasn't too late as there was a lot to do yet to make it secure for the winds and cold that was to come. This is the time for the Elk season and it is in the middle of November. We had to make a plank counter there to put the clipboards on, as there were several different areas that had to get information from. Most of this was for the biologist to get data to help them manage the Elk herds in this part of the State. All during the hunting season, all hunters had to stop and report the kill or if they didn't get any animals. Also, when the season started we had several people there that put in a shift every day for the next ten days.

The tent would open at about noon each day and close some time around midnight. Later in the evening, the enforcement division would send some of the men in to help. The main thing here is that some of the hunters would wait until after we closed the tent to bring through some of the illegal game. It was discovered that some of these people would wait to come through after we closed the tent so that was where the fun came into play. All of the agents would leave and take a different position on the roads and place a sign on the side of the road that said all cars must stop ½ mile ahead for checking game kills. They would leave a fence gate open for them to pull off the road and a chance to get rid of the illegal game that they may have killed. The agents would be parked out of site and when they would see a car pull off the road they would move in to witness the unloading. When they pulled off the road, it was just the beginning of their troubles for the night. They would be arrested and taken into jail, there most of them posted bail and would have to come back for a trial.

One time after this, my boss and I worked the same area but we were on patrol in the hills. We got word from someone that there was a large camp of hunters that had hound dogs with them and they were using them to run deer and Elk out of the trees. The car that we had to patrol with wasn't equipped to go that far into the hills so we went to Yakima and got the big four-wheel drive truck and we got up there and sure enough, there they were. There wasn't anyone in camp but it wasn't very long and we could hear the dogs baying as the hunters rode horseback into camp with the dogs running wild. They had all been given a ticket and were instructed to pick up the camp and to appear in court that evening. It didn't take long for them to do as they were told. The court was scheduled for seven that evening. When my boss and I arrived for the court, I think all of the towns' people were there to see what was going to happen. We knew after seeing the crowd that we couldn't make a case here. After the judge heard our case, he dismissed the case. You could see that the judge wasn't going against that group of friends.

It is a great relief to be out of the office for a day or two and go do something to help the regular Game Wardens that are out there with a large area to cover. Those of us that go out there have a good time meeting people that are some of the best people in the country. They are the hunters and the fishermen that pay our wages from day to day and month to month and year to year. This is the agency that doesn't get any tax money even if we are State employees. That to me is the real reason that I, for one, enjoy the work. I have said it before we are the happiest group of people that work in State government. I am back, the computer had a senior moment and I thought that I had lost everything but with a stroke of the right keys and all is well.

Then there was another time Mr. Condon went with me on the truck so that he could help handle some of the job. Just out of Longview, Washington, there had been a large amount of fish trapped in some small ponds and we went down there to see if we could get the fish out of the pond before they died. The Department was always looking for this type of feed for the fish hatcheries where we raised fish in ponds at many different locations in the State. There wasn't any of the fish that could be eaten except, there were some small sturgeon that looked like they would be eatable so we took two of these and put them on ice for we had to travel about four hundred miles before we would get home. We kept them in ice and when we got home, I took one and my boss took one. As soon as I got home, I cleaned my fish and was going to have a great fish fry. I made steak out of them and when they started to cook, they stunk up the house so bad that we had to throw them out in garbage. I think it was a week before we could get the smell from the house. These came from the Columbia River that had made this pond and the fish had been in this swap type so long that the cooking came out like you were downwind from this strong odor.

Then the next time when I was just getting started to drive the truck, Mr. Condon would go with me to get out of the office for a day or two at a time. I didn't mind him going with me, as he would help load and unload. He was also interesting to listen to when he told about some of his college days in the State of Washington University in Seattle. As he would tell me that his father was the university Dean for many years. He was a very large man over six feet tall and weighed about 300 lbs. He was also a very conservative person at home and at work. He would let the employees know when they were being wasteful. I was told that a lot of the office people would check out scissors from the supply room and it wasn't long before they were back asking for another issue of the scissors. Then the question was how long ago did you check out these scissors? I don't remember maybe someone took them from my desk. That slowed down the taking of any supplies home. Somehow, the scissors would show up on the desk. It was a rough time the State didn't pay very much and there was a shortage of a lot of things as it was Wartime.

Another part of my job was to take what packages that had to go parcel post. I had to take to the office that was in the Smith Tower down town. I could wrap the packages but had no way of weighing them and getting the stamps put on for mailing. Then there was another job that was a time taking job but someone had to do it good or bad. That was to haul out of this same building bags of Wheat that weighed as much as 150 lbs. per bag. This agency was the Department of Agriculture Grain testing station. They received the small samples in by mail and after they were tested, the grain was put in large burlap grain bags for me to haul out and store in the Warehouse. The Game Department gets this for nothing but we had to haul it out for them. It was good for the Game Department as it helped us at the bird farms when it comes time to feed the pheasants. Back in the 50 the Department had to save everything, they could in order to put more game in the field. That was drilled into us that the more we could put in the field made that more happy hunters.

I am still driving the truck for the Department of Game as I went to work for them September 15, 1945 and now it is about June or July of 1946 doing the same thing. I sure had a good time learning the State of Washington. When I wasn't doing any driving, I was helping in the Warehouse, that way I was getting acquainted with the operation. I said that one time back I would work my way up as I saw the opportunity. Well, this is the way that I saw what was going on here that the old Warehouseman was getting tired of his job. It is now about 1947 and I have been in the Warehouse for a year and a half. It was about 1948 or 1949 that the Game Department purchased property on Fairview Avenue and built a nice four-story building, two floors of Warehouse and two floors of office space. There was also a parking place for the employees on that level. The two floors of the Warehouse were below street level but open to the alley, and then there was a two-door shop on this alley level. I felt that this situation was a very nice with everyone in the same place. Then they asked me to be on the planning board as they were planning on a larger Warehouse and adding a two bay vehicle repair shop. That was good thinking on their part. I had proved to them that I could run a shop and make it pay for itself and save a bundle of money besides. It would be a good place to save money as before all the work was farmed out to some independent shop whenever the repairs had to be done and the cost was high to say the least.

The past year I helped my boss set-up a paper trail that would give a copy of every one of the repairs that were made to any of the State game vehicles. With that, I had a good record of what each of the 200 vehicles was costing the Department. It wasn't to put the independent shops out of business. The shop would do a lot of the fabrication jobs. And, the other was that we would take delivery of all new units and get them serviced and install the special equipment that would be needed. This would work out very well with two good men to do the work. One of these two was very good at fabrication with steel or wood and the other was a good man at several things and one of them was he was a good welder. The first man was a good one to build things like building a new bed on any of the trucks and many other things. The second was good at welding and installing special items to the equipment; he also did the greasing and oil changing on our hauling trucks. Before we moved to the new building, the activities were in several places in Seattle. I had the Warehouse on Yesler and the engineering department had their operation in Georgetown area. The main office was located on the 12th floor of the Smith Tower building. The office moved to this location in 1945 from the Lloyd building. The move was soon after I had gone to work for them. It was a rough job when you had to take everything down elevators and up elevators to the new place working in the alleyways. You had to have someone stay at the truck at all times, if not someone would have the truck unloaded before you got back for another trip. The people that lived in the alleys had a habit of picking up things that weren't nailed down.

This old Warehouseman had been with the Department so long that I think he didn't know just how long he had been with them. He did tell me that he had worked for the Game Department when it wasn't a State agency. Before 1933, each county in the State had their own division that looked out for the wild life and the fish. It was in 1933 that the State established The Washington Department of Game. That included all of the wild animals and all the fresh water lakes and streams that this agency would be responsible for the management and regulation. It was set up with a board of six directors. There were three from the western Washington and the other three were to be from the eastern part of the State. The Governor of the State would appoint some new members to the board. At this point, I am not sure just how this worked. It must have been a good piece of legislation that lasted for about sixty-two years. I think that every new Governor that came on board would try to change the system and give this job to him so that the Agency would have to operate on the money from the general fund. That would give him some power over the agency. As it was set up, the Game Department had their own fund and there couldn't be any monies transferred from this fund for any thing but the Game Department.

This is one of the reasons that I loved to work for this agency. It was run like a business not like a State Department. The agency could not run over the budget because there was no way to get any other monies. The law stated that we had to live within this setup. If the Department would have any money left over at the end of the biennium, that surplus went back into the Game fun, not the general State fund. The Game Department had to be self-supporting. At the time, I went to work for them in 1945 this was one of three agencies that were self-supporting. The other agencies were Parks and the Liquor Departments. I have mentioned it before and I will mention it again, these agency employees were just like a good family they got along well and would help their fellow man any time. This agency had the best longevity in the State. The women had about 12 to 14 years with the agency, the men had 18 to 20 years, and they were very proud of this fact.

Back to the old Warehouseman that was thinking of retiring. So, he told me he had a 1924 Chevrolet touring car that he had been using once in awhile but was always in a garage. It had a good top with side curtains. He wanted $ 100.00 dollars for this car. I sure needed it to go to work with. We had one car and I left that home for my wife to use when I was out of town so much. This old car I thought that it would be just right to park it on the street while I was gone and then I would have a car to get home with when I got back from a trip and would leave the truck in the Warehouse. That would be much better then taking the city bus. I had that car for several months and when I had to leave town for a few days I would leave it on the street. This Warehouse wasn't in the best of neighbors. Across the street was the red light district. There wasn't much activity on the street but I think it started after dark. As I didn't have to work at night, I cared less as to what went on over there. Just so they left me alone I wasn't about to interfere.

When the new Warehouse building was being built, the contractor had some troubles with supplies for the job and was running late. We had to be out of the building at the old location of the Warehouse that we had been renting now before the new building was finished. So, they had to move me into the building with all of the Warehouse supplies. This was an open covered building. There weren't any windows or doors so they had to hire a night watchman to keep the stock from disappearing.

The Game Department hired an unemployed Greyhound bus driver that turned out to be a kleptomaniac. After about a week or two, one of the construction employees came to me and asked if we were missing some ammunition that I had stored on the second floor of the building, thinking that it would be out of sight and out of mind. Also, we had covered it with other boxes so that it wasn't a temptation. I then checked the inventory and found that we were missing several cases of shotgun shells. This hired night watchman had made this construction foreman a great deal on a case of shells, it was less then half of the purchase price for a case. When my boss had found out about it, he took the information to the enforcement department and they set up an undercover situation. They had asked the foreman to tell the night watchman he would take the shells on a given night and we would have several agents there in hiding so that they could see the transaction take place. Then, just as the trade was being made, they stepped out and found that the shells that we were missing were the ones he was offering to this foreman. Needless to say, we took his vehicle and everything in it and he was arrested and taken to jail. Before we took him to jail, we searched the vehicle and found that there were some other items in the car that had been stolen. Some of the items were from the Greyhound bus company.

It must have been about the spring of 1957 that the Warehouseman retired and I took his job. This was a big up grade for me to go from a truck driver to the Warehouse manager. I sure did like the raise that I had got when I moved up the ladder. I had started out at $75.00 a month and payable once a month. I had a couple of small raises while I was driving but when I went into the Warehouse, I think it went up to $200.00 per month. Now that I am stationed in one place and that was in the city all the time so there wasn't any travel allowance. It wasn't but a short time after taking over the Warehouse that I wanted an audit taken to be sure that I wouldn't be accused of stealing any stock so my boss sent in some of the office personnel to take the inventory with me. After that was taken then I could feel safe to go ahead and start to fill orders. One of the things that disturbed me the most was the consuming chore of keeping track of the stock. When I talked to my boss about it, he was all in favor of revising the current system, so I worked up a card system. That way all I had to do then was to take an order after it had been filled, pull the card and delete the amount of the order and then when I got new stock in all I had to do was add to the card. Then there was another flaw. Any of the employees could come in and check out any thing they wanted. It was like some thing free for the taking. I felt that I was some day going to be asked to account for the stock that went out of the Warehouse. I discussed it with my boss and he was in full agreement that this should have some accountable form that needs to be approved by the department that these field people worked for so I could charge that department with what was checked out of the Warehouse.

My boss took it up to the director and it was agreed that some form should be used and when he took it to the division head, they all agreed that we should have a checkout form. The department of game did have a small form that was used in the office supply room for the office personnel to check out office supplies. The boss and I worked that form over so that it could be used for anything that changed hands in the department. It was called the Form 5, it had to be used to get anything from the Warehouse or from the office. Not only was it to be used to get supplies but also it had to have the division approval.

When the above went into effect, I soon found out that I had made some enemies in the Department. Some in the office and some in the field that didn't like all the paper work. It was just a short time, one of the field men came to the office, and when they went home, they stopped at the Warehouse to get their order filled. One of these men came in and started to take what he wanted from the shelves and put in the pickup. I asked where his order was, his remark was I don't need any so, I went to the truck, removed the items, and informed him that was it, he wouldn't get anything until it was handled properly. The other fellows started to pick on him and he got mad and left and never did come in after that. Here was the same person that tried to get me fired when I moved him and he had the damaged furniture that he himself had packed.

I continued trying to upgrade the bookwork in this Warehouse. After I got the card system completed, it saved me about fifty percent of my time. With that savings, I could do other things in the Warehouse. This Warehouse had a very odd lot of supplies, some new, some old and some older then old, that had been saved from the time when the State Game was formed by the legislators in 1933. The State at that time had taken over all of the County Game operations in the State. That is where much of that stuff had come from. Then there are some of the items that were still being used each year. The one that I am thinking about is the fish planting backpack cans that had been handmade so the fish were planted by each planter would carry one of these cans on their back. They could never carry very many fish, as the fish would die if the oxygen ran out in that small amount of water or they would have to change water when the temperature got up over about sixty degrees. At that time, the carrier would find a place along a creek then put new cold water in this backpack to save the fish. What I am saying is that there is a time when some things should be saved. Then in the same breath there was a lot of this junk that had to be there taking up space for so many years that some of it had been eaten almost to the point that you couldn't tell what it started out to be when it was in good shape.

After the saving of time on the entry of stock, I was able to work on some of the extra little things that needed some attention. To me the first thing that I had to give some time to was the old trade-in vehicles. Some of these came in all dirty and some of them were hardly running so when the dealers would come in to bid on these trade-ins they would hardly give more then $20.00 for the unit. All it took to get a lot more for them was to clean them and make some small repairs. Then clean the windows inside and outside. There were several of these that the dealers would go up to $100.00 dollars for the trade-in value. That would add up to a good sum by the time one year had gone by.

A very good example would be when the Department had issued a new Ford pickup to one of the Game farmers that was being used in the Okanogan area. It was there for just a short time when the Department transferred this man and his wife to the West coast. It was about mid-January that they had loaded up their belongings to move to the other job. It was very bad weather and they had to come over the Snoqualmie Pass. It was such a storm that it was hard to see anything and when they didn't make a turn in the road they went over the bank. It had rolled over, end over end and went down in the lake backwards. Being it was nighttime they had the lights on and when the truck had stopped, it was underwater about ten feet but the headlights were shining through the water so that a school bus driver had spotted that light. She got information to the State Patrol, they had contacted a wrecker, and also some divers to get that car out and to see what could be done about the man and his wife. Of course, the man and his wife had died in this wreck. The divers reported that the women had been killed instantly, as there had been a steel bar that was being carried in the bed of the truck had come through the cab and struck the woman in the head. She was still in the cab but the man was some fifty feet farther on down the bank into the water. He wasn't injured but had died by drowning. It was assumed that he had got out or was thrown out and as he tried to get out, he went the wrong way to get back to the road. It was very sad, as they were an older couple being moved so that they didn't have to work in the cold and snowy conditions of Eastern Washington.

This happened a few months after I was promoted to a Warehouseman, from a truck driver. After the truck was taken out of the water, my boss sent me up to the Snoqualmie pass, where the truck had been taken. It was there that we decided to have our lowboy trailer go up there and bring the truck into the Warehouse. There had been considerable damage to the unit but the more I looked the truck over, I felt that it should be fixed, as it was a new vehicle with about 2000 miles on it. I called several body repair shops in to get a price on fixing it up. In those days, we were buying these new pickups for $1500.00. Almost all of the shops came in with bids of over the price of the new purchase price. When I discussed this with my boss I told him that I would get prices for the repair parts that will be needed and I would do the work in my spare time with a little over time as I could do it. After getting the best prices I could find, the total came to $400.00 and the Department gave me the job. It took several months but had it on the road and that truck was later, about five years, sent to the Warehouse to be traded in for a replacement after it had over 100,000 miles on it. I didn't put much over time on the repair because they didn't pay any overtime but I am sure that it got me promoted to a higher job soon after that when I took over the automobile shop and the fabrication part of the shop.

We were just getting settled in at this new Warehouse for the long haul when things changed. In about 1955 there was a lawsuit filed by the Olympia businessmen that all State agencies had to be located in Olympia. This department along with many more had to move out of Seattle and other parts of the State and bring the head office to Olympia. The Department of Game set up a new office in Olympia but that didn't satisfy the directive that had been handed down. As I remember, it was in 1958 that the main office was moved to Olympia. The Warehouse and the shop were left behind. The reason was they didn't have a large enough room for my Department. That was sure a bummer as it cost so much to operate in two different places and so far away from the main office, was also costly.

This left my crew and me in the Seattle office for the next two years while they were looking for a place large enough to house all the Warehouse operation and the mechanical part of our operation that was in Seattle. The Seattle Warehouse and the auto shop were a large operation that worked real well for the whole Department. It was my job to keep the shop busy and to order supplies in the amount that we could deliver the supplies as the trucks was going that way.

The new space needed in Olympia would be about 50,000 sq. feet of space. That is the reason that it took over two years to find the right space. It turned out that the space they got for my division was an old cannery that had been empty for a long time. I think that they purchased this building because they wanted more space in the main building so what happened was they used a large section of it for the Engineering Department. That didn't bother me any as there was still plenty of space for me to put the front section in to the auto and truck repair and also give me room for the fabrication of tankers and the building of some of the hatchery and Game Farm items that would need to be built some place else. Maybe in the local area and that would have been a cost much higher then what I could do the job in Olympia. One of the main reasons was that we were able to get raw stock of steel and wood for half price by getting large orders.

For two years, we stayed in Seattle while the department was looking for and purchasing a large building for the balance of the total Washington Department of Game. It was a trying time for me as I had been in Seattle for nineteen years and I had been paying for a nice house and had it fixed up to what we wanted. During this two-year period, we would take the weekends and go to the Olympia area looking for some place to live when the move did take place. We did discuss what we were going to do was look for some small acreage some place with-in 20 miles of my work.

The department had bought a large old cannery that hadn't been in use for many years and it was close to the office so that made it very good to have all the operation back, together again. Even though it wasn't under the same roof it had its good points also, when it came to making all the noise that a shop and a storeroom forklift and trucks running. Now I didn't have to shut down the operation at any time. We had a lot more storage room, in this building then what we had on the two floors in Seattle.

We did add all the total shop operations in the front of this building by putting in a large hoist for doing the grease jobs and also whenever we had to work on the underside of any unit. Then across the isle, we put in the fabrication part of the operation. This building had very high ceilings and there was a good size room above the main floor. Under that room is where I had fixed up a nice place to have the office, it had enough room that I could have the second desk for the secretary.

I didn't have a secretary all the time but when I did have some special job that had to be done it made it very easy for them to work. This is the first time that I have had a secretary. The lady that the office had sent over to me was a regular in the main office. This came to me with some surprise when she said that she was Seventh-day Adventist. I am sure that she did this to find out if I had any objections. When I told her that didn't make any difference to me as long that it didn't interfere with the workload. I told her it wasn't my faith, she asked if I would like to read a book about the eating pork. I informed her I would read the book so the next day she came with that small book about why you shouldn't eat pork. I took that book home and as I read it, I would look up in my bible and see if the quotations were the same. I found that they did differ in as much that they didn't always quote the total or they took parts and used that when this book was written. After getting it read I took it back to her and told her just what I have mentioned here and she didn't have anything to say but we were good friends ever since. And she would be assigned to me from time to time.

It is now June and we have moved all the supplies from the Seattle location to the Olympia building. The same crew has come with the move and we are ready to give it our best. I have my same Warehouse man, the mechanics are the same ones doing the vehicle repair, and the other was the fabricator of new things that have to be built from iron or wood. This person was good at both. Then I had three truck drivers, one of the drivers was the large semi-hauler and the next was the one that had a double axle truck. That was the one that did most of the fish food hauling and the moving of the personal from one area to another as the transfers of these people came to us. Then we had the smaller truck that was a single that hauled the small orders and the shorter trips. The first driver had three different types and size trailers that he could use to fit the need. A flat bed that was used for hauling hay to the Game Ranges that had to have baled hay hauled in the season to the ranges that had winter-feeding to do for the elk and deer. Then he had the lowboy for hauling heavy equipment, then there was the 6000-gallon fish planting tanker. This was my pride and joy as I had designed this tanker after the need to haul fish for greater distance.

This tanker was needed before we left Seattle where I had got a budget approved to get a surplus tanker so I found that we could get one of the aircraft gasoline semi-tankers. I don't remember what it cost, but wasn't very much for me to run a test on this tanker to see if what I had in mind would work so that we could haul more fish at a time and also for longer distances. I wanted and did put an air pump on this tank. To distribute the air into the bottom of the tank we put four-inch cup grinding stones that were fastened down to the bottom and the small air tubes were fed into the stones from underneath the tank. We also installed overhead aerators over the top of the tank, the same that were used on the small older fish hauling trucks. The most important part of this was the way to load this tanker that sat up about 12 feet from the ground. With the smaller tanks, we loaded them by bucket brigade. There was one man down in the water of the rearing pond that would dip the bucket into the water where the small fish had been crowded up into a small area of about four foot square. He would hand this to the next man and then to the third person that was on the truck. The difference is now, how are we going to load this tanker that is much higher? I lay awake night after night thinking of how to handle this large amount of these small fish that is about six to seven inches long that had to be planted in the streams. I thought about a vacuum system. When I mentioned it to the Supervisor of the fish division he threw up his hands and said this would kill all the little fish. In some of my other things that I had done, I was sure that it would pull the load into the tank. As for the damage to the fish, I would have to test this to be sure that it would work. This supervisor was very good about it but stated that I should be thinking of some other system because he didn't think it would work. His idea was to build an endless chain system that would have small buckets fastened to the chain as the chain would be put into the water and the buckets would pick up the fish somewhat like we were doing it by hand. I gave this some serious thought and was planning on it if the vacuum system didn't work. The endless chain system would be a very bulky and heavy piece of equipment to move around, as compared to the vacuum system. The only thing that I had to do was to make the tank hatches on the top airtight and then add a four-inch coupling to the rear of the tank that would be above the water line. Then put a valve or two in the line where the pump that was already there would pump the water out to create a vacuum on the top of the water, when it reached about 15 inch of vacuum the fish would be sucked up a four-inch hose and into the tank. The procedure would be, the driver of the truck would pull the tanker along side of the pond and fill the tank full of water, then lock down all the hatches and have the hose attached to the fitting at the rear of the tank. Then the operator at the hatchery would put the end in the water where the fish had been crowded up so that it would be almost nothing but fish in this small area. Now we would reverse the water and let the water out of the tank forming a vacuum in the tank.

When the tank had been finished, we took the tank to the nearest fish hatchery to make the test. The supervisor and I went to the hatchery to see if all would go well or as planned. It worked as I had planned. About one minute after the fish started to go up the tube he called a halt to the loading. He asked that we open up the hatch on the top and see if the fish were all dead or not. What a good sight, the little fish were just as happy as they could be swimming around like nothing had happened. I was watching as the loading took place and the man in the pond holding the hose. When that vacuum started to lift the fish, they started to swim away from the end of the hose but there was no getting away. This six thousand gallon tank would haul three thousand pounds of fish. It was later calculated that we could load that load of fish in fifteen to twenty minutes. Then we could also haul them for several hours without stressing them. After using this tank for a couple of seasons, they gave me enough money to have a new and larger tank built. It was on that tank that I had figured that I could improve on this hauling tanker by putting on refrigeration that would give us a greater hauling distance. This would allow the truck to load up fish in eastern Washington then haul them to the western part of the State.

This vacuum loading system that I had put on the tanker was a revolutionary thing and I didn't think in those terms. Soon after, this new tanker was built by one of the largest tank builders in the Northwest. This company was also a large builder of the Septic tank pumps. It wasn't long after our fish tank was built that I saw that the septic pump was using the vacuum system to lift the sludge from the under grown tanks to their tank truck. That is when I realized that I could have patented this, I would have made a bundle of money. It's to late now, so why cry over spilt milk.

Working for the State of Washington Department of game is one of the most rewarding jobs of all jobs. My job as Warehouse supervisor was a very interesting to say the least and not a dull moment. Each day was a new experience. The job consisted of running the Warehouse and the shipping of supplies the mechanic shop and the three truck drivers that had to have their trip scheduled daily so that the shipment would reach the destinations on time. A lot of the hauling was to the fish hatcheries where there they had to haul the food. This consisted of frozen viscera that we had stored in a waterfront frozen food locker. Speaking of this frozen fish food, I remember one time in the winter when I was hauling supplies, I had a load of this frozen viscera on my truck and when I got to the State highway scale house on the other side of the Snoqualmie Pass it was open. When I was weighing in the scale officer said that I was over the weight to go over the Swauk Pass. He informed me that I would have to unload about a third of the load. So, I asked where he would like me to put this material. When I told him it was a load of viscera in frozen blocks, that stopped him for a while and he said what is that? When I told him he said, "I don't want that around here so you can go, but if the scale house on the other side is open don't mention that I let you go." I didn't have to tell anyone any thing, as the station wasn't open. If I had left those viscera there on the ground, it would have made a terrible odor in a short time. Even though we were a State agency, we didn't get away with any thing. Our trucks had to go through the Scale House and be legal with the weight as well as all of the other safety codes.

Now that the Department had grown a lot, we did have larger sales of hunting and fishing licenses, that extra revenue was what we needed to get going with the demand of the sportsmen. That was our first endeavor was to give the sportsman all we could, as this was the only income we had in those days. This agency was one of two, self- supporting agencies that didn't get any hand out from tax money. I recall that after I had made the trip to the Chelan fish hatchery I was sent back to Cle Elum, Washington to haul some material to put up a game check station one mile East of this town where the Scale House was that wasn't going to let me go farther but had a change of mind. This was to get the station setup for the Elk Season that was to begin in a few days. The material that had been sent to the area was to have everything in the truck but when I got the location there wasn't a hammer. I went back to the town to get a hammer and I asked the storekeeper to charge it to the Department. The storekeeper said, "It isn't worth waiting for several months for my money I will give you the hammer." I was going to pay for it but I didn't have that money on me and still have some for a lunch. That struck me as ridiculous that venders had to wait that long when they did business with the State. Later when I got in the office as the purchasing officer I looked into the problem and found that every one of this type of a purchase had to be approved again after the invoice had been submitted and the order had been written then a copy was sent to the field to be verified again. That was the long time that it took to get these vendors paid. I changed the system so that when an employee had been given the authority he signed the sales slip and we would pay on that transaction within three days instead of the three months. This worked out very well for the Department because the vender would give us a discount if paid in ten days.

I was very pleased with how things were going now that I have been in the office for a while and made a few changes to the fastest growing agency. This Department was held back for all the years of the World War II. It was understandable when you think about it, there were a lot more important things that took front row. There were many of the upper echelon and supervisors that went to the War and there wasn't that much time in the day for very many people that were interested in hunting and fishing. There wasn't much money to do any expanding or the personnel to do the work. When I went to work for them it was just a few days after the end of the War. The equipment was in need of a lot of repairs and/or replaced. All of the fleet of vehicles were in very bad shape with over hundred thousand miles on them.

After the main office was moved then I went to the Warehouse and got things lined up for the main job I was hired to do and that was to get fish feed to the hatcheries and game farms. The agency had this old

1940 3-ton Dodge truck that had seen its better days when I came to work. One thing about it, it was slow and would pull any thing that was loaded on it. Because it was so slow, it would take me many hours to make a trip to some of the distant places that I had to go. This truck had a speed of about 35 to 40 miles per hour and I was sure that it would make that speed if there was a tailwind. As long as I am talking about speed there was one time that I was going east down the long grade to go over the Colombia River at Vantage, Washington. The weather was a little cool and the engine was a little cool, I had to shift gears to a lower gear to keep from using the brakes to much, as they would fade out if the drums got to hot. When I let up on the throttle to shift, the engine died and the truck seem to take off like a bullet. I had finely got the engine started and by that time I was able to get in a gear. We were traveling at a good speed down this winding road. It was a good thing there wasn't any traffic coming at me on this two-lane road because I was cutting the corners all I could to keep from going in the ditch or go over the bank. It felt like it had been going about 50 or 60 miles per hour. It was not a good feeling, believe me.

I was coming back from Spokane, Washington late one night after coming down from Snoqualmie Pass and just before I got to North Bend, Washington there was a sign on the side of the road that read all trucks stop at the scales. To me this was rather unusual that the State would be doing that when they had their signs that told the trucker to stop not a sign on the side of the road. When I got closer, I could see that the station was dark and there were men running around from truck to truck checking with large flashlights. As I got up to them, they were the Union bosses checking on the members and giving the non-union drivers a bad time. When they came to me, they gave me a bad time that I was driving for the State. The one comment was they would have every driver in a short time. I had trouble with Unions before when working for Boeing. When working for Boeing during the World War II the Union wanted me to do things that would slow down the production so that they could hold a strike to get better wages. Well I thought we were to give it our best here at home because the men on the front were fighting hard to save this country. Before the War ended I had it up to there with Labor Unions trying to run my life.

Time to get back to the business of writing. My family and I have been on an eleven-acre farm in the Centralia area. We had to move to a place some where in a commuting area of Olympia, Washington where my work was. The agency was located in Seattle for the years of 1933 until a court ruled that all State agencies had to be located in Olympia, the Capitol of Washington. I wanted a small acreage in the Olympia area so that I would be close to my work. It didn't work out that way, as there wasn't much in the Olympia area that looked good to me. Then I branched out and went south of Olympia heading closer to the Centralia area. Zelda had a lot of relatives in that area. It was only three miles from town that I ran on to this place with eleven acres on the old highway, it was run down but that was just what I needed to keep busy and have room for my daughter to have a horse and for me to have a calf to raise for our winter meat. I was raised on a ranch in Montana there we always would butcher every fall and put all kinds of meat away for the long winter that we would have.

This owner was selling on his own so we came to an agreement signed the earnest agreement then we went home to Seattle and put our home up for sale. This was a large home, two stories and a full basement on a corner lot overlooking lake Washington. Being on a corner, I had this place looking like a park. That turned out to be the wrong thing to do. When the real estate office would show the place some of the lookers said we didn't want something that looked like a park and too much work for them. After it was on the market for a few weeks, I took it off and did a little change in the property. The house was located on one of the lots, the other lot was on the corner so all I had to do was remove the front steps, and I installed new ones on the street side that was on the end of the full-length porch that had been glassed in. I then put it up for sale again as the same home for the same money and it sold in three days. It was good but the sale was on government papers and they made me reduce the price by $800.00 dollars. I didn't loose any thing because I had sold the corner lot for $5,000.00 and on a contract at 6% interest. Paid $11,500 for the place in 1950, that looks like a good profit. When I got through with this, there was about $16,000 net. That wasn't all profits, as I had put in a lot of work and expense in the place over the years that we had the place. Now came the waiting period and it was a very long wait of over six months before I got the money so that I could pay for the little farm in Centralia. Had to make several trips to Centralia to try and explain what the hold up was. This man that had the farm had gone out and purchased another place so they were on him for their money. That wasn't the only problem. I was told by the Department of Game that I was to be in the Olympia Warehouse by the first of July 1960. The deal wasn't closed yet and I had to go down to Olympia and batch and sleep in the Warehouse for the next 30 days. It was the first of August that I did get moved, what a relief, when that episode was over.

After getting moved into our new place, there was a lot of work needed as it had been run down badly. The first thing was to put in a good, up to date heating system in the house. The system that we took out was the old oil stove. I think this stove was built in the year of 1920 or maybe earlier. It looked and stunk like it was 100 years old. Then it was the water system that was badly needed. They had a small electric water pump in the basement and the water came from a sand point that had been driven in the garden area behind the house. The sand point was only 30 feet deep in the shallow water that I am sure it wasn't fit to drink. Yet there was a 50 foot deep, good well down in the hay field. I installed a five - hp pump there and dug a ditch for the pipe to bring all the water us ever needed up to the house. Then the next chore, were fences to fix before we had any stock. The barn was deep with manure that had to be hauled out and the corral had to be rebuilt. All this time, I commuted to work in Olympia. With that load, there never was a dull moment. Now that the major things have been repaired, it is time to start living like a farmer. I was born and raised as a farmer. The fact is I thought that I was going to be one, up until I got married. It is amazing how one's life takes sudden change. The first thing I thought was I would need so much more if I were to support a family. I had a long talk with myself regarding what I wanted out of this new life. I came up with the solution. Build up this little farm and keep my job with the State, it has a lot of perks as they say in the government language. Each working day I would drive to Olympia, Washington and return each day.

It didn't take very long when some of the State employees knew that I was driving they wanted rides. I had one lady that worked in our office then I had four from four different agencies. I had a large Cadillac four-door sedan and with the passengers paying me each month for the rides, it paid for all the expenses. There was one time on the way to work at about seven o'clock in the morning one of the ladies got sick and called for a quick stop, she jumped out of the car and ran for the brush. I am sure she made it in time, as there wasn't any odor on her when she got back in the car. One of the best ones was the lady that was always late and she would come running out of her house with some of her cloths in her arm and a piece of toast in her mouth. After she got the toast devoured, she would ask that I turn the rear view mirror and she would finish dressing. This didn't happen once or twice, it was many times. Most of the time the passengers would all sleep all the way to work. The only one that sometimes went to sleep on the drivers shoulder so the driver saw to it that the youngest and the best looking got that front center space. I always had a carload for the rest of my working days at the State of Washington Department of Game.

It seemed like it took forever to get the farm in order. One of the first was to get a calf so that it would eat up the grass and get larger and fatter so we would have our winter meat. We went to a couple of dairy farms and asked if they would save the day old caves that they were selling to people like ourselves that wanted one or two to feed up for butchering. Most of the dairies would save the heifer calf and raise them to fill in the milking herd, as some of their older cows were not producing enough milk to pay for their keep, they would send these old cows to the market. This first year we got one-day-old Holstein bull calf that we brought home and feed it by bottle for a while until he got old enough to graze in the field. Then he did start to grow and got so big that he was hard to handle. Now comes the time to butcher this animal. Here is where we hadn't planned on the next move. Our daughter, Sharon, had made a pet of this calf. She had it named and there was no way she would like to eat her pet but also understood that we couldn't just keep this calf because it was getting larger each day.

We told her that we had to trade this calf for another so that we could have the meat for the winter. I told her a small fib, and I think she did know that wasn't going to happen. Anyway, the calf was butchered and was taken to the freezer plant where they made up all the meat into steaks, roasts and hamburger. This was very good meat and it lasted all winter with some left over for summer.

This little start of raising some stock was only the beginning of the animals that we had on the little farm. Next came a horse that Sharon wanted from the first, but the fences had to be fixed first and also the barn had to have some care like putting some doors in working condition. Then came the cleaning of the stalls and making some repairs to each of them including the mangers had to be made over to feed horses rather the stanchions that had been for cows. After that was finished, everything was in order so that we could have a horse and Sharon had a good friend up the road about half mile that had horses and had been riding from the time they were small. These girls were back and forth and staying overnight from time to time. Well, they had this extra horse that was an old horse that any small child could do anything around him and he would never move if they were in any danger of getting stepped on. He was an older horse and had been trained some time to perform in the ring to the point that the rider wouldn't have to do much of any thing once he got started. The neighbors loaned us that horse for as long as we needed it or until they would have to have him back for some reason or other. These girls were just young girls that loved animals and would like to ride in shows to show off their horses and how they looked, doing all that as show off's. You would be surprised how serious they were and worked very hard with a lot of practice. I thought this was great, some thing like this would give them plenty to do, and I am sure that it kept them from getting into trouble like so many young people do when they don't have enough to do.

Now 1962 my daughter is happy with her horse, her mother wants one now. When you have two women wanting the some thing, I didn't have a ghost of a chance. Looked around for several months until we saw an ad in the paper that a girl in the area had an Arabian mare with a colt at her side. She wanted to sell the mother and we would have to take the colt and care for it until the colt was old enough to be weaned, then she wanted the colt back. When it came time to return the colt, the girl wasn't able to care for this colt now that it was getting like a horse and about time to break it to ride. We had the horse for all these months it seemed like ours any way so we bought this colt. It was to be the one for Zelda and Sharon had the mother horse. It was enough that they had all these horses. I had ended up with the borrowed old horse for myself. I wasn't proud, I took that horse in parades and rode in some shows. I wanted something that had a little more of a challenge and more lively. I didn't have too much money to be putting into these playthings so I kept my ears and eyes open for a sale where someone had to get rid of a good horse. Well I finally did find one that was located in the Bald Hills area outside of Centralia, Washington. He was a good - looking horse, if he had some meat on his bones. He was a young horse but wasn't treated very well and hadn't had enough to eat. I guess I felt sorry for it and bought it for one hundred dollars that was for him to deliver the animal to my place, which he did the next day. After I put this horse in the corral, he looked even worse then he looked the day I saw him. I was so ashamed of that horse that I would let him out in the field where no one would see his condition. I fed him well and he got some meat on the bones then he was put out in the pasture. He was a well-built quarter horse.

It is now the time to put a saddle on him and see just how good he is. I hadn't ridden him before so was not sure what he might do. I was prepared to have him buck but he didn't so I started out of the corral, and that horse wouldn't go past the gate area. He would just back up when I took him up to the gate, several times only to get the same treatment. When Sharon got home from school, I had her take her horse and we would both try to ride out together. No, that didn't work either, then we rode around in the corral for a while and I could see that this young horse wanted to follow the other horse without any problem. That gave me the idea that this horse may have been a trail horse. How right I was, as we were riding around in the corral. Sharon took the lead and we went out that gate like it was the common thing to do. It took weeks and weeks going through that gate until we got that horse trained to go through by himself when someone was riding. I could lead him through but could not ride him and get through that gate. This got to be such a job that I thought about selling him to the glue company. After all that time, he turned out to be a very good horse. Then the next trick was to load the horse in the back of the truck that

I had built a covered box on the truck so we could haul three horses to the shows and also ride the trails. I did get rid of this horse and got a good-looking quarter horse that was a spirited animal. I had put him in one parade and that was a mistake. He went along good while the parade was on the move but when it had to stop that silly horse would turn around and see where he had been. If it hadn't been in a group of horses, I would have put him in his place but quick. He would think twice before pulling that kind of a trick again. I did ride this horse in several 25-mile competition rides. These rides took place up in the hills that went almost straight up at times and then down very steep grades. Part of the trail was over logs and rocks. I would say that this horse sure knew how to put his feet just where he wanted them. I never had him trip or fall from this kind of a train. The entire trip he would prance and dance every step of the way. After the ride, he would be so warm and have foam all over him. It would be about an hour to walk him around to cool him off before I could load him in the truck.

This horse did have a bad stubborn streak in him. I am sure that he had never been loaded into a truck or trailer. I had worked for weeks to train him. It came down to the fact that he wasn't going to go up in that truck. I put the truck in the corral and put some of his oats in the truck so that he would get use to this and it didn't do any good. I think he would starve himself first. As time went by, I had to see that we were going to have to change things so that we would be able to haul this animal to any shows or trail riding. I had seen a rather unheard of way to break a horse of this type of a mind. You could pull all you wanted to and there wasn't a chance of getting him to move. Then one evening I got things all set up to put him in the truck. I got Zelda and Sharon to help me. I got this horse as far as he would go then Zelda and Sharon had a long rope that they laid on the ground and started to move closer to the horse. As they got closer, I could see that he didn't like what was happening, when they got within about ten feet of him he took one long lunge and went into that truck. Now that we knew how to do that, we took him out of the truck and put him in and out about a dozen times. I was sure that this would have had him so trained that there wouldn't be any trouble from this time on. This was still anything but easy to make him load. So, we had to get out the rope again and we went over, all of the same things, for every evening for a week before that dumb animal got it through his head that it was best to do what we wanted. I had no trouble after that.

Now we had a good truck and three horses so one weekend, there was a group of riders going to go to Mt. St. Helens for a ride around Spirit Lake. We had heard that it was a good trail and it would take about four hours of easy riding to making the trip. There was a State park up there that we had a good place to park, load, and unload our horses. There must have been a dozen outfits there that were going to make that trip. Not only was some of our club members there, there were some other people that I hadn't seen before. That didn't bother us at all, the more the merrier. As we were to start to make the trip, we didn't get a quarter of a mile and the Deer flies were so bad that the horses couldn't stand it very long and some of them were even bucking in order to rid of these pesky flies. We had our lunch there at the park where it was in the shade area and the bugs weren't that bad. After lunch, we started to load the horses. Well, you guessed right, that horse of mine would not load. I was up in the truck trying to pull on his bridle and he would not move.

There were some of the other people there that saw what was happening so they took a long rope and came up behind him. When he saw that, he made one lunge from the ground up into the truck. It happened so fast that I didn't get my foot out of the way and his foot hit me in the arch of the foot. I thought that it was broken it hurt so bad. We had some sixty miles to go to get home and this was on a Sunday. We got within a mile of Chehalis and I ran out of gas. There was a gas station not far from where we were but the fence was too high to climb over so I had to walk around that fence to find a phone to call Sharon. She and her boyfriend had gone ahead and were waiting for us at the house. I told them where we were and for them to bring us some gas from the garage. They got there about the time that I got back to the truck with this sore foot and almost unable to walk on it. I think if I had had more then ten feet to go I would have had to crawl the rest of the way. I sold that horse and got out of the riding for good. After that when the girls wanted to go to the horse shows I was able to take them without the hassle of loading that silly horse.

Well, back to the work at hand. I had been commissioned to be able to make arrests and perform any thing else that had been given the enforcement division. All of the office men would be sent out to do enforcement work as was needed when there was a special need to help the field officers. Like the opening day or weekend when so many hunters and /or fishermen would be out in large numbers. I did enjoy that it gave us a break from the office routine. Mr. Condon and I would get assigned to some place in the State and it could be anywhere they, the office, wanted us to go. This one time when the boss and I were working enforcement in the Moses Lake area, there was the most terrifying windstorm that hit the West coast of Washington. This happened on October 12, 1962 but we were over on the east side of the State and didn't know anything about it until breakfast the next morning.

We didn't get to call home very many times because I was making about $125.00 a month so couldn't afford to make these calls. After breakfast, we heard that there had been a terrible windstorm that had hit the State in the southwestern part of the State and had winds in the hurricane force. This had hit down and left destruction in its path. When I called home I had found out that the storm had blown down trees and had destroyed our chicken house, blown down some fences that left a great deal of trash of broken branches a foot deep in the driveway. Both garages had lost shingles and some of the fences were down. Sharon was having a few of her girlfriends in for a slumber party that night. It was early evening when the storm hit the Centralia area. The phones were dead and the power was out so Zelda had a house full of scared girls but it wasn't very long when the girls' folks came to pickup the kids. The next morning Charles had come down from Seattle to help his mother clear the driveway. My boss and I had been released to go home and help there, but when I got home things were somewhat cleaned up. That windstorm has gone down in the Washington weather books as the worst storm we have ever had in the States history.

The next thing I had to do was take count of how much damage was done so that I could report it to the insurance. There were many large trees down and a lot of fences that had to be replaced soon so the stock wouldn't get out. Then the chicken house was a total loss because it been moved from its pillars and had also been twisted in the center. Some time later, I had to build on the barn for storage area for hay. I looked this old chicken house over and made up my mind that I could cut off one end and that part I could move into place to make this hay storage area. I had this old 15/30 model McCormick Deering tractor that I could pull this over to the barn so that is what I did. It was sure much cheaper then building a new one. It was so nice that Sharon, my daughter thought that would be a good place to hold a high school dance before I messed it up by filling it with hay. It wasn't long she had this party going and did they have a ball. I will guess that there were at least 50 kids there. I know that it took Zelda and I busy making sandwiches and keep the cold pop and lemonade on hand. When I would go out there, the noise was so bad that I am sure that all the bugs and spiders left.

It is now about 1965 and there was the time that something else had to be done. The taxes had been going up to the point that I had to make some kind of a change. There were eleven acres of land, we had been playing around with some cattle, and one time Zelda had thought that she would like to raise some day old calves and feed them to sell them as veal when they were about four months old. She had been volunteering at most of the nursing homes and they need veal for their patients. Then I took part of the barn area and built some small spaces to keep the little calves in, because they must be kept from running around in order to have good tender veal. While Zelda was doing that, I was still working at the Department of Game in Olympia, Washington. I was still having a load of passengers that I picked up in the mornings and delivered them home every evening. It was sure a bad job but someone had to do it.

In the summer months it was a large job to keep the grass growing in the pasture. We had a large sprinkler system but the pipes had to be moved almost every day from one place to the other. The main well was in the middle of the 11 acres of land. The main water line was a four-inch that went from the well all the way to the east half of the land and there were two lateral lines that went ninety degrees to the main line and they were five hundred feet long each line with thirty sprinkler heads. These two lines had to be the ones that were moved each day until you had one forth of the pasture watered.

We hadn't been at this place very long when our little daughter was wanting a small dog. So, we went to the small farmer next door. He had a dog kennel and sold several different breeds. We came home with a small white dog that had a brown spot on its back about the size of a silver dollar. She named it Penny. This was a very nice loving thing. She was a cross between a Chihuahua and a short hair terrier. When this dog was old enough, Sharon had her bred to a Chihuahua and when the time came, she had four nice little pups. This was the starting of Sharon getting into the raising of these small dogs.

Most of the girls that had horses would all get together, and then they would ride around the Fords Prairie area from home to home. This lasted for a long time while they were young girls, then when they got to be older their needs changed. Sharon joined the Job's Daughters, and then she started to get a job to keep busy. I think her first job was working at the Dairy Queen ice cream store. She wasn't happy to have this job but she got a job also working in a tack shop in Centralia. That was while she was going to high school. This girl was a workaholic, not only the schoolwork but also two jobs and leader of the Girl Scouts Horse Club in between times. I must say she would never give up. She had a boyfriend by the name of Glen and I am not sure when they got married, but it was after they both had finished school.

Glen & Sharon decided to go to Ellensburg, Washington where they were going to Central Washington College. They had gone over to Ellensburg and found a mobile home they could rent and the next move was to get their furniture and belongings to this small town for them to get educated. I think if there was one thing that had to go was her old pump organ that was about six foot tall. She found one of the "U-Haul" trailers that this organ would fit in and it was large enough to get all the junk they owned in so they towed it with Glen's Jeep. I had an older Cadillac that had a hitch on it so we followed them over and when it was unloaded, I hooked it to the Cadillac and brought the trailer back for them. I couldn't help to discover the high trailer had such a great drag when pulled into a hard headwind. That car had a lot of power but I could not get over forty miles per hour going up the mountain pass bringing the trailer back for them as their school was starting the next day, this would save them a trip. It was sure a good thing that I filled the gas tank before starting home. With that headwind and going uphill, you could see the gas gauge going down as you drove.

Now that we are home and the trailer has been delivered to the rental place, we must take a look at things now that both children are out of the nest. All I can say is we will miss them both very much. Sharon is married and going to school in Ellensburg and Charles is also married and living in Skyway that is just south of Seattle.

This time of life, when we are alone in a large house, it seems that we cannot get use to it yet. Now it is 1963 and found out the oldest grandson has arrived, what a little baby he is but I am sure he will grow up to be a good young man. The kids named him Dale, after his Uncle that was killed on the job with the railroad in Spokane. That was real tragedy for all the family, especially for Zelda, his sister. He was her little boy, as she had to take care of him when he was a baby.

It was in August of that year that we took the normal vacation and went to Montana. This we did every year when we went back to visit all the families. Zelda's family was the closest to western Montana then we would work our way East and South. The first place was her sister Lucille and her family that lived out off Lewiston, Montana about thirty miles north. The little town of Danvers had a population of about three people. It had a large elevator for the farmers to take their grain into storage and for shipping it by rail when the grain was sold. It was an area of small and large wheat farmers.

We being city people now whenever we went to their places they would always have fried chicken right from the farm. They knew that we did enjoy the chicken, when it was fresh, not the store purchased that may have been on the shelf for days or weeks. The men were always busy at this time of year harvesting the wheat before some hailstorm would come along and wipe out a complete crop in just a few minutes. When that happened the whole year's labor and cost went down the tube. That being their only source of an income they had to do without any income for the rest of the year with the hope that next year would be better. There isn't a farmer that takes the largest risk in being able to feed his family for the next year. They live on the leftover from the year before, if there is anything. Most have several different crops that they do get some feed for the cows and horses. That was why they have milk cows and then they have the chickens and all they have to do is keep the hens laying eggs and the cow's milk well. So, things go for the farmer year after year that way. They are the biggest gamblers in the world to just survive.

My bother-in-law and sister-in-law were good farmers with a lot of acres in wheat. They must have had 500 to 1000 acres. They weren't hailed out in this area as often as they did in some of the other areas. One of the times when we took the vacation and our son was only about six years old, he was so interested in every thing, which went on while we were there. There was one time my sister-in-law was getting some chicken for the dinner. These were the large fryers and time to be butchered. She would get two or three of these, take them to the chopping block, and chop off the heads. This was the regular way that was the most humane way to kill the chicken. Our son, Charles, was there watching her do this. So after some time Charles caught some of the little chicks and did the same thing to them only he wasn't that good with the axe and he made a mess. Zelda and I didn't find out about it for many years before we were told and that was so long afterwards that you couldn't have punished him then for what happened when he was so young. Then there was another incident that took place a short time later, and maybe it was this time when he was six. When we first arrived there at Zelda's sisters place, it was in the evening so after dinner Walter, Zelda's brother- in- law, asked Charles if he wanted to sleep in the saddle tonight? Charles being a city kid and also western make believe cowboy was so excited his face lit up and he said that he wanted to. So, they went to the barn and got the saddle and put in on the floor in the front room. That kid was just like he had got a new toy. Yes, he did sleep there that night and several nights while we were there. To this day, he is still an all-western cowboy. He has played guitar, watches western videos and is a great fan of John Wayne.

Back to WorkThe gang, Warehouse man, two truck drivers and two mechanics and I had a lot of work to do in this new place, Olympia. It was an old cannery and it had to be cleaned out and fixed up so that we had a good bay for a shop and then we had to have a hoist put in so we could lift the cars and trucks to service them. One time the drafting engineers sent down a blue print of a large steel work that had to be fabricated in the shop to fit in the fish hatchery. When the shop man took a look at this blue print, he came to my office and showed me that there was a mistake in the sizing. When I took it to the Engineering Department to draw it to their attention, the engineer told me that they didn't make mistakes and said, "You build them as I had put it down." This job was going to be very difficult with that kind of an attitude. This was a large order that took several tons of steel and it took a month to put together. These pieces were something like a short ladder and the lower end was to span an open drain cannel. When the job was finished I had one of the truck drivers haul them to the construction site. The next week when the construction crew started to install these fabricated pieces of steel, they had to send them back to the shop and said that we made the mistake. Well, I thought this would happen so I didn't return the blue prints. You guessed it, the Engineer came down to my office and started to give me a bad time, when I pulled out the original prints they backed down. I had the returned beams unloaded in the shop and we did modify them, which took about a month. As a result of the past action, I had no trouble with them after that, as a matter of fact, they would come down for information from us as what we were able to construct in the shop. We asked them to show them to the shop and they can tell if they were able to do the job with what equipment we had.

The building that they purchased for my operation was a good buy as it was just across the street from the main office and there was plenty of space. The front part of this Warehouse was rebuilt to make one section an automobile and truck service area. After getting every thing out of the Seattle building moved to Olympia then we all got into the act and did most of the remodel. We really put the truck drivers to work for the next couple of weeks and also the mechanics and the Warehouseman. We hauled the large forklift down first so that I would have some thing to unload the trucks with and to relocate the loads as the material came in. Being the boss I took the job at the Olympia station while the rest of the crew did the packing and loading in Seattle. After getting all moved in we had to start making the changes in this building that meant we had to take out some of the internal walls and some concrete machine bases that had been left there when the building was vacated. Some of the internal walls had to be removed then built up to change to fit our operation. One of the things was that the main vehicle service area had to have a large hoist that would handle the large hauling trucks and also it had to be used for automobile serving when we had to grease and change oil in these smaller units.

This job was hired out to the low bidder. They had to break out some old concrete and they had to dig a hole for the hoist main cylinder that went down in the ground about 12 feet. It was very interesting when they got down to the digging I saw that the this building was built on a sand bed fill-in and they had driven piling down then poured the cement floor over these pilings. Now the next thing was to keep the salt water out of this hole when the cement was poured around this cylinder. What the contractors did was to put that cylinder into a waterproof plastic bag that was twice as large as the cylinder. When the cement was poured into that bag there was no way that the salt water could get at the cylinder and start the rust action. I thought it was a great way of doing it. Then there was the chore of taking out some of the concrete bulkheads that we installed for the cannery machinery was mounted on. The Warehouse crew did the work in between time of our regular work. There was a lot of work to be done when you move a Warehouse full of items that it took to make the Department of Game function with in their budget. This would help the sportsman more birds in the field and more fish in the waters of the State. In those days we didn't have the sacred cow to get more money to operate on.

After several months of getting all the stock put away and the mechanics in their stations, now we can focus on getting to the job at hand. I feel proud of the job that we can do and save the Department a lot of money. I made reference to some of the work that our jack-of-all-trades did that saved a great deal on building some of the odd thing that we had to build. If we were to contract this type of work out the bidder not being familiar with the system would only bid very high as not to loose any money.

Then I had the other mechanic that did the service work on the cars and trucks it wasn't very hard to keep him busy al the time. If it wasn't the normal greasing of the trucks, it was the deliveries to the installations that the State had in all parts of the State. After the move to Olympia, we had to make several more loads to be hauled to these installations so I got a couple more trucks and then we had three drivers that were busy. I had built up to the point that we needed three different size truck to do a good job of getting the supplies to the 12 fish hatcheries, 10 Game farms and 7 Game range areas that were scattered out all over the State. There wasn't any special type of a driver to handle these different trucks. They were all good at their job. One drove the tractor-trailer truck and he had three different trailers that he could switch to so that we could haul heavy equipment on the lowboy trailer then he could use the fish planting tanker to haul fish with in the spring. Then we had the flat bed semi trailer that was used for hauling odds and ends.

The job here in Olympia was bit more work for me but they did give me a secretary from time to time as I needed one to do some of the bookwork and the filing. It wasn't that I didn't know how to do these chores it was a need to give me a chance to get some of the purchasing done. Now that we are here in Olympia we are sixty miles from a large share of the stock that we used that we couldn't do anything but go to Seattle to buy and to pickup the items for our stock. To have it shipped or mailed was more expensive then going after the merchandise. The three truck drivers that I had were busy hauling the large loads and the longer hauls. I had a good pickup that I could haul any of the items that I would have to purchase when I was in Seattle. One of the main shopping that I did was at the federal surplus store that was located in the south end of Seattle. As a State agency we had a second choice at the merchandise, as the different things were available. The State schools were the first to go in and shop for and take any thing that they wanted or could use. After they had about a month then we came in to pick out what we could use. After that, I think it was open to the public. A lot of these items that I would get at this surplus were in good shape and could be used for many things. They didn't look good but the were priced right.

Just after the War ended there was a lot of this surplus that was new and we could get it for a small sum. When I was driving a truck during the first of my employment with the Game Department, they had purchased a caterpillar dozer that was in a crate ready to be shipped to where it was needed but the War ended and this wasn't needed any more. This dozer was at the Tacoma depot center so I had the privilege of getting the job of hauling this to the Chelan fish hatchery. I got the hauling papers and went to Tacoma and when they went to load it they had me wait for a while until they could get the crane to load it with. It never entered my head that this machine was crated and it could be started until it was uncrated and the seals were removed. This machine was lifted up by this crane and I had to haul it just the way it was put on the truck. The truck wasn't built to haul this type of equipment but it wasn't the total weight, it was where it was located on the bed of the truck. When I got to one of the State scale houses I was over loaded on the rear tires. They did let me go that way to my destination, as there wasn't anything we could do abut this dilemma. The fun came when I got to the fish hatchery there was only one-way to get this off of the truck. We had no crane to unload with so I had to start taking all the seals off of the dozer and all the straps, parts and crates. Then had to get all the heavy grease off so that I could get the engine started and back it off on a bank that I had planned to do. It wasn't that I had to get back on the road in a hurry. My boss had given me the job of getting this tractor running and working it at the hatchery while the office was looking for someone to hire that was an operator and I was to have some of them come to try it out. I was the one to make the decision as to who got the job, which made me feel like a big shot. After getting this dozer off of the truck, it was planned that I start the digging for a basin that was up the hill from the back of the fish hatchery. This was some rough hard dirt and difficult to make it move. The engineers had surveyed the area that I had to get started to dig this hillside out and push the waste out of the way but not so far away that we had to use this dirt for some on the back fill when the job is finished. Then it was back to hiring someone. It wasn't very long when the new operators were to come out to the hatchery and show me what they knew about running one of these large dozers. It was caterpillar D 4. The running of this machine was what I was doing just before I came to Washington. I had been working for the State of Montana Water Conservation Department during the depression days. I was classified as a heavy equipment operator.

Now that the new Olympia warehouse has been set up to our needs, we can settle down to a normal day. Come to work at 8:00 AM and go home at 4:30 PM by taking off one half hour for lunch. Now, that was a very nice schedule for anyone. I was in charge of six men and one-woman part time. I had mentioned before that I had the two mechanics and three Truck drivers plus the Warehouseman. Most of the materials would come in and stock would come from Olympia now that we are here in Olympia. When we were in Seattle, we were closer to the suppliers so we could haul from their Warehouse to ours, as we needed. We got better prices and we saved on Warehouse space of us. It was a big bummer when we had to move to Olympia away from the large suppliers. The suppliers had to add extra on the orders that had to be delivered, with the extra round trips of 120 plus miles and time to make the trip. It's time to quit crying about the move from Seattle to Olympia and get on with the situation.

My boss, Hal Condon was giving a lot of thought as to when he would retire. With this on his mind, he was giving me a lot more purchasing to do on my own to learn the business. He had told me it was for my own good so I may have a chance to take his job when he did retire. I sure did appreciate the chance to be considered for his job. Of course, he didn't have the say as to who would get the job. That was up to the Department of Personnel. When the time came, I would have to take the test as anyone else would to get the job. I did have an advantage as I had been doing this kind of work for many years. Those years were some good training and it is called the way up, learned by hard knocks.

Mr. Condon and I got along very well and I would put in several hours over what I had needed to do but that didn't bother me I was use to doing several jobs whenever I could get them. I had grown up on a farm in Montana and the day wasn't over until all the days' chores were done. More times then not we worked fourteen to eighteen hours a day seven days a week. The pay was fifty cents a day or $ 15.00 dollars a month when I was working out for some other farmers. At home you felt lucky that you could work off your board and room.

As I have said, the department is now working things from the office here and not anything in Seattle. Now the Department has the nice almost new office building that will have to be sold to the highest bidder. This is where I lost track of what the new owner is ding with the property and I don't care much. I do know that it sure upset a lot of families that worked for the State of Washing Department of Game when we were forced to make this move.

I took a few years to get things in order so that we could have some visitors. The first group was all of Zelda's relatives that lived in the close vicinity of our little farm. There must have been forty of the aunts, uncles, cousins and one of her sisters and their family. We had card tables set up all over the house. This being in the evening we couldn't use the outside so that made this small house seem smaller. I think every one had a good time at the house Warming. After this evening we did go on living and continue to improve the place. As time goes on, the world changes. It seems to be that the taxman is the first to wake you up when it comes to increase the property tax. When I first purchased the place the taxes were $ 50.00 dollars a year. I will admit that was very low for the times. It was about two years and the assessor came to the place and I was home. He stopped in the driveway and stood there in wonderment. At the time I didn't know who he was but when I talked to him, he said that he was out to reassess the place and he took out a picture that had been taken about 10 years ago. It was no wonder the taxes were so low. Then I found out the difference when I got the Statement the next time, the bill was $ 400.00 dollars a year.

With the taxes going up every year, we talked about doing some thing with the property so that it would help to pay the taxes. The first thing I tried was a small rental business. I did some research on this and found that there was a need for lawn and garden power tools and also I had some cement equipment that was what I did. Put up a sign and it wasn't but an hour that some one stopped and was interested in one of the lawn mowers. At the time I had only two mowers that I was using on my lawn. Then I was sure that this venture was going to be all right. The first Saturday evening I went to the auction house and they had several old mowers so I bid on them.

Every one was feeling sorry for me that I needed so many old mowers. Before the night was over I had purchased six. When I got them home they all but one worked very well and the sixth one wasn't too good but I did spend a lot on getting it to run good. Now I am on the way of renting equipment. This venture turned out to be a good one. I had planed doing this for the few years that I had before retirement. In getting started now, it should be doing fine as a job after retirement. This rental thing did turned out to be a great thing for the area. I was very surprised that there was a need like this in this area. The one thing that was to my advantage was that it was on a very heavy used road before the new road, now called I-5 that is in a different location. That one time it was the only road from Seattle to Portland Oregon called the 99 highway. At this point I had about ten years to go before I was to be ready to retire from my job. After a couple of years doing this and it was getting to be more then I wanted. But yet it wasn't good enough to hire someone to run it, so I closed shop only to go in another direction. One thing for sure we had to do something as the taxes were going up beyond my paycheck.

It was just at the right time when I was thinking of doing something else the neighbor to the south of us had his place for sale for a long time so I had the idea that if I could buy that piece of property that would give me five acres more to add to what I had. That would give me a total of sixteen acres to build on. I had thought before that I would like to build a mobile home park. Zelda's cousin was a draftsman for the government and they were down to see us and we got to talking about putting a park in and he thought it would be a good idea. So, we measured the land. It wasn't very long before they came down from Seattle and he had a great drawing of the plot that would give me 109 spaces.

After purchasing this place, it took several months to clean the place up. This place had a barn, chicken house and a rundown house. The fist thing was to get the house ready so that could be rented. Then I started to clear the land of the buildings and take out fences so that we had a clean piece of land to work with. The first thing was to move an old chicken house from the place to the back of the property so it would be out of the way when the construction would start. There was some fun when I went to move this building that was 20 feet wide and 80 feet long. I had an old farm tractor but it was too heavy to move this building. So, the next thing was to cut it in half. The old tractor did move it but it wasn't easy. By this time the house that came with the property was rented and I was getting some money to start the project. I had planned on leaving about 150 feet set back from the roadway. That area was to be for some business some day. I started the layout and measured starting from the set back. The first thing I wanted to do something that I knew hadn't been done, was to place the lots for mobile homes at an angle so that each resident wouldn't be looking directly into the neighbors windows. Then the next thing is to get a permit from the county that didn't take very long so then I had my work cut out for me. Just foe some fun I had asked some contractors to give me a bid on putting the total area of sixteen acres into the mobile home park. They were to put in all of the roads, water, power, and septic tanks and put a carport with storage on each lot. The low bid was $ 120,000.00. That made me a little nervous as I looked at all of that money. I checked with a friend of mine that was in business in Seattle. We went to lunch one day and he told me to not to use my own money but to burrow it.

Of course, I didn't have any money like that, so I would have had some problem of getting a loan of that size. As I told him, I couldn't see doing that. I was sure that I couldn't sleep with that kind of a mortgage. I didn't get the loan but started to build a few at a time and pay for every thing as I built. The other thing was that I was not sure enough as to where are the customers coming from If I did build all of it at the same time, that was a worry also. I had a good idea that I would get people that wee coming into the area to work on the Centralia Steam plant. This plant was just getting started to build to furnish electric from coal. Then my concern was the I might get some homes in then when the plant was finish they would al be moving out of town leaving me with a large mortgage and a lot of empty spaces.

With that behind me now I am going to do the job myself starting with a few at a time and forget about any large mortgage. The first phase of the job was started on the south fence line. This group of 12 spaces that first was to lay it out as to size of each lot and where the power lines were going. After getting the lay out marked then I had to get the power poles put in, one at each lot. That I had to have that contracted as the poles were too have to handle by hand and also the holes were too deep to dig by hand. After getting the electrical supplies I made up all the circuit boxes with all the fittings that went on each pole   Then came the locating of the sewer lines and the building of the septic tank would be placed and how deep and how large of a tank for 12 trailers. I calculated it to be 12 feet square and 6 feet deep. That would give me the right depth to give it the proper slope to the lines to drain correctly. Now the location of this tank was put in the center with six coming from each end of the group.

The building of the tank was very interesting. I dug this hole by hand seven foot deep. It wasn't that hard to dig as the soil was didn't have a single rock or any hard pan. The next step was to pour a bottom slab so that I could build the walls. The walls were concrete building blocks 8" x 8" x 16" That I motored each block in place. After that came the fun part. I had to put a top on this tank with the proper lid and covers, two small lids one on each end of the tank and the center hole so that a person could get into the tank if service was needed. The tank being 6 foot by 8 foot, it took a lot of supports under the form of plywood that I used. There was so many supports in the tank that you could hardly get through do any more work in the tank, not that it would be needed at this point. I had a small cement mixer that we used to complete the tank.

With the tank finished, we started to dig trenches for the water, power cable and water lines. Now is the time to stake out the road and lot lines so that we know where to put the fittings. With this first group of spaces we already have the power poles in so each lot had a pole that the 200 amp circuit. The building of the road was an effort when you didn't have the proper equipment for this type of work. I had an old 19/20 McCormick steel wheels that I thought I could use to make a temporary road. Well that didn't work out at all. There was an old plow that was with the tractor when I bought the farm. I did go out in the park and start to plow the sod but it was too big of a mess. After doing all of that, I was walking down the area and I found several silver dollars that I had turned up with the plow. After that I got to looking around as to where would they have come from when most of them were still shiny. I looked for a while and I found that I had run over a large glass vase with the iron wheels then I had scattered all over the area.

The next day I went to town to see if I could borrow a metal detector to see if I could find more dollars before I had started to do more on the park as I would be laying down a lot of concrete and didn't want to cover up any money. Well, that didn't work out as the metal detector was set up to find steel not silver. One weekend my son and his family came down to see us, and my two grandsons' went with my son and me to see the area where I was going to build. At this time, I was telling the kids that I had picked up a lot of silver dollars out here where I had did the plowing. These kids were about 3and4 year old. They ran all around here and when they came back to us, I happened to look down and there was another dollar. Oh, Grandpa give me that, I said you would have to dig in the dirt to find them. I had a ditch that I had started digging so I told them to dig in the area. After digging a little while, they didn't think that was a good idea because they hadn't found any. When I was using the metal detector and walking around in the field, the neighbor from across the road came over to see what I was looking for.

When I told them what I had found they gave me some information on this finding of silver dollars. There had been some other owners of this property. They were there when the first people had been doing something to the soil and they these people had taken off some $ 800.00 and the next owners had taken off $ 400.00. The story was that the first owner didn't trust the banks in the early 20's and all the wages were paid in cash money, as the story goes this man would bury it in the roots of the trees. After he passed away, the next owner logged off this five acres area and scattered this silver all around in the dirt. After taking the trees down the stumps were blasted out of the ground. That would sure send them flying in every direction.

Now is the time to get back to building the park. As I mentioned, I tried to do the roadwork with my unacquainted old equipment well I gave that up and hired a man with a good grader to build the roads. I think I paid him $ 50.00 dollars an hour. That was the best thing I had ever done. That man knew his job very well. After four hours of work, he had all the sod moved from the roadway, and now it will be ready for the gravel after I get more of the spaces finished. It was September 3, 1969 the first and second renter had come in to the park even though the space wasn't finished but they wanted to be down there away from the road and he offered to help me finish it and some of the others. Then it was September 8, 1969 that I got my second renter that took the number 1 space. From that time on people would see that we had a park and they were coming everyday wanting to get a space. That meant that I had to get busy and finish this first phase of eight spaces. With so many wanting spaces, the next phases were larger numbers and I had to hire more help to put things together. All of these people that I took in on this first phase had to pay $ 35.00 a month, and with that I furnished the water and garbage but they had to pay for the balance of the utilities. Then in 1970, I had to raise the rent to $40.00 a month. Buy 1974 I had to raise the rent to $ 45.00 a month.

This is the most interesting project that I have ventured into. Although I have had other businesses and human race was involved. This was close to every ones family when you have a park like this. Also, this being a family park there was almost every renter that I had, had young children. When you have that type of a facility, you soon have animals that children love. It didn't take long and it happened. Several of the families got dogs, puppy dogs, and from there I had a lot of trouble. The residents was starting to have ill feelings for all the neighbors was trying to keep the pets in the yards. I had so many complains that I had to go to each home and inform them that the dogs had to go but the kids could stay. And that was now not some time down the road. It wasn't more then two days and I didn't have the dog problem any longer. I didn't have any thing against the kids or the dogs. All and all I had a nice group of tenets. I got along with them very well as long as they paid their rent. I was continuing to build more spaces as time went by. Now it was a little easer to build as there was some money coming in.

After having the renters for about four years things were going very smooth and every one is paying their rents, some on time and some a little late but I did get it one way or another. There was one space that a young couple had taken this space and they had a new double home setup on this lot. They had been good about paying every month. They had been there about six months and then this time the payment didn't come on time so I went over to see what was the problem and they had moved out lock stock and barrel. They must have left in the night.

I talked to the neighbors and they didn't know when they had left. It was a few days later and the dealer from Tacoma had called and wanted to know where this couple was that they hadn't paid the payment for two months. He was informed that he would have to pay the monthly rental on the space if the trailer wasn't moved. At that time, he wanted me to sell this trailer for him and he was going to have an open house and try to sell it. That was fine with me, so he had the open house and didn't sell the place so he still wanted to leave the home on the lot and he agreed to pay the space rental. After three months one morning after I had gone to work in Olympia I had a call from Zelda, my wife that the crew was there taking down the home to move it from the lot. I had asked her to go over there and inform him that the home will not be move until the rent has been paid. He was in the door way and when she told him how much the bill was He wrote out the check and through it at her and said that he would cancel it. Zelda called me again and told me what had taken place and the check had been written on an Olympia bank. So she came up to Olympia and I took the check to the bank and asked if there was funds in the bank to cash this check. The funds were there, so we got the money and when we got home the home was gone and I had my money. I f the rent had not been paid and he had the chance to cancel it and the home was gone I would have called the sheriff and reported a stolen home. Well I didn't have to call the sheriff. When he got the Mobile home to his shop, he would want to cancel this check and to his surprise we all ready had the money.

I did have a group of the spaces in different stages of being available for rent. I didn't have rush on them as I did when I first started the project. In place of six I had eight at this phase of building. It was about 1972 I had a salesman stop as I was working in the park and he asked if I would sell the park as it is today. I hesitated for a moment and said no I'm' not ready to sell. He said that he had a buyer in Portland that had sold his auto shop and would be ready to pay cash. He had left and as I got to thinking about it may this is the time to sell. This same salesman came back the second time and I gave him a very high price, thinking it wouldn't sell for a long time with a price that high on the place. I was wrong, this person that had sold his shop took the place if he could move into one of the spaces that wasn't finished. He agreed to finish this space that he wanted. After this buyer got moved in he went to work on finishing this space.

The finishing part was to build the carport. I had all of the rest of the work done on this place. Now it left the other eight spaces that I had to finish and with a move of considerable amount of good old hard to come buy items. We had only 60 days to get rid of this stuff. It was decided that we would take the most of it to the auction that was just up the road from our place. The auctioneer was Milo Fiske (no relative) I had to build a trailer or should I say rebuild the one that I had that was used around the farm and it wasn't fit to go on the highway so I dismantled this old Junker and built and built a good heavy box on the frame. I knew that I would have to do something about moving to Olympia and getting read of all this collection of stuff. If I didn't do this I would have had to rent a trailer. After checking out the fees for the rental I could build a trailer for less money and still have the trailer to do other hauling. This trailer had an eight by twelve box that would haul a large load. It took me two days to get the material delivered to the auction. You wouldn't believe haw hard it was to get rid of so much of this collection that it had taken me thirty years to save this stuff. I think I shed a tear or two about that time. The only reason that it went easier was that we were all ready making plans to move the Olympia area where we had a lot in a park that was set up to be used by the Airstream trailer club, which we were a member of this club.

We had been planning this place for some months. We did have the lot purchased and had intended to use the lot to park our trailer on when ever we came to Olympia to help build this park. Now with the sale of the place we had to get out and buy a Mobile home to put on the lot. We found one here in Olympia. Now we had cash, we paid cash for this home, in the total price delivered and set up on the lot for $ 24,000.00 dollars. This Mobile home was a year old and had been use as a model so we saved about $ 4000.00. After purchasing the home now we had to get the power on at this lot we have in the Airstream Park.

Charles and I went a pole company at Rochester, Washington loaded it on the pickup and hauled it to the lot. Now was the time to dig the hole to place this pole into. To put a 15 foot pole in that hole was a great chore, that pole had to weigh at least 300 pounds. All we could do was roll it around and get it started in the hole then tied ropes to the upper part and then try and pull this pole. When we got the pole in an upright then we had to keep it plumb and put the dirt in all around it and then had to tamp the dirt as a little dirt was put in the hole. That was a full day's work. What I ha left to do was get the electrical box and the cable installed on this pole so we could have power to have the home brought in and set up. This home was a double wide 24 feet by 74 feet long. This home was a two bedroom, double bath and a large front room and a good size dining room with a good kitchen and a family room.

Then back to the ranch as they say in Montana. There was a lot of work to be done at the park in Centralia with only 60 days to be moved out and into this new home. Besides finishing the park and getting the junk hauled away to the auction. I did take week off when it came time to make the final move to this new place were we planed to live for many years after retirement that would be nine months longer to work for the State of Washington. This move was December 15, 1973. There wasn't any time for us to get some place to store Zelda's canned things because this is wintertime and things could freeze and we would have a mess. We had the little Airstream trailer so we filled it with every thing that would freeze. Zelda had her mother here and we were going to have her stay with us, so she could be taken out of the home in Centralia. It was the middle of January that we went and picked up her mother so she could get to see her bedroom and where she would live here with us. Of all things that night it stormed badly and we lost power to the house and there wasn't any heat. Grandma got up in the night and fell in the doorway from her room to ours and she couldn't get up. It was getting daylight by this time and when we got her up it was to cold to stay in the house so I went to the trailer and turned on the propane heater so we could get her dressed and we could take her back to nursing home.

49

There was about two feet of snow some of the roads were closed. We got Grandma back to her old place and she was happy.

When we got back to Olympia there wasn't any power on yet so we too a hotel for the night. It is going to be different now that we live much closer to my work that means that I don't have to get up that early. What I am looking for is the day I can retire. I will have to work for eight months yet. That is the full 30 years of service I have had this job. I loved every day of it. Even this is a State job I worked with the agency that didn't get any tax money to operate on. In place of building the mobile home park I will be starting to build up this place for a long time stay, maybe the last move we will make.

The first thing I will have do is to get the skirting installed before I retire as I plan on taking a long trip as soon as I get the retirement papers so that I can travel. When I bought this RV the Airstream trailer that meant that we would have a place to put our head down when the day was over and it would be the same bed not a different like going to the hotels. The both of us have relatives that span half way across the country. We do plan on staying at each place until they kick us out. I wouldn't be surprised if they wouldn't want us for long time as we will be plugging their power and using their water. I wouldn't do that with out making a good donation for this small amount of usage we would have. As I set in to getting this Mobile home all set up with the yard in the shape that I would like and could live with. Then build a shop so that we could have some storage as well I would have a place to do some woodwork and some mechanical. As soon as that was built we had to put an awning on the back door side of the home. That would also serve as a carport and an area to work on the vehicles when needed. Then we had an awning installed on the other side of the home. This would give us a small patio to have a couple of chairs to lounge in. When I had the concrete poured I hired it done, as I didn't have the time when I was still working and the time to retire was coming up on me very fast. When I came home from work the day that were to pour the first concrete slab, I took look at the job and they had it with the slope to the house so that any water would run under the house. You can bet that this old man came unglued. I got in touch with the contractor in the next two minutes and informed him that this had to be all taken out and it was to be put back the correct way. It didn't take long for the crew was out there and they were busting out all of that slab that was 12' X 30' and 4" deep then they had to haul it away as I didn't want the waste around to only get in the way. They did know that the sooner they could get it out the easer it would be. This concrete was setting up and getting harder by the minute. The next day when I came home the job was done correctly. The next chore was to build a small shop and a place to store things. This was a 10 x 10 that I built myself. There was no problem on this as I had been doing this kind of work for several years.

Now that the outside of the home was taken care of it is time of the year that the outside had to have a lot of work. First was to get some soil hauled in so that we could have a garden like we did when we were on the farm in Centralia but this one had to be considerable smaller. When we were in Centralia we had 16 acres of land and here we have a lot that was 60 foot by 120 foot. The land here is nothing but rock so I had several loads of good soil. With that leveled and some lawn seed planted it was time to work on the sprinkler system. I wanted it so that we could go traveling for several days or weeks and the plants would get water. Also we had neighbors that would have done the watering but I didn't want to depend on some one else to do my chores.

Things are shaping up so that I will be ready to travel the day after I retire. The first Airstream trailer was a little 23-foot single axle. After using this for some time it wasn't the one that I felt was good enough to live in for some long trips. The main reason was that the bed had to be made up each day and the bed taken down each day. It wasn't bad just for a weekend but several months the answer is no way. We went to the dealer in Tacoma and he didn't have any thing so we went Everett to the other dealer and he had one but he was at a trailer show so we went to the show and found this dealer. We then purchased a 28-foot with twin beds in the center and a bath in the rear. The dealer was to do several things to this trailer before we would take delivery. He had given us a week and we were to come and pick it up so we went there and he hadn't done any thing to the unit.

51

This man was some place else and the only one there was a lady that was answering the phone. She called him and he said that every thing would be fixed when I brought it back to him the next week. I wasn't going to leave there with out the trailer so I made up the hitch from his stock and then I traded my new batteries for the no good ones that was in the trailer. After getting it home there wasn't much to be fixed so went ahead and loaded it for a long trip the next day after I would retire. I never did go back to the same dealer. I was convinced that he never did get around to doing the things that he told the customer. After the trailer was loaded we took a small trip to the ocean for a few days and found out that we had put in a lot of things. That was what we call a shake- down trip. There was one other thing that I had to do was put some heavy air lift shocks on the rear of this 1973 Oldsmobile Tornado two door car. What I liked was that it was a front-end drive. Then when I would pull into a camp ground I would be ask how I liked this front wheel drive when pulling the trailer. They would invariably State that it was almost impossible to use as tow car. Then later on down the road I had found out that this car was tested by Oldsmobile, they hooked up one and took the rear wheels off and drove away without any problem. I pulled a trailer with this car all over the U. S. for 150,000 miles with out any major problems. I did have a flat tire on the rear wheel one time down south on a narrow road. So I took up the sway bar and raised the rear of the car just enough to be off of the ground and drove almost 25 miles to a tire service station. It didn't harm the tire as they just took a nail out and I was on the way again. I did have a problem with the heating of the engine. That was expected, as this car wasn't made with the heavy radiator because it was for street and highway driving not for pulling a heavy load. There wasn't much I could do but take it easer on the hills and some times I would have to pull of to the side of the road and let it cool off. Then I heard of a place where I could get a kit to put in a water-injected system. I ordered that and installed it. The first time I had the engine starting to heat up I tuned on this system and the engine cooled down where by I didn't have to stop on the road any more to let it cool off. Then a little later I found out that the water injection did another good thing, when I went to replace the spark plugs there wasn't any carbon on the plugs. The year of 1985, I retired the old Oldsmobile and got a, almost new, Chevrolet Suburban to do the towing.

Every thing seems to be in order now for the day that the Department will give me my party and say good-by. I am ready and will leave the next day. This trip is planned to be about nine months long. We are heading East on I 90 going all the way to Chicago where we will visit one of Zelda's nieces. It's going to take some time before we get that far. The first day out we made it to Lake Easton State Park Where we will stay the night this about a 150-mile trek. I didn't intend to make a lot of miles in a day, after all this is to be retirement time. We didn't have to get up to the alarm clock as I had been doing for the past 50 years. This type of travel will be some new life for us even though we have been a member of the club for four years we didn't get the time off work for any travel but just for a week end and then back to work. As I continue this righting I am going to try to insert what my wife Zelda had written in her journal that she had kept on every trip and mile we traveled. The only thing I will have a hard time reading the writing as she would do a lot of the time would write as we were going down the road. At time that would almost be impossible when some of the roads were very rough, partly because when pulling a trailer you do get somewhat of an extra shake. I am sure that some of those times she didn't write. Then when there was some thing to look at I am sure she took out time again from making any notes.

From here there will be the Journal that my wife had been saving for some reason or another. As I said good luck in reading, if there is some voids it is my problem.

If you see the time has changed it is because I am getting this store ready to publish it soon. This making change is a long time consuming job. If this is boring don't tell any one, try and get in touch with me. Today is the 2005 - October 5th. At 8:00 PM and it is time for bed, Good night.

From her journal- Sept. 4th left Olympia and camped at Easton State Park in the cascades a lovely place. Sept. 5, 1975 parked at Leo Geer's place in Moses Lake, Washington her brother's place and had dinner with them. Sept. 6 Parked at a KOA Park in Idaho in the mountains. Sept. 7 we were in Boulder, Montana. The next day we went to the school where her little brother Claude Geer was for the handicapped. Sept. 8, we camped at the Bozeman Hot Springs. Walter and Charlotte Cline visited with us that evening Then on September 9, we had Gertrude Cooper from the nursing home to our trailer for noon dinner. In the afternoon we had some work done on the car and then we had to go in the pool, as she wanted to test a $ 35.00 swimming suit. We left the next day for Ryegate to stay for couple of weeks with my dad Roy Fiske. Then on Saturday we went to Billings to see Mavis & Carl Burg who were visiting Becky her sister also Dana & Warn Holmes were there and we all had dinner with them. The next day we went to have dinner with Evelyn & Floyd. This is looking good; we get a lot of meals as we move around the country. We were resting at Pops (Zelda would call him) in Ryegate. Ronald came in and we had a good visit in the yard. It was a lovely after noon. Pop made a meat loaf and I fried some eggplant that we didn't like. Then Mary & Gerry came to town in the evening. She didn't say how long the evening was but I am sure, when us kids get together there is much to discuss. From here we went to Lewistown to see Zelda's sister and family, at their farm in the area of Danvers, Montana. When we get in this area there are so many relatives that it will take weeks to go any farther. That is all right with me after all I am retired and no job to go to. Now it is the 16th Of Sept. we arrived at 4:00 PM at Russell and Debbie Sliuka. That was as close to Zelda's sister's place that was up the road about mile but the roads were to rutted and large rocks that was in the way for a low car that I was pulling the trailer with. There was another thing we had to go over a cattle guard that was also built for trucks and tractors. These farmers live 30 miles from any other town and the town of Danvers was just grain elevator and a school. There was a train track that came in the get the grain when it came time the sell or ship out of the area.

After we got the trailer set for living in we had the kids and all come out to greet us. Zelda writes that Jennifer was a sweet, loving little girl that is 4 months old. Lucille and Walter and us went into Lewistown had dinner and met Gerard and pug DeBuff (cousins) and waited for the train to come in from Boulder, Montana that was bring Claude our brother for a visit. It is raining tonight and early morning it is now 12:50 AM the 17th of September a good day. The men, Walter and Leonard were unloading material that had come in to build a shop and a storage area.

Lucille, Debbie (Russell's wife) Claude and I visited, looking at pictures then getting a chicken dinner and all enjoyed the evening. With the rain it prevents the outside work so we all went to Winifred, Montana to see the other brother and his family with a new baby and a new farm for them. Crops were all looking good. Sure hop that this holds out so the kids can get on their feet and start to live as good as expected of farmers' life on the farm can be. A farmer is biggest gambler in the world. There is one thing that makes them keep going is that they are working for them selves they are the boss. September 18, it rained all night and we got ready to move to the next place. We left for Ryegate and it stormed all the way to Harlowton, Montana. We had dinner in Ryegate café saw Helen Bettinger Fox. Then she writes that we saw the twins and David Capenters. How cute they were. Had a good chicken and dumpling dinner then talked with Pop for the evening and read some in my book.

Just another day September 19, 1975 Zelda did the laundry and baked a bread pudding and then some sweet and sour meatballs. Then after dinner she and I went to Harlowton to see some of her cousins Emerald Miller at Polly Riggs place. Emerald is in bad health with cancer, hope and faith sustains her. Had dinner with Polly. Then we visited for a while then we left for home. That is to my dads place where the trailer is that we call home now for some time. We didn't get home until 11:00 PM that is late for us to be out running around. Then the next day we went to dinner at the senior citizens in Ryegate had a very good meal and then met a lot of the old people that we hadn't seen in years. Mary Ellen Williams, Myrtle Bartz and Stella Sterling. Marie & Ronald came home with us then Marie cut and set Zelda's hair but had a very nice visit it is 10:30 PM now will study my Bible lesson and read a little before bed time.

The next day we got up and had our breakfast. While traveling we had a rule that we never did have a breakfast with the people that we were staying with. That way I could sleep in when ever I wanted to. Now it is September 21, went to Evelyn and Floyd's place again. Visited for a while then went out to see Nick, Tex, and Ronald. Ronald and Marie have done beautiful things to the old home place. We did miss the windmill. Ronald, Marie, Evelyn, Floyd, are such nice people. Of course there will never be another Pop like our Pop. Zelda had cooked some steaks for Pop's dinner and prepared for the move to Billings tomorrow morning to where Evelyn lives. Evelyn gave Zelda a lovely Montana agate. I will have it set in a ring. Also a Camilla set - pin and ear rings of Mom Fiske's and agates for Leonard. He also got the coffee grinder, Old lantern and old churn. She gave some 15# or 20 pound of hamburger to Evelyn for the Senior Citizen Saturday noon dinner. We have been on the road for 18 days now and we have covered about 800 miles and visited about 50 relatives so far. Now we are leaving Ryegate and going to Billings Where we may find a valve that is needed on the Airstream trailer. We got a place to park at the KOA; an RV campground that is located on the Yellowstone River This will be the second time we have had to rent a place for the night. This is the way to go until some one says no we can't have you using our power and water. On the complete trip we never did have any one turn us away. Every one was more then happy to have us. The one thing that I would do is help them at their farm work and Zelda would help in the kitchen. While here in Billings we had a couple of my cousins that came down to the park to see us. It was nice to see them and we had a great visit. They were Marie Fredrickson and her sister Katherine Schariff. They had welcomed us Warmly. We are going on to Gillette, Wyoming tomorrow. My wife is saying she is tired of travel all ready, may be new country will help and get more interesting as we go from one place to the next.

September 24, 1975 - Will be leaving Billings in the morning and heading for Gillette. On the way we stopped at the Custer's last stand Of Harden, Montana. She took pictures and sent some historical post cards to Dale, Cary, and Roy. Wyoming proved to be as I had pictured it from Zane Grey's books. Red hills, Mesquite and Cotton wood trees then the Bad Lands are all there. Stayed in the yard of Cleo's mechanic shop. Parked the trailer there and went to there house for dinner then visited for a while then went back trailer for the night but would leave in the morning for Sundance, Wyoming and found there was a KOA so we stayed there to see the Devils Tower. If you haven't seen this it is the most spectacular thing that I have ever seen and it was worth the trip up there to see. They have an 11/2-mile walking path that goes all the way around it. It is one half-mile in diameter and 500 to 600 feet tall. It is a rock formation that the rocks that have fallen down are all in heptagon shape. On the backside of this rock there is, what is left a ladder that some one had built on the side of this shirr mass of stone. There were a lot of birds, animals and wild life there. Hears is where Zelda wants to go home. We came back to the park after having a good salmon dinner at Matea's restaurant lounge. When we got back to the trailer and found a flat tire. We just unhooked the car and went to the tower, didn't see what was wrong in the trailer if any. We found that the door of the refrigerator had come open on the trip today and things were tossed around pretty bad. Frozen meat fell out and broke the door at the bottom. This is the second time in these few days that she writes that she wanted to go home. I don't think that she told me how she felt. Fixed the flat and left camp in a wild wind wanted to visit some sights but storm too bad. Got just two miles from Wall drug, South Dakota and parked for several hours in a rest area as the wind was blowing so hard it wasn't save to be on the road. We had some thing to eat and then went on only to give up at the next KOA park just down the wind was getting to be rough. Hope the wind calms down by morning want to get to Sioux Falls, South Dakota. It is much like western Montana in scenery lot of farms and huge herds of cattle. She writes that she thinks the people are much more friendly then In Wyoming.

Time does fly when you are having fun. It is now September the 27th 1975 and we are now leaving Sioux Falls, South Dakota. Here we parked at another KOA park that was close to the Airstream dealer here and they didn't have the valve that I need. Then the next morning we took out still going east. This day took us through the State of Minnesota We saw a lot of nice farm land with rolling hills, groups of trees. Zelda said it is boring traveling here. Today we camped just before crossing the Mississippi River. We went a rest area and the State Patrol invited us to stay there as there wasn't a camp ground any where close to this area and it was getting late in the day. It was a lovely place with a lot of trees and color being this time of the year. They really had the fall colors, very much like the falls we have in Washington. Here we could identify some of the trees like the Elm, Maple and Oak. We left Minnesota heading to Sparta, Wisconsin where Zelda had an older relative. We didn't have an address for them so when we got in town she went to find a telephone and that was hard to find. The town was an old town with very few businesses. After that hassle she did find the phone but when she got them on the phone they were both to hard of hearing that we didn't get to see them as we wasn't able to make them understand just what was going on.

We got tired of trying to make a connection her in relatives here in Sparta so we went on down to LaFage, Wisconsin. It was a nice drive down covering the central part of Wisconsin. The roads weren't the best. Heading to my cousin Keith and Madeline place that is about 10 miles north of LaFage but it was impossible for me to figure out their road system. I will try and give some kind of a way this worked. They used the township and the range with some other numbers to mark where some would get their mail. With all of that we drove all the way into LaFarge and found out that they were way out in the country. I was able to get close then I called ahead so they would meet me and I would follow them to the house. Then the roads were getting narrower as we got farther south and the bridges also got narrow to the point that they were a one-way traffic on them. They had a very nice place on a hillside and without any place to park the trailer except in the driveway. In order to get the trailer level we had to get a lot of wooden blocks and build up the lower side as I remember it took about a foot and half. After all of that we had a great dinner with the family and few extra. We meet Don and Sally, Harry and Lynda. Zelda said she thought that Sally, Dons wife was very sweet. Keith's wife Madeline was a great skipping rope person and she was good at it as she was selling them for people to use as an exercise system. She sure took it to heart and she was very thin as it was. Zelda bought one but I don't thing she used it very long as I didn't see it around after we got home. Zelda also give some thought to how she felt about some of my family. Up to now we were visiting mostly her family and she hadn't seen these people before. Keith and I had a good visit. She thinks that they are very busy with their own affairs however Keith gave me the impression that he was a big wheel and likes it. I don't know how she came to that thinking. I may have told her about him when we were going to school.

You could find Keith in the book and me out in the field. I was no match for him when it came to the books. Mater of fact we were with in a two-month apart in age, I was the oldest of the clan. Keith was out of grade school three years before I could make it. Then when we were in High school I was just coming in and he was going out. She writes that the boy's seemly successful. I will write to Sally and Don they are to me genuine good couple. I also liked Harry and Lynda very much, my kind of people. The family all came to have dinner at Keith's place and Zelda supplied the Washington grown beef roast. The next day we went to Alberta's to have a dinner. Alberta is another cousin of mien. And what a cook she was. I think that it was all from the farm to the table. After this big dinner some of the crew walked off the dinner to climb a large hill that was on the place. It looked like I didn't go it looked to big for me to waste the time. She also wrote that, I wander why our ancestors left this for Dakota's and Montana.

We had a short trip to go this time when we were to see one of Dad's sisters that lives in Viroqua, Wisconsin. We did wonder around the hills and up and down to get there. We had to have some more directions. At Gathums a lovely young man who graduated from the St Martins College in Lacey studied the map that Keith had given us and kindly directed us to Aunt Blanch's farm. She was alone now and here son-in-law was using the farm to have a milking dairy. What a dairy it was he had that barn so clean that it was better then a lot of homes. This was a lovely place when my uncle was alive and operating this place they had a cheese factory for many years. We thought that this was one of he better places in the area even if it was very old. Zelda said that this is so lovely that she could come and stay for a week. Don is so neat the place is beautiful. Lucille his wife is lovely and Aunt Blanche is just like Minnie, Blanche's mother that lives in Montana.

I want to put down but it is 12:45 and I want to be up in time to see Don do his chores it won't bother him or the cows. We were just about ready to leave and found that there was a flat tire on the trailer. It was a good place to have this flat. I removed the wheel and took it into Spring Green, Wisconsin to get it fixed. After getting it fixed it was late enough that we had lunch with Blanch, and Don and Lucille joined us. They are really very lovely people. Hope to meet them again. We never did get back there again. Now that we have the tire fixed and our lunch it was time to head for Chicago. Even with the late start we got to Chicago at 6:00 PM we arrived at Betty and Ron's place. We had some meat and cabbage balls for dinner and after dinner we had a long visit into the evening. Betty was the daughter of Myrtle & Don Snyder, My brother-in-law and sister-in-law. The next day Betty took us all around Chicago to see the Sears building the largest in Town. Then down along the lake with it's many boats. We then stopped at a Chinese restaurant where we were to meet Ron for lunch He was there and he had a couple of his associates with him. After lunch we walked up State Street in Chicago. It wasn't the best place in town it was very noisy and it was ethnic, disheartening and displeased me. Then we looked at some of the residential areas that Ron was interested in buying. Then in the evening Ron went to his tennis practice so the girls Betty and Zelda had a good visit and talked a lot about Betty's mothers health, Eccentrics maybe this helped Betty to give here a since of mind. Betty is a wonderful girl and she could have been mine. I was wise enough to refuse. The lord works in mysteries ways his wonders to perform. We stayed at their place for several days parked in the driveway. Betty and Ron took us to the Terrace Inn for a dinner. Then again there was also two of Ron's assistance joined us. I had my first taste of snails. The group at the table informed her they were very good eating. You should have seen her eyes when they brought the dish to her with a small pick to get the snail out of the shell. We were sure pampered and were taken to the nice places in town. After this great dinner we went over to the dance area. I don't know haw it happened but I got roped into doing the bump with one of Ron's friends because they were good dancers. Zelda didn't say she got sick from eating those snails but she didn't say she was hungry either.

Now that is Saturday October 4, 1975. Where is the time going? Here it is a month and we are having fun every bit of the way so far. We arrived at our daughters place in Highland, ILL at 5:00 PM and Sharon was there to greet us with a good welcome and a hug or two. Then the next day we tried to find a sewer line so that we could empty the tanks as need. The need was there just now. When we were in Chicago the tanks got filled up so when we were getting ready to leave I was checking over the maps and couldn't find any place discharge the tank. Zelda's niece said she would call the city hall they might know of a place. When she got hold of some one, she was informed that there wasn't any place in this area and then went on to inform her that the trailer that was parked in her drive way was illegal. In one of my travel books there was a place to empty that was about have way to where were going so that would work out just find. To get to this place was somewhat out of the way by about 50 miles. When we got to this place they had trouble with the septic tank and had a machine in there at the time to replace the old one and there wasn't any way that we could have a place to dump the tanks. So when we got to Sharon and Jerry's place I had to do something soon. If you were ever in the area there isn't any bushes to hide so I had to find this sewer line. It didn't take to long to find the line so I cut a hole in that and put in a fitting so that now we have all the services that we needed as we were going to stay with them for a long time but would be living in our trailer. Went to a lake for a picnic lunch. Sharon had taken cold slaw and tossed salad and had some deep fried chicken and had a keg of beer the host and hostess were tavern owners.

We spent the next day getting things set up and tying down the awning and making a small place to sit under this awning. Then we had a hard time getting the trailer level. That country is almost flat but this area had a lot of slope when it comes to level this small trailer. Sharon and Jerry were both working so by the end of the day were snug as a bug ready to stay for two months. Zelda got up early to work out the colt. Seems that it is useless as there isn't any one really interested in him. She filled the water tank and picked Fly eggs off the colt. By the way this area has the most bugs and flying insects that I have ever seen anywhere I have been. The next day we went to Highland to get some service on the car but couldn't find a place. I will have to do some looking around at a later date. First things first. We have tried to find some repair parts for the trailer every place were could find some one that did this kind of work or had any parts so that I could do the job myself. We found that in St. Louis there was a dealer and we went over there and he had every thing that I needed to make the repairs. As we were down town of St Louis we went over to Sharon's office and met here boss and had coffee with them. It was a very nice office and Sharon seems to like the work. Sharon is a good, fast and accurate in here work. On October

9th Zelda wrapped package for her mother and also mailed a package to Livinda. Then did the usual things, cleaned Sharon's house and worked with the colt. After that she did her own house then went to St. Jacob to see the place but there wasn't much to see.

By October the 10th she writes that Leonard is getting restless he and Jerry do not have much in common Leonard talked of moving on he feels we are imposing on Sharon & Jerry. Jerry told me I must keep him busy. Then on the eleventh Jerry and 3 others hauled hay. Leonard, Sharon and Zelda went to town. Zelda said that she didn't spend anything no money, our banks still fouling up our paychecks. At least the Statements are slow coming. Then Dottie, Sharon, Leonard and I went to St. Jacob for an auction. Jerry and Joe went fishing. Joe and Dottie are Jerry's aunt and uncle. On Sunday Jerry and Sharon took us to an auction house they were interesting. Had dinner in Trenton restaurant not good but bad. The next day we didn't have much to do so Zelda put up 24 pints of apple jell for Sharon. It is getting Warm here now the temperature is reading 92 degree. Made some drapes for Sharon's front room and cleaned up the mess then Jerry fried some stakes for us.

The next day I did Sharon's and my laundry, baked some cookies. With all of this going on it got in Jerry's hair, must begin living in our home and let them live in there's. Will start that Monday. Friday we are going to leave for a weekend in Kentucky. Will get the trailer off of the blocks and prepare for this trip we may go and see if there is some sightseeing we could do. Must also take Sharon's tape recorder in for repair. I must realize there lives are there own and we must always be here when needed I have feeling Sharon wants us to stay. But wants us to stay out of the way. Time has passed, it is December 11, perhaps I had expected too much of this visit. We have had some surprising Shocks and some developments that were defiantly unexpected. I am not sure that Sharon knows what she is doing; I know that she wouldn't take advice from me. Jerry may become a man worthy of this world and maybe not. He seems to try but doesn't know how or what to do. He doesn't endeavor to improve himself mentally.

Their friends are all tavern people. Both of the kids are going to the tavern three to four times a week. No food in the house but pool must be played and Jerry has to have his bottle of beer every night or some wine. He must be three sheets to the wind when he goes to bed. He leaves for work late in the morning and Sharon leaves at 7:30 for her job. Jerry feeds the horses at nights but never cleans the barn. Some time feeds and waters the dogs. Neglects necessary work, can't see the work that has to be done. No initiative but spends the money instead of paying the bills. I don't believe Sharon has any to spend and has to account for every penny. I did that to Leonard too. They may make a successful marriage but doubt it. There sure is a great change in the life stile for Sharon. I have made drapes, jelly, cooked, mended, cleaned house, and refinished furniture. For no thanks. I guess that they expect it to be done. The Thanksgiving was the most unsuccessful, so our first Thanks giving at Sharon's home. Friday morning they took off for Jerry's folks in Kentucky when there was 10" of snow that morning. The next day we had a high wind of about 75 mile per hour that broke some windows in the house but the Airstream did OK. Sharon is very dissatisfied with things I do. I do try to stay out of their hair. With a diet of corn and not knowing how to cook Southern dishes and fried corn, etc, I am pretty unpopular. On my birthday the kids went to an office party, so Leonard and I went to see Tammy Wynette also Conway Twity and Loretta Lynn. I was disappointed in all three including the belly dancing. I received a birthday card from Sharon, found it on the kitchen counter. I think it explains something?????.

This week of December we have some Christmas shopping to do then go to St. Louis to see the Gateway to the west, the most fantastic Arches you ever will see. They are built all of stainless steel. We did go up in them and took some pictures from there, what a site. Then to see the oldest old Cathedral, what a beautiful piece of history. These builders had to be craftsmen to do such fine work. Then we went over to the Anheuser Bush Brewery and to see the Clydesdale teams. This is the largest brewery in the world with millions of barrels of beer a day. They have a lot of beautiful parks so I guess that is where some of the money goes to help keep them up. We also saw a lot of slum areas in St Louis. That is why it is the answer to one question of mine, why, does every time one opens their mouth there is a can of beer to fill it. The brewery also makes a lot out of corn, Starch, syrup, oil, and margarine. There is corn and beer everywhere. I am feeling like a hog that is being fatted for market. That's a terrible way for guests to feel and very rude.

Went to Horse Shoe Lake today December 11th to see the Cypress trees that grow in the water and all of the geese that was there. It was a beautiful day. The geese were very large with a wing span of at lest 36 inches. The Cypress grows in shallow water about two to four feet deep. When the water is clear you can see the formation of the root system. These trees have a very delicate lacy foliage in the summer. After the day was closing in on us we started for home by the way of a town by the name of Centralia. We wanted to see what the other same name town looked like because we lived the other Centralia that is in Washington. We walked blocks after driving around town and found a restaurant, called the Green Grill and it was also a tavern we were hungry enough to stay, as the language was very foul. I don't understand Illinois I must have lived a very sheltered life. It was like they had been waiting for us to return because they took off for the tavern 15 minutes after we got home. I am so thankful for having a good family and many friends like Charles, Irene, Dale, Cary, Roy, Aunt Jo, Doris Johnson, Zona & Dick Busselle, Betty and Ron Kowsly and my friends in the garden club. Also Edith Kopa, Peral Johnson, Erma and Millie and all of the other dear members, Edith & Lillian and dear friends from the Washington Land Yacht Harbor. Here is the list of the Harbor friends that we are to meet with Ester, Lavinda, Fred, Stad & Maxine, and Hal & Margaret Condon. With out their letters and phone calls I couldn't have endured. May god forgive whatever error I have made. A lovely Christmas dinner that Sharon had prepared and will have the tree in the morning all of us receiving, mostly their hearts desire. Except me, I wanted to go home. Had a lovely Christmas night at Dottie and Jo's place. They had cookies, fudge, and a punch drink.

I had a feeling that the weather was going to change, so got the trailer all hooked up and I turned it around so that we were headed out of the driveway in the morning. In the morning there was about foot of snow all over the ground. While waiting for breakfast I shoveled out the snow in front of the car as it was up a small grade. I sure didn't want to put on chains just to go twenty feet. We sure had a great breakfast this morning at Sharon and Jerry's specially after all the work to do to get ready to move on. This meal did the trick. From the time we left the yard we were in about 18 inches of snow. It was a bad place just a short distance up the road that we had to go up a rather steep grade to get on the highway. I had to watch the traffic on this road to make sue that I didn't have to stop at the entry or I wouldn't have to been able to get started again. With no cars in site I hit the gas and made it up on to the road with out any problem but had the snow, that hadn't been plowed out, for about fifty miles then the road was good and could make some time. We checked in a KOA park here in West Memphis, Arkansas for the night it was very nice and quiet there and the weather was getting to be a little better. The next morning we started out for Texarkana, Texas it s the December 27th, 1974 we traveled southwest through part of Texas, a small part of Texas the first day. We traveled for all of seven days getting across the State of Texas.

When getting close to Midland we saw a lot of signs and they were telling us that the annual date festival was on and be sure to look us up. We stopped there and had a hard time finding the festival but we did and it was some card tables set up in the mall there. We wanted to purchase some of the dates but they couldn't sell any from them you had to g to one of the outlet stores. That was a bad deal so we left the town with out the dates. I remember that we gassed up and was thinking of staying there for the night but when I saw that the clouds they didn't look good so we drove for several more miles to get over a mountain range and the weather was better so we stayed there for the night. This was a seven daylong trip across the State. We got to El Paso, Texas we stopped in Anthony that is close to the border. After we crossed the border we go into some of the worst roads that we had ever been on. I t was so rough that I was driving at a slow speed to prevent being shaken up and to save the equipment. All at once I saw that the red light was shining in the mirror so I bulled over and got out of the car to see what the police wanted. Just as I was out of the car the policeman waved me on but I saw that there was a small car that was traveling right on my rear bumper some thing I couldn't see in the mirror. I am sure that little car got a ticket. Then December 30th,

1974 we stayed at one of the KAO parks there and then drove down the Organ Pipe Cactus National Monument. We thought that we would stay down there for the night but it didn't look to good so we came back and continue to go on our way west.

Now it is the New Years Eve and we have made it to the fine neighbor place in Yuma, Arizona. We made this meeting long time before we went on this trip so they were waiting for us to show. It was about 4:00 PM when we got there and Mr. Steal was out in the yard watering his lawn and garden. I noticed that he had a lot of tomatoes in his yard and I said to him, " It has been freezing, almost every stop we have made since we left Illinois so I think you should cover the tomatoes". The next morning the garden hose that he had left on the lawn was stiff as a board all the water in it was frozen. After getting set up Mrs. Steal had baked a pie that we had for the evening desert and was it ever good. It was like being home. Then for the New Year we went to see a parade in town with the Steals. The next day we just rested up a little and then we drove around Yuma and decided to move on to the Wind Sand Stars Park just a short distance South of Indo, California. What a nice park with a lot of older people that was down for the winter sunshine. What really made it so nice there was that there were a lot of the same people there that came here from the Land Yacht Harbor where we live. The Condon's welcomed us with a fine dinner in their Airstream trailer Sunday night. I was sick with Colitis for a good three days and then begin to recover gradually to feel better. Then Zelda was commenting on how she feels, as we were getting closer to our friends and closer to home. According to her journal. This is the first of many trips that we took after retiring. We left Olympia September 4th 1974 and it is now a new year January 4, 1975. It sure did feel good to be back with the Airstream friends and others that we have known for many years, like the Condon's, Pinckerton's, Schmelings, and Bogan's. My homesickness has left me, went site seeing every day gathering raisins, dates, grapefruit and played shuffleboard every day. Every body loved me. No longer among strangers it was most beautiful with these people. Then the next day we went up on the tram by our selves. The weather was just great and we never gave it any thought as to where we were going so we were dress like it was summer but when we got to the top there was snow and not that Warm. When we were down at the bottom waiting I was in short sleeves shirt and a lady asked me if we were from Alaska. I had seen some of the people with heavy coats and couldn't believe what I had seen. To me it was Warm all over the area.

There was a large going away party for two families that were going on down the road to see more or maybe they were looking to see what was over on the other side. After the Bogons left we moved into there space for a month. Then the Condon's were given a going away potluck party and they left for home after that and we left the next day for a different. We went up to Desert Hot Springs, where Mavis and Carl Berg is close by at Tamrick Park. While we were in the area we visited my cousin Mavis and her husband several times. They came over to our trailer several times also. This day February 2, 1975 the Bergs came over for spaghetti this day. Then there was times that we went over to their trailed and had waffles for dinner It is just 22 days from today when we start for home I can hardly wait. Charles and family have been so great. Betty Jo and Ron in Chicago great. Have thoroughly enjoyed their kindness and loving care. February 11th 1975 we are in a dull camp. Nothing doing her so we went for a walk out in the desert took some pictures of mountains then walked to the small store and got some milk. Then we took a swim in the pool and played some pool. If I remember this was a camp that had been full of Canadians that have come here for many years so that put us as strangers and they were a little bit bashful to talk to us. You guessed we left this camp and made our way toWards home. Very homesick want only to go home. February 13,1975 - We are still on the road but we are heading for home little by little. Today we went to Pioneer town and to Crist Park up at Yucca Valley. It depicts biblical scenes of the time of Christ. It was very interesting to say the least. At one o'clock had my hair done, then we went over to see Mavis and Carl Burge.

Then on February 14, 1975 we met some of the Airstream folks and took a tour to see the Queen Mary that was used to transport World War one soldiers over the seas. It was a very good display of what was one time as the way to travel. I was a little upset as they had taken out all of the engine room and all of the boilers. It was a nice well cleaned up room that was a large part of the ship when it was in operation. There were 40 passengers on this bus and when we went to a restaurant be for being taken back to our park. With that many people it took forever to get every one taken care of. Zelda writes I guess it was a great day for some. We got on the ship and had a small lunch before the tour started at one o'clock. I know how they make a lot of money as the hamburgers were $ 10.00 dollars and they weren't that big either. I didn't find it that interesting. Didn't get home until 1:00 in the morning. Sunday she took it easy and read the bible for a while then some read some letters. The day was full of wind and sand. Then went to Carl's to ask them to join us to breakfast at Samboos in north Palm Springs. Then on to the Date Festival. Saw a lot of different thinks and then went to Sandy's restaurant in Palm Desert, got home to the trailer at 10:00pm. February 16 a holiday, will wash some clothes and vacuum the trailer. Then went for a drive up one of the many canyons to see a lot of the different colors in the rocks and in the bushes also. The next day we went to a Wally Byam Airstream breakfast, there we met Alf and Suzanne Nordon. The Nordons were members of the same club as we belong to and they lived in the same park here in Olympia, so we ended up joining their club that day. Leonard would want to go into Palm Springs and park on the curb to watch the Cadillac cars that would be going up and down in town. It wasn't that they wanted to show off the car but they were busy going shopping and spending some of their hard earned money. After leaving southern California we headed home the Washington Land Yacht Harbor where we live.

Now that we are home it is time for the honey dew this and honey do that. I am not sure what the male specie would do if they didn't have the good woman keeping us kids in line most of the time. It was December 1973 that we moved from Centralia, Washington to Olympia, Washington, we had purchased the mobile home several months earlier and had a lot of the work done that had to be done before we were to take this trip that had been planned for many months. Even though I had to work nine months yet to get my 30 year's service in for the full retirement pay. We traded in our small first Airstream trailer that we had for one that was a little longer and that had twin beds so that you didn't have to make up the beds every time you used it. This getting up and the first thing make the bed and then get your breakfast was for the birds. We went out to the dealers and didn't find what we wanted until we stopped at the dealer up north of Seattle. .

When I was talking to the person in charge they informed me that the owner was at a RV display about forty miles to the north so we drove up and talked to this dealer and he had one that was just what we were looking for. He had just taken it in on a trade so it looked very bad but there wasn't any thing that couldn't be fixed. We made the deal with him and he was to have two weeks to get the trailer ready and we would pick it up on this given day. When the time had come we drove up to his lot and there was the trailer, he wasn't there and couldn't be found that day. The only thing to do now was make the changes that we had agreed so I changed the batteries and the hitch so that I could get this trailer home to Olympia. I had no choice but to do what I did as I had taken my little trailer with me and wasn't going to male another trip. I might add that this turned out to be a very good trailer and we had put thousands of miles on it. WE had that trailer about ten years.

This is a new chapter in our lives. It is 1979 and I have been voted in as the President for the year in this club of Airstream travel club. I was elected in 1975 and then worked the way up the ladder to become a President. It is a good thing because there is a lot to learn to run a club as large as ours. At this time we had a membership of 1500 trailer. We were the second largest in the world. It was my job to get volunteers to put on one breakfast at each of the weekend rallies. Out of this number of trailers we would get about an average of 100 to 200 trailers and we would feed 200 to 400 people. I discovered that it took a large crew of people to handle that many hungry members. The first lady and I had a lot of work ahead of us if were going to make things better in the club. We got involved as much as we could do and then some at times. This group of people was the greatest.

My first lady and I will now start the year of being the top dogs in the club, if any thing goes wrong it will be on our heads. Just before taking office was surprised to hear one of the members got up and made a Statement that sounded good to me so, this Statement was that we should increase the number of home spaces so that more of the members would have a chance to get a place. After the chair asked the group to take a count of who wanted some thing like that or who was against. When he called for the vote I looked at the numbers and it must have been at least 2/3 of the group wanted us to expand the mobile home park. I, being the up coming President had already head what the members. Now I do have my work cut out for me. When I had my first meeting I did have to do some thing about this expansion so I nominated a feasibility committee of three people and making the out going President Chairman of this committee. I had a very active group; they had come up with a good deal in a short time. The property that is to the south and the east was available. The subdivision owner and contractor was a little short of money and they made us a very good deal on the purchase of the land it we were to consider a price and were would take the deal if his earth moving crew were hired to do all of the leveling and putting in all of the utilities. That meant that he would do the grading, building the roads, installing septic tank, water lines and electric service for one price of $ 10,000.00 per lot.

Now that we had some direction we had to find out how many of the members wanted to put up that kind of money. I appointed a couple that had done some of this kind of work before so the turned out to be a big help for this expansion. (They made it happen.) They sent out a notice to see how many now are interested in this program. At this time we had about 800 members after a group of members started their own units, the first being the Eastern Washington group and then the North Cascade group. The return was about 300 reporting they could be interested in the near future and some were ready to go now. After that survey there was a need for some money to pay for the mailings and the paper so we asked the group of 300 to send in $10.00 dollars for us to get started on the project. Of those we got 100 and that gave us some working money.

The reason for this move was that the club and the powers to be wouldn't let us spend one penny on this expansion. They didn't think it was a good to have more people here in the park. It seemed at the time that I had to hold evening meetings about one or two a week to be sure that things were going as planned. As the program went on every thing was working out very good. Now it was the time to put up or shut up. The owner (Hodges) had come up with the figure of furnishing the property, doing the survey, getting the county permits, laying out the lots. Putting in the roads, water, electric and installing all of the septic tanks. All of this for a sum of $ 10,000.00 per lot. Now we put out a notice to all of the members that they would have to send us their check for this amount and the money would be put in escrow until the job was finished. I believe that 38 had sent in the money but it was more then I expected. The job got started just a short time before I had to go out of office, then the next President, Floyd Steel did a good job of making the working of this expansion to the Washington Land Yacht Harbor. All of these spaces were on the south side of the park. The first lady and I ended our services as of October 1, 1979 what a year it was, and I feel it was a good one so many of the members have said.

Even though we had a lot of good help for the past year, it is a great relief to be free again. The first time I retired from working but now I am retiring from club duties. Now I feel that we can travel a lot more and go to places that we haven't been before. With a daughter in St Jacob, Ill., it meant that we would be traveling back and forth from home to visit there at least once a year or maybe every other year anyway. As time went by the road got longer and longer, until we didn't get to go only once in a while. Our daughter and family were young and had to work like a trooper so that didn't let us have much time with her and her family when we did get there. It was 2800 miles each trip and the same when we came back home. Because of their heavy schedule we would have to sit around in the trailer most of the time while we were there and that isn't any fun or I must say it got old fast when you sit around doing nothing. Soon after getting out of office we got things ready to go to Southern California and Yuma Arizona for the winter.

This next segment will be what Zelda (my first wife) had written in her notebook. I will have to abbreviate some of the places as she had done. Some may not make sense but it is the way she saw it or had put it down at the time.

It is now April 23,1980 and we had been on a long trip east and down South for the winter. On the way home we stopped to visit with one of our greatest friends, Bruce and Martha Roberts that live on the Klamath River in northern California. They have this summer home that is on the river where the fishing of Steelhead (sea run trout) is good. We meet their son and a number of the people that live around there. Leonard fished all day with the aWard of one fish, about a 15 pounder. As we came over the Siskiyou the mountains were covered with sagebrush and other desert vegetation but on down the Klamath River near Crazy horse creek. Now the forest becomes green again and vegetation is profuse however, not so dense. We have had a great visit at the Robert's place and I did get to fish some and Zelda did get to visit with Martha so in the morning we will start for home. We will stop at the Colliers rest area for the night then continue on to Salem the next day. April 24 1980 we left the rest area and stopped for gas and emptying the holding tank in Ashland, Oregon. Zelda made good marks for all of the greener that is in the fields here in Oregon. We didn't find my sister Arlene home so we went on up the road and found a good parking area just off of the road that was a very nice place. The weather is cooler tonight, had rain in the night. She is saying that the weather in this are and in Washington is our kind of weather.

We are getting closer to home but have to stop in Camas, Washington. We will be visiting with my uncle and aunt. Both of them are getting up in years and have to depend on some one to take them to town. After the shopping we got home to Bill and Agnes my Uncle and Aunt then we turned around and went to have dinner back in town. Now it is the morning of April 26th and we are having breakfast with Bill and Agnes in their home. We left there at 9:30am and headed for Kinswa State Park. Found a space with full hookups. Then to our surprise there was Jarvis and Edree Brown there doing some fishing these were from the Land Yacht Harbor the same park that we live in. I did a little fishing in the afternoon with out any luck. But went home to a great meal of pork chops. Will go the fish hatchery to fish again down stream from the hatchery maybe there could be some fish there that close to the hatchery, no it didn't work either, no fish. Then Sunday April 27, at Ike Kinswa now the temperature is at 79 degree unexpected. Leonard spent 6 hours of unsuccessful fishing. Zelda made a good start on the sweater vest she is making for her sister with the extra time she had, vacuumed the trailer and did her nails. Leonard and I walked for an hour to night and on returning the evening was so balmy we put light for the patio awning on the trailer and enjoyed a few more hours of this summer weather. The Browns joined us with a nice visit. Then April 28, 1980 we planned a trip into Mossyrock this morning while there Zelda bought six packages of diaper sweetener for use in the trailer holding tank.

Also, some food items but was disappointed in what was available. We visited some of the other parks in the area then on the 29th I fished and Zelda cleaned the trailer made preparations for the return to Olympia at the Washington Land Yacht Harbor our home place when not traveling. She walked before dinner for half hour and I slept, as wasn't feeling that good maybe not getting any fish had some thing to do with it. Had a light dinner and retired early. April 30, 1980 up fairly early to get thing going as this is the last leg of this long trip of about 15000 miles we are feeling much better this morning. Zelda changed the beds and laid out all the items that must be toted back into the house when we get home. We called to the Browns and left Ike Kinswa Park. Arriving in Centralia, Washington to pickup a box of pheasant eggs from my brother-in-law that runs the State Pheasant farm. These eggs are very good for eating but not for hatching. They candle all of the eggs to determine what eggs are fertile. We arrived in Lacey about 12:00 noon. Had time to have a quick lunch and started the laundry, put all the food away in the refrigerator and freezer. The neighbors welcomed us home, Whitney's and the Carrols. In the evening we went it the Hawks Prairie Inn for dinner and finished the laundry to tired to read or watch TV, just went to bed.

May the first and there are a lot of Airstreams on the Terraport. Zelda finished the laundry and ironing so she went shopping for food. Now she must get prepared to make some thing for a potluck meal at the hall. Then she potted up a lot of plants to be sold at the bazaar. This is one time that we have this money making for the year. She took 12 rhubarb plants sold them for $ 1:00 dollar a plant. 15 tomato plants at $ .50 cents each and a lot of her house plants and this all sold for a total of $ 70.00 dollars from this one booth as there was many others that was working to help the club. May the 2, 1980 Friday there was a board meeting at 10:00am, Leonard had to attend as the past president. The meeting went well and then all the booths were opened up for sales to start. We went out to eat Mexican food with the Butts and Whitney's on the west side of Olympia. Returned home in time to attend the Friday night program it was the rhyme band made up of the members of this unit of Airstream trailers. They were the hillbillies as one has never experienced appeared. Zelda said I should have been with them. Traveling, I can't practice. Have been asked to perform at the St. Helen Rally jointly with Oregon unit in June. Will miss that as our daughter and family will be coming, it has been 5 years since Sharon has been home. We stayed for coffee and cookies and a lot of visiting before going home and to bed. I was very tired.

May the third 1980 Saturday morning up and dressed and waited in line for my pancake breakfast. They didn't seem to be so good. John makes better buckwheat pancakes. Noise very loud, hastened home a few preparations and back to the hall to sell more plants. They were all sold by early afternoon. At 10:00 AM we had the membership meeting, Ruth Steele, Bus and Edna Carrel sat in the front row, also Max and Marion Jordon, all such nice people. Very good meeting. At 5:00pm Leonard and Zelda hoisted a table at the potluck and had as our guest, Mr. & Mrs. Roger Hagg the evening entertainment, a barber shop Quartet, they were great. At the end of the program they always wish those that have had a birthday in the month of the rally were recognized. Leonard and some others that I have forgot who they were had a birthday and the anniversary Zelda and Leonard stood up, as the month of May was our 43rd year of marriage. Now it is midnight and we did get to bed, another rally almost behind us. Now it is the fourth day of May 1980, Sunday and the dedication day of the Washington Land Yacht Harbors expansion of the residential area.

This park is a park for Airstream RV members that would like to have a place to park and live for short period or live here full time. We now have 133 spaces and when the expansion is completed we will have 200 homes. As I was about to take the office president there was a vote on to enlarge this park, it couldn't be done without going through channels. When I saw that the large number of the members was for this expansion so as soon as I took the office I appointed a feasibility committee of three members so I asked Ray Melheart the out going president to chair this committee. It was about two months and they had come back with a good report that we could purchase some land on the south and the east of this park. Now we are on the go except for some of the members that didn't like the idea and would not support it at all, there only reason was that we couldn't use any of the club's money and they meant it. Now that didn't stop us from going ahead by asking the members at large how many would but up the money in escrow to do the expansion.

The next step was to form a committee to take on the job of putting it all together. Roy Wilson and his wife (sorry can't remember her name) but they did a great job. They first had to find out how many of the 1200 members were wanting to get a space here at the Harbor. There was about 600 came back that they were interested. Now we were on the way to making this harbor a nice large place so we didn't have to work the older people to death. This is a volunteer organization. This was run without any hired help. Because we didn't have any money to work with we sent out a request for the interested people asking them to send in a sum of $ 10.00 dollars to be used for postage and permits or some of that kind of an expense. This was a donation that we had wanted so we didn't have to have some single member pay it out of pocket, you couldn't expect some member to pay for all of this with out getting it back by the end.

When this request was sent out, the return was somewhat smaller like only 100 would get first to get their names put in the drawing for the lots when finished. The project did go on and was competed but had to do it in three phases. This Sunday May fourth was the dedication with Eerie Faulk gave the sermon for the church serves and he was marvelous. Then Renwick did give most satisfying preparations also. Zeta Short on a very shot notice did a splendid job with our large choir of 26 participants. We chatted with the people after church then went home to do some gardening before it was time to go to the dedication of the new addition to the LYH (Land yacht Harbor) at 2:00 P.M. Zelda was in her new pink sun hat, my mulberry shirt pale blue and green went to the dedication. Leonard, Roy Wilson, Floyd Steele and Ray Melhart turned the first shovel of soil on the grounds. Does anyone know the efforts and sweat, worry and mental aWareness that has gone into this? Now that the dedication is over it is time for all to buckle down and go to work on this badly needed expansion.

We are very thankful for what has taken place here today. God bless our dedicated members and relieve the hearts of those older dear members who so apposed expansion. May all of the LYH family forget and beam with happiness to forgive and forget and go on loving more and more. I would hope that the older members that did appose would understand that with out them there wouldn't have been this LYH (Land Yacht Harbor). Mat 5, 1980 Today dawned lovely sunshine that awoke me and I staggered from bed to prepare for the day. It is Leonard's birthday and he is 66 years old now. Whitney's and the Harrold's and us went to a Mexican food place for dinner. We had to leave early as we have some more guests coming. They were the Mr. & Mrs. Neil that are friends of Don and Myrtle Synder's who wanted us to sell Amway products.

Leonard always falls for these funny quick money making deals. They came at 8:30 and I felt sorry for the young couple they are trying to make a living selling Amway. No we didn't go for this scheme. Leonard has been in bed since 10:30. I have been catching up on writing in my diary, as I was too busy since Tuesday last week. Tomorrow will be Tuesday May the 6th and it is my mother's birthday, this is Zelda's mother that is in a nursing home in Centralia, Washington. Will I be able to celebrate it with her> its 1:00 PM. My mother doesn't know me but I cut her hair and talk to her, does she know I am anxious for her? Will Leonard go with me tomorrow, yes of course he will. I must go prepared to cut her hair. I would like to take her some ice cream and a flower. May the 6th - Up at seven AM, Leonard out shortly after. Cooked a breakfast of whole grain cereal and dried fruit cooked with the cereal, very good, milk no sugar and a small glass of grapefruit juice and toast raspberry jam and coffee. Leonard had to go to a nominating committee meeting at 10:00 AM. I weeded, transplanted, plants, watered and turned some soil, but I have no cover such as barley or rye to use as a green crop. Charles came by with the keys for his Cadillac that Leonard is working on.

I have managed to finish the replanting in the flowerbeds and watered all. The wisteria seems to be doing very good, must get several bags of Pete moss for the patio flowerbed. Leonard has raised many petunias in the green house and my beds should be showy this summer. The apple trees are doing well. Planted my cabbage plants today, 5 of them. This morning May 7th, 1980, we spread four bales of Pete moss over the flower beds of the front patio, watered it down and more water will be necessary tomorrow Leonard transplanted or replanted 146 petunias for the our open yard space. It will be very pretty. Leonard went to the Harbor committee meeting not too spectacular. Lois Whitney brought me four books to read this morning. Then Clare came by and returned two cubes of butter. Leonard and I walked the Harbor and retired for the night. May 8, 1980, Zelda planted a lot of the garden with vegetables, Leonard and John and several other members repaired the roads in the harbor. John Whitney and Vernie Harrold and I went fishing on the Cowlitz River to fish for Stealhead. They would be leaving at 6:30 so I had to get up at 5:00 and get lunch and coffee made for the fishermen. Zelda said she was very tired tonight but had a good talk with Martha and Bruce this morning, Martha is feeling better. We are planning a big day of fishing, celebrating our 43rd wedding also mothers day on Sunday at Charles place. Charles and I went fishing, Cary sick but went to work. Dale sick and went to bed. Then Irene went to see her Grandmother how has terminal cancer. That left Zelda here on her wedding anniversary looking after sick kids and her husband off fishing. When Irene got home she had a wonderful dinner then Leonard and I came home at 10:00, the weather is cooler.

On May the 13th, 1980 Zelda woke up with a bad sore throat and coughing. She thinks that she got it from the boys (the grandkids). They were sneezing and wheezing on Mothers Day. But the end of the day she was feeling better and said that she would be well tomorrow. Irene's grandmother passed away yesterday. I don't know if we are expected to attend the funeral or a memorial or not? We sure don't get any information from them; maybe we will be sick and can't go. Clare Berg tried to find some sewing material for Zelda but failed, so I guess I'll go shopping in Federal Way. Will cut out a dress tomorrow. Leonard did some repairs on the trailer and is now making a stand for his drill. He is so thrilled with it. Zelda want to walk tonight. Will sneak out when every one sleeps. I can feel at peace and think better and get the world and me back in balance. May 14, 1980 - Still fighting a sore throat, but the garden and yard is looking good and will get pots of mums today. We are getting a rhubarb from Donald until mine is ready for use.

May 16, 1980 - Leonard and I walked the new addition to the Land Yacht. Not feeling good to day. Had a bad night with eye's watering and mattering, sore throat and all my limbs hurt feel worse Leonard is doing all the housework. Mt. St. Helens blew this morning at 8:00am. What devastation. Leonard is being a good nurse going out and got the news of the Harbor and brings it to me. Not feeling very good today.

May 19th 1980 - Felt better this morning. Up early as my back was killing me from spending so much time in bed. The mountain blew again today but only slightly. Will mail the paper to Sharon to read of the volcano. Eyes bad watched TV with closed eyes?

Gertrude Pinkerton called to invite me to conduct the Bible class. I refused. I am not desirous of doing anything for a year or two, as I am still tired from the past year as President and First Lady duties.

We moved to Orting, Washington on a part of the land that our son Charles and Irene had bought on the Puyallup. River. They had bought two ten-acre lots and I put a small mobile home on one of the tracks of land. I had planned on building a stick built home. It was November of 1989 that I had a double by-pass surgery. That made me order a small mobile home, that way I could have a place to live and I could build on the sides of this, which I did. On one side I but on a large single car garage and on the other side I put on a sun porch and had the front entry there as the front door and a deck. After the concrete support runners were installed we had the home delivered. After the home was setup by the dealer then it was the job for me to put the skirting all around the home.

We had moved into the new home and I used the awning on the travel trailer to use as a place to make up the formwork that had to go under the house. The rain didn't seem to ever quit. I put the sawhorses under the awning and made up the skirting in sections then installed them under the home. When the framing was finished then came the treated paneling. All this winter the rain and wind were giving every thing a test of strength. There was one night the winds were very strong that it broke off tops of trees and large branches. We had some land on the roof of the house but we were lucky that the big one didn't hit the house. This storm was one for the book and one top of a tree came from about 100 feet down and hit my Suburban on the right hand door. This top was about 29 feet long with a but-end of 10 inch in diameter. It came straight down and ripped door panel completely off of the truck. Then there was another time when the rain came down so much that the river was raising very fast. This could have been a threat of flooding and our homes would be going down the river. We could hear the fast moving water coming down the river at such force that you could hear the large rocks in the river rolling along with the water. When I say rocks these were the size of a small home.

I went out there at about midnight and could see the dike was about go. Where I stood on the dike I could see large rocks and earth fall off into the river. These chunks were about 100 feet long 10 feet deep and up to 10 feet wide. The dike did break though shortly after I was there and the water did get up to with in five feet of my new home that I hadn't finished yet. As a result of this the county wouldn't fix the dike and some time later there was word out the county was going to condemn the property. All any of us wanted was to have the dike fixed. We went along for a few years and the river didn't flood any more so we thought that the one that did was one that was very rare and we didn't have to worry and maybe the county would fix that dike but they never did. Then in the year of 1994 January 30 my wife, Zelda passed away after 57 year of marriage. I stayed around the house for about six months. On my 80th birthday I went to a dance in Puyallup and found that there was a nice group of people that was there just for dancing. I was sitting around wandering how was I going to get to dance. Then the dance instructor came over and talked me in to going over where the gang had been gathering. I was surprised that this lady was one of the church members in Orting, Washington and this lady was the one that was giving dance lessons down town Puyallup in the evenings. I went down there and took some lessons. That sure helped me a lot as I hadn't danced for about 20 years.

Then I purchased a motor home. I then took off for about a year of travel to visit my relatives. This was a most interesting trip any one could have taken. I had started going to some of the dances here before I left on this trip. Now that I am on the road I would look up dances. At this point I was just keeping myself busy, it wasn't that I was looking for a girl, but several of them thought that because I was single maybe I would have a chance. All that I was doing was getting someone to dance with.

After getting to Sharon's (my daughter's) place, Norm and I would go looking for places to dance. Norm was also single after his wife passed away a couple of days after Zelda passed away. Norm was Sharon's father- in-law. Just before purchasing the Motor Home I had sold the trailer and the tow vehicle to a lady that was about my age. She was from California and I thought that she would buy this unit and go back to where she came from but then she wanted me to show her the way to hookup the trailer and put it at her house. That was when I thought that this poor lady would never be able to handle this rig. Then I found out that she needed this to be able to buy a place in the Land Yacht Harbor. It had been only a few days that she had found out that I could do some carpentry because she wanted the garage inside rebuilt. In place of going back and forth to my place on the Puyallup River, I got my Motor home ready and parked at her house while I was doing this work. She was a very positive type of a person. The first thing that she wanted was the garage floor carpeted then wanted me to build cabinets on most of the outer walls that meant that I would have to but them on top of the carpet. She was the boss so I did as she asked me to do. It wasn't long after I had done that job she called and informed me that the washing machine water line broke and there was water all over the place. I had a carpet cleaner that had a large capacity tank and also a shop vacuum so I put them in the car and did we have fun chasing this water around the room so that it didn't do any more damage then what it had done already. From there I had asked her to go to dances with me then it was going on drives around the country. It was getting to feel like she had found someone that she liked very much and I was getting the same feeling. After being married for 57 years I couldn't think that it would happen again. I did have some reservations, as I was 79 years old. Then I said to my self she is all most my age. But it turned out that she was only about five years younger then me, which I could handle.

I didn't know what I was waiting around for but we got married September 5, 1995 in the evening in her house. There was a party going on for one of the neighbors that was leaving. They had invited us to partake in this party not knowing that we had been planning on getting married this evening and we were going to make the announcement at this party. The party was going rather slowly and we didn't want to tell them until after the cake and ice cream had been served and eaten. The minister was to be at her house at 8 'O'clock which was next door to the party. Earlier in the evening I had packed my suitcase and had it in the trunk of the car so I backed the car in her garage and put her baggage in the car with out any one getting suspicious as to what was going on at this household.

My wife to be had gone to a lot of work fixing up the front room of her house for the wedding. It was by candlelight and she had one end of the room fixed up with flowers on both sides of the place where the Bishop was going to stand while he did his duties under the light of the candles. At the last minute we had to change the front setting because the bishop had to read the ceremony and couldn't do it in any other way. While they were doing all of that we were a little late getting married and I hadn't thought about it until some time later there was a chance to get out of the marriage. That didn't stop us from going through with this chore. Right after the wedding we had planned on going to Seattle air port to get a hotel then go on our honeymoon from there. The next morning we left to go on a long honeymoon. Left the airport headed north to Canada then on to Banff there we turned around and came down into Montana to the east of Glacier park and stopped at all of my relatives on the way.

This wasn't the last of this honeymoon as we went east to where my daughter and her family live. Now we turned around and headed back to the West coast to start a life in Olympia Washington. Now what is this old couple going to do from here out. It didn't take long to figure out when we sat down and took an inventory. She had two houses and a car and the Airstream trailer. Then I had a house that was full of 54 years of accumulation, two cars, a Motor home, Lawn tractors. I went to an Auction house and they came and relieved me of most all of the things that I had in the house and the yard. It was like giving away part of your life, not getting anything for most of it. This is June the third 2004. It seem that I have trouble getting time to write lately

As we go and do our daily chores and nightly duties we continue to keep going another day. My life is getting shorter each minute as it is for all of us; I am now past the 90 years old but still going, not so fast but getting there day by day. The one thing that I always try to do is keep busy, just some thing different then sitting around twitting you thumbs. I do have some yard work to do gland that gets me out of the rocking chair day after day, or do some repairs to the house or maybe the cars, what ever works is what I like.

Back to the story of my life and a few other people that I mention from time to time. As we turn the pages of the calendar it is now July 2004. My wife and I are getting up in years as they say. It seems that if we don't have a doctor's appointment it is going to some ones funeral. I will now move on to the time after we got married that was in September 1994. After getting settled in for a long grind. After a few months we got into the traveling again and we started to trade Motor homes until we found the one we both liked and we still have that 1995 Airstream class "A" 33 foot long. It had 5000 miles on it when we purchased it and now we have 45,000. We also have slowed down on the travels. One of the first long trips was to go up into Canada then into the Yukon for a lot of miles then over to Alaska. Now I am working on inserting some writing that I have done on the laptop that I carry with me when we travel and what we did on that trip. Then I have a journal about a trip to England by airplane and then I rented a car to travel in England. The thing that makes this fascinating is we both kept a separate daily report as to what we did and what we didn't do. After we got back home I took these books and put in the form of, She Said and He said, for the

10 days we were over there. I plan on including other writing to this document. If I can get it to work?

I installed an upgrade to my computer and the other night, I thought that I had lost everything when I couldn't get to this point after the upgrade. I can't write, what I was thinking by this time. I am still trying to get some of my work up and running. It is somewhat a large amount change that I will be suffering with. Well, I am not up to what I wanted so I think I will have to find some one that can show me how this little trick is. I didn't know that to write some other parts of a document was such a chore. It's been a long, long, long time since I have been on the computer that I have almost forgotten how to run this bug. What am I looking for is the way to insert some other writing that I have on my laptop. It has been a year now and I have not found a way to get the other writings in some kind form so that I can us some of the other material. For the time it had taken up to now, I could have copied each of the inserts that I want to put into this book. I might say that I do have several other things to do besides just writing, like traveling and going to some of the relatives. And some of them do have lots of work that I can do to save them of getting some contractor, that isn't cheap at the least.

In between times we have had to have some work done on the Motor Home that has taken some time getting things done right the first time. I do the most of that kind of work but there is some now that I can't handle very easy. In May I have turned 91 years young and going to keep it up as long as I can. I am still working on merging some of my writings into the large ones and then make up a new book. Now it is July 2005 -7PM and I have a little time to put down a few words. We have the Motor Home ready to go on this trip of about 6000 miles. The first is to get to Montana for a memorial then the next day will be a family reunion in Billings, Montana. After the reunion on the 6th of July 2005, we are headed for the hot area of the United States, which is in the south central Illinois to see my daughter and her family, which I haven't seen for about 6 or 7 years. Even with both of us in the upper years of life, life seems to take longer to get things done. The past years we have been closely connected with Winifred's family.

Leonard Fiske

THE NEXT SEVERAL PAGES, IS WHAT I CALL, TIMES OF OUR LIVES, WHEN TRAVELING.

Oct. 29, 1996

Some times we get things together so that it looks good when in print. I thought I would run a test to see if I have figured this thing out.

I wanted to have the two-line spacing and the indents on both ends of the letter. It seems that I am not getting things right. Now I am going to run the spell check to see what will happen. The spell check worked out find.

In order to keep this journal from being so dry and boring I am going to tie each day together as if it is one writing. The next day must not have been worth putting down any words October 31,1996

Some times I wonder when I will get used to this computer. Today we did a little looking around the area here in Yuma, Arizona for a place to park the Motor Home for less money then the three or four hundred dollar a month. Our motor home is so equipped that we should be able to survive for a few days a week or maybe more. Nov. 1, 1996

Here it is another day at Yuma Lakes campground. We will be moving from here in the next three days. Then we are going to the desert for a while, hope to get to do some painting there if the wind don't blow.

We did some shopping here in Yuma, Arizona. First thing is to find out where you are after you have made a few turns, first one way then go back the other way only to find that you have passed this store several times. You wonder were all the people come from because this park has several hundred spaces and they are filling up.

Nov. 3, 1.996

Now it is Sunday, time to go to church. We saw a Christian church on the road to Yuma. It was an out door sermon because it was a western days program. You can imagine we didn't have a sermon it was mostly singing and the playing of guitars. The instruments were all right but there was too much of the same thing. This was not the type of church that either one of us cared for.

We are now at the Imperial dam area parked on the BLM land. We are on a high plateau looking over the valley at the dam and waterways. This water is now on it's way to the Imperial Valley of California.

Nov. 9, 1996 Today is one of the hottest days since we got here. Today we had to do the regular thing is to dump the holding tanks and take on fresh water. This is one of the rituals of spending time in the Motor Home or any type of a recreational vehicle. We have a generator on board that makes it an easy way to live for a short time. The annual fee here is $50.00 dollars for the season ending the 15th of April. There isn't any of this packing them in so tight that one couldn't put out your awnings. Here we can park almost any place. At different areas they furnish a place to dump and a place to get fresh water at no extra cost.

Nov.13, 1996

Today was a day of all days. The day started by us wanting to go to town and get the mail then we were going to get an AC/DC television, then we wouldn't have run the generator all the time. The mail had one very important letter, that Winifred had an offer on her house in Lacey. Then we had to look up a place that had a fax machine. We went to a title company and they were very gracious. Winifred called Noreen the agent and she faxed the papers from Lacey to the Yuma title company she signed the papers and faxed them back to Lacey. The job finished in about one hour

We looked at several television sets trying to save a few dollars. We went to the best company that was going out of business and found that they had one that just fit the bill. While we were in the title office Winifred asked that I go and get the papers of the TV and study them. Low and behold the box didn't have the power cord, we had to go back to see if we could find a cord, because the cord that was missing was the 12 volt one. This being an AC/DC the TV wouldn't be of much value.

Nov. 19, 1996

This is a new day that started out yesterday when we left the Quail Hill area and went to the Foothill area to look up a repairman that could fix the generator. We parked on the street behind his place of business so that we would be there the first thing in the morning. We were there but the mechanic was late so didn't get on it for one half hour. When he did get to work on the generator it didn't take but thirty or forty minutes. This evening as I am writing this every think seems to be working.

We left Yuma at about noon and drove to Quartzite, Arizona where my sister and brother in law are parked out in the desert. We stopped there to see them then went on up the farther into the desert where we can paint. Maybe there will be less dust. That is some think you don't need on paintings.

We had full holding tanks all the way to Quartzite and I think Winifred got a little sick from the odor because she is all worn out tonight. She is laying on the davenport reading the USA TODAY paper.

Nov. 20, 1996

We are here in Quartzite. Things seem to have been a very quiet day. Nothing so disastrous has happened. Winifred painted a nice picture, which she plans on giving for the 40th wedding of her nephew Larry and niece Doris. I wish I could do so well on the painting. It seems that I have some problems yet with the black water tank. It fills up rather fast. I just reminded Winifred that to night is our shower night. We do this whether we are one the road or at home. I am going to shut this off tonight regardless if it is a short message for one day or not.

Nov. 21, 1996

This was a good day. Temperature was a high of 82 degrees today with a little wind from the southwest. I did take the Motor home down to the dump station and leave the black and gray waste in their tank. Then filled up the drinking water tank with fresh water. This is one of the regular duties when you park out on the desert. I did a little painting on the old picture that I had started last year when we were here in this same place. I have a little more to do on it, maybe some high lighting really doesn't think much of this picture, it just doesn't seem to do any thing for me.

Nov. 22,1996

It rained most of the night, not hard but off and on, there was water standing around this morning when I got up. There was no rain all day only some clouds until later in the afternoon they were all most gone. As I am writing this note as the wind got a bit hard and whistling around the Motor home. It sounds like when I was a kid in Montana only there would be snow drifting this time of year.

Other wise the day hasn't been bad. I did change the gasket in the toilet bowl. It was not to bad of a job I think it took about half an hour in this crowded area to work in. We went to town couple of times. As we went past where Lucille and Roy are camped we didn't see them. Talked to the neighbor and they said that they were home but was in and out so we missed them every time we went past.

Nov. 23,1996

Not much went on today. We sat around a little then went to town and did some shopping at the flea markets. There wasn't very many of the places open yet. We did find some thing to buy. The one think was a fitting for the black and gray water dump valve where I could hook a hose on and flush out the tank. Guess what, it didn't fit so had to take it back. It seem that I have to take so many things back for one reason or the other. Last night I typed some on the computer and the battery went dead, so I had to redo it today.

Nov. 24, 1996

Today we left Quartzite Arizona heading for home with the first stop in Riverside California until after Thanksgiving. We arrived just a little after noon. We are set up here with electric power. Snug as a bug in a rug. The weather was great no wind, as mater a fact the wind generators wasn't turning. There were a lot of these generators in the area west of Indio, California. There had to be hundreds on the hillsides. They are a massive piece of equipment with three-blade propeller. I will sign off now for a few days while we are at Larry and Doris Ashe's place here in Riverside.

Nov. 26,1996

Last evening Larry Ashe worked on this computer to get the clock set up with the correct time of day. Now I have been playing with it and find out that I have a lot of fonts in this letter writing to do most any thing. Now I would like to find out how to put a space in to insert a picture of different sizes. What ever I did it didn't work.

Nov. 29,1996

Yesterday was Thanksgiving Day and we are at Larry and Doris Ashe's home in Riverside California. What a day we had yesterday. The first thing was we went to a hotel to have brunch. This brunch was prepared by their daughter and son-in-law. They had rented this room for the family as a 40th wedding anniversary before the large Thanksgiving dinner that was held at the Sharon and Elray home in the afternoon for the same group of relatives that counted up to twenty one people. What a great crowd of noisy ones. But who cares when you are having fun.

Now we sit here recuperating from the busy but tiring fun day that had just finished. Winifred and I were the oldest people so we have the excuse to rest. Being the oldest has its good points. They didn't ask us to do any thing, how nice that is even when we were able to do most any thing. We did a great job of eating that delicious food.

June 2, 1997 Mon.

Our first stop on the trip was on the banks of the Columbia River on the Oregon side of the river. We sit here in the shade of a small tree at 4:00 PM watching a tug boat go down the river with a load of sawdust. Then we have planned to go on to Utah, then through Yellowstone Park, then on to Montana.

June 3, 1997 Tue.

We were up and ready to leave the camp this morning at 8:15AM. We are traveling on route 84 east to Salt Lake City, Utah. We had a little discussion regarding where we are camped tonight. I think it is Hammett, Idaho, at a State Park. This discussion I lost. We were at the State Park, but it was at Glenns Ferry.

They didn't have a pull though space, in the upper area of the park, so they put us in a rather new area that was closed but the Ranger took us to this large area where we were the only one's in the area. Here it cost us a sum of $16.00 dollar for the night with full hook-up. It was tops of the RV parks. We came total of 340 miles today. It was a nice drive, all good roads and great weather.

June 4, 1997 Wed

Shame on me. I am running late, here it is June 8th and I am going to try to remember how the day went. On this day after the typing got to be four days old. We did get started down the road by 8:30 AM, even though this was a nice place to park, we had to get on the road as planned. We only drove 301 miles today. As we entered into Utah the roads did get very rough and it did slow us a little. When we got closer to the place where we were to turn off of the freeway I got caught in a right turn only lane, when it was time to turn left. Then had to go to the next off ramp to turn around drive back about three miles to get back on the freeway. Then back in the far left lane so that we could reach our destination here in the suburb of Salt Lake City, Utah.

June 5,1997 Tour

We had a good night parked on the street at Winifred's dear friend's place. The next think was to get set up in the street because there wasn't room in the driveway or back yard. These people are the greatest. We are in Mormons country and these people are of the Mormons faith and they live it to the fullest. This couple is in their upper 80's but they look in the 70's. George gets around very well and his wife does have some problems with her feet so she has slowed down some.

June 6,1997 Fri.

Here we are at the George and Mary Smeath home parked on the street and hooked up to their power. We are like a bug in a rug. The weather has been a little Warm. When we first arrived the temperature was in the upper 90's I did have a small job that I was most happy to do for these good friends. The patio door screen needed the bottom rollers. George and I went to the store and found a pair that we thought would work and they didn't so I had to modified them. The door does work but not like it should. If I had my grinder I would be able make it work better then when it was new. We are enjoying the girls cooking. You see we have three ladies in the household that keeps the three hunger men satisfied with food under Mary's directions.

89

Also today we all went to Springville to see Frances Smeath, my editor of my book. I talked to her the night before and she had it finished. I picked up the material from her and then we took them all out to lunch a good lunch. Then returned to Salt Lake.

June 7,1997 Sat.

I have the story edited now Frances wanted me to read it and make correction that I thought it needed. I spent the most part of the day reading. I did have to change some of the wording to fit the type of story and sound like the lingo that was used in that day. She did a great job to take my mess and make some sense out of it.

June 8, 1997 Sun

First thing to day George and I went to Smithville and Had Fran make some corrections to My Story. That took about two hours then we returned home. Then we went to a Mexican restaurant for dinner. Then did some visiting until time for bed. Some time in the night some body thought it would be real funny to paste some raw eggs on the side of this new Airstream Motor Home. I sure hope they slept well after trying to devalue this beautiful Home. That has a value of $ 100,000.00 dollar. Maybe they where jealous.

June 9,1997 Mon.

It was raining a little, but I worked up a piece of the Smeaths lawn area that was bare of grass where a large tree had been removed. Then George and I went to town and got some planting mix and some fertilizer. I finished the seeding and watering that completed the job. I finished jut in time because the rain started and hasn't quit yet to day. That wasn't the worst of it, in the night it really did rain. The thunder and lighting and rain pored down all night. The weather report was 2 ½ inches.

June 10,1997 Tue.

We got up the usually time and got the Motor Home ready to travel. Fill the water tank with fresh water. Then hook up the little car, and then unplug the electric cord. Coil that up and store it in the compartment. The only thing left to do before we can travel is to raise the hydraulic jacks that are built into vehicle. Now we are on the road I drove to the county maintenance yard where they have a place to dump the holding tanks.

June 11,1997 Wed.

We arrived here a Hedy's place that is a little closer in the big city of Salt Lake City, Utah. This place is in a nice neighbor hood. The only thing it is a little noisier then what we are use to where we live.

June 12, 1997 Thus

The plans are to go down town Salt Lake to see some of the sites. We returned from the downtown area to day in a hard rain. It is a good thing that we had the umbrella and coats. Yesterday the temperature was in the upper 80"s and the day I think it is in the low 70"s with the wind and rain it felt much colder. I am typing this while Winifred my dear wife and slave is doing the dishes. You must keep them busy or they will get in trouble.

June 13,1997 Fri.

What a great day this is. Here it is raining this morning just when we planned on taking the buss to downtown Salt Lake City today. The first thing I had to do this morning was to check the refrigerator, it seems to go of at times. Then have the other amusing thing, one of the compartment on the out side leaks water. It has stopped raining so I think we will take the car and check out the traffic. The traffic wasn't that bad. We went to the museum and found part of it closed for repairs. Well some you win and some you loose. It was a good day any way after all the fuss that the weather did this morning. Today we didn't get wet and the storm held off until later this after noon.

June 14,1997 Sat.

Winifred wanted to see another one of her Mission friends that live to the north of Salt Lake City, Utah. We took Hedy Holt with us and drove to Helen's place. After arriving the three girls took off afoot to talk over old times. They went over and walked in a park that was close by Helen's house. After they returned home Helen had a great dinner

91

ready to be consumed by this Hungary group of four old people that included me. After eating and the dishes were washed Helen took us to the cheese factory that to me was a very poor place. We didn't stay there very long boat went to an old farm place that the university Utah was fixing up as one of the old pioneer farms with the same late 1800's and early 1900's way of life. One of the first we saw was a one room log cabin that was about 12' x 12' that a family of seven had lived in for many years until they could build a larger house. This house had the old country cook stove a table some benches and wood crates on the walls for the pantry. Then they had fixed up the next larger house that was a five-room house with kitchen, bedroom and front room down stairs then two bedrooms in the attic area of the house. It was also furnished with every thing that made it a workable place. In other words you come could move in and live the as the pioneers did in those times. They had many pieces of old machinery from the old steam trackers that pulled the large plows that turned over the native sod so the new people could start farming, as we know it today. We left there and drove home some 90 miles, it was a long day for people in their 80's.

June 15, 1997 Sunday:

It being Sunday we didn't do any thing. Hedy went to church, I took her because she walks but was late then I got lost a little getting back to Hedy's house. That afternoon we went out to eat. Winifred and Hedy got to visit for awhile while I got some thing picked up around the motor home before we took of to the repair shop where I had a eight o'clock appointment to have the refrigerator worked on. Also on Sunday the microwave oven went out.

June 16,1997 Mon.

This shop didn't repair this, so I got a man to come to the parking lot to do the repair. He found that a fuse inside if the microwave blew. We had you lunch there and took off for some place, as far as we could go or wanted to Drives. As it turned out we saw a Federal campground along side of the Fonrenelle Reservoir. This was a nice place, it wasn't open yet so it didn't cost. There were only three other campers in the place. We would of made it farther except we mad a wrong turn in heavy rain storm and we ended up out in the country heeding back into Utah. I didn't want to tell any one but now I have.

June 17, 1997 Tue.

We took our time this morning before leaving this good campground. Then we headed north on highway 189 north to Big Piney then 351 to the junction 191 where we are now at the Wind River Campground. It isn't time for bed yet, so I will talk Winifred into playing some cards. Last night I thought I would skunk her but the last had she took it easy. I didn't have any thing to brag about and was sure this would be her game.

June 18,1997 Wed.

We took our time leaving the Wind River Campground. Winifred wanted to do the laundry here because we didn't know when and where we would have the opportunity again for a while. We didn't drive very today, after leaving Jackson we found a Federal campground called the Gros Ventre It was close to the Gros Ventre River. We walked down to the river and it was running at its banks. We didn't feel like we were in danger at any time. I was having the same old problem with the refrigerator of not staying lit. It was decided that we would go into Jackson and get the metric wrench that I needed so when we got back, I took the burner jet out cleaned it then started it up. I t had run all day with out going out. Just as I was typing this I looked up at the controls and things had gone out Winifred jumped up and punched the buttons to transfer the operation back to the propane.

June 19, 1997 Thus.

We are now parked at the very elite $ 40.00 dollars a night to park the motor home. We do have full hookup, grassy lot just out the door. It has paved roads and it is a newly built last year. This place is in the town Yellowstone, Montana the west entrance to the park. The plan is now to go back in the park tomorrow and get a space in the park at Madison, and then use the small car to tour the park. It is very difficult to stop at most of the site seeing places with the large Motor Home.

June 20, 1997 Fri.

Today we took the tour of the park using the small car and went the long loop. It took the full day to make this trip. We got to see some fantastic scenery and the most interesting was the Parks grand canyon The colors were out of this world, they don't have to take a back seat to any place in the world. There was a lot of wildlife and people as well as a lot of road that we saw on this trip.

June 21, 1997 Sat.

Today was the day to tour the small section that is in the north part of the Park. This was a much shorter trip, in fact we went out of the park and drove up to the little town of Gardine. About 60 years ago this six miles from Gardner to Gardine was known as the firing line when the Elk season was open. The Elk would come out of the cross the road then they legal to harvest as game for the taking by those that had an Elk license. I was up there one time with my brother-in-Law Floyd Lord. The day was super cold, the temperature was at the 63 degrees below zero not good for the taking of the Elk. This six miles was known as the firing line because all the area on the right going north was the Yellowstone Park closed to hunting. Then the other side was open. During first few minutes after eight o'clock the hunters would kill up to 500 animal. This was in the winter when the snow was about four to five feet deep. They say that the hillside would be red from all this killing. Later I had heard that this type of slaughter was corrected by opening part of the park so the concentrations weren't the same along the road. We arrived home a little early so we rested a little after dinner.

June 22, 1997 Sun.

We left the Madison federal park this morning at 8:00 AM headed for Big Timber, Montana. Arrived here at 11:30 got a space here along the Boulder River. We are backed into space 5 on the bank of this river. About 3 weeks ago this park had to evacuate all the traveler to high ground. The owners had a four-hour notice. They told me today that every one was on high ground before the Park was flooded. Now as I type this I am looking out the window at the river it should be renamed the wild river. No I don't feel threatened here because the season has ended. I would think the area would be in a drought. That's the way life is here in Montana. The plan is to stay here for the next 14 days.

June 23, 1997 Mon.

I got a little behind in my typing. Now it is a difficult to know just what we did after a few hours when things cool off even in hot weather. Today Winifred did the wash so we can be clean when we leave this place. This is a very nice park to stay in but we have these itchy wheels under us and wouldn't want them to feel bad because we didn't move on. It is a beautiful campsite. I mentioned that we are backed up to the Boulder River that is now getting down to its normal size after the bad flood they had here three weeks ago.

June 24 1997 Tue.

Today we left camp mid-morning traveled to the little town of Harlowton, Montana that is located forty miles north. We saw lot of green grass with many bands of sheep and several heard of cattle. The hillsides are the greenest that I have ever seen for many years. I hear that this part of the country was hit with a bad winter with lots of snow and rain. It has been that way all over the country from coast to coast.

June 25, 1997 Wed.

This is another day and we took the little car, headed East to Billings, Montana. There we visited my sister and her husband. It is a pleasure to visit there because he is totally blind and he does all the watering his lawn and has a garden that is out of this world. Every thing is in nice rows. I is well watered and not a weed in that garden. He can tell by the feel of the plants what they are. We had a good day and back here at camp now. I am closing this off at 7:15 PM. I think we will play a few hands of cards before we call it a day.

June 26, 1997 Thur.

It was late when we got up this morning. Winifred fixed a good breakfast of hash and eggs with toast. Then we rested up for a while before taking a ride up the Boulder River. There were a lot of good sized ranches up this canyon. I had heard that several big name people had a place up Here on of those would be Tom Brokaw the anchor on NBC television. Then there is a movie star by the name of Brook Shields. That is getting pretty close to hob knobbing in the upper class. For me any way. Also today we some thing that didn't look like I was regular ranching activity. First we saw a place off of the road that had several cars parked. It wasn't a ranch junkyard because there were signs Crew Parking. That is when Winifred mentioned that it was for the crew when they were shooting a film or making a movie in the area. We didn't go over a mile and at one of the entrees to a ranch there was a guard at the gate. Sure enough, the gate man said that Robert Redford was making film about training horses. Then we went on up the valley to where the good road ended and that is where we turned around. At this point it was 20 miles from Big Timber, Montana. Then at 4:00 PM we had another good meal, they call this supper in Montana, of boiled cabbage, carrots, celery with some baloney thrown in for the flavor.

June 27, 1997 Fri.

We are still here at the Spring Creek Camp Just out of Big Timber, Montana. The Boulder River behind us has been receding steadily now it looks good. Good enough to want to fish in it. After breakfast I took the Motor Home to the place here on the campgrounds to dump the holding tanks. This we must do every few days because we don't have the confidence of the sewer dump at our site. I been looking forWard for this evening When the Park puts on a Rainbow Fish fry supper a full meal that will cost $ 7.50 a plate. In checking the time it will be an hour yet. The hour is about to start the dinner, oh I forgot, this is suppertime in Montana. Here comes a good-looking thunderstorm with a lot of rain. We just got our dishes filled the rain started to come down. We had to pick up our meal at the outdoor area then we ran for the shelter. All in all it turned out to be a very good supper.

June 28, 1997 Sat.

Today was going to be a good day because Evelyn and Albert Kraft my sister and brother-in-law would be coming from Billings the RV camp at Big Timber, Montana Where we have the Motor Home parked. They arrived just a little after 9:00 AM. While we were waiting for them, I had some chores to do. First I promised Winifred that I would vacuum the carpet then put up the gazebo. I had put this thing up once so it turned out to be a little job but I made it before the company came. We sat around all morning until noon then Winifred set a great picnic type of lunch on the picnic table. She had put on a new blue flowered tablecloth with a small pot of red roses as the centerpiece. The food consisted of potato salad, ham, potato chips, pickles, celery, cheese, peach Jell-O, and fresh tomatoes that she had forgot to put out. We all had a good day and the weather held off with its habit of raining each midday.

June 29, 1997 Sun.

This is the time to go to church but we looked in the phone and didn't find any of our faith. Then we decided to drive to Bozman, Montana. This is the town that I had spent every summer of my high school days. While we were there I looked up my Uncle Walter Cline. His place is what II called home when I was away from home when I couldn't get a job some place else. He is the husband of my dad's youngest sister. Walter is now 94 years old getting around very well with a walker other wise he is feeling good. The thing that put him in the walker was that about 2 years ago he fell and broke his hip. We took him to lunch and had a good talk about the past. It was great to see that he is happy where he is living in the retirement home.

June 30, 1997 Mon.

I think we have seen almost all the important places, like looking up relatives. This morning Winifred did the wash, including the bed sheets, so that is out of the way for a while. This PM we decided that we would go to Harlowton, Montana in the morning. In order that we can get a early start we picked up thing around the Motor Home so that there isn't much left to do tomorrow.

July 1,1997 Tue.

It was a good thing that I did get the outside work done yesterday. There was thunder and lighting storms all night with heavy rain that left water standing all around, in big Timber. When we got ready to leave the rain was rather light so had no problem getting hooked up with out getting wet. We are here now parked in the city park where the rain is coming down real hard. You should see the mess on the Motor Home and the little car after going through 10 miles of road construction. You can't see out of the rear window it is all covered with mud. After all of the mud the little car we tow, you couldn't make out the color or the name for so much mud.

July 2,1997Wed.

We are in Harlowton, Montana today at the city park waiting for the Rodeo to start tomorrow. This is a very quite place all night then this morning about 7:00 AM all of the contestants along with their horses started to fill up every space in the park and the roadways. The park attendant had a hard time trying to keep all these vehicles off of the grass and RV parking spaces. Went for a walk around the park didn't think it would take this long. It is now 7:30 PM with the weather looking very dark in the north west of the park sure hope that it doesn't rain tonight. The arena is such a mess with sloppy mud.

July 3, 1997 Thur.

It didn't rain last night, thank God, maybe the arena would dry up a little bit. It was so wet it is still a mud hole. The show must go on ad they say in show business. We are here in the city park yet and many of the relatives have found us. We had 11 people in the Motor home at one time, it was sure good to have that many come and visit, I love my family members. They have always been very supportive. We all attended the street parade downtown, it was small but different then what we would have out on the coast of Washington State. This was typical western flavor with genuine cowboys and cowgirls. Then there was the sheep wagon that my friend built and used when he use to heard sheep about 50 or 60 years ago. Then we all went to the dance at the Moose lodge. They had a great western music and a nice crowd not over crowed.

July 4, 1997 Fri.

Today is the day we've been looking for. The day of the big Rodeo in Harlowton, Montana. It has been many years many years since I have been to one of these events. I think that Winifred found that it was different then what she had seen for some time too. It was a good show even though the mud did have its drawbacks. I think that it slowed the action down somewhat. It seemed to make a lot of rider miss the target when trying to rope the animals. The weather turned out to be very nice not to hot or not to cold and no wind. My bother Jerry and his wife Shirley came by in the evening And we visited a while then they took of with their fifth wheel RV and was going to camp at the Dead Mans Basin over night then on to Roundup, Montana to finish selling more of their household items before they start traveling full time. We were very tired by 9:00 PM that we went to bed and I sure did sleep.

July 5, 1997 Sat.

Today we were slow getting started with showers to take breakup camp then to a place to dump the holding tanks the take on water for the next few days. After getting all that done we went to see my cousin Warren Holmes that is in a nursing home here in Harlowton. Then I found out that there was a friend of mine in the same home. I saw the two of them but not sure the knew who I was. I did feel good about going to see them because maybe they did know me but couldn't respond to my talking for some reason or other. After leaving the area I discovered that the air conditioner on the engine was turning out hot air only. This was one of the hot days so didn't need all that heat. It was only a few minutes Winifred got so Warm she had to strip down to her under wear then she soaked towels in cold water lay on the bed covered up with the towels. I drove 15 miles East to the town of Shawmut, Montana. Here I took thing in my own hands. I took the heat control device out of the dash and sure enough the control cable was bent so that it wouldn't change the temperature from hot to cold. After I straightened the cable in turned out the cold air. By this time it was time for lunch. In this small town of about 50 people they have a small restaurant and a little groceries. We had been told they had the best food in the area. We went there and ordered a small hamburger. You know that burger hung out all sides of the standard buns a good ½ " all the way around that bun. It was also very thick and for $ 2.25 each. The normal burgers anywhere else in the country would cost at least $ 5.00. We then continued on the Ryegate, Montana then out to my brother Ronald's ranch where his wife, Marie, still lives. My brother passed away some eight years ago.

July 6, 1997 Sun.

What a day! What a day! Quoting Winifred Fiske after arriving home to the Motor Home that is parked at Marie Fiske's Ranch. We were invited to the Big Snowy Mountains that lay 30 miles North of Ryegate to spend a day with Wegner family at their cattle ranch in the mountains This ranch belongs to Kenneth and Shirley Wegner. He purchased it from his folks when his folks retired to the city this makes the second generation to live on the land, or as some people say live off of the land. The have to a little of both in order to survive. Soon after we arrived there Ken and some of his family took Winifred and I up the swimming Women Canyon to where he had his cows pastured for the summer on Government land. I was surprised to learn that he had to fence his stock in the area that his stock was pasturing on. He was showing us some of the steep grades that they had to haul posts and wire, it looked almost impossible. When it came time to haul the posts he had to take the horses and use the as pack horses. The tie on some posts and wire to the pack saddle and lead the horse up the hill. If they didn't do it that way, they would have to carry the material in one post or a spool of wire at a trip. Can you imagine how had that would be to carry up a steep grade that is almost impossible to climb with out any extra load. To reach this turn around place we went over about 5 miles of rough roads that the truck he used was a four-wheel drive. We navigated up and down over rocks and holes that were two to three feet deep. We forded the Swimming Women Creek several times The fording wasn't that bad as this creek is about 10 or 12 feet wide and 6" to a foot deep with good rock base. It was like going home to be taken up this Creek. Shortly after moving from the Homestead My brothers and sisters with my mother would go there to a church camp that was in almost the same area. Then Ken took us to a log cabin that had belonged to Ted Unger. It was about 1930 that I worked for him to move this log cabin. I think he was given a cabin that was down on the prairie East of Rothiamay, Montana to it present location. At the time we moved this cabin we took the old rotted roof of then numbered each log as it was removed and put on an old truck and hauled up the Swimming Women Creek. It was building about 12 X 16 foot. I am sure that we had to take several trips to get it moved. I also remember that some the logs were to heavy to lift on so had to roll them up on the load. After getting all the logs hauled the job was to put them back into a log house again. Using our numbering system in reverse. I t was hard to believe that the cabin looked very good after all it has been there 67 years Then Ken took us past the place that I lived in the winter of 1937 when I was first married. It was a homesteaders log home. I was working for the Butcher in Ryegate feeding the cattle cleaning barns and when he needed any animals for slaughter I would load up one of the fattest steer and take it to town. It was a good stock hauling truck that he had me use. We lived in that two room log house all winter at temperature way below zero and snow up to two feet deep. I had all the food we needed from the meat market and the groceries that we needed from his store. As for wages, I can't remember but I think it was thirty dollars a month. It was sure a good job. I was my own boss if I wanted to sleep in that was my business. This job also included the feeding of the animals hay and keeping the water holes in the creek open so that the cows could get the water. After all of this rough road and all we returned to the most sumptuous ham dinner with all the trimmings just like a thanksgiving dinner. I have had some other meals that Shirley had made. It is like second nature to her when it comes to cooking. She also showed us some of her oil paintings. She does animals and people real well. After the dinner we got to go horseback riding. Four of us took a ride Ken his Son Winifred and I. I was to believe that Winifred had ridden a horse much but she was like a prow except when we started down a small short hill to the Swimming woman Creek. She wanted to stop there but was convinced that it wasn't that bad. After that we went up and down a few more hills with out an other word from her. Now it was getting time for these old people to head for Motor Home that had been parked at Marie Fiske's ranch.

July 7, 1997 Mon.

I had found out that they were having trouble with a leak under the kitchen sink. After taking a look at it I could see that it has had it's day many days ago. When I removed that old pot metal garbage disposal had simply fallen apart. Audrey Fiske and I went to Harlowton, Montana and got a new disposal. After Getting it installed, that didn't take very long, I hadn't read the directions so I missed one little point. I had to make another test to see if I had any leaks, so we started up the dishwasher and the water wouldn't pump the water out. The soapsuds came out all over the floor. My first thought was that the drain line had plugged up some how. This is the place for sunsets and sun rises. I just took a picture of a sunset at 9:15pm it had a lot of red with some trees in the fore ground. This should finish the day. Tomorrow I hope that is another and many more.

July 8,1997 Tue.

The first think to do today was to finish the job that was started yesterday. I read the directions for installing the disposal. The dishwasher didn't have any thing wrong with it, it was the dummy that installed the disposal. It had been many years since I had put one of these in. This was made as a universal type. If you had a dishwasher you must remove a plug at the dish wash inlet. After doing that every thing worked just fine. Winifred was doing some washing while I was completing the kitchen sink job. Then about noon we had a call from Mary, who lives just down the road from where we are parked, the information that we got was that if we hurried we could eat lunch at the Hooterites colony. Well some thing went wrong because when we got there I think the lunch was over. We took a tour of the bakery and had a sample of some kind of a German Scottish cheese puff. Mary and Winifred had two each then I had one that was plenty for me. By the time we got out of the place it was mid afternoon. It was to late to have lunch and to early to have supper. Winifred and I were going to go for a ride in the country but had to get some gas first. After getting the gas I went into the store the back door at the same time Mary came in the front door. She wanted to know if we were hungry If we were she wanted to take us to supper so we went to the small town of Lavina, Montana 15 miles east of Ryegate had a good meal. So things do turn out for the best after awhile. The only thing that went wrong this time I road in front and Winifred in the back. She was suffering from heat so Mary turned up the air and about froze me out, as luck would have it there was a quilt in the back that used for protection from the cold on a hot day in Montana.

July 9, 1997 Wed.

Winifred wanted a sunrise picture so I got up at 5:00 AM to get that picture the after breakfast we wanted to go out to the old homestead.

After trying one way we had to turn back and go a different way then couldn't get to the Homestead. Too many deep ruts in the road or trail that was a road. We returned from that little trip of 60 miles got to the Motor Home and found out it was lunch time at the Senior Center in Ryegate had a good meal for $ 2.00 each. Then went to the Motor Home and hear we are in a air conditioner running full blast. Outside temperature about 95 and the inside is holding at 80 degrees. It should be a little cooler tomorrow.

July 10, 1997 Thur.

We hit the road this morning leaving Marie Fiske's ranch so that Marie and her daughter Audery can get back to normal. Then stopped at Mary Fiske's place just a half mile down the road to say good-bye before heading to Billings, Montana, to see my sister Evelyn and her husband Al Kraft. Mary Fiske was married to my youngest brother Gerald for a time. It didn't get near as hot as it did yesterday. It was raining a little off and on during most of the day that helped keep the day somewhat normal. We got setup at Evelyn's then went out to have some thing to eat at 5:00 PM. The restaurant that we went to isn't one you would right home about as the greatest place to eat. Evelyn, am sure, thought that it was a great place. I hope that she doesn't feel bad that it turned out the way it did.

July 11, 1997 Fri.

It seems that when you don't write each day you can't remember what took place. I began to think it may be old age, at 83 I guess it could be to some to think about. Now what was it that we did do that is worth writing about? We did some visiting then some shopping here in Billings. Then Evelyn made a great dinner of new potatoes just out of Albert's no weed garden. Then she made the best creamed pees and potatoes that is always good any time. We finished the day by going to the Elk club for a dance and we stayed for about two hours. The music was good and the floor was crowded.

July 12,1997 Sat.

We got up a little later then usual this morning for some reason. Then we went to the downtown Museum. It was very good. Had great film talking about the homestead days in Eastern the area that I didn't know that much about. Although I had heard that I had very poor farm land and it did take a lot of acreage to run cattle or sheep there.

July 13,1997 Sun.

We had thought about trying to find a church to attend to day but the day slipped away until it was to late. Then Evelyn, Albert, Winifred and I decided to go out to the Oscar's dreamland. This is an old farm that the owner was a collector of old time farm machinery. Starting in the later 1800 through the mid 1900's. Steam, gas, oil and horse drawn items. Then they had set up a small town the old day store, church, school house, Jail, barber shop, printing shop, Mayors home in though days, It was very well done most all items were painted to there standard colors and a large number of them would run and they have been running them every year. I don't think I have seen so much good equipment in one place. Then there was a video of the equipment be used as they had been used in the early days. It was most interesting for a lot or most of the machines I had used or I had seen them used in my day of working on the farm and homestead, here in Montana. Then went to a dance at the Elks in Billings where we danced to Fern and Wayne playing western music. This was another good dance that we attended.

July 14,1997 Mon.

What did we do today? I have to give it some thought as my mind is in low gear for the moment. Now that I have had couple of minutes to think about it. We had a lot of company that came to see Evelyn and Albert. Then we had a great lunch that Evelyn had fixed. In the after noon it was planed that we all fix sandwiches to take to the dance club tonight. In the early afternoon Audrey and Marie Fiske came just in time to help make the sandwiches. With them to help Albert and I didn't have much to do but stay out of the way. Then at 7:00 PM we went to a dance again this was a group of 65 years old or older. This time we danced to the Roller again good music.

July 15, 1997 Tue.

We left Billings this morning and drove as far as Spring Creek Camp where we had stayed on the way east in June very nice camp on the Boulder River that is just behind the Motor Home. It is a little Warm today but we are parked in space 2 in the shade of some large trees. What a life but some one has to do it. After getting parked and after lunch Winifred and I had a terrible disagreement one of the worst in our marriage. It was over a small thing. As I was walking to the bathroom she held out a cup for me to put down in the cabinet. I took it then set it on the kitchen sink and went to the bathroom. That's when all hell broke loose. I have never seen her this angry at any thing. As I sit here ready to shut down the computer I don't know what will happen next. After a day of silences, we went to bed and made up by forgetting what had happed I never like to go to bed angry with any one, not even your wife.

July 16,1997 Wed.

We just rested up a little doing nothing for the most part. Winifred did a wash and I cleaned bugs off of the front of the Motor Home. That was about all I wanted to do in the line using the elbow grease when you are not use to it. We left the Boulder Creek Camp ground about 9:00 AM. Stopped to fill up with gas. Also had to dump the holding tanks before going to the next stop, which is the Chalet Bearmouth RV Park. It is only a short distance of 33 miles from Missoula, Montana we are parked alongside of the Clark Fork River in Western Montana. This area is where the Lewis and Clark Expedition took place in the 1800's. This is a very beautiful River. It is about 200 feet wide with a smooth flow.

September 3, 1997 Wednesday

Left Lacey after Winifred had her dental work done, when she had couple of teeth filled. We took off for Ocean Shores arriving late in the afternoon at Charles and Irene place. Our intent is to mow the lawn, repair the lawn mower, I had to put a new drive belt on this mower before I could mow the lawn. Then the plan is to take care of the blown down trees that where in the yard. It is one of the large pine trees that about 20 feet tall and almost 20 feet in diameter. The wind had just laid it down and just missed the house.

September 4, 1997 Thursday

I repaired the lawn mower by putting the belt on the drive pulley. It was sloppy but I did get the lawn mowed. Now I take my time at installing the new belt. After installing the belt I started on the fallen tree by cutting it up in small pieces and Winifred was going to stake it. After a few minutes the neighbor next door came over to help. I think he felt sorry for Winifred so he started hauling the cut material and stack them. Winifred went to the Motor Home to do her chores. When lunchtime came, would you believe she came out with chicken salad sandwiches and drinks. It was a great treat plus taking rest at the same time. I was doing this by chain saw. The job just about worked me to death, the neighbor would take the cutting away no matter how fast I would cut.

September 5, 1997 Friday

This is Winifred and my 2nd year of marriage. We are at Ocean Shores so we take advantage of the location and take a drive up north to Kalalock. We went by the way of Aberdeen for a special lunch at the lodge that looks over the Pacific Ocean. We returned by the way of the coast route that was a little closer but slower. After a little rest went to a dance but that wasn't a good music so came home. That wasn't the end of our anniversary we had till midnight.

Sept. 6, 1997 Sat.

After all the travel and dance we were faced with a nasty problem of one of the holding tanks was full. The day started with moving the Motor home to where with could empty the tanks. After that we had breakfast then went down town Ocean Shores to get a burn permit they would only issue permits one day at a time and bun from sunrise to noon. We then went to an art show at the convention center, I thought there was much more do-dad's then true Art. Came home to the Motor home had lunch then worked on cutting up some trees that had blown down. Got a lot more to do to get things cleaned up.

Sept. 7, 1997 Sunday

The day started out a little strange about 6:30 Winifred asked If I wanted t get up," I said no," so she got u with out a word and took her shower then got dressed. I waited for her to say she was finished. I don't know how long she had been finished but heard nothing I got up and she had been finished for a long time. I think she was angry about some thing because there were no words spoken for a long time. We hadn't planed on having a large breakfast as we had reservation at the Silo Motel for brunch right after Church at 13:30 p.m.; it being Sunday we hadn't planed on doing any regular type of work. Late in the afternoon I did install the drive belt on the lawn mower. It took an hour and a half, now it works like new. I was sitting outside in the lawn chair when Winifred came out disgusted about some thing, started out to walk. I asked where she was going. I didn't get an answer so after a few minutes I went out to the road and could see her going to the Ocean, When she saw me she waited for me to catch up then completed the walk.

Sept. 8, 1997 Monday

January 3, 1998 Saturday

It is 10:30 in the morning and we have the Motor Home loaded ready to take of on a trip, the first for this year. We have stopped at the Eagles Nest RV Park in Illwaco, Washington. Had a good trip so far today. We have parked and had our dinner. It is a little cool out side, about 30 degrees. We came through some snowstorm but I don't think it will snow to night.

January 4,1998 Sunday

We had a good nights rest at Eagles Nest Park in Ilwaco. Left there about 9: a.m. on the second day of our trip south this year. It rained and the wind blew like mad, the temperature stayed around the 30 degree. It wasn't that comfortable most of the night. It seems that I was awake most of the night. To day was one of the same as yesterday, lots of rain and wind with very poor visibility. Also he roads were very rough and winding and a few ups and down on small hills. The conditions and the weather slowed us down so much that we had to find a different place to stay to night. If the roads and weather had been good we may have gone as far as Klamth, Oregon where there was an other Coast to Coast Camp was then we can use our membership and pay only $ 4.00 a night instead of the going rate of $ 25.00 to 30.00 per over night stay. This time of the year we haven't had any trouble getting a place. This Park called the Osprey point RV Resort in Lakeside, Oregon, only two years old, very nice. This is one of the Camping club America that is one of the membership type of campgrounds that I also have membership in it and the cost is $ 5.00 per night. The two memberships cost me $ 200.00 per year, it doesn't take many nights out to get the money back.

January 5,1998 Monday

We didn't have much luck at getting one of our membership campgrounds today. There was one listed but when we got there at 3:00 O' clock the place was closed so had to look for some thing else. Got back on the freeway and headed south, after 20 miles we spotted a Campsite in the town of Rick, California. This was a place that looked very junky but they did have a pull threw space. Even though it didn't look like much I took it, and they had the power that we needed because the temperature is still on the cool side here on the coast route # 101. After leaving the other closed park we tried one other that was close by. I never gave it a thought that it would be closed but it was and here I am in the driveway and found the there was no way I could turn this 33 foot Motor Home around with the small car attached to the back. We had to unhook the car then fund tat the batter was dead in the car so had to push the car back out of the way then back the Motor Home out of the drive way then get the little car attached again. I might add that wasn't the thing that I enjoyed. Now to give some information on the trip itself for the day. We left that beautiful place.

January 6, 1998 Tue.

We started out today at 9:00 a.m. and drove 7 miles South of Orick and there was one of the membership campgrounds, called the Redwood trails these camps cost $ 4.00 per night. Because we needed to dump the tanks and fill up with fresh water we took the opportunity to get all this done before we get to our friend place in Santa Rosa, Calif. There we have to park on the street in front of the house. It has rained almost all day some times harder then others, water everywhere. Winifred had made a good dinner of some white fish we picked up a market just down the road about 14 miles. So I sit here telling my little story. Putting this on the laptop that I carry to record this day-to-day activities while it is fresh on my mind. It seems that if you let it get cold, the mind doesn't seem to see it the same.

January 7, 1998 Wednesday

Today we got started from this camp at 8:00a.m. Heading south again. We now have about 240 miles before reaching the first stop in Southern California. We had some good weather today, the first in several days that we have been on the road. Some parts of the road were slow going when going through the giant Red Wood forest. Some of the road was very rough and the other slow up was very twisty. I am glad that we did go by the coast route in place of Highway 5 where there would be mountains to go over with the possibility of snow. The coast route we didn't have any snow just a lot of rain and son wind but not that bad. We arrived here in Santa Rosa at three o'clock today.

January 8, 1998 Thursday

We are still parked here at Loomus and the Nuzum families Winifred's great friends. They have been friend for many years. In fact they seem like family to us, we feel at home here, I hope they feel the same. Ruth and Hank Nuzum, Winifred and I went to lunch, about an hours drive over to the ocean at Bodega Bay. We ate at the Tide's restaurant It had great food with a great price. The place was being remodeled with a view of the bay by all customers while dining here. The weather has been mild with just a trace of rain today. On top of the large meal at the ocean we had the usual good meal here last night. The women here sure can put on the food.

January 9, 1998 Friday

We slept in today as there wasn't much planned. Had good soup lunch here at the Loomus family. Then in the afternoon the Nuzums took us to see a long time friend of their that has had Polio for many years. What a pitiful thing to happen to a nice young lady. She has machines that she has to live with or she wouldn't live and around the clock care. Then we went past the Cosco Company and the crowd was so bad we didn't stop went on back home. On the way we did stop at a store called "trader Joe's" and what a crowd there was there but we did get some things then came home. It also rained almost all day but not hard. After a short rest we got ready to go to Flo and Willard's place for dinner. The Nuzums took us and then Millie and Ross were there also. We had a good time and a great dinner with a lot of reminiscing by Winifred and her long time friends.

January 10, 1998 Saturday

The day started rather nice with just a little rain but picked up later in the day. We went over to see Connie and Bert Tate about 9:00 a.m. and found they had just got up. Bert had to take his daughter to work this morning and then he had to do some checking on some of his jobs. Connie, Winifred and I sat around all day visiting. The girls did the talking to catch up on old times. I sat there and went to sleep couple of times. It wasn't that I was bored just sleepy. Winifred got to talk to Brad and some one by the name of Ed. From the conversation he was a buddy of Smokey when they were young ones. We got home, I mean back to the Motor Home that is parked in front of the Nuzun's home. On the way home the little car started to feel like the brakes were going out but we made it back arriving home about 8:30p.m.. Then we finished the day by going into house and watched the Olympic ice skaters qualifying for the One that would be going to the next Olympic. That lasted until 11:00p.m.

January 11, 1998 Sunday

We got a late start for bed the night before so we slept in. After getting up late and going into the house we were going to church with the Nuzum's but the weather was so bad we didn't go, so sat around the house. Some of them watched the foot ball games and I did some checking thing on the car and fixing some of the latches in the Motor Home. Then I went into the house and helped the football watchers do their thing. This evening Fred and Diane served a great waffle dinner.

January 12, 1998 Monday

We left the Nuzums and Loomus home this morning at about 9:30 a.m. to visit with Flo and Willard. Oh did it ever rain once on the way and the worst was just after we got the electric cable hooked up and got in the house. It came down in sheets. Then it has cleared up a lot with the sun out but there is a wind blowing so I don't think it is very Warm, although the thermometer is reading 56 degrees. We have had a great lunch then came out to the Motor Home for a nap while Flo and Willard took their nap. Winifred is still sleeping time away while I have been typing the report of to day's happenings. Now a large cloud has blocked the sun and it looks like rain.

January 13, 1998 Tuesday

The weather was horrible all day so sat around and visited. Flo had a great lunch for us and then again we had dinner. If I recall we had good soup and a lot of the sheep headers bread. If you don't know what this kind of bread is, you don't know what you have missed. It is baked on top of the stove in a large Dutch oven. The lid must weigh at least 3 pounds. When the bread is finished the dough will bake until it raises the lid about 1 inch off of the pan. In the afternoon we went to a place where they manufactured the stint like the one I have in one of my vessels of the heart. This was a very fantastic place, they have about 1000 employees almost all Asians or Mexican. They go to all measures to be sure that the stint is the finest that can be manufactured. They test the metals the stints are made of to make sure it meets their high standard. Every phase of the operation is inspected. These stints are made of a special alloy. It is a mesh cylinder about 1/8 inch diameter on up that would fit the larger vessels. It is a rather new company yet they are building a new complex beside the older one but several times larger. The way they are going it might be a good investment. It sure doesn't look like they are going to give up soon.

January 14,1998 Wednesday

Today we didn't do much because the rain is still coming down like it isn't going to quit. Willard had a Doctors appointment in the morning so Flo, Winifred and I went shopping over at Cosco's even if it was raining cats and dogs.

January 15, 1998 Thursday

We are moving on down the road today. We got up a little earlier then usual because the Halls had some thing going on for the day and we had already planned on leaving for Riverside. We got started about 9:00 a.m. I am getting sick of this constant rain. I didn't check the mileage but am sure we traveled about 200 miles. I had checked out the membership parks and found this park called Somerville Almond Tree RV Park.

January 16, 1998 Friday

This is such a nice park that we paid for two more days so we could rest up a little. The weather was sun shining all day and the temperature was 60 degrees what a contrast for what we have had for the past 2 weeks of rain and cold. Then on top of that the sun was hiding all the time. Today I got the satellite dish out and put some new legs on it then hooked up the box. Some thing that I had not done since we left home. You know I couldn't get things to work so I went over to one of the neighbors trailer that had a dish like mine to find out what he had his settings. He came over and we got the dish sited in and that's all that was wrong. Then we sat around and talked. In our conversations he seemed to like some of the same things that I had written in my book. At about seven o'clock he returned the book and had read it all and was very impressed. This comes from a complete stranger. This makes me feel that there is some thing in the book that appeals to more then the family.

January 17, 1998 Saturday

What a day this was. The sun shone all day and the temperature was in the low 70's. I did a small job in the Motor Home getting the bedroom TV going. I think the only thing I could find was the, power cord wasn't making contact in the socket. Then this afternoon I sat in the sun for about an hour. This is some thing I could take a lot of.

January 18, 1998 Sunday

Today we must leave this nice park, located just off of I-5 called the Somerville's Almond Tree RV Park, Coalinga, California. We arrived in Riverside, Calif. at 3 p.m. at the Larry and Doris Ashe home. It is always a pleasure to visit here. The weather was great here when we arrived but this morning it had rained in the night and now it is cloudy and 56 degrees. I don't know how long we will be here before heading for San Diego to visit Winifred's brother and niece.

January 19, 1998 Monday

We are parked in front of Larry and Doris's place now and will be here for a few days yet. Yesterday was a slow day not much going on. The weather was nice and Warm and we drove to the Nordstrom store to return some shirts. Then back home, took a rest later in the day. Had a great fish dinner.

January 20,1998 Tuesday

Weather was just gorgeous all day temperature was in the upper 60's. I really enjoy this kind of weather. The four of us did some shopping and picked up some items for me to make a small repair in the Motor Home. One of the drawers under the dinette seat had come out of the slides so I needed a small piece of wood to make the repair. We stopped at Camping World and Home Base. At home base I got a small piece of wood 1" X 4" X 3/4 to fix this drawer.

January 21, 1998 Wednesday

The weather even better then yesterday. A lot of sun and Warm. Then I fixed this drawer that had broken then I find that the other drawer under the other seat will soon have to be repaired like the first. Did some visiting then I washed the Motor Home in the afternoon.

January 22, 1998 Thursday

Winifred did a lot of calling to the Dr.'s in Lacey and here in Riverside so that I could have some blood drawn to find out if my enema has come up to standard. We got the approval and we went down to Larry's Dr. and I gave them some of my blood. They are to have the results by tomorrow. I don't know what will happen if the test is bad. I hope we don't have to go back home for a few more days.

January 23, 1998 Friday

We still have no answer about my blood test results. It seem that one said that they had Faxed the report to our Dr. At the Lacey Medical Center and they claim they had not received it as of 6:00 o'clock today. Now it is to late to contact the Lab here in Riverside to check this all out so we must wait until Tuesday. This has upset out plans to the point that I wish that I had stayed home until all the Dr. Calls had been taken car of, if there is a time that such a thing will happen. Now for some thing on a better note. The weather is still great with the sun shining all day and we could go shopping again today. We had lunch out at a Mexican

Restaurant, not one of my favorite places but I was out numbered three to one. You can't win them all you know. This evening we had a good dinner as usual, Doris seems to take things easy and the first thing you know the meal is on the table. I feel that we have stayed here to long, but this pace is like going back home you are so welcomed all the time. When we got home found that the Motor home had slid off of it's jacks and in doing so the step got damaged when it hit the curb.

January 24,1998 Saturday

Winifred did some washing of the clothes. I had small job to do. The first one was to empty the holding tanks then I repaired the step that got damaged when the Motor Home slipped off of the jacks. It turned out to be a rather easy job. I borrowed a come-a-long from Larry Ashe then hooked one end to the frame and the other end to the step. The results were just right, now the step works like new. The day isn't finished until we do some shopping. Well the girls went shopping while us boys stayed home. Then we ended the day with a good salmon dinner.

January 25, 1998 Sunday

Winifred and I slept in a little this morning, and then at 10:30 we went over to Sharon and Elray's place for some more great eats. Well day the wasn't over, we returned home to watch the Super Bowl game. Then Carole and Jan came to Riverside to see us and they were here also to watch the Super Bowl game. Every one here was watchers except me. For the life of me I can't see what people see in a butch of big bullies shoving each other around.

January 26, 1998 Monday

We did some small chores, like going over to the Church of the Later day Saints for Larry and Doris to do some genealogical work on Doris's family tree. Then we stopped at a restaurant for a lunch. It was a good place to eat. Then we came home to rest then in the evening we went to a fancy type place and had dinner. This was a birthday dinner for Winifred, Larry and Doris We all has fish, all was great accept Winifred's. That was about as small a piece of fish I had ever seen put on a table

January 27, 1998 Tuesday

We left Larry's and Doris this morning after eight days of picking on them. I bet they will miss us and not being able to see that Motor home sitting in front of their house. We have made it to the end of today's drive. We checked into the Bureau of Land Management just south of Quartzsite. The fees have doubled since last year but we took the seasonal permit that gives us the right to park on any BLM lands that has been long- term visitors' area.

January 28, 1998 Wednesday

We didn't get a very early start to do any thing today. I think the past week may have tired us some even though Larry and Doris were gracious hosts and we did enjoy them very much. We went too much and ate too much. We did go up town here in Quartzite, Arizona to look around at some of the booths. It there in one there must be thousand and several million people. The weather is very nice with the sun shining all day and no wind yet. Temperature is 40 at night and 70 in the daytime

January 29, 1998 Thursday

We got up early to take on water. The BLM has a place here in the desert that they supply water to the first come. For some reason they shut of the water at about 10:00 or 11:00 in the morning. All of these RV's that are out there on the desert have to get water somewhere. They come there with containers as small as a gallon up to the large motor homes that could take on two or three hundred gallon. We were late yesterday so didn't get any water. Today we had our breakfast then went to get in line. We hit it good there were only three ahead of us but when we got there the water was Warm enough to take a bath in. After getting the water we took the little car and went to town to check out the sales table and the booths. I was looking mainly for a small inverter to use to run the DDS dish system so we didn't have to run the generator whenever we watched the TV. I found one of the 300 amp. Just what I was looking for and it cost $ 75.00 just out side of the sales area. After we got back to the Motor Home we took a little rest. I hooked up the inverter and had good TV for the news. No noise now. The question now is how long will the batteries last, or how long can we watch the TV before every thing shuts down.

January 30, 1998 Friday

I had a bad night, had to go to the bathroom about a dozen times, didn't get much sleep. My bowls have been loose for the past two months ever sense I was in the Hospital. I don't think it is the water or the food because I haven't changed things that way. Have been blaming it on some thing that I picked up when I was sin the hospital in October and November. I had two black stools early in the evening. In the night I had thought that I would like to be back home closer to my Doctors and the insurance coverage area. The present system seems to make it a hardship on the people who travel or go out or their area.

January 31, 1998 Saturday

We left the desert this morning, going south to Phoenix to see my cousins Don, Sally, and Shirley Fiske. It was only 150 miles but it took us along time to find where they lived. I think we went about 50 miles out of the way and in some very heavy traffic with a lot of stop and go. We managed to get there and we parked on the street in front of their house. This is a very nice part of town very expensive homes in the area.

February 1,1998 Sunday

Being Sunday we are here doing nothing for the day. One of the reasons is this is the time to rest so that we can get a lot done starting Monday. The weather has been the best very few clouds and a lot of sun. Don, Sally, and Shirley were guests in the Motor Home most of the afternoon and we sat around visiting.

February 2, 1998 Monday

This is the day of work when you have work to do. Winifred started the washing in the house then took her sun bathing after she took her shower a then I took mine. Then I started to do the washing. We finished the washing just before supper. When Shirley came home from work at noon then we went for a ride with her to do some shopping in

Scottsdale for some beanie bag animals. She went two different stores and the second store had a limit of three per purchase so each of us bought the limit. Of course Shirley paid for them, I don't think I would like to start that kind of a collection. The for dinner Shirley took us all to a Japanese restaurant that they fixed the food right in front of you at the table. They also showed off their skill in handling the spatula and knifes.

February 3, 1998 Tuesday

Today was a nice day except there wasn't any sun. Started out with 40 degree and reached a high of 69. Winifred and I went shopping and picked up some food at Cosco for some of the meals that we are having while staying at Don's, Sally's and Shirley's place here in Phoenix, Arizona. We did look for a place to dump the holding tanks. After we got home the next door neighbor came over to see the Motor Home an in the conversation He said that we could use his clean out drop just outside of his house.

February 4, 1998 Wednesday

Before we were up this morning the local police game a knocking on our door, it's time to move the Motor Home from the street and put it in the driveway. That is just what I did after I had breakfast and went next door to empty the holding tanks. Some people have a way of telling you what to do. The day was one of those miserable ones where it rained most of the day with a lot of wind. I am kind of glad that we are here at my cousins' place rather then out in the desert. Winifred fixed a great fish dinner for all of us. She does better when she doesn't have me around to tell her how to cook.

February 5, 1998 Thursday

Well today Winifred is still cook and we had spaghetti with spinach, tossed salad and the desert was a jell-O. In the afternoon she was telling me that I must keep talking about how good the souse was. During the meal Winifred wasn't eating her meal very fast just picking at it until some one made a comet about how hot it was. Then it came out that she had put some hot pepper in the souse. Up to that point I was sure that it came that way because I wouldn't know the difference in these sauces. Today was a good day some clouds and the temperature was on the cool side. We went to look at one of the retirement homes in Sun City, it was very nice and the price was just a little less then what we have in Olympia. Winifred had a phone call this evening from the Burke's that live in Sun City West and they are coming down tomorrow and have lunch with us.

February 6, 1998 Friday

We were to have 10:00 a.m. guest today from Sun City West. It was the Burkes and they didn't show until after the noon lunchtime. I have to excuse them as they brought a nice cake to celebrate the two girls birthdays. The main thing is that Winifred and her friend Dorothy got some good visiting in talking about old times. Then in the evening Shirley, Don and Sally took Winifred ad I out to a fish place and it was a great meal. Then we went to one of the mauls to shop and pickup some Beanie things. Because that is what Shirley and Sally collect as a hobby. We were told that some of these you can purchase for $ 5.95 and they may get up to $ 1000.00 for them. I would say that is nothing to sneeze at but how long will this go on and the market will fall off just about the time all collectors get a good number on hand.

February 7, 1998 Saturday

We left Shirley Fiske's place this morning heading for Quartzite, Arizona to be on the desert for a few days. On the way I stopped at a truck service place and had the Motor Home greased and the oil changed. Then filled up the propane tank. We got out to the desert about 3:30pm. And found a place we thought was a good place parked and put the levelers down but the ground was too soft for them so I was stuck for a while. Now we are parked and not putting the jacks down here on this kind of ground.

February 8, 1998 Sunday

It poured down rain all night. It hasn't rained here on the desert any time that we have been there so I wondered how the ground would react to the water. I thought about in the night that maybe the Motor Home would settle in the mud or maybe be washed away in one of the flash flood type or gully washes I think it is called. It rained most of the morning but rather nice in the afternoon and set up the dish for some local, home news, weather reports. It didn't seem to be that great in the Pacific Northwest so think we will stay in the desert for a while. We may stay here at Quartzsite for a few days then down to Yuma.

February 9, 1998 Monday

Today was a good day a few clouds but the sun was shining most of the time. We went up town but played out doing some of the shopping. We did get a couple of cast iron ornaments, one duck with a bell and the there was a bucking cowboy with the bell. These can be used as a dinner bell or it can be used as a doorbell. We also got a sign that has the name "Fiskes" made from a piece of wood, very well done. It will probably be used over the back door as a doorbell. The in the afternoon Roy and Lucille came over for a while. They are also here on the desert only up the rod a little

February 10, 1998 Tuesday

Winifred's 79th birthday today and we are out on the desert at Quartzite, Arizona. She didn't have any idea what I was getting her but I slipped away from the Motor Home and went to the flea market that is being held here. One of the other times when we were looking around at these tables we found a small 32 caliber hand gun that she thought she would like so yesterday when I went to see if the gun was still there and it was so made an offer and the owner excepted it. This morning while Winifred was getting dressed I got the gifts ready. We had brought Connie's gift from home then I had found a rice steamer and the gun. I thought she was going to miss the gun that I had put in the bottom of bag that the steamer was in. The weather was good today some clouds. The temperature was in the low 60's. We also went to the little town of Blythe, Calif. and had lunch at the Sizzler and what a good lunch for under $11.00 all we could eat.

February 11, 1998 Wednesday

Another day on the desert. Weather started out with some clouds for the first hour, then the sun shone all day. While the sun was shining helped the solar panels do their thing and charge the batteries in the Motor Home. Yesterday we did run the batteries down to far because in the mooring the fan on the furnace was running with out any heat. This tells you that the power is down so the gas burner wouldn't light. We did some site seeing in the countryside today. We saw more and more desert not much of a change in the scenery. We called home to have our mail sent to Yuma, as that is the plan now. Before I close off on this writing I have to tell you that Winifred put up a very good dinner meal with chicken and baked potato and a green salad.

February 12, 1998 Thursday

Yesterday we moved from Quartzsite to the Yuma area. We are parked at the Imperial Dam are called the Quail Hill. We found a place out on a point that looks west and north a good view. The weather here is a high of 72 and the low is 56. It sure is good sleeping time.

February 13, 1998 Friday

It is now 8:00 a.m. and the weather is a little cloudy but Warm now at 66 degrees. We are getting ready to go to the town of Yuma, Arizona for the day. On the way into town, for some reason, we stopped at some of the R. V. Parks to find out how much they were getting per month week day and annual. After stopping at three different ones and found this park that we paid for a month. The Park is called, " Desert Paradise". It sure is a clean place so we went back to the Imperial Dam and had lunch then moved into this park. I had all the hook up's with concrete patio and a place for the little car that we tow along side of the Motor Home. After getting set up we went to town and got our large bundle of mail.

February 14, 1998 Saturday Valentine Day

It was a good night and we rested real well and then slept in until 9:00 a.m. and missed the breakfast that was being served at the club house. They had a yard sales here in the park so went to some of them I didn't see any thing that I wanted or couldn't get a long with out. Winifred got some books. Then we went grocery shopping after lunch we went and washed the car, some of that 4000 miles of mud and water that had collected the past six weeks on the road.

February 15, 1998 Sunday

Another lazy day. We almost slept in to long as we had planed on going to church at the hall here in the Park. We made the 8:45 church time but were disappointed with the type of service that they had. In short I didn't get much out of it. That will be the last time that I will attend here. Then we called the kids Smokey and Charles & Irene. They were both were very pleased that we called so they know how to get a hold of us in the case of an emergency. All seemed ok at both of the households. The weather here was a hard rain last night with a lot of wind. In fact it blew quite hard all day and was cold all day.

February 16, 1998 Monday

The first thing this morning after we had breakfast we drove across the border to Mexico jus south of Yuma, AZ. I went there for the main thing was to find out about what they can do with my teeth. The number of people was over whelming. There was so many that it was almost impossible to move. I did get in to the Dental office and got an appointment for Feb. 24th at 1:30 a.m.; the weather to day was like what the south should be like this time of the year a low of 50 and the high of 72 and no wind.

February 17, 1998 Tuesday

It rained and the wind blew very hard most of the night. Then the day wasn't much better only I think that it rained even harder. As of this evening there is water standing all around the park. Winifred did get the wash out of the way even if we had to run from the rain every once in a while.

February 18, 1998 Wednesday

This was a great day with lots of sunshine. I did get some repair work done on the Motor Home. I have been trying to fix a small leak at the compressor where the air hose attaches so it can be used to air the tires or inflate the front boots.

Leonard Fiske

February 19, 1998 Thursday

Today didn't start out to be very good weather with a lot of clouds that didn't go away all day. In the evening it started to rain a little but it doesn't appear to be any flash flood. For the last three days we have been looking for a good grocery. There seems to be a shortage of food stores in the East part of Yuma. There is one large IGA store at the Fortuna Rd. It is so crowded that you can't move in there. I didn't take the time to compare the prices but I am sure they have seen the chance to raise the prices where there is not any more completion then they have.

February 20, 1998 Friday

A lot of high winds and clouds today and the temperature didn't get over 65. We came down here from Olympia to get away from some of the cold and rain. So far I don't think the trip was worth all the travel for what. I did some work on the little cars tow bar. I would like to get some kind of winch on the tie back strap. Then I over hauled the toilet buy putting in a new gasket ant securing the seat down so that is tight.

February 21, 1998 Saturday

First thing we did was go over to the clubhouse and have a pancake breakfast with sausage and eggs. No rain today but the wind was rather cool. I do not under stand this kind of weather. I am not going to say I should stayed home and faced that kind. When the sun is shining, we do enjoy the weather.

February 22, 1998 Sunday

We looked up some churches here in Yuma and we attended the Methodist. I did not feel impressed but the regular minister was on some assignment and the guest speaker did a good job but rather dry. Then after church we went to see the largest area Flea market. There were so many cars lined up I don't think you could have got in for several hours

February 23, 1998 Monday

I for got that I didn't write any thing for today. It must have a very exciting day when you can't remember any thing that happened or didn't happen. All I can think of is that the wind blew all day and got harder as the evening came on to us. We did go to the post office and mailed special letter to Brad at Dean Witter office with the travel check that we finally got after waiting for four months. I wonder if that is the way they make extra money by placing this in the bank and draw the interest for the four months. The calculation insurance cost us $ 400.00 dollars. This calculates out to about the $ 400.00 plus the interest on the $ 6000.00 at least an extra $ 200.00 or a total of $ 600.00. It they had a thousand cancellations they could net about $ 600,000.00 dollars

February 24, 1998 Tuesday

The day started out with a breakfast party at a restaurant in Yuma for the Mooneys who are going to leave for home Thursday. The ones tending the party was Ernie and Goldie Krouse. Art and Blanch Vail and Leonard and Winifred Fiske and Dwaine and Lee Mooney. After the party was over we went to Mexico so that I could get some dental work done. I am having two teeth capped. They have put in the temporary in to day and I go back in a week for the permanents caps. I am getting this done plus cleaning for $ 320.00 dollar. We got back to the camp ground at 4:00 o'clock this p.m. and moved from space 256 to space 30 that is on the north fence row away from the main road. At dinner time we had a phone message that there was a death in the family. When I called Charles it was Lucille Slivka in Lewistown, Montana that had passed away. It was a blessing because for the past 4 years she has been in a nursing home and didn't know any one. I hope she didn't have to suffer very much.

February 25, 1998 Wednesday

This was to be a day to ourselves. It turned out that we were going to the large swap and meet here in Yuma. When we got there they weren't open. To find out they were open on Thursday, Friday and Sunday only. We stopped at a gun shop on the way home and then that evening we went to a potluck here at the park, to me it was a flop there were only 16 or 20 people out of some 500 people that live in this park.

Leonard Fiske

February 26, 1998 Thursday

We didn't get up very early today but after breakfast we went to the large swap and meet and found that the crowd wasn't very bad. We saw all of the place and purchased some small items that we could carry home. Then after a nap I took a piece of candy and pulled out the temporary caps that I had put in yesterday so we took off for Mexico to get them glued back in their proper place rather then in my pocket. Guess what we had for dinner to night, yes it was soup

February 27, Friday

This was the stay home day but the first thing that I did after breakfast was to go over to the lumber yard for a small piece of wood to install two latches on the bedroom drawers. That small piece cost me 22 cents. All I needed was this small piece for a shim behind the latch. I finished this job in the morning then after a good lunch I took a nap then started to redo a job that I wasn't happy with. The other day I thought that I had fixed a leak in a fitting on the air compressor. Most of the time this afternoon was looking for the brush that I use in the soapy water to test leaks.

February 28, 1998 Saturday Last day of this month.

Very nice day and wee went to the gun show here in Yuma. It is to be on for two days just this week end. We got there soon after it opened and we got to see most of the show before a lot of the crowd got there. We found a good holster for Winifred's new pistol and I found real nice 22 caliber target pistol. We got home to the Motor Home just in time for lunch then had our rest then we went to the car wash and washed the little car. After we got back from there we polished the car. We hadn't any more then finished the car when it was time for a free going away dinner at the Park club house. It was a good meal. We met Ernie and Goldie Krouse so we had dinner together then after dinner we came to the Motor Home and had a good visit. Today we have used up 59 days of this new year of 1998 and we have 307 days left of the year. I don't know what that has to do with any thing but I but it in for what it is worth.

March 1, 1988 Sunday

This is our day of worship so we went to the Mormon church in the morning. I have trouble understanding their faith. I am sure it is because I haven't been many of the services. I am use to having a minister preach a sermon not the congregation giving their stories of their life. After leaving church we got home and had a very y good Sunday dinner. Then had a short nap then took a drive up in hills and into a large valley called the Dome Valley. We drove around there a little and found they had a large area of truck gardening plus a lot of hay fields. Also we saw a very large feed lot for cattle. This area was at least 2or 3 section of land and thousands of cattle.

March 2, 1998 Monday

Today is the kind of a day that most every one here has been waiting for that is Warm and sunny and the temperatures in the upper 70's like it did today. We went groceries shopping this morning then laid around taking in the nice weather. There wasn't even any wind that is unusual for this area. This evening we went out for a Mexican dinner and found this good one that was dawn town on 4th Ave. and 27th St. here in Yuma.

March 3, 1998 Tuesday

It's only yesterday that I didn't write any thing and I have forgotten what I did all day. Oh I remember now we went to Mexico for a dental appointment that was to be at 11:00 and we didn't get in until 2:00 but they were short of help and I didn't have any thing to do so why make a big fuss. I sure have more time then money, well now that I have said it at my age of 83 who's to say. Very nice Warm day just what we came down here for. I guess I had better not complain.

March 4, 1998 Wednesday

Got up late and then went grocery shopping for food for the Ashe family that is coming down from San Diego , Calif., it is Winifred's brother and his two children. We went to the Farmers Market and what a rat race that was. Then we went back there after lunch to see if some of the other type o merchandise was some thing that you couldn't

125

get along with out but it was almost 3:00 and most of the venders had packed up and was gone. The weather was great today the temperature was up in the upper 70's.

March 5, 1998 Thursday

We had to do a little tiding up before our company from San Diego would get here some time in the afternoon. Winifred did the washing and I did some odd jobs around the Motor Home, like putting out the awning, picking up odd and ends then I vacuumed the carpet. Then we laid around an waited for them to arrive. It wasn't very long when the came got setup in their space then we satisfied awhile before we had a great dinner chicken, rice ad a Jell-O desert. Every one seemed t be filled and satisfied so about 9:00 o'clock the went to their motor home as we went to bed.

Mach 6, 1998 Friday

This morning our guest came over and had breakfast with us. We had fresh pealed oranges and waffle. After breakfast we all went to the swap and shop then went to lunch at the home town buffet. after all of that we came home town a little nap then Winifred and her brother bill went for a ride in the done buggy. Then I took Carol and her bother to old Yuma but found that the car parade drivers were having a party in the area so most of the area was blocked off. We turned around and came home. It was then that we heard about the difficulty that Winifred had getting out of the done buggy. Any way they seem to have a good laugh out of it

March 7, 1998 Saturday

To day was the big day for Winifred and her brother, and his two children, Carol and Jim. We first had breakfast in the Motor home then we went to garage sales for the first thing and they were thrilled to some degree. This was the largest of the swap and meet places in the Yuma area. From there e we went to one of the smaller swap and meet areas with a lot more junky then the first one and they thought that was to real good just like going to yard sales only they were all in the same place didn't have drive al l over town. We ate in a Mexican restraint then came home to rest. We had so much to eat that we came home, had a rest then had a snack for dinner. The weather was just great not to hot and no wind. The wind seems to blow a lot here, I suppose that if the wind didn't blow it would get very hot. The last few days the temperature was in the upper 70's.

March 8, 1998 Sunday

Our guest were going to leave this morning but decided to stay over one more day so they could go to see the Yuma terrestrials prison that was used in 1872 every one except me thought it was fantastic. After the tour we went out to the swap and shop again. This was the junky one and they thought this was better then the day before. Bill bought some more wrenches here so that made him happy then we came back to the motor home for some rest then Winifred made a great dinner of chicken and rice and jell-O for desert.

March 9, 1998 Monday

Winifred's brother and family did get going today, as Carol had to get back to work. After they left we took a good rest just laying around. Then late in the afternoon we went over to get in the shuffle board game and we did play. Winifred did great but I did very poorly ending up in the hole. I am not going to tell you how much in the hole. The weather got Warm today up in the high 70's with a lot of wind. Took some pictures of some of the few flowers that are in bloom on the desert

March 10 1998 Tuesday

We have three days left before we start for home. We went out for breakfast this morning at an all you can eat for $ 2.99 each and it was good also all was Warm. Some of these places have to much food out and it gets cold before it is used up. the weather was in the upper 70's but there was a lot of wind until mid after noon then I was able to put out the awning. We did a lot of laying around some time sleeping and I think that Winifred was reading most of the time.

March 11, 1998 Wednesday

Now we have two days before we pull up roots and move north. We have been down in the south for almost three months and this is about the fourth day that it felt like what we came her for, heat and

Warmth. Today has been the hottest run in the mid 80's with just a light wind. It is a good thing we had the wind or I don't know how hot it would get. probably in the 100's. We had a two other couples dinner get together at a all you can eat at 2:00 P. M. and we ate so much , that we didn't have to cook any thing this evening. Winifred and I did a little shopping for some groceries then came right home, as it was getting very hot out there. Then we laid around in the shade until it cooled off some. At this writing the temperature is 68 degrees and it is 7:20 p.m. with that I am going to sign off for the day will be back next evening. Good night.

March 12, 1998 Thursday

Well, I changed my mind and will be leaving for home tomorrow morning. Today it got Warm in the upper 90's. This was the first day that we had to turn on the air conditioner. I was feeling a little Warm but Winifred can't take the heat or the sun. We did a little shopping this morning to get some oranges and grapefruit. We were told about a place way out south of town and we had a hard time finding this place. After checking with a walker we had over shot the place and got into the end of the road. There is where we ran into a road crew working up the road and we got into some mud where they had watered the dirt down

March 13, 1998 Friday

The old saying, on the road again that is what we did today. We left Desert Paradise Park and headed toWard home. We came 187 miles to day and stopped at this Country Hills Park south east of Beaumont, Calif. it is a nice park. It is hard to visualize the differences from the desert to this very hilly terrine They have built this park by pushing the dirt out of the banks and made a level spot for about 4 or 5 spaces. The roads go with the terrain of the land some very steep with roads running in all directions. Around the hills up and down, some one had to put a lot of thought into this before starting the job. We are sitting here cozy as a bug. The weather was very Warm when we came though Indio but about the time we checked in here the wind blew and it got down right cold in a mater of minutes. Then I here on the news that about 50 miles west of here they got 2" of rain today and we came through nice weather all day.

March 14, 1998 Saturday

At 5:45 this morning things didn't start out very good. Winifred woke up a little before me and raised the rear curtain to see the moon. She wanted me to look at the moon and I didn't understand that it was the moon she wanted me to look at. Then I said put the curtain down you are letting in cold air. Things didn't get very good after that, I think she thought I was giving her orders. So, I got up to get ready to travel when she wanted the keys to the little car so she could go home. As I thought more about it there is no way I was going to let her go all alone. I would never forgive myself if she got into trouble on the way. I was sure that the car would make the trip but she does have a time finding her way. She is a good driver but her eye sight isn't as good as it use to be. We did get going by 7:00 a.m. I drove hard and fast until we reached the park we had reservation at Somerville Almond tree Park. This is the same park that we stayed at when we came down in January. It is a very good park well laid out with all drive thro spaces. The weather has been good to us today. Started out a little cloudy then some sunshine and very little wind. That was for a short time just after I left Riverside. We sure did run into the bugs on this trip it almost blocked out the windshield so when we got setup and took a bucket of water and washed the front end off before they would stain the paint. I am going to try to get to Red Bluff tomorrow night.

March 15, 1998 Sunday

When I started out this morning I thought that this would be a hard drive from Beaumont to Red Bluff but I drove hard and steady and arrived at 2:00 p.m. here in the Elks parking lot It is a nice with a lot of room but the highway noise is some thing else. There is no way you can rest in peace here, I hope the night will be a little better. I got the dish set up so Winifred could watch the 60 minute program on TV. Winifred made up a good dinner of turkey that she wouldn't eat but I had her share, boiled potato's, asparagus and some salad but I couldn't eat that much then some carrot and later we just had the good chocolate pudding.

March 16, 1998 Monday

We didn't plan on going very far today so we had a late start. Stopped at the Collier Rest area had lunch and I took a little nap. We got into Talent, Oregon for the night. This park was to be one of the membership parks I found out they had dropped the company, we took the park anyway so that Winifred could go to Ashland where she lived many years ago. After getting set up we went to Ashland, drove up the streets that had a park that is almost down town area. We thought we would find some place to eat while we were in town. You won't believe that we drove up and down the streets and found one but wasn't open yet so we went to many more places then finally back to the place that wasn't was open when we got back there it had opened and it was worth the wait. The food was good and plenty of it. The weather was almost perfect today all the way with sun shining and no wind.

March 17, 1998 Tuesday

We are still on the way home from the south. We stopped at Ashland, Oregon Where Winifred and her son had spent many years working and growing up. It is hard for me to believe that the weather has been beautiful all day and here in Salem, Oregon where we are now at my sisters place. There is a light wind and it is cold or maybe we had to much hot weather still in our system from being down south on the desert. I must say this trip home we have seen a great change in the gasoline prices. On the way down south in January the gas prices were steady at about $ 1.29 per gallon, now on the way back at the end of March we have seen a low of $ .93 cents and a high of $ 1,62 cents. I have filled up with gas three times and paid .99 cents, 1.09 and 1.29 I don't seem to hit the low prices all the time. I think I had better shut down this machine before my eyes go shut and I may loose all this that I have written tonight.

March 19, 1998 Wednesday

We arrived at my sister's place in Salem, Oregon just after noon got hooked up to the power then had a good visit with my sister Arlene who has been alone for several years and I think she was glad to have some of the family stop by even if it was for a short time. Winifred wasn't feeling very good had a sore throat so in the morning Arlene and I went to breakfast and had a good visit. About 11:00 a.m. we took off for home in Olympia. We arrived at 3:45 p.m. just in time to pickup our mail that the gate lady has been picking and holding it at the gate. There was five paper shopping bags full of this so called junk mail that had accumulated in the past two and a half months that we were down on the desert and in Yuma.

March 19, 1998 Thursday

Now comes the chore of unloading the Motor home. Winifred's sore throat had gotten worse and it is now a full blown head cold. She helped a little the first thing in the morning but had to quite and I was all day doing the unloading of the little car and washing the Cadillac that had been stored in the garage for all this time.

May the 19, 1998 Tue.

It has been two months sense we got home from the south. How time flies. I have been working on the little trailer that was just like a pile of junk when I had to have one to met the rules of the Harbor here when I wanted to come back into the Harbor to live. I just thought it would explain what goes on here when we are home. If it isn't one thing it is some other that keeps us jumping.

May 21,1998 Thursday

This has been an unusual day compared to the past several weeks. I have been working on the little trailer almost all the time trying to get it ready for sale. Winifred was getting tired of this kind of living. Most of our married life for the past 2 1/2 years I have been under foot most of the day and night. Today we loaded the Motor Home and took off for the ocean over the memorial day week end We are at Charles and Irene's place here in ocean shores. I am going to try and do some cleaning up around here. Mowing the lawn and cleaning up of some of the tree branches that was left behind when the City crew around the roads trimming all the trees back to the property line. They use a large machine that is like a rotary mower only it is turned up at a 90 degree and it butchers the trees and leave a lot of trash and the trees look hideous with all the branches off of one side of the tree. Most of the time there are snags, broken and split you wouldn't believe what a mess it looks like now. I under stand they are doing this preparing to put in a sewer system

May 23, 1998 Saturday 7:05 p.m.

We are still here at Ocean Shores I have mowed lawn yesterday and to day. I don't think I have ever seen the grass so high. I had to mow it three times in order to get it down to a clean cut. Then I had to go over it the last time and spread the cutting so that they wouldn't kill out the grass. When I finished the mowing, this lawn looked like a hay field that was ready for the bailer, but no bailer around here. After all of that I quit and took off the rest of the day. I just laid around the Motor Home and didn't do any thing. It seem like a waste of time when you have to take out time when the sun is still up. At 84 my health isn't what it use to be. I do get tired more easily. My body says to go ahead but my heart has a different idea. I do feel a little off from the normal sense October 9th 1997 when I had pneumonia and a congestive heart failure. It sure seem to take a long time to come back to normal.

May 24, 1998 Sunday 4:20 p.m.

We are here in Ocean shores yet and will be going home Tuesday. Today was a day of leisure. We had a good night and slept in a little this morning. Finished our breakfast at 9:30 a.m. Winifred watched TV. and I read a book for awhile then went to sleep for a short time. Then we went for a walk then went to town and had a good Mexican dinner. It rained all night and into the early morning before it let up, but now it is a real nice day.

May 25, 1998 Monday 6:30 p.m.

Today is memorial day to honor our dead. Winifred and I are still here in Ocean Shores. The weather and time didn't give me much time to get every think done here at the house. I did get some of the work done as mowing the lawn. Didn't get any of the trimming or any of the street area cleaned of the trash that was left when the city chopped all the brush back to the property line. I did get some of the mowing on the street where there wasn't any trash. We did go for a little ride this afternoon and went to what was the great Johnson's Store. This store has been known for its small store with the most items. It has been said if it has been made this store would have it and they weren't over priced. I have seen thing on the shelf that had to be 50 years old like Aladdin lamp parts wicks and mantels. That is just a few that I can think of at this moment.

June 26, 1998 Friday

Well it has been one month and one day since we have been on the road. We left Olympia this morning at 10:00 A.M. and arrived here in Moses Lake at 3:30 P.M. It was a nice drive today the weather was good to a little rain going over the Snoqualmie Pass. Here we are at a nice Warm temperature of a 73 high at this time of day I can read the sign up the street and it reads 68 degrees at 8:00 P.M. At 5:00 this evening we drove out to Soap Lake for what we heard was the best place in town to have dinner. I must say it wasn't that bad, a little pricey for a small town after all the town is a health town. They claim the lake has healing minerals in the water. They ,at one time had several bath houses that would cure most any ailment. This is what I had heard.

June 27, 1998 Saturday

We left Moses Lake at 9:00 a.m. today. The weather has been cooperating nice with no wind or rain. In the afternoon the clouds came in just as we were entering Montana but cleared some during the mid afternoon. We are at Haugon Montana parked in a free camp ground that has been put in on the grounds of the ten thousand silver dollar place. I looked for a rest area as we entered Idaho but found none so we didn't have lunch until right here in the camp ground and it was rather late to take to the road again so planed on staying all night. It's not often you find a free parking Places were the first ones in here and now it is 7:30 the place is filled up. This park looks like they had been doing some up grading but I am sure that they didn't have any one here that knew just what is needed when it comes to building for the newer larger RV's that are using these parking places. Today the parks will have to make many pull through because the unit are getting larger. There are a lot of motor homes that measure 30 to 45 feet in length then they all are pulling a car , truck or van behind them that adds upWard of an addition 25 to 30 feet. It is the last resort that we want to unhook that little beast that has been following you all day

June 28, 1998 Sunday

We left Haugon Montana this morning at 8:30 a.m. heading for Harlowton Montana. It was a nice day and the traffic wasn't bad today as it is some times during the week when there are a jillion trucks for miles. I think we could have broken the gas mileage today because we had a hard wind at our back all day. It was 5:30 when we arrived at the city park here in Harlowton. We were here last year and enjoyed the stay. After the days drive Winifred fixed a good supper, baked chicken, corn, potato's. I will be giving you a more on the activities here for the next week. This is not a bad place to stay for $ 8:35 per night. We have grass all around and we are in the trees with electric. I will be back tomorrow night for a little more gabbing on this lap top.

June 29, 1998 Monday

Hello! here I am back. This has been a lazy day after the trip from Olympia that started a few days back. It was not very existing but the little car had to be washed so took it up town to the car wash. I don't mean to belittle this little town of Harlowton. I have been gone for a long time so I can call it one of the small hick towns of Montana. That doesn't mean that Montana has the sole right to this name. After getting the car washed we went to see My cousin in law and found out that Warren Holmes wasn't any better then a year ago when we went to see him in a nursing home here in Harlowton. Warren has been in this home for almost five years. I pray that I don't have to end up that way. Of cause we don't have that choice. Just before lunch time we came home for lunch. As we got out of the car Audrey and Marie drove in behind us. They had seen us turn into the park. Some times I get a funny feeling that I couldn't get away with anything even if I had the idea. We couldn't visit very long as we had an appointment with a real-eState lady to go out in the country to look at a 600 acre farm. This is not for us it is so we can tell Charles and Irene about what we have seen. I wasn't too impressed with the place. It sounded good had the Musselshell river going through the property. It had been left un worked for a long time. The ditches were grown in with weeds and grass. When I asked about the water right she didn't indicate that even though the river ran through the property that didn't give them the right to take all the water that was in the river. The hay crops seem to be short and run down. Indicating that the fields were very old. There was no drinking water on the place, it had to be hauled in or drink the rain water that had been run into a cistern. The roads were very poor and that was mainly because the road went through some low land that would flood during any high water times and this year was one of the times. It's a pretty place with a lot of green brush and river bank grasses. There is no buildings on the property and it is long way from building materials. Transportation of materials would probably cost half as much as the building would cost. Tomorrow we are going down to Roundup, Montana to see my brother who has retired from barbering to see if he knows of any property down there. (you hear that barbers know every thing that goes on in the area) only kidding Jerry.

June 30, 1998 Tuesday

We made it down to Roundup and met Jerry and Shirley at a restaurant in town. We asked them about any places that we thought would fit Charles and Irene's type of farms. When we asked Jerry he didn't know of any but Shirley spoke up and said that the Prudential Realtors would probably know. We went up there and we walked in the office and the lady at the desk asked us our name and she said we had a Fiske in here about a month ago but I don't think it was you. After we put two and two together, Charles and Irene that had been in this office when they flew out to look at some farm land that they had picked up from the internet. It is had to believe but we then talked with the salesman and he was the one that had talked to Charles. His name was Jerry Fraser from the town of Lavina as we talked more his grandfather was the person that I had known. Then the more we talked he and I knew many people. When we talked about who married who it almost meant that we were related way down the shirt tail. He had just taken a new listing of a piece of property 640 acres that was priced at $ 325,000.00 we went out there and looked and it didn't look bad. It was about 9:00 p.m. when Audrey came in and informed us that Mary Fiske had had an accident coming out of Billings. The report in the paper said that she had pulled in front of an East bound vehicle and hit her on the drivers side of the car. The car was mangled so bad that they had to use the live jaw on the car to get her out.

July 1, 1998 Wednesday

With so much activity the last few days we took it a little easy. We drove down to Ryegate to see Marie to see if there was any word about Mary. The only word that they had was that she isn't responding to what is going on around her. They say if you take her had there isn't any indication that some one is there, I guess she doesn't talk or sees any one. I sure hope that she hasn't just given up.

July 2, 1998 Thursday

I am not sure that it is the age that makes me unable to remember what we did yesterday. I have to admitt that must have forgotten so it must not be of any value.

July 3, 1998 Friday

It is now the day before the 4th and we had company of several of our relatives. The first was Evelyn, my sister and Albert, my brother-in-law, then Audrey, my niece and Marie, Audrey's mother(and my sister-in-law). Then Frances, my cousin and Linda her driver. Linda is the youngest of Warren and Dora's family, also cousins. Then there was Ken and Shirley with their three children. Now it is getting close to lunch time so they all threw up a quick pot-luck type lunch. At about 3:00 p.m. Winifred and I decided to drive up to a large ranch at Rothimay. This place had a new log house on it and the owner was running 750 pairs of black Angus cattle. It wasn't one that I think I would want but maybe Charles would like it. He is the one that we are looking up these places for. All our company had left some of them went to evening Rodeo and some went to their rooms here in town after we rested a little we went to the Moose lodge for a dance. Most of the people that were at the pot-luck were there at the dance. Winifred and I came home early like 10:30 p.m. we old people can't keep up to this late hour group. We haven't heard of any change in Mary Fiske.

July 4, 1998 Saturday

The big day has arrived here at the park here in Harlowton, Montana. The first thing this morning after breakfast we started to get things ready for the gang that was here yesterday. While I was doing the dishes and then I made the cold slaw while Winifred went to the telephone to make some calls and get her walking done. Evelyn and Albert came about 10:00 a.m. so we went to the parade with them so we could get a good spot on the street. After the parade was over every one of our company came down for a pot luck meal again. We were just finishing up when the Rodeo started. The rest of the family wet to the Rodeo except Evelyn and Albert they didn't want to see the Rodeo but went back to Billings then Winifred and I went over to the show. We didn't stay to long as she got to feeling ill. When the show was over we all had a water melon here at the Motor Home then every one went home, I think. We got all the party thing done and in come a thunder storm that lasted about an hour. There was a lot of rain and wind in this storm. It is now 7:40 p.m. and time that I take my shower.

July 5, 1998 Sunday

The big day is over and here we are getting ready t0 leave Harlowton and head East. The intent was to end up at Glendive. We got to Ryegate in time for church but no church so we got to talk to The O'Tools that live across the street. in our conversation we found that there was a house up on the hill that use to be My uncle Harry's dairy back in about 1932 or 1934. Then we went down the town restaurant to meet Tex and Sharon we visited for a while but it was a short visit because they were on the way to Shepherd to deliver a saddle. After they left it was lunch time so we went to have lunch, had just got our lunch when Audery and Marie walked in so we had them for company. After lunch we went to the place on the hill and know one was home. We left our card then went for a drive to look at Mary's place to see if there would have a place to park. It wasn't bad but decided to stay all night at the Ryegate city park it had one electric outlet so we hooked up and it ran the air conditioner so you can't beat that at the price. I can't find out who to pay what else can a person do.

July 6, 1998 Monday

We made it to Glendive today and we are parked here for the night. We got a hold of the real estate people and wee have gone over the park with a fine tooth comb. We got here at 2:30p.m. and was the third RV in the park today at $25.00 per night. It looks like 1/3 full hare at 7:30

p.m. and they stay open until 9:00 p.m. and then they use a sign in the window for the late one's to go park and pay in the morning. The roads are all gravel but very good. The ground is all level here and it has city sewer and city water. The park uses most of the 13 acres but could be expanded using the other 5 acres or there could be homes put on this area. I am going to quit now and finish later.

July 7, 1998 Tuesday

We left the park at 10:00a.m. headed to Billings and stay at Evelyn's place for a few days. The day got rather warm for Winifred but I think she serviced ok because the air conditioner in the Motor Home was working very good. Last year I had trouble shifting the temperature from hot to cold. I had that fixed at Valley I 5 REV. and they did a very good job. It was rather hot when we got to Evelyn's. I got the little car un hooked and then backed the Motor Home into their drive way. It is time for bed so I will shut this thing off. we didn't sleep very well last night. It is thundering and trying to rain at this moment.

July 8, 1998 Wednesday

Most of the day seemed to be trying to reach the different Real Estate offices. It was rather warm yesterday about 97 degrees. Of course this is Montana in the summer time I did go over to Wal Mart and got a air filter for the little car. It had been getting hard to start it must have a lot of that road dust getting into the air system while being towed behind the Motor Home. It wasn't a bad day not to tiring. Then in the late afternoon Ken and Shirley, my niece stopped by here after Shirley had to wait for 3 hours in the Doctors office for her appointment. We had a nice visit. Shirley is the daughter of my sister, Evelyn.

July 9, 1998 Thursday

As a result of the telephone calls yesterday we had a phone call, I think was about 6:00 this morning I know that I was still sleeping. We got up and got ready to go to Ryegate, Montana, to see a piece of property that we looked at before but couldn't get into the house. We were lucky as we drove up there and the owner was there so got a chance to see the inside of the house also looked over all of the property. It has a potential of making a good RV park. The property has 1200 feet on Highway 12 and the south side off the acreage could be sold off as home building lots. We looked over this property before lunch time. Evelyn, Albert, Winifred and I got through looking at the place, as we were to meet Ken and Shirley for lunch at the restaurant that is just across the road from this property that we were looking at. As we walked in there was Marie and Audery there having their lunch so they joined us all in the large room to the back of the restaurant. I think that before the lunch hour was over we had 15 people including the children . It seemed that half of the Fiske clan gathered there for lunch After getting back to Billings, Winifred got a hold of the Real Estate office in Roundup and we had him get to work on checking some of the things that we didn't have the answer for. The first was could we get a road in and off of the property from the road. The next was is the lower part of the ground a wet lands? Also would the city give a permit to subdivide the property?

July 10, 1998 Friday

It was agreed that the first thing we would do was to go down to the hospital to see Mary Fiske who has been there in ICU with no change in her condition since her accident of June 30, 1998 at the intersection of highway 3 and the Zimmerman hill. Evelyn and I went in to see her then waited for all the family to get there and then after a long wait the Doctor informed us that Mary's condition has not improved but was deteriorating. As result of that meeting the family decided that there wasn't any chance the she wouldn't ever get any better. So I think that they are going to take her off of the respirator to see if she can do it on her own. I feel that was the best thing, as I looked at her I couldn't believe that she was alive. When she was hit she must have taken a sharp blow that did something to the brain or the nerves. It was about 12:00 noon Evelyn, Albert, Winifred and I went to the Red Robin for lunch. It was a good lunch then we went to Evelyn's where we are parked in their driveway. All we been doing this afternoon is sit in the Motor Home with the air conditioner running. I haven't heard or seen any thing about the temperature but it must be in the 100's.

July 11, 1998 Saturday

Here we are still at Evelyn's and Albert's place. If we don't get to moving soon they will want us to register to vote in Montana. May be the tax man will show up at the door. That's enough of that now we get into what we did today. The first thing was that we went shopping for shoes and shirts. I didn't think that I would need any of the above. Some how I was persuaded to go to the mall, we get there and the stores were not open so we went to the other mall. We ended up at the J C Penny's store where we purchased 2 pair of shoes and 2 shirts. I maybe shouldn't put this part in writing. When Winifred went to pay the bill by credit card they discovered that the card was an old card, When we went there to buy this stuff she said that she that she was going to pay for it on her card when her other car didn't work we used our joint card. It was a lot of fun even if she was a little embarrassed. Then in the evening we were invited to a wedding reception in one of the Billings City parks. The wedding was one of Albert's niece's that was getting married. As every one was gathering at the park a thunder storm was bring in hard winds but very little rain. The wind blew so hard that people was holding thinks down for several minutes. It was a great party with all having a fun time storm or no storm. These kid were local so they must have been use to this type of weather. We got back to the Motor Home about 8:00 tired out

July 12, 1998 Sunday

Guess what we slept in this morning after the past hard days. Evelyn and Albert asked if we wanted to go to church with them this morning. We went with them to church then when church was out we went to a Mexican place for dinner, I have had better but this wasn't that bad ether. We got home just as Jerry and Shirley drove up. They had been to breakfast with Mary Fisk's Family as many of them was there because May had passed away yesterday. We told that the funeral will be for Mary Wednesday Morning at 10:30 in the Ryegate School Gymnasium. It is getting late so I am going to shut this thing down for the night.

July 13, 1998 Monday

We left Billings this morning at 10:50 after about 2 hours of running around Billings for a place to dump the holding tanks in the Motor Home. What made it a disaster was that we took the little car a couple days earlier to check out the places so that we didn't have to do this running around with the big rig. Well it turned out that we wasted out time. A short time before I got there some one had dumped some thing in the septic tank and plugged it up so no one else could use it. I have seen and heard that some RV'ers are careless and they have a loose fitting on the end of their hose and it come off going down into the trap. We arrived here in Ryegate at noon and got our famous place along side of the city park. The price is right with electric no charge. I wanted to take a look at the 17 acre place here in town. My nephew Tex Carpenter was cutting the hay today and I got to talk to the owner again about some of the bounders of the property. I have tried to sketch out a lay out of where the road and house is located on the property. there was some more thunder storms that came through here at about 6:00 but none at this hour

July 14,1998 Tuesday

For the past 10 to 15 days the temperature has been in the mid to upper 90's. When you have this type of a situation it will most always bring in the thunder storms. It is 7:30 p.m. and it doesn't appear to me that the thunder storms are going to come this evening. We are still parked here at the city park. We have had some company today and the temperature is hanging at the 95 degrees. The Street tar is so soft that it gets tracked into the Motor Home. It took me almost al afternoon to clean the carpet. This is a nice place but that tar should have been covered heavier coating of fine gravel.

July 15,1998 Wednesday

This day was a nice day but a sad one because we had to bury one of the family members. I had written on June the 30th that Mary Fiske was in a terrible auto accident coming out of Billings. She was in the Billings Hospital for 10 days and didn't show any improvement then on the 10th day the Doctor gave the family the facts of the situation. As he explained it there was no hope. So they took her off of the life support and she passed away that evening at 6:30 p.m.. Today we had the funeral here in the Ryegate school gymnasium. There was a very large crowd, a very good lunch after the service. Then most of the close family went out to the farm where Mary had lived for many years. There I saw some of her family side that I hardly knew having seen them once or twice. Today has been another hot day. It seems that this country has slipped south about 2000 miles. When I use to live here 61 years ago there may be two or three days of this kind of heat but not this weeks and weeks running. What else could I say after this some sad and some pleasures. It is to bad that the families have to wait for a death to get together. Some times it is the only time you see some of the other side of the family.

July 16, 1998 Thursday

After a few days in Ryegate we took off for a new place to park. We had planned to stop at the Big Timber camp ground that we had liked very much, when we arrived the place had changed hands but they were booked up for 10 days s we changed our mind and headed for home. We drove 377 miles, it wasn't that bad the weather was very Warm close to the 100's but there wise there wasn't any wind to hold you back. Wash are now parked at the Chalet Bearmouth that is on the Clark Fork River. This place in on highway 90 about 40 miles east of Missoula, Montana.

July 17, 1998 Friday

We left the campground at about 7:30 a.m. and arrived in Olympia at 5:10. I would have been home earlier but after we go to North Bend the traffic was nothing bur stop and go, it had to be the Friday afternoon and people going home after work. We saw only one accident on the road and that was after we got on I-5 going south around the Tacoma area.

July 18, 1998 Saturday

We had several small chores to do around the house and some to do at the neighbor and Winifred had the washing to do. The plan was to stop there for a day or two then go to the ocean at Ocean Shores and clean up Charles and Irene's place. Winifred had Smoky her son over with his dogs that Winifred just loves.

July 19, 1998 Sunday

In the morning we went over to Charles place to inform him on what we found out about farms or ranches there. We had been looking for him to buy. He and Irene think they want to over there and have a place that will give them some income. I must say that if you have to put up much money this would be a tough go. The people that have lived there all their life are just making ends meet and they have to put in long hours. We finished up with our chores and got ready to go again.

July 20, 1998 Monday

This morning we had some small things to load then we could get on the way to Ocean Shores. It was lunch time when we got to Aberdeen, Washington so stopped at a well known restaurant called Duffy's not a bad place to eat. We got to Charles and Irene's place parked the Motor Home then mowed some of the grass that was mostly weeds. I did that because Winifred's son Smoky was to come down from Olympia for a few days and I wasn't sure when he would come. After the large lunch or dinner we had a dish of strawberry short cake for the evening meal that was plenty.

July 21, 1998 Tuesday

Today I finished the mowing. I forgot I spent about two hours on trying to get the dish setup with no luck. After the grass was mowed I did get the dish setup buy changing some of the settings, now it is coming in very good. This makes Winifred happy but I think she got weaned from it some because we didn't have TV all the time when we were traveling the State of Montana. Smoky still didn't come today. I must have heard it wrong when I said that he was coming yesterday. I got the vehicle wash equipment ready and Winifred washed the whole Motor Home. She had to work hard at it, as we hadn't washed it during the month long trip into Montana. Then when she started to wash the windows there was the hard water marks on the windows they we had picked up some place while we were traveling.

July 22, 1998 Wednesday

I started to do some pruning this morning to help the place look better after the cities mutilating crew came around the whole Ocean Shores area and cut limbs, trees and brush back on the right of way to the property lines. It was one of the worst butchering jobs that I have ever seen. The whole area was de-nuded on all streets. Smoky showed up about 10:00 a.m., but he stayed just for the day then went home about 4:00, he will be back next week maybe will stay a few days this time.

July 23, 1998 Thursday

After Smoky left, Winifred didn't feel too good. I think that she misses him very much. I do know that she and her son were very close as I was told they would go tent camping very often. As we went to bed, Winifred told me that Smoky and his wife Mildred weren't talking any more or having meals together, which may be what was giving her some of her problem. Then she thought that I was unfair, that I like to work outside and do repair work. She thought that I should stay inside with her and keep her company. That's what I did today but I will have to figure out some other way. Maybe she would like to help me with some of the chores. It may be difficult since I have worked so much of my life by myself and some jobs it is hard for two people to do the same thing. The first thing this morning was to empty the holding tanks after breakfast. This is a job that we cannot avoid, they hold only so much. If Charles and Irene weren't going to sell the place, I would put in another drop back here where it would be easier for me to use. We did go and look around the area and saw duck 1,2, and three. Then stopped at the city library then we finished the day with a good dinner of corn, baked beans, Cole slaw and topped off with strawberry short cake.

July 24, 1998 Friday

This wasn't the best of days. It started out that we went into town to get a burn permit to clean up the east side of the property where the city butchered up the brush and trees. Winifred was going to help me with the burn after she got the Motor Home inside windows cleaned. While I was watching the fire, she went for a walk with her handbag on here shoulder. I just happened to see her and all she would say was she was going for a walk. I couldn't leave the fire at this time so after over an hour I had put the fire out and went looking for her. She was on the beach studying the waves and birds. I just waited for her to come for home and she did about 12:30 p.m. We road home together with out a single word of conversation and here it is 7:00 p.m. and there hasn't been a dozen words spoken. I don't know what the problem is at this time. The balance of the day I have been watching the fire to make sure that it doesn't start up again. Then I washed the Motor Home windows on the outside and took a little nap. This evening after she fixed a good dinner I went out to pickup the equipment in the shop.

July 25, 1998 Saturday

The day started out with no one talking. Then after breakfast, the minds started to move a little. It seems that I have been working too much of the time during the day light hours. Winifred said right after breakfast, "well, it's time for you to get out to work." I think that is what broke the silence we had for much too long. As a result, I stayed in the Motor Home all morning then we got out the paints and started to do some oil painting. I sure didn't get anything else done like cleaning up the yard and doing some pruning. I seem to be happy working or repairing something but my wife thinks differently about it.

July 26, 1998 Sunday

This was a very nice day. It started out with most of the problems forgotten. We went to church this morning then into town to try a new place only to find out that they were having buffet only so we had breakfast the second time. That's all right we called it our lunch. Then for this evening, we had breakfast again. It seemed that I craved some cereal, so that is what we had and a bowl of fresh peaches. We did some garage saleing this afternoon and found this place that had some leftover items from his store that he sold last year. Winifred got several greeting cards that were $ 1.00 each and I found a couple of computer books also, two dolls. Then after we were home a short time I thought about this yard sale place. They had a cabinet for a key board that slides out, I thought about it at the time we where there and I didn't think I needed it that bad because it was to long. As we were taking our naps it came to me that this can be cut down to fit the place that I want to install it at home. I got up from the nap and went over there and looked it over. It could be cut down so I offered him $ 3.00 and he wanted five, it was worth that but I saw some aluminum brackets there and wanted him to throw them in for the $ 5.00 but he wanted $6.00. I paid the money and I am sure I got a good deal.

July 27, 1998 Monday

We are still here on Charles and Irene's place here in Ocean Shores. The temperature got to 74 degrees today and the TV said it was 95 in Olympia so we will be staying here a few more days where the weather is almost perfect just a little cool in the morning. I have been burning again this morning. The same trash that was left around after the city mutilated so many of the trees. I hope that some of the people are happy with the horrible job that was done to the beautiful city of Ocean Shores property. I for one think it was one of the worst jobs. I am sure there must not be any competition for this kind of workmanship. That's enough crying over spilt milk because there isn't anything that can be done about this sloppy work when the lot owners didn't have any say about what the job would look like when the job was finished. As far as I know, the lot owners have not been billed for the job but I would bet that the city fathers will figure it in on the sewer job or some other place.

July 28,1998 Tuesday

Here I am putting off what I could do today and find out that I put off this typing and now I can't think what happened a couple of days back. This was the day that the tanks are filled and need to be emptied so that was the first and most important thing. After that, the hookup was in order and the clocks were set again, the TV cable was connected. Now we are sitting good for a few more days. If I thought we were going to use this place to park for any length time I would install the drain pipe to the septic tank from the place that I wouldn't have to move this 100 feet each time that the tanks were full. Then we got out the oil paintings that we have been carrying around for some time and never took the time to get down to the painting. We found out that we had forgotten a lot of the art of putting oil to the canvas.

July 29, 1998 Wednesday

We got up a little late and then Winifred fixed a good breakfast. The we went to town and got the newspaper and a few groceries and Winifred picked up a special paintbrush that she needs to make some clouds on her painting. We both did some painting in the afternoon only to find out that we need do more painting. I think that I didn't do my painting any good yesterday so the next time I do the painting again I am going to have to do some correcting.

July 30, 1998 Thursday

I woke up early and it was a little cool so while the furnace was warming the place up I worked up Winifred and we played abound a little until I turned over on top of her and we had a little sex until she said that it was enough.

We did something different today. Left Ocean Shores went to Aberdeen then on to West Port. When we got to West Port there was a chainsaw carving show going on with dozens doing the carving with the standard chain saw that is used in the wood for falling large trees. With all those saws running at the same time the noise was something. We returned home to the Motor Home at 5:00 p.m. just in time to get the local news on TV. After making some pop corn and cleaning up things, I went to the task of doing my writing as I try to do at the end of each day.

July 31, 1998 Friday

We had a light rain last night so the ground and grass was just right to be mowed. With this condition there isn't as much dust, that is a plus. I mowed all of the lawn and the street edges. It was time to empty the holding tanks. I did that after breakfast, while I was parked over in the place where I could reach the drop place. Then I mowed this part of the lawn so that I could park back in the same space then hook up the power and the dish, now I am ready for the next few days. Now that I am located for a few more days, I finished the balance of the lawn. Winifred was out in the large part of the lawn getting ready for Charles and Irene when they come on Sunday. She is planning a lawn party with all the fixings. She has a table made from sawhorses, a piece of scrap lumber, a couple of blankets and to top it all off the centerpiece of flowers from the Motor Home table.

August 1, 1998 Saturday

We are still here at Charles and Irene place at Ocean Shores. At lunch time there was a beep on a Ford pickup and it was none other then Smoky with his two dogs. One thing he got here in time for lunch so his mother didn't have to make two lunches. Winifred and her son are so much at home in this setting, eating lunch outside, in the open air, with bees and bugs to share the food with and in this case with the dogs also. I am sure that Winifred has missed this type of living as they use to do this very often then I came along and it wasn't my style. I wish she would do more of it with her son. Then about 3:00 p.m., he had to leave for home in Olympia. Then after Smoky left, I made the cole slaw that was to be used for the Sunday yard party when Charles and Irene would be here to do something on the place where we are parked. They arrived at about 4:00 p.m. so we got the chicken out of the freezer and we opened a can of pork and beans so we had the Sunday dinner in the Motor Home in place of the lawn and we had it this evening because they have to leave for home in the morning. You just don't know how they have scheduled there time. Maybe Winifred and I don't understand that the working people today have to keep their nose to the grindstone. Everyone is rushing from place to place these days. I must say that I am glad that I am not in that rat race. I have to question all of this rushing. It seems the faster they go the more behind they get? I think I have rambled on long enough for this day.

August 2, 1998 Sunday

We had a busy start this morning as Charles and Irene were here and they had a lot of work on their schedule. Winifred & I got up a little earlier the usual. The past weeks we have been sleeping in until after 8:00 o'clock, we say we are on vacation and we are full timers at it. The first thing after breakfast Charles and I made a trip to the town of Ocean Shores. We got there just as the hardware store opened and got a new lock set for the door on the tower of his house. They were busy getting things ready to put it up for sale and this one door on the second floor of the deck was rusted up so bad that we had to break the old lock. Before the noon hour, the Real Estate man had come and looked over the place. The kids were loaded and they headed back to the big rush of the city of Auburn, Washington.

August 3, 1998 Monday

Did a little bit picking up of our equipment and I worked on the upstairs toilet of Charles and Irene's house here at Ocean Shoes. After that, I did a little on work on one of the lawn mowers but I have to do something about the carburetor, it is hard to start. Then Winifred and I drove up to Kalock for dinner. It was 180 miles round trip. The drive was great but the food wasn't that great. Live and learn. Tomorrow morning we head back to Olympia to see what there is there that we didn't get finished when we left for Montana the first of July, 1998.

January 12,1999 Tue.

Today we are loading the Motor home for a trip to Southern California and Arizona where the sun may be shining. We left at 12:30 p.m. after getting loaded and getting some phone calls made. It was while we were having our breakfast that Mildred called and was worried about Smoky(Bob) Cavanaugh that he hadn't called in for some time. This upset every one, as he was duck hunting over in the Moses Lake area. After many long distant calls to the other hunters home and to the Regional Office in Ephrata to see if they could locate these two hunters. After many more calls Winifred was satisfied that they were all right for now, so we took off for Salem. We did get at my sisters place at 3:30 p.m. just before she got home. This evening Winifred made several more calls to Mildred and the other hunters home in Gig Harbor. We did get some more information. The other hunter had called his wife last Thursday evening, that hadn't been mentioned last evening. What a three-ring circus this whole thing has turned out to be, couple of grown men not considering their families by just doing what they want to and not keeping their loved one's informed.

January 13, 1999 Wed.

Today we left my sister Arlene's place in Salem, Oregon heading south before a storm might come in the mountains that we still have to go over. I don't want to get into any snow with this Motor home or freezing weather. We made good time, weather was great and roads dry all the way. I did stop in Ashland at Les Schwab to have my front tires rebalanced only to find out that the right front was out of round and would have to buy a new tire. I had them put it back on. I am going to find the tire manufacture to see if I can get some kind of an adjustment. It has only 20,000 miles on what is supposed to be one of the best tires built. That's according to the company that makes them. We have parked for the night here in Yreka, Calif., a good park but did cost $22.00 a night with $2.00 dollars off when you are a member of the Good Sam Club.

January 14, 1999 Wed.

We had a good nights rest last night even if the price was a little high. We got started this morning at 8:30 and was on the way south on I-5 freeway headed for Santa Rosa, Calif. Winifred had planned the trip here in Calif. that we turn off of the freeway at William and take a short cut and come into Santa Rosa from the back door. When we first started on this short cut I thought that I had been on this road before. Well, it wasn't very far when the road got steeper and more crooked. In fact, there was a time when I looked in the mirror and thought that the little car that I was towing wanted to pass the Motor home. The trip was a lot longer then I had calculated and we didn't get into Santa Rosa until about 3:30 and it was after 4:00 when we got to Connie's place. We couldn't park any place on the street in front of her apartment so we had to go several blocks and then we parked an a mall area an unhooked the little car so we looked around and found an old restaurant had closed just a half block from Connie's place. There still wasn't anyone home so we are sitting here on this old parking lot. I have driven a lot of miles over many State roads but never had I had any harder drive then this was. It was so bad I feel like a sailor that comes ashore. I still feel the sway as I type this and it has been three hours since we landed.

January 15, 1999 Friday

We are in this parking lot that is half a block from Connie's so we can walk there with ease. The weather hasn't been the best, cloudy and sprinkle off and on but rained hard for awhile this evening. This place is a large parking lot with an old building on one corner and I see a sign on the place that it's for lease so may be that is why we haven't been run off yet. Winifred and Connie went groceries shopping yesterday afternoon and guess what I did? I took a nap for about an hour. I think it was a hangover from the day before. I did take the little car to the car wash, as it was so thick with mud you couldn't see the color. What a mess it was after about 700 miles of road grime that we had been through. Lots of rain plus the sand that had been used on the road for ice when the early storm had gone through several days ago

January 16, 1999 Saturday

We are still here on the parking lot, not a bad place. We do have to run the generator a little to keep the battery up and have to run it for the microwave. I have solar panels on the top of the Motor home, but they aren't helping much when we can't see the sun yet with this cloud and rain all the time. It is rather convenient to be able to visit Connie and Burt as they live in an apartment where there isn't any parking area for much less then their vehicles. Monday we move over to the other side of town to some friends of Winifred's. Being Saturday we were able to visit with Burt and Connie for awhile then Burt had to go on the job for a short time during which time Winifred got to visit with her daughter and I did a little sleeping and some writing in this journal. In the evening, we had a great meal that Burt and Connie put up. It was make your own taco with all the fixings. It wasn't what I could eat very much off but enjoyed it and didn't stuff myself.

January 17, 1999 Sunday

The day started out with the rain still coming down as if we were home so why did we make this trip. We went over to Burt and Connie's place this morning for his nutritional food. The breakfast consisted of pancakes, hash browns, eggs and all most fat free ham. What a meal. In the afternoon, we had a good visit with Burt, Connie and her three children that live in the area came to see us while we were still here. That was real nice of them to take time out from there busy schedules. One of the boys named Charlie came all the way from San Francisco, Calif., that is about 60 miles.

January 18, 1999 Monday

This is what is called," Black Monday" holiday. It is wet and nasty again with a few clouds and some higher elevation fog. We are getting ready to move from here and go across town to friends of Winifred's this afternoon. We went over to Connie's at about 9:00 o'clock just in time to catch Burt leaving for work and Connie had already left for an appointment that she had. So, we went back to the Motor home and waited until about lunchtime. We went back and she was home so we took her out to lunch at the Sizzlers, not all that good but we got filled up. Then we road around town to look at some city or county park so

Winifred could find someplace that Smoky could park his truck and visit around here in Santa Rosa. Now it is getting to be 3:00 p.m. and we are still on the parking lot but we soon left there heading for the next stop on the other side of town. We had the little car unhooked so Winifred drove the car and I followed her, as I didn't know the way to well. There had been a new road put in over a hill for a housing development so we missed the first turn off and got lost for a while. She then told me to stay put and she would scout out the road to find out where we could get through to her friends house. She came back and I followed her to the destination with no problem only a little late but I got set and the hook up all done before dark. We had been on the road and parked for seven days without being hooked to any electric power. I had solar panels on the roof for this extended time without the battery being charged from line power. All this time we had very little sun so that didn't help under this situation.

January 19, 1999 Tuesday

Here it is 9:00 a.m. and we are here at the Nuzums and after a good nights sleep we have had breakfast and I have caught up on yesterdays writing and beginning today's. Nothing to report at this time so will close off until tonight.

January 20, 1999 Wednesday

I didn't get at the writing this morning it seems that I was a little late getting up. We didn't have breakfast until 9:00 a.m. it was maybe because we were up to long last night. This traveling does put a crimp in any ones schedule. Some of the time we may travel longer or we may stop earlier. We are here at Hank and Ruth's Nuzums. We always park here in front of their house. We have done this for the past three years when we are on the way to the South. In doing this, Winifred gets to visit with her very good friends and I get to rest a little from the driving. It breaks up the trip some at the same time.

January 22, 1999

We are still here having a good time with lots to eat and wonderful hosts. Today we wake up to a nice day. Cloudy but no rain. Last night after dinner Fred Lomis made some homemade candy. It is one of his favorite brittles, but this time he used Pecans in it in place of the peanuts and it turned out real good. The night before he made peanut brittle for the first time in their new microwave oven so wasn't sure about the out come, well it was eatable but with a burnt taste. Because I have had a lot of trouble with the same thing about it was either burnt or it tuned out sticky and chewy. This is enough for today.

January 23, 1999 Saturday

We sure had a great dinner party last evening here at the Nuzum's place. They had invited two other couples, long time friends of Winifred's and we had a good visit after dinner. Then this morning we had a great breakfast with the Nuzums and Lomis. I saw Fred making some sweet rolls last night that were served for breakfast, were they ever good. As I write this, the morning is almost gone. This is a little short but it is also a day with some hard rains. I guess it is over maybe for a few hours.

January 24, 1999 Sunday

Today was a good day that started out with a light breakfast. At 8:30 a.m., we went to the Methodist Church here in Santa Rosa with Fred and Diana. This was the church that Winifred had gone to way back on in her life. It was a great sermon. The minister was a very good one that you wouldn't or couldn't go to sleep. After church, we went out to brunch, not a bad brunch but I have had better. Then we went to Fred and Diane's place for a little rest then they had most of their children and parents in for the dinner meal. For the past week Diane had made a new meal every day so Fred said that there wasn't enough room in the refrigerator to hold any more so tonight's meal will be all the leftovers. After all the family had their fill there was still some food left. The meal was delayed a little while, as one of the family was to pick up a six-month-old beagle pup. Those kids were all wrapped up in that dog, I don't think they ate anything this evening.

January 26, 1999 Tue.

It rained hard all night and part of the morning. At this point I am not sure why we left home except to visit friends. We are now here at Flo and Willard's place in Santa Rosa. Having a good time eating very well and sleeping well. What more could you ask for? It is getting to be

4:00 p.m. and they aren't awake yet so I wonder when we go to eat. I'm not hungry yet so maybe that is a good thing. Maybe it was best that we had lots of good food because we are going to be late eating this evening. Willard found out his truck is ready at the garage so he and I went across town some distance away.

January 27, 1999 Wednesday

Did some visiting and the first thing in the morning I had to take the Motor home to the Michelin tire dealer to see what is wrong with the right front tire. This is the tire that I had to have balanced the day before in Yreka, Cal. They told me the tire was bad, that it had internal cord slippage. So today the tire company told me that they couldn't make any adjustment on the tire that the problem was something else. They took the wheel off and put it on the balance machine and showed me the wheel was what was the problem and he showed it to me while it was running at a very slow speed and I saw that the wheel was out about 3/8 of an inch. The next thing will be to take it to the dealer to see if I can get anything out of them or at least find out how this can be corrected.

We had a good evening meal as usual at Flo and Willard's place. I almost forgot to mention that Flo had gotten a tow train for Christmas but was having so much company and house full of guests.

January 28, 1999 Thursday

We got up rather late and after breakfast we did a little visiting and then went somewhere but I don't remember where. Maybe it was the Family Geology Center to look up some one of the families, Winifred's and mine. This evening we had another great meal and did some visiting again. At 9:00p.m. I got sleepy and went out to the Motor Home for the night, course I let Winifred come along only if she would be a good girl.

January 29, 1999 Friday

I should not let this day go by with out saying anything, but I can't recall what happened 24 hours after the fact. This may sound funny but to me it is a sad thing not to remember when that is all that you have to do. I can make an excuse that the friends that we are visiting have kept us very busy. Mostly eating and sleeping. I don't think that that I have had so much time to just do nothing and sleep a lot.

January 30, 1999 Saturday

The last couple of days I have been playing around trying to set up this typing the way that I would like to have it. As of this time I don't really like the layout. Maybe I can get the time some day to make it work when I don't have to eat or sleep. We had all the plans made for today that the women were going to the Family Genealogies Center in the morning and Ross and I was going to the gun show at the fairground. After walking all over the grounds there wasn't a show today. The sign stated gun show from 9:00 a.m. to 5:00 p.m. but didn't have a date on the sign. Then after we had a snack, we had a naptime for two hours then drove around where Winifred had lived and sold many of the houses and I saw where she had planted some Redwood trees that now were about ninety feet high. At one time she must have owned many different houses and all different sizes.

January 31, 1999 Sunday

Today is the day of rest, go to church and thank God for putting us here on earth.. I do believe that I was put here to do a job, whatever that may be. I don't feel that I have finished that job yet, even though I am getting up in years, many people are getting older.

I went with Winifred and her friends to the church where she had spent many years. I am not of the same faith so I went to the first hour then came home to the Motor Home as I had some chores to do before we take off on the next leg of the trip that we are on this year. They got home about 1:30 and started to get leftovers on the table and we had great meal. We had the same great bunch of her good friends for this meal we were instructed that we had to eat up all the leftovers. Then the rest of the evening we sat around and had a great visit. It was nice of them to all be there as we had planed to leave the next morning. The weather was nice but the wind was cold like winter as it is their winter there.

February 1, 1999 Monday

The day started out with a great breakfast with Ross and Millie where we have been parked out side of their home on the street with our electric cord plugged into there power outlet. It makes this type of travel a little less expensive. We sure do appreciate these kinds of friends and then they feed us to that is real super we the best of all worlds. We left Santa Rosa this morning and reached our destination here at 4:00 p.m., the same place we usually stop at when ever we are in the area. It is called the Somerville's Almond tree R.V. Park.

February 2, 1999 Tuesday

We signed up for three days more at this very nice park. The first thing that happened after breakfast was that Winifred got all the wash done and put away before noon. I think a traveler must do this occasionally to rest. We also empty tanks and take on a supply of fresh water. Also, we look around the area and learn about the way others live. We are parked about 12 miles from the town of Coalinga, Cal., one of the first oil well areas in California dating back to the 1890's. This afternoon we went to the R.C.BAKER MEMORIAL MUSEUM and it was a very well put up place with a good showing of how this way of life was like back in 1870 with the archival of the Americans. I don't know how much oil is being pumped now. I didn't see any of the pumping arms moving. I think that the main source of livelihoods is in the truck gardening and fruit trees. This was an arid area with very little rainfall then the State built a cement cannel from some source of water supply to make this area a great producing of the vegetables and orchards.

February 3,1999 Wednesday

We are still here at the same campground and resting. So, this morning we didn't have breakfast until 10:00 a.m. then did nothing until this afternoon when we went over to Coalinga, California. We went a different way. North on Highway 5 about 10 miles there was another little highway traveler's service area. One of the largest there was the Harris Ranch it had everything from Motel, Restaurant, gift shop, Gas service Stations. Ever thing that I looked at was very expensive. We thought we would like a cup of coffee but it cost $ 1.75 for a cup. The meals would run from a low of $10.00 to a high of $ 30.00 a plate. After seeing this, I wasn't hungry any longer. Then went across the highway where there were several more eating establishments and went to the Red Robin good all you could eat for two people was $15.00. Then went to Coalinga to see the what is called "Iron Zoo" a unique group of oil pumps decorated as animals, clowns & more. I, for one, wasn't impressed by this type of art. Ugly oil pumpers that dot the hillsides and mess up the natural land area. I am sure that all of this is heaven for many people in the area and gave many families a living. I must confess that these wells not only gave the employment but also helped to keep our oil supply home instead of importing.

February 4,1999 Thursday

Another day of leisure for this old couple. Next week Winifred will be 80 years young and next May I will be in the 85 league. I can say that both of us are feeling very good and some times act like kids. I did a few things around the Motor Home like vacuum the carpet, clean the windshield for the trip tomorrow to Riverside, California. We always stop here on the way to the sunny south. Doris and Larry Ashe are one of the best host and hostesses.

This was truly a day off from work and for dinner we went to Harris Ranch Restaurant. This is an Old pioneer ranch that must date back in the 1800's and now it is a full service area that is along highway 5 about half way between two areas of civilization There is 400 miles of nothing and this place is located about the half way point that gives them a great advantage. This ranch has a Motel, gift store, bar and two Service stations. These people don't have it all to themselves because just across the freeway is some tough competition.

They are a little pricy but they can get this because of the way they display the fact that it is an old ranch and all the decor is of that era with a lot of old time pictures of the days gone by. Plus, they have a lot of the old hand tools that were used to survive.

February 5, 1999 Friday

Left the Almond Tree Park at 9:30 today headed for Riverside, Calif. where the next stop will be at Winifred's nephew and niece's home. This is where we always stop at when we travel to the South. Here we park in front of their house on the curb. It had a rather steep grade but with several blocks under the front jacks, we get along very well. This Motor Home has the automatic leveling jacks on all four corners of the vehicle. We did get a little lost as we got within about 5 miles of their place. I was afraid that I would go past the turn off of Spruce Street. Up to this point I hadn't seen the Spruce street exit so I took the downtown exit and that put me about 9 miles past in a different direction. Then on top of that, I was getting low on fuel so when I pulled off to gas up they gave us directions back to where I had made the mistake. We didn't loose too much time as we got here about 3:30 long before dark. They were waiting for us but thought that we had changed our minds about coming today. We didn't miss a great dinner that we had at about 7:30 p.m. of breast of chicken with a backed potato. Every place we go they have heard that I am on a low fat of 20 mg. per day. I feel a little funny about that so many are concerned about my health but I am grateful that they do, it makes my eating more enjoyable when I know that I'm not over doing the fat part.

Yesterday when I pulled in here I didn't get the coach set true level so today I blocked up the front jacks and raised the front about 6" inches so now we are set good for a long stay but that wouldn't be good manners to stay too long. I sure wouldn't want to wear out such a good place to stay.

February 6, 1999 Saturday

Right after breakfast we had to go shopping so I could get the car wash soap and wax to wash both vehicles that were so muddy you could hardly tell their color. Winifred and I went over to the closest store the K-Mart and they didn't have what I wanted so we went looking for a Wal-Mart. After getting the directions here at this store, we got a little lost. We found out later we took the road to San Diego instead of the one to Indio. Here again, we were within about one mile of where we wanted to go. Then we started home we saw another K-Mart store so we got the car wash soap and wax that I wanted. The rest of the day I spent washing vehicles and were they ever dirty. I had to wash them twice to get them to look good. After that, I was very tired. Then at seven this evening we went out to dinner and had a very good codfish meal. We came home and had a little ice cream before bedtime.

February 7, 1999 Sunday

Today is the day that we are going to have an 11 year olds birthday party in the park across the street from where we are staying. Some of the guests came and started to set up the picnic but after a little while, the wind came up cold and chased the party into the house. I was glad of that because I was freezing, but Larry and Winifred were enjoying the cool air. I have not been able to understand why they both like temperatures between 50 & 60 degrees. We ended up with a great party and the 11 year old had a ball opening his gifts. We had a lot to eat and after the good meal the birthday boy had gotten a quiz game that he and his sister had fun reading some of the questions and the old folks had to answer, the kids really got a bang out of the fact that we missed a lot of getting the right answers. This is the first night in a long time that we are giving up before 9:00 or 10:00 p.m. I for one can't take those late hours

I might add that we all talk at once and as loud as possible. I am so grateful to be apart of this family & I love each & every one of them,,,,,,,,,,,(Winifred)

February 8, 1999 Monday

It has been a heavy overcast all day today and that must have had an effect on my ambition. I sure didn't get any thing accomplished. I was going to wash the Motor Home widows on the outside and thought that I didn't have the correct clothes for that type of a dirty job that it could be. Went to Wal-Mart and found a pair of trousers and a medium weight jacket in case the weather didn't warm up to suit me. We did a lot of visiting this afternoon and evening. Then came the good part when Doris had fixed the dinner of the good chicken that she has always served, this time she had garlic bread that was all so very good. After dinner, we talked until 10:00 p.m. about every thing in the world but didn't solve any major things. After retiring, I read a couple of chapters in a book when Winifred went to sleep I also gave up and we both had a good nights sleep.

February 9, 1999 Tuesday

This morning we rose rather early so that we could go through the process of preparing the Motor Home for unloading the holding tanks. This means that I had to lift the automatic jacks, unhook the power cord and the dish cable. Here, at this place, it is really handy because Larry has a drop in the median in front of his house that all I have to do is backup about 75' feet and hook up the waste hose that takes all the waste to the city sewer line. Then I pull ahead, level the coach and everything is back in order for several days more. After that Larry and I went to town, as he had to get a blood drawn, then make some other stops. When we got home the women had rearranged the inside of the house and started to set up the tables for Winifred's 80th birthday celebration that will take place tomorrow afternoon. We are going to take the hard workers out to dinner this evening. As I sit here we are waiting for Larry and Doris to get ready to go out. At this moment we had a very hard rain and wind come down that you couldn't hardly hear any thing else. We had one of these this afternoon but it didn't last but a few minutes. The sun didn't shine all day today. It seems that this bad weather has plagued us all the way from home.

February 10, 1999 Wednesday

This is the big day of Winifred's life, it's her 80th birthday with one of the nicest parties that any one could ever have. It started out with a telephone call to her Son singing happy birthday. That started her day for sure, it was the first time she had heard his voice since the first of January about a week before leaving home for the south. As you recall, he was to be home four or five days after leaving to go Duck hunting over in the Moses Lake area with a friend and he hadn't called home. We spent a couple of days to find out that his friend had called his wife and that everything was fine so we took off for the south. Back to the big day. She had several of her kin call her and wish her the happy birthday over the phone. Then at about 2:30 p.m. everyone was there and there was a little time before the big feed so they played some kind of a game that was like bingo but just like it. While they were doing that, I took a lot of pictures with the camcorder. Talk about the noise then when this game was being played. When dinner was called, Winifred and I were seated at the head of the table. Then Doris and her daughter served the most delicious baked filet of salmon that you ever tasted. Then came the time for the gifts and cards. The gifts were a large book on cooking Fat Free, from Doris with three cans of canned Tyson chicken, a large electric barbecue from Bill, Jan, Jim, Carole, tulip plant in a small pot that we put on the table in the Motor Home, also a jar of lemon curd from Jan and then the most important was the huggable bears from Pam and Larry Lee. Not last but least a promise of a Scanner for the computer and many cards. Then came the beautiful Happy Birthday carrot cake. Of course the cake wasn't large enough to put 80 candles on so they used the numeral of eight zero. By the time the party was over the time was getting to be 10:00 o'clock and was Winifred wore out with all the excitement all day. I am sure it must have been the best and most enjoyable birthday that she had ever had in her honor. Especially with so many kids and relatives putting it on. It must have been 11:00 p.m. when we finally got to bed, it was all great fun.

February 11, 1999 Thursday

At the party, there was a change in the plans as to where we will be journeying to next. So, it ended up that we were to go to Palm Springs, California for a few days. After everyone gave us the directions to the next place some 60 miles away from Riverside, I thanked them very much but I can't keep that much in my mind for very long. Then in the morning, we had heard that there were high winds in the area that we were going, then we had made many calls to the State Dept. for some information that only took lot of extra time. I don't like to be rude but I have trouble being scared with this kind of information. In my travels, it seems that if the way gets too bad the highway crews close the roads. I also don't like to get myself all worked up about "maybe this or that could happen to you down the road". We did leave Riverside as planned and we did find that the wind was blowing hard but not to the point of destroying the Motor Home.

February 12, 1999 Saturday

I have a few minutes now so thought that I would get this started for this day. To begin with, it is hard to write about some thing that hasn't happened yet. The plan is to go and do some yard sale shopping this day. I say this day because it could mean most of the day when you go with Carole on one of these trips to look at some one else's junk. I don't mind it when I don't have room to cart it home that way the thought of purchasing is different. Sure enough, we started out this morning when Winifred went for a walk and saw a yard that was open for business. Would you believe she saw what see wanted very badly? She hurried back to the Motor Home to tell me the great find. She gave me the directions but I missed a part of the location and had to come back to the Motor Home to get her then Carole followed a short time later. Winifred had seen a set of dishes that she thought was just the right thing for our home in Olympia, Washington. The first thing that I thought of was, do we have to carry these the entire way home? After looking at them and checking I found that they had only two pieces missing, they were asking $ 40.00 so because of the missing pieces I offered them $ 20.00 and I ended up getting them for $ 25.00. That made them a great buy even if we do have to haul them 3000 miles before we get home. As I said earlier, it took most of the day to get worn out on this shopping trip. Finally got a little rest then we used Carole's large bathe tub and the Jacuzzi, it was nicer then we have in the Motor Home with all of that fancy equipment we didn't get any cleaner. Had a little snack at five thirty with some of the neighbors coming to Carole's house here that she manages for the owner that lives else where. Carole and her Brother Jim are cleaning up the place so that it can be rented again. I remembered after I had shut down the computer that I hadn't mentioned the weather. This has to be the best day since we left home the 10th of January. I didn't get any official reading but I am sure that it had to be in the upper 70's or low 80's. I got to thinking that when the weather was bad I probably had mentioned it several times.

February 14, 1999 Sunday

Today we left Palm Springs and went back to Riverside to be here and help Doris Ashe celebrate her birthday that will be tomorrow. It isn't one of the big number dates so I think it will be a slow quiet one, I hope. I don't think I can take another like the past week was. We are here now in Riverside with the sun shining all day and not windy, at this moment the temperature is 60 degrees. After arriving here, I unloaded the holding tanks then went to the gas station and filled up with gas that cost $ 1.06 per gallon.

February 15, 1999 Monday

Here is another big day of more birthday celebration. This time it is Doris Ashe, it is her 61st and holding very well for some one that old. It had been planned that the four of us go to have lunch some place that was nice. We had a great surprise as the party grew to 11 before lunchtime. We all met over at a different place then what we first had in mind. It was called Scott's Seafood and a very nice place with good food. Here each of us had ordered a different meal from the menu. The other place that was first considered said that with a party that size there would have to be only one entree. Nothing could be ordered from the menu. To me that sounded like they didn't want groups diners. We had a good time and Doris got several great cards there, then in the evening, she had her big gift that Winifred and I gave her. You should have seen the time they had in opening this rather heavy package. We had used the plastic bag to wrap this gift. I did put a little amount of wraping tape on to hold that plastic bag from sliding all around. First Larry was going to help with his pocketknife that didn't work out to well so he got a pair of scissors. Then when he got down to the main box, it was taped up so much he used his knife and the scissors. They accused me of doing this inside wrap. When we finally got this box open, it was a Tiffany floor lamp. The weather was a little cloudy mixed with a lot of smog, I guess that's the way they have to live here in Riverside.

February 16, 1999 Tuesday

Now the partying is all over it is time to think about where we are going next. After all the partying we took our time, this was a rest day and the time to get the thinking cap on correct. Winifred was checking on her brother Bill to see if it would be ok to stop at his place, not knowing how he was feeling, I guess he caught a cold when he was in Riverside for some of the partying. We did stay in Riverside today, did some laundry, and then took Larry and Doris out to Coco's for dinner, which turned out to be as good as they usually are.

February 17, 1999 Wednesday

After calling to find out how Bill was and how bad the roads were, we got started later in the morning. We got to Winifred's brothers place early in the afternoon so Winifred and her brother could have a good visit. While they were doing that, I went over to town and got a hair cut from a very good barber. Her brother sure wasn't feeling very good but Carole had fixed the dinner for all of us then brought it over for all four of us. I think that was very good of her. She had cooked the chicken with a Yorkshire type of sauce or something like that and it was very delicious to say the least.

February 18, 1999 Thursday

After about several hours of calling the highways for road conditions we were informed that there was a road closure and high winds. Then Bill called some friend of his that live in the closed area and found out that everything was just fine so we took off for Yuma, AZ. We arrived in the mid-afternoon at Algogonus, Mexico a border town. We went in and checked with the Dentist there where I had some work done to find out about what had to be done or could be done with a tooth that Winifred had broken off at the gum line. She was informed that it would cost $ 350.00, as they would have to do a root cannel, put in a pin, then a cap. Then we just stayed there alongside of the road for the night it was a little noisy until about 10:00 p.m., but otherwise it wasn't that bad.

February 19, 1999 Friday

We left Yuma area this morning heading for Tucson, AZ. We got just about there and pulled into a RV park where we had stayed once before when it was a Coast-to-Coast membership park but now it isn't so had to pay much more then it should have been. This time when I pulled into this park I could feel that it wasn't the same management. The first give away was that it was almost empty compared to the last time we stopped there. The park was filled up and there was an over flow area that had at least 100 waiting to get a space and the park was a large park with about 200 full hookup spaces. I am getting fed up with this park system. You pay an annual fee to your home park and a fee to the Coast to Coast and yet I have very poor luck of getting into any of their parks. My annual fee's amount to almost $ 500.00 dollars a year. We did go to a great fish and chip dinner all you could eat for $ 6.00 a plate. I almost forgot to mention the kind of weather. When the weather was bad I made comment on it so I will tell you that today, sun was shining all day with the temperature got up in the mid 80's. This was the first day that I got out of my coat and the long sleeve shirt.

February 20, 1999 Saturday

The first thing we did was take a shower this morning so we could take advantage of a place to take on water and empty the holding tanks.

Then the park volunteers were putting on a breakfast for $ 2.00 so how can you go wrong with that. We left at 11:00 a.m. heading for Tucson arriving here at the Oracle Park the same one I had stayed at when my brother Ronald and Marie were down here from Montana, it was the last time we had traveled and stayed at a park before he passed away just a short time after this trip. There has been a little change in the area but the park hasn't changed any at all.

February 21, 1999 Sunday

Today we are in this park in Tucson, Arizona to see if we can't make contact with some of my family that lives here. It is my sister Evelyn's daughter, Patty Lawson, and her family. She has two of her sons that live here, Mark Lawson and Brain Lawson. She has another son and family that live in Virginia. All of this family I have had very little contact with because of the different areas that we live.

We have been waiting for some of the family to contact us here in the park. When we got here yesterday, I had called Patty to let her know and she was to let her family also know. We had to go to the grocery story for a couple of items. When we returned there was a note on the door that Mark and family had stopped to see us and we must have just missed them. So while waiting I had some things to do on the Motor Home but had to get some parts from Camping World. On the way down yesterday a motorist motioned to me that there was some problem with the Motor Home so stopped and found that the sewer hose holder had come loose and let the hose end out and then started to unravel. The hose was a 10ft long and when I stopped it must have been 200 ft of this trailing behind us. Winifred is watching her T V as we have our direct TV dish with us so she can get her regular programs from any place that we stop. That is when I get to do this writing each day.

The day started out early this morning so that we could go to the swap meeting and get back before it got to hot. Winfred can't take the heat I sometimes think I have done her an unjust for making her come into this kind of a torture. The weather got up to mid 80"s today not much change over yesterday. On the dish we had tuned onto our home TV station and found the weather was wet, cold and lots of snow in the higher elevation.

Leonard Fiske

February 22, 1999 Monday

Today we left Tucson about 10:00 a.m. after going to see Mark and Brian Lawson at their office just a short distance from where we were parked. When you go to visit these young people it is for a short time as they have jobs, thank god they are working to make a life for their family. It was good that we did get to see them for a short time, although this time we may see them in July when there will be a 50th wedding anniversary for my sister Lucille and Roy Merriman at Noxon, Montana. I am sure that we will try to make that trip some time when we are helping Charles and Irene move the hardware from Auburn to Ryegate.

We arrived here about 1:00 p.m. at Shirley's place here in Phoenix, Arizona. I thought that I would back into the circular driveway. Last year when we were here I drove in the driveway. Which put the door on the street side and when we leveled the Coach the step was very far off the ground. We had been parked out on the street and the patrol made us move from the street. When I backed into the driveway this time, it put the door on the upper side so the step isn't very far from the ground. That makes it easier to get in and out. When I put the jacks down to level the Coach, things didn't work as it should. It ended up with the left rear corner too high and the Coach was in a bind, so when I started over to lower all the jacks the left rear wouldn't come down, or the jack itself wouldn't retract, as it should. After working with it for some time, it came down with a bang, shaking and bouncing some of the dishes out of the cabinets. I was on the outside and Winifred was in the inside. When I called to her, she was in a state of shock and it wasn't something that was normal. The best I can describe it , maybe a strong earthquake. We left it like that tonight even if it was out of level. Winifred was still shook and I was tired of working with this any longer.

February 23, 1999 Tuesday

Well, we survived the night and after breakfast I got the book of instructions out and found out that I could release a valve at the pump and that would allow the trouble jack to retract. After doing that, I wondered what caused this to do what it did. When I checked the power unit, I had discovered that the fluid in the reservoir was way down. After putting in a quart of fluid, the system worked fine. I then went through the process of normal leveling, now all is well and the coach is level.

February 24, 1999 Wednesday

After a good nights sleep, we both feel much better. When I started to get breakfast this morning, I remembered that one or two of the drawers in the kitchen was loose and would be almost impossible to open. So, after breakfast found that some of the screws had come loose because they were loaded to heavy with canned goods. That meant I took the effected drawers out and repaired the slides. It took the better part of the day as I had to look all over to fine the needed bolts and screws but got it done by dinnertime.

Before I sign off for the evening, I will say that the weather was very nice with a few clouds and mostly sun shining. Temperature was in the mid 80"s today. Had a good dinner in the house that Sally had made then had a nice visit. They both work all day so we left about 7:00 p.m. now it's time to say good night and happy dreams.

February 25, 1999 Thursday

We are here in Phoenix at my cousin Shirley's place. Winifred did some laundry today and we went to town to do some shopping. Yesterday I went to a drug store to find a pill cutter and the one that I had purchased didn't cut the pill in half, it only cut about one third of the pill off so today I took it back and got my money. Well I didn't find another one so had to go back to that same drug store and buy the same type of a cutter. I hope it works. We had promised Don Fiske that we would get him one of these after seeing him cutting a pill in half with a butcher knife.

We got back to the Motor Home in time to get a little rest before they had gotten home from work. Dr. Shirley Fiske came home last and she took us out for a Mexican dinner. Everyone seemed to think that it was great. I shouldn't make any remarks about the food when I don't have any idea of what it should be like. All I know is that it isn't one of my favorite meals. The weather is nice during the day maybe a little warm for Winifred but I do enjoy the warmth even if the nights do get down to 40 degrees. As the sun comes up it brings the heat with it and that's what makes it better then when the sun comes up and the cold stays cold like it does in the mid and eastern parts of the country.

February 26, 1999 Friday

Today we moved from Phoenix to Sun City Grand of Arizona. I have heard that this is where the richest of the rich live a life of playing golf. We are now at Frank and Dorothy Burkes. We were at their place two years ago when they lived over in the Sun City West area. Now they are in a newer section called the Sun City Grand. I think that these people have so much money that they move to a new and better place ever so often just to have a new golf course. Not having to live among them, I am not sure that it isn't those with more money they have just moved up the scale of worth. This is not degrading them for having so much money. They do pay a lot of taxes, I am sure some of it dribbles down to some of the less fortunate.

It was close to lunch when we arrived and Dorothy made a good light lunch. It seems that now at our age we do some funny things, like taking a nap after we eat. We are all over 80 now, but thank God we are still going strong, but maybe a little slower at times. In the evening we went out to eat at Coco's. This wasn't as good as some of the other Coco's that we have been to.

February 27, 1999 Saturday

The Burke's showed us around the new area of some of the delightful areas of this place then at lunch time we stopped at one of the Visa places on the golf course where we had a good lunch on them. After getting home, we did take a nap like good little kids. Then in the evening, we went to eat up town. The first place was one of those where you enter and wait in line for hours then get in front of a board that has a menu that is a mile long that you have to select from. I tell you by the time you go through all of that you aren't hungry any more. We didn't try to go there so went down the street and found this nice place, got right in to a sit down place, and had a great meal.

February 28, 1999 Sunday

The girls went to church this morning and Francis and I went to the store to get a birthday cake for Dorothy Burke on her 80th . This was a surprise and when we brought the cake in after dinner, she really was surprised or she was a good actor. The evening wasn't a very exciting evening with the women watching TV and Francis sleeping in his chair. For me I found a book on the coffee table and read some of that when I wasn't sleeping. Maybe it was the burnt ribs that we had for dinner. Francis had gotten a new gas barbeque and he had forgotten how hot they are so when he looked after about 45 minutes they were badly burnt. They sure were fat free that I had to have anyway. I did eat several pieces and they weren't that bad.

March 1, 1999 Monday

We left the Burkes place and headed southwest to Yuma where we have a reservation waiting for us. Got away at about 9:00 a.m. and got to Yuma park grounds at 1:30 p.m. it was about 200 miles.

Got setup on space 33 for the month of March. Winifred got what she wanted was a space on the North wall area. The weather here was 93 degrees and hardly any wind. I shouldn't complain because that's what we came down here for was the hot weather.

March 2, 1999 Tuesday

Just settling in for a months stay here at the Desert Paradise RV Resort. We did do some shopping and going to the post office to get our mail. We went to three different post offices before running it down, we found it in the main Yuma office. Temperature has been up in the area that I like and Winifred hates, it has been in the upper 90"s

March 3, 1999 Wednesday

Hot again today up in the upper 90's.

March 4, 1999 Thursday

Today is a little cooler, I think it got up to a high of 70 degrees. We went to some of the flea markets in the area. It looks like we are a little late in the year. We found several stands that were loading up their wares and moving on to some other place to pedal their wares. Of course, this was in the middle of the week so maybe the weekend may be better.

Leonard Fiske

March 5, 1999 Friday

When we were at my cousins in Phoenix, Dr. Shirley Fiske had won a week at a very nice new time-share living resort that she couldn't use so she gave this time of a week to us called the Scottsdale Villa Mirage. They assigned us a good room on the second floor that over looked the tennis court on one side and the parking lot on the other. It was a studio apartment that had a small dinette with a good-sized bed and a great shower. We were there a little ahead of time so went out to have lunch. After driving around for a time we found a Mexican sandwich shop that wasn't one of the best we had ever been to when in a strange area. There is one thing we didn't plan on going back.

I found out after the first day that , you purchase one of these apartments and you get to use it for one week a year, if I understand it correctly the purchase price is $ 20,000 for a week of use but for how long I don't know. The apartment that we had had a value of $ 1200.00 for the week.

March 6, 1999 Saturday

Saturday we did some running around the area only to get lost several times so gave up and went back to the apartment for a nap. The way the engineers design the areas in a lot of right and left then around a curve and run into a dead end. It was just a wasted day as far as I am concerned.

March 7, 1999 Sunday

The only thing that was good to mention was we went to Church and after Church we had a good lunch at a place that called themselves Coyote Gardens or something like that. Then we drove over to Phoenix and had a good visit with Don and Sally Fiske.

March 8, 1999 Monday

Here again we went driving around the area to see some of the building that is going on ,in so many areas at the same time. It was some thing that you can't imagine the vastness of this kind of a boom and the amount of money that must be in the area to continue. We didn't get much sleep as we were both sick for some reason.

170

March 9, 1999 Tuesday.

After a full night of misery, we had decided that we would go back to Yuma where we had left the Motor Home in the Desert Paradise resort. We were loaded and ready to take off and then I saw that there was a flat tire on the little car. Then the chore of unloading everything out of the trunk because the spare tie was in the bottom under cover so that it wouldn't be seen or be in the way. This spare was one of those that was temporary and couldn't be driven very far. We checked out at 10:00 a.m. then headed for home looking for a tire repair shop. They fixed the tire in short order and we were on the way at 10:30 a.m. to Yuma. This was a very nice day and the traffic wasn't very heavy so we made good time arriving here at the Motor Home at 2:30 p.m.. Winifred was sick most of the night where I was lucky that my illness lasted about four hours then in the morning I felt a little tired but wasn't that bad that I couldn't drive home. Winifred laid down the front seat and slept all the way home. Arriving home, we found that all was in good condition, only that the space next to us had a different vehicle and they had parked in my space but there was room for me to get in anyway.

March 10, 1999 Wednesday

Believe me this was the day of rest for this old couple that was tired out from this fast life hob-nobbing with the upper class.

March 11, 1999 Thursday

Now that we are rested up, Winifred did the washing of the bedding and the clothes and I did a few of the small jobs that a person has to do from time to time when you travel this fashion. The first for me was the removing the collection of bugs that was on the front of the Motor Home. I did get the bugs removed from the front that took most of the day.

March 12, 1999 Friday

Today I started the task of putting a wax on the clean front end of the Motor Home that I had taken all the bugs off the day before. I started with a type of paste wax that was almost impossible to remove after putting it on. I did a small area then got out a different type that seemed to work very well. Then the dreaded job was the washing of the windows on the outside. I have known that I would have a tough job because I had gotten some hard watermarks from some sprinkler system where there was hard water and it left marks that are almost impossible to remove. I have tried to clean those marks off with all the cleaning compounds on the market with no results. Went to a glass company and they sold me a can of cleaner that would do the job but was a slow process. This material had a small amount of buffing in it, which means that you have to rub and rub more and more. Gave up the job until I can get some power equipment and maybe that will do a first class job with out so much elbow grease.

I had better mention the weather. When the weather was bad, I would mention it down to the degree. Now that it is nice, we seem to forget about making mention. Today it is real nice with just about what the world ordered. It was about 66 degrees with some wind maybe a little more then I would like.

March 13, 1999 Saturday

Just a lazy day. We went to town and made some copies of the 1099 forms that we had collected and sent them to the accountant for her to do the taxes for the year 1998. Then we went out to the Hometown Buffet. Had a good amount to eat then went home to the Motor Home for a nap in the afternoon. What a life, eat and sleep how can you beat that.

March 14, 1999 Sunday

The day looks like a great day and it was a great day . Went to Church at the Methodist out here in the Foothills area. It was a good service. After Church, we came home and had some lunch, a nap, then sat around for a while. We were thinking of going for drive when we had company then Art and Blanch Vail who are our neighbors in Lacey that lives in one of the other parks just up the road. They have a park model and come here every winter.

March 15, 1999 Monday

We talked about gong to Mexico today and get there early. What we thought was early didn't turn out that way. The parking lot at the border to Mexico was half-full, I would guess there were one thousand cars. We did some looking around and didn't spend much money then came home. While we were down town, we had lunch at one of the best Mexican restaurants in the country. After we had a nap I washed the little car then just sat around until the wind drove every one to putting up awnings and nailing things down because it was blowing hard with a lot of dark clouds. It looked as if it was going to rain but none so far. I hear the western show that Winifred has been watching is coming to an end, then it could be bedtime. She always wants me to read to her every night and I don't think I have missed one or two times in the past three and a half years of marriage.

March 16, 1999 Tuesday

In the morning, we went out to the swap meets and found that they were closed so came home and did a little napping for a while. Then late in the afternoon went over to the clubhouse and tried to play a little shuffleboard. That didn't turn out to be a good venture with the wind blowing the wax off of the board. Of course, I think that I did win, but how anyone will find out, I don't know.

March 17, 1999 Wednesday

Today we decided to take a ride out to the Imperial Dam area where we had parked a couple of years back. On the way, it was time for lunch so we stopped at the Yuma US Army proving ground where they have a very good restaurant that had good food and priced right. Then after lunch, we drove up to the Quail Hill area where we had parked. Not much change but maybe the same or more RV's still are parking there on the BLM land. We came back by the backroad through the date section of Yuma then home to rest before we had to go to the Methodist Church St. Patrick's day Baked Potato with all the fixings. It was only $ 5.00 per plate and I think it was worth the money and it is for a good cause.

March 18, 1999 Thursday

Winifred takes a walk every morning after breakfast while I do the dishes. She can out walk me any time, as my legs seem to get into trouble when I push it. We did go and get some groceries for the next three days while Winifred's brother Bill Ashe and her niece Carole come here at the park for a while. I think we will be doing the town in an old people fashion.

March 19, 1999 Friday

We started out the day with a breakfast while waiting for Winifred' family to arrive from San Diego, California. At about 2:00 pm. they came and got set up in the space next to us so it was very convenient. When all was said, we ended up going out to dinner at the Town Buffet where we could eat all you wanted. It was a good meal and every one ate more then they should have. You have to get your money's worth.

March 20, 1999 Saturday

Winifred and I had planned a trip to the Army proving grounds that is located 14 miles North of Yuma. Then we went to the Imperial Dam area, then stopped at the Army Base restaurant for lunch.

March 21, 1999 Sunday

We had breakfast in each others Motor Home's then planned on going to the big swap meet. Winifred didn't want to go so the rest of us went and there was the largest crowd that I had ever seen there. We shopped for one hour then every one met at the gate. We all had purchased a few items then headed home. After sitting around visiting for most of the afternoon then we had a good chicken dinner that Carole had fixed up and it wasn't bad at all.

Then every one was looking forward for the Academy Awards that started at 5:30p.m., and didn't give up until, I think was after 11:00 p. m. I couldn't take all of that so went to bed.

March 22, 1999 Monday

The first thing this morning was to give the guests breakfast in our Motor Home as we had done in the past. After breakfast our guests, Winifred's family got their Motor Home ready to go home. They said they were going to stop on the way home and go to Mexico.

March 23, 1999 Tuesday

Today we slept in for a change. It really wasn't that bad, it gave us an excuse to do nothing. So, when we had the chance, we took it without any questions. Isn't this just some small talk? The weather was warm around 92 degrees above zero, but the nights are on the cool side that we have to turn on the heater in the mornings to take the chill off.

March 24, 1999 Wednesday

I woke a little early this morning so we got up and had our pills and some orange juice then we went down town to have breakfast and go to one of the banks to cash a personnel check. I went to a half dozen banks here in Yuma and there wasn't one that would take an out of town check. Yesterday had the little car over where the swap meet is held to get a price and find out if they would make a nose cover for the little car, maybe it would save the windshield and the front end of the car. They made a template yesterday and they had it ready this afternoon at 2:00 p.m. It turned out good and it only cost $ 180.00 dollars. When I priced one at home they wanted $ 460.00 dollars and it would take six weeks for delivery.

March 25, 1999 Thursday

We had a wash to do and we talked about what else is there here in Yuma that we couldn't head for home(Olympia). Then I discovered that I had forgot to have a small opening put in the nose cover so I took it back and they put that hole there in just a few minutes. They put the cover on then marked the place, cut and bound the cut area. Then we decided to leave tomorrow.

March 26, 1999 Friday

Left Yuma at 8:30 their time and headed for home. What a beautiful day all the way, sun shining and little amount of wind until we started north on I-5 then we had some head wind. We arrived here at Coalinga at Almond Tree RV Park and checked in at 4:30 p.m. after traveling some 472 miles in the eight-hour time. This Motor home drives and handles like a car. You can sit there and cruise down the road with ease.

March 27, 1999 Saturday

It is time for us to leave the park and go on our way to the next stop. We left the park at Coalinga at about 8:30 a.m. and made it to the rest stop junction 96 and I-5 nice large area. It is called the Collier rest area. Again, we had put on about 400 miles when we stopped here. We plan on staying here for the night. This is a rest area off of the highway. There aren't any hook-ups, just a place off of the road. We had left the so called south where the weather was in the upper 80's and lows were in the 50's at night. Here it was 36 degrees and we almost froze to death before morning.

March 28, 1999 Sunday

Because we almost froze, we got an early start today. At seven this a.m. we were on the road heading north for home in Olympia where we arrived at 3:30 p.m. We did take out some time to have a sandwich at the Oak Tree restaurant in Woodland, Washington.

To recap the weather from the time we left Yuma until we arrived home it was one of the best trips home I had ever having. We left in the sunshine and that stayed with us all three days with only a little wind in the Los Angeles area and a little today at mid Oregon coming through the mountains. Last but not lest we did get some small amount of rain as we were coming into Salem and that was just a small amount, that gave out until we were about 20 miles from home. As I sign off from this trip it is raining a good lot now at 7:00p.m. That ends another trip under our belts.

I will continue when we take the next outing if it's only for one day or several months, see you all back at the barn some time down the road.

April 30,1999 Friday

It's 1:00 p.m. and we are ready to travel over to Auburn to help Charles and Irene get the trucks loaded for their move to Ryegate, Montana where they are going to set up the hardware store. This will be the first of several before they have all the collection of their.

We arrived at Charles and Irene's place to find they had a good share of the truck loaded. They had a friend of Dale's helping because Dale wasn't feeling very good, coming down with a cold. They were doing a good job, but when Winifred got in there with her gloves on things started to move. All she had to do was call out "hep hep" and everyone started to move like they weren't doing before that. It didn't take long and we had the shelving all on the truck. It looks like the truck was over loaded at this point but we had about 6 foot of space to fill up so we put in some bulky thing that has to go. Winifred and Tony, Dales buddy, was a great help. By this time, it was about 5:00 PM so we quit for the day.

May 1, 1999 Saturday

Charles and I spent the early morning working on the hitch and ball that was on the rental truck. The rental company had welded the hitch ball to the receiver so had to cut that ball off and get another the correct size to hook up the large trailer that was loaded with stock from the store.

Dale came and helped today and we finished loading the truck and got all of the hookups completed and ready to roll by 4:00 PM. I had my instructions of how to feed the four dogs and the three cats also how to pick up the droppings each day. This is the kind of work that not every one can handle all alone, but I must do my best. The weather has cooperated all day except a few shower that didn't hold us back any

May 2, 1999 Sunday

Today was the day of departure and they were gone by 7:30 a.m. Charles on the lead with the large truck and trailer and Irene following driving the loaded down pickup truck. When they left, they wanted to get as far as Missoula, Montana the first day. If all went as planned, they should be in Missoula about now after nine hours of driving. They haven't driven long trips for so long I bet they are two tired kids. Winifred and I are parked here in their front yard waiting for them to call. It is now 6:30PM here and 7:30 in the area that they should be in if all went well. They left here this morning in good condition, equipment all good so there shouldn't be any problem. It could be that the going was slower then expected so they didn't get as far as I think they would. I have heard on the TV that there has been rain and snow in some of the area that they have to travel.

May 3, 1999 Monday

Today we did some looking around the area to find a place to unload the holding tanks of the Motor Home and also fill up with Propane. Then we planted some of the trees that Irene had, but didn't get time to plant, and Winifred planted some of the smaller flowers in the flowerbed.

Then in the afternoon, we had three calls on the log splitter that was listed in the Union paper that comes from the Boeing plant. The third party called at seven PM and said he was on the way, he got here in the dark and purchased it and we loaded it on his truck and he was on his way.

It worked out fine because we had been waiting for Charles and Irene to call us from some place on their way to Montana we didn't get that call this night. Maybe it will be the next night.

Today we had planned and did take the Motor Home to the Eagles where we dumped the holding tanks then we went over to the Propane co and filled up with propane then back to our housesitting place. It took just an hour to do that so it gave us some time do a little job around here that Charles had asked if I ha time was to fix sump pump system. Whenever the pump came on the water would come out of the down spout fitting. I found that by cutting this rain drain system pipe off and put a piece on the drainpipe and cap off the other end so water couldn't come back and out the wrong place. Now the drain from the roof will dump into the sump area then be pumped, as it should be.

Well we had a call at 6:00 PM from the kids that they had mad the trip but very slow in places. They said at the hills and passes they were going 15 miles an hour with the load that they were carrying and pulling. They sounded happy and they had got to Ryegate, Montana yesterday evening and got most of the load unloaded by the time they had called this evening. We were sure glad that they had made it and now when they finish unloading the rental truck they have to take it to Billings, Montana then return to Ryegate and unload the trailer.

They said that they had a mailbox now then they will get the trailer licenses from the courthouse before they can leave to come home. We will be dog and cat sitting and feeding for several days yet.

May 5,1999 Wednesday

It was a fairly good day today with some clouds this morning, Today is my 85th birthday and we are still house sitting or animal sitting maybe it should be called. The first thing was that Winifred said that I could do anything I wanted to do because it was my birthday. I had selected to do a little job here at Charles and Irene's place while they are gone to Montana and won't be home fore several more days.

Charles had the old garden tiller, that I had given him, in the front yard with just a tarp on it and I thought that it would take a long time to get it started, but it started after only a few pulls on the rope. Then I had in mind that I should till a piece of ruff ground that is in the back yard. It had a lot of rock and clumps of grass. This tiller has the front tines, the ground had a lot of rock of all sizes so we did a lot of dancing around when ever you would hit one of the large rocks. All turned out very well after I had picked out the rocks and the large clumps of grass. Then in the evening, we went to the Elks down town Auburn and had dinner of spaghetti all you can eat. It was a good meal and we had met some very nice people there. I think they were looking for some members. I shouldn't be talking like that. Forgive me. I will chock this up as a great 85th year dinner.

May 6, 1999 Thursday

I had to finish the job that I had started yesterday. It had to be raked and a few more rocks picked up. It did take almost a half a day but finished that then started on the job of salvaging the old travel trailer was being parted out there was only the floor and chassis left so we got started on ripping the floor off and started to clean up this mess, burning some that could be burned. It has been raining off and on all day so didn't get all done as planned

May 7, 1999 Friday

Today we really got into the job of cleaning up the old chassis and got all the flooring off. Had started a fire to burn up some of the waste and sort out the aluminum for Dale my oldest grand son to sell at the salvage yards.

Then at lunchtime, I had a call about the boat loader that Charles had put in the union paper. It wasn't but one minute later when there was another call. The second caller came out this afternoon and purchased it. The fellow didn't have any intention of buying it because when he wanted it he had to go back to town and get some money. It is getting to be 10:00 PM and way past my bedtime. Good night.

May 8,1999 Saturday

We were thinking about Charles and Irene, wondering where they were now. They must have all of the loads unloaded now and on the way home. I think they may be home Sunday late.

After I got the old trailer chassis cleaned up, I took it out to the road so that some one might see and want to buy it. Then I came back and cleaned up the mess that was left behind. I sorted it out and put the salvage aluminum to one side for Dale to sell. The burnable material I hauled to the burn barrel the plastic foam Winifred and I put that in garbage cans. After all of that I got the rote tiller out and got about ten feet and the belt or some thing went wrong that the tines stopped. I put the tiller in the shop for Charles to fix when he got home.

Thinking the kids would be home by Sunday so we worked hard at putting thinks back where they were and the last was to get the lawn mowed which I did and every thing looked good

I had hadn't thought about hat they would be home tonight, I had just finished my shower and got into bed when Winifred called to me the kids are home. Irene came in but I didn't see the pickup and the trailer. Then found out that they had to be pulled in by a tow truck from Ellensburg, Washington because the truck was acting up. It would run but barely and had no power so they were wise to have the tow truck bring them in rather then get stuck out on the pass some place at a late hour of the night. The driver unloaded the pickup then Charles left the trailer the on he road until the next morning as it was getting dark by now. They sure did make good time to be able to get here in the day and a half driving time

May 9, 1999 Sunday

After breakfast, I helped Charles move the trailer off of the road into the yard and parked it in front of the shop doors so that he can get started to load the second load for his new lactation in Ryegate, Montana.

Then we got the motor home ready to go home to Olympia for a while as I had more work that I had to do on the little trailer that should be finished so the new members of the club will be accepted into the club. You see this trailer was one of the small ones that I had purchased to restore then sell, but this one I turned soft and sold it to a fellow that needed one to become a member in the club

May 13, 1999 Thursday

I didn't get the little trailer ready to be moved when we found out that Charles and Irene were loaded up to make the trip to Montana so here we are sitting in their yard ready to feed dogs and cats again. They are all ready to head out in the morning. This time they have only the pickup and it is pulling the trailer that is loaded with store inventory. I wish them good luck, as it is a load for that one half ton truck with the 350 engine. There is one thing about it the motor home is just like home here. It is better then living in their house when they are in the process of moving thing out.

May 14, 1999 Friday

We are sitting here at Charles and Irene dog and cat sitting for the second time while they are taking another load of the hardware store inventory. It is 7:00 PM and we haven't had a phone call yet so they must be still on the way. I sure hope they didn't get in trouble and was able to get over the mountain passes.

We didn't do a great deal today, sort of getting lined up for a few things that need to be done around here. Charles did say that he would like to have some work done on the kitchen lighting. So today I did take some of it apart to run down the reason the one light doesn't work. We went to the store and I got a piece of molding and some quarter round for the job. While we were out went to the Sear's store and purchased a new Coffee maker. The one we have in the motor home started to make a lot of noise coming from the clock that is built into the works and I didn't want to tear it down and then couldn't find the parts.

May 15, 1999 Saturday

The first thing that I did was to go to McLendon's in Sumner, Washington to get some lights and look at the decorative material that lets the light through and hides the ugly lamp fixture. For one thing, they don't come in a size that you could use here in this house. I did get the lights and there was no way they would fit in the area so had to return them. That took up a lot of the day. Now to correct that I will have to put another wood divider in the framework so that we can use this new size of material. It's late in the day now so it will have to be done Monday. I did get the lawn mowed between the rain showers

May 16, 1999 Sunday

Today is the day we take off and do nothing but rest up for the next week. After breakfast, we took a drive from Auburn to North Bend then to Snoqualmie Pass on High Way 90 East. On the way we stopped at the Snoqualmie Falls that is a real site, the water must drop over 200 feet then continue on its way to the Puget Sound. After having a cup of coffee at the summit, I got the idea to stop at the falls again and have Sunday dinner. We went to the dining room and found out that the next sitting would be about an hour from this time. They said that a lunch was being served upstairs so we went there to find that it was in the bar, we had a television behind us, and someone wanted that turned on. Well that took care of that. We left and drove back to Auburn where we had dinner at Trotter's. We had a good dinner of Salmon that cost us $ 22.00 as compared to a figure of about $50.00 at the Snoqualmie Lodge. When we got back to the motor home, we had a little time before the dos and cats had to be fed at 3:30 each day. What a hard job that is while the owners are moving to Ryegate, Montana. I haven't been able to get much done here around the place with the rain off and on most of the time.

May 17, 1999 Monday

What a day this was it rained most all day some times harder then other times. We are still here in Auburn, Washington sitting dogs and cats. I did get a little done in the kitchen when I finished the ceiling lighting area by putting a divider piece in the overhead recessed area. These were designed for the time when the diffusion plastic was made in long lengths of at least 6 feet long. Today the market has only a standard sizes 2 foot X 4 foot. After finishing that job, I started on the cleaning, with my pressure washer, the porches and cement walks and apron to the garage. It now looks like new concrete again. This is four days the kids are gone on their move. We haven't heard from them but expect them to come rolling in tomorrow afternoon or evening.

May 18, 1999 Tuesday

Well, the kids didn't get home yet and it is 7:30 PM. Today all I got done was to pressure washer the front concrete and the back deck. The weather was fairly good today with just a few sprinkles just enough that I did put on my raincoat. I was bound to get this cleaning finished before the kids got home. Winifred helped a lot today by spelling me off. To hold the trigger on the washer gun made your hands tired. The place is looking better for selling of the place.

June 9, 1999

Today we are at home in Olympia, Washington getting ready to go back and do the final sitting job I think. I had just got running this new laptop computer. I made the deal that the store would take the documents off the old one and install them on this new computer. Now I think that I can work this on the road and then when I get home I can print things the same as I do on the desk machine.

April 11, 1999 Friday

Today we had to go to Auburn, Washington I think is the last time to help load a large semi-trailer that is 56 feet long. Charles plan is to get every thing in this trailer. This is supposed to be the last trip with their belongings. When they return from this trip, they will be taking the dogs and cats then they will have every thing in Montana.

June 12,1999 Saturday

I woke up this morning at 4:30 AM and now it is 6:30 pm. Dale, my grandson and a friend of his, named Tony was great help. They are both 300 pound and very strong. They should be they are in the prime of life. I helped with the light boxes and gave them orders as to where to put the boxes. This truck was a large one and it doesn't look so large now after working all day loading.

June 13, 1999 Sunday

We thought that we could get this all loaded by last night but it wasn't so this morning got started by 7:30 and got it loaded by 3:00pm this afternoon. After the house furniture was loaded, then came the large items from the shop. First, we put on the table saw followed by the other woodworking equipment. Last but not least were the lawn mowers. The last was the cases of paint that was some of the hardware store stock. The last bit of work was that Irene and Charles was getting their cars loaded with last few items including one of the cats. They got started at 3:30 to get a head of the truck that was going to pickup the trailer Monday morning.

June 14, 1999 Monday

Every one is gone now so Winifred and I are sitting here waiting for the truck driver to come and start the trip to Montana with Charles and Irene's years of collection. The driver got here about 10:30 and was on his way. He told me he would be there in Ryegate Tuesday noon. I would like to be there when they open the truck to see how much of the load had shifted. I packed most of it so I am sure that didn't fall down. Now we have one more item that will be picked up tomorrow.

June 15, 1999 Tuesday

As of 3:00pm this afternoon, they came and picked up the old truck and it will be taken to an auction that is held in Auburn, Washington. This place is getting sort of a lonely place with the house empty, the yard is being cleaned up. This evening Dale came over to get some of the thinks that is mother had given him before she left for Montana. I have tried to talk Dale into taking some of the old antique things that are still here. If he does take them, the place will be almost cleaned out. The more of this we can get rid of it will be less for Charles to do when he gets back for his last time at this place. Yes, we are still here to take care of the dogs and cats. It's going to be tough to see them leave but I am sure that they will do all right and I hope they will be happy doing what they want do with out some one ginning them more taxes. Washington seems to be good at taxing every one to death.

June 16, 1999 Wednesday

I didn't write yesterday so now I have to think what we did here while we are house, dog and cat sitting. With every thing gone there isn't much to do. After talking to Winifred about this situation senior moments as to what did we do, we loaded up all the old RV items and took them down to Rochester, Washington to get rid of them and clean up the yard at the same time. The above items were what came out of the RV that we had parted out when the woodwork in the body had rusted out and it was falling down around you ears. The salvage was the chassis, windows, stove, furnace, shower stall, toilet and three holding tanks. I didn't get that much for them. I wanted to get rid of them you couldn't leave them here at the place that was being sold I got only 50.00 dollars for all. It sure wasn't very much but if you took the same load to the landfill, it would have cost about 50.00 dollars so this makes it sound a little better.

On our way home, we stopped in Centralia and had a great lunch at the Winter Kitchen. We go there every chance we get, it has an old fashion atmosphere, and the total place has the early 1900's theme. From there we made it home to the trailer here in Auburn after stopping at the house in Olympia, Washington. There we checked the answering machine for messages and pick up the mail. Then we still got back in time to feed the animals by 3:30 PM.

June 17, 1999 Thursday

Didn't do much we slept in for a while then after breakfast we went to town to see what some of the antique shops had in them so we could get some idea as to the value of some of the collection that Irene had here. She had asked that we do this checking. One party may be able to give us an answer as to the value if any of two old radios and an old washing machine. I think I had better let this new computer cool down for the night.

June 18, 1999 Friday

We were expecting them to come home today but they didn't get here yet and it is 7:15 PM. Because there isn't any bed or any thing to eat, they will stay at a Motel some where on the road and come here in the morning. The most we did was take care of our selves and the dogs and cats. We had a little rain today, not very heavy so things didn't get very wet. Now the weather is great sun shining with no wind and sixty degrees, very pleasant.

June 19, 1999 Saturday

Now we start with the fact that the kids did get here at noon today that takes the suspense off of us. There sure wasn't much to do around here so I got one of the lawn mowers out and tried to fix the power drive system. After taking, some of the parts of I could see that it was something that required taking a lot of the drive gears apart and I didn't have that much time so some one will have to use it as a push only machine. In the testing that I did this morning I did mow some of the lawn and it wasn't that bad.

After Charles and Irene got out of the truck they had so much on their minds that had to be done it wasn't any way they could do any talking at this time. I don't think that if I were their age just retiring I wouldn't have made a move as large for all the tea in China.

June 20, 1999 Sunday

Today is the day of the last load. In order to make this an event6ful day Winifred had invited all of their children and family to be here at noon for a picnic. Yesterday when I mentioned it, she was all upset and said they can come and have a party if they want to I won't be here I have work to do. It hurt Winifred very much to think that some one wasn't interested in a picnic. Winifred was trying to give her a going away party with all the family was to be attending this picnic for a few hours after eating.

It all came out beautiful with every one coming plus three that came but didn't change the result of the party. There were a lot of pictures taken and Irene was so excited that she took or had taken every one of the pictures down and had them proceed in an hour and she did seem pleased that the party went on with out a hitch. As I write this, I did have a good time and enjoyed it very much. I must do say that I wish them lots of luck in the large move and be happy that they did the right thing.

I must end to days writing to state that the weather was great for the most part but after the group went home the rain has come in and hasn't given up for the past six hours.

June 21, 1999 Monday

The last night here, as Charles & Irene have the last thing in the trailer so tomorrow the cats and dogs will be loaded in the vehicles for the final trip to Montana. We also will do the final chore and leave here right after they leave. We could have gone home earlier except I want to get a last picture as they load the animals.

Charles & Irene have been here for the last four days getting all of the last minute things taken care of before they leave for good. Tonight the four of us went to get a fill of Chinese food and it was very good.

June 22, 1999 Tuesday

It happened this morning, at about 8:30 AM Charles and Irene took off for Montana. With the cats and dogs and the last of the odds an ends put in the trailer, they left this place to never return.

Soon as they were on their way Winifred & I got ready and went back to Olympia so that we could get ready to take a long trip of about 8 to 10 thousand miles East and South then return some time in September if all goes well. There was some good lumber left there so when we got home we called Winifred's son Smoky. We got a trailer for the hauling of the lumber and he could use some 4x6x8 treated timbers. He took his truck and I took the trailer. There was more then I could haul and Smokey couldn't get all of the timbers on his truck so we are going over and get the rest with my trailer at 9:00 AM tomorrow.

June 28, 1999 Monday

We have been home for a few days getting ready to head out for all points East and South. Today we went as far as Spokane, Washington and stopped over night with Milton & Helen Geer, I haven't seen them for about 4 years. Winifred had never met them before so she got a chance to visit with Helen and said she had enjoyed them very very much.

After a great dinner, we went outside and Winifred found out that there was some bad odor coming from some place and we traced it down to a bad battery in the Motor Home. One of the batteries in the Motor Home had shorted out internally and was cooking there with the gases coming out of the battery. Not a good situation so I got some water and poured that over the battery to get it cooled down. I was afraid that it could explode and cause some real damage. The next morning I took the Motor Home and got a new battery. That took care of the odor and also set me at ease for the balance of the trip that we are on.

June 29,1999 Tuesday

We left Spokane at 10:00 am and headed North on highway 2 going to Libby, Montana to see Judi and her daughter Tiennie that she had been wanting to see for several years. They do live some distance off the beaten path where we don't travel normally.

June 30, 1999 Wednesday

We left Libby this morning heading for Noxon, Montana to see my sister Lucille and Roy for over night then we will be heading to Harlowton, Montana.

July 1, 1999 Thursday

We arrived in Harlowton, after a ward drive of about 500 miles, it was about 4:30 pm when we got to the park and it was a good thing that we got here when we did because we did get the last space that is on the end of the camping area. This has turned out to be the best place in the park. The other trailers and campers can't park close to us only on one side that leaves us a little more room to have a family reunion. The weather is wet, raining and cold for this time of the year in Montana.

When we arrived, Don and Sally were already here and had been here for several days. These are the cousins that we told last winter when we were in Arizona that we would meet them here on or before the 4th of July for the rodeo and a Fiske reunion at the same time.

July 2, 1999 Friday

Today is the day to beat all days. Don, Sally, Winifred and I went for a drive to Ryegate to look up a few of the places that some of the families had homesteaded and where some had lived in their later years after retiring from the ranching and farming for many years

Over the last few months we have been hearing a lot of different stories about some of the relatives that live here that have been having health problems. Marie and Audrey Fiske, we were told were both getting Alzheimer's disease, so we tried to check with those that were real close to Marie and Audrey to find out just what is going on around here. The four of us went to Ryegate to see if Charles and Irene were getting settled all right. When we got to Ryegate, we found out that they were in Harlowton, Montana checking to see if we had arrived yet from Olympia, Washington.

When we stopped at Marie's place, we went into an unlocked house to find the TV was on and the little dog was in a chair watching the TV. Then we went to Tex and Sharon's place up the road a short way but no one there either. Not that we needed them but just wanted to visit and see if we could get some straight stores on what was going on with Audrey as her mother had been put in a home in Billings, Montana. On the way back we stopped and Audrey was home with the dog and they were both watching the TV. The day is almost over now so we headed for Harlowton where our RV's are parked at the city Park. The day was long but it was very enjoyable. This was a good day when you could show some of the younger kinfolks.

July 3, 1999 Saturday

After a good night sleep we didn't do much but prepare for the family reunion that we were to have tomorrow at noon. I wasn't sure how many we could get to this gathering because my sister was the one that was making the contacts but she had a very serious problem with her eyes when she started t blind about two weeks before this party. Now she can't drive any more and she is married to a blind man so this will make things very hard for the both of them. Also, it is time to empty the holding tanks

July 4, 1999 Sunday

This is the day of the before mentioned reunion. It is Independence Day and the big Rodeo that is always held on the 4th of July weekend each year.

A lot of the family members did get the message and came but there were a few that was unable le to get there. The last count that I had was 22. The weather was horrible and very cold that made the gathering stay a short time out was so cold that no one wanted any of a large watermelon that we had planned to have.

July 5, 1999 Monday

We got up and had breakfast then packed thing then took off to the East on highway 12 to Ryegate. We parked at the city park where we had park last year when we were here to check on property for Charles and Irene but this time is to help them get the hardware store going. I worked about six hrs. today but did get a lot done, that is Charles and I Rene did, I was getting myself aquatinted with what we had to do when you work with a all brick building. This is some thing that I have never did when remodeling.

July 6, 1999 Tuesday

We are here in Ryegate, Montana yet helping Charles and Irene get the hardware store building going. Today I am still on the wrecking some of the walls to make room for more shelving and not so many small rooms. These walls are all lath and plaster so we have to beat the plaster off the remove the lath. Irene is a good picker upper of the trash. And she can also use a hammer very well. Charles goes on his way of putting up the stock shelves.

July 7, 1999 Wednesday

We got a large part of the walls down and Charles got the rest of the shelving put up on the North wall. We got as lot done but it is in the stage where it doesn't show very much. The weather is a little cooler today with the temperature topping out at 92 degrees

July 8, 1999 Thursday

It is 8:05 PM. We had to move from the city park area where we had been parked. At lunchtime, we had a smart young lady come to the door and told us that we would have to move because the Telephone Company was putting on a free hot dog meal today that the tent people were coming and they would need to use the power that we were using. It so happened that this out let had only one service. So that meant that we would have to go with out our air conditioner. It is bad enough for Winifred to go the heat for a very short time let alone for half of the day and into the evening and maybe longer. So, we went out to the Mary Fiske place to park and we are here for the time being. After dinner, we went into town to see the big crowd of 500 people that this lady was saying would take over the city park. Winifred found this lady and I am sure that she told her what she do with the party. I counted what crowd was there and it couldn't have been over 50 so when Winifred ask where the 500 people was and she replied she didn't know the just didn't show.

That is enough of the above and we did get a lot done in the store. I am still working on taking out some walls. And Charles is putting up more shelves.

July 9, 1999 Friday

Today the same old stuff, removing walls in the Charles and Irene's building in Ryegate, Montana that will be a hardware store. We have a nice setting here at what is known as Mary's place tat is three miles south of Ryegate. This is where we moved to when we were run out of the place in the park in town. I didn't work so hard today and my ankles didn't swell as much so I think that the running up and down the stepladders could have caused this swelling.

Weather is hot, in the 90's thank goodness that we have a good air-conditioner

July 10, 1999 Saturday

We have been working hard so thought we would take the day off and go to the Snowy Mountains where Ken and Shirley Wegner is living on and old pioneer ranch that his dad had lived his whole life and now the younger generation is caring on raising cattle and Sheep.

They showed us around the place and they we about to vaccinate a bull that they had just g into the shoot so we went with them to the corral and Winifred got to see how they take care of and animal that needs to have some medicine from time to time. Then we went in the house and had a great lunch of dumplings and vegetable soup with a brown gravy. Was that every a great meal as they had some hay bailing to do yet today we left early afternoon and came home.

July 10, 1999 Sunday

Charles was having some problems with the Motor home that they are renting so the first thing I did was to see if it was some simple thing that I could fix. The hot water heater wouldn't come on, so did some checking and found that there wasn't any current and we couldn't find the fuse panel. The water hose was leaking very badly. Then Charles went and got the owner and he came down top see if there was a blown fuse. Then he was looking at an inline fuse it looked good and when he put in back in the heater started up.

Then I went to the store to see if Charles was going to do any thing today. He said that his toe hurt to bad and he was going to take it easy today. It was about noon and his foot was getting worse. I mentioned that he had better get to emergency at the Hospital in Billings. I guess it got worse so they went to Billings They gave him some shots and sent him home. They were late getting home and he had to get his foot up for the night. The next morning they had to go back to Billings for more shots then had to go to the Doctor in the after noon.

July 12, 1999 Monday

Charles and Irene went to Billings this morning after going to the hospital they went to the Doctor. He isn't through yet. He has to go back tomorrow for some tests. They got home about four thirty this after noon. He was feeling better and I think the doctor told him he had to stop smoking, I sure hope he does. They came out o Mary's place where we are parked to give us the news. He does have to go back tomorrow and get some more test to see if they can determine the amount circulation that is getting down to the foot. The infected toe doesn't heal.

Didn't do very much today. I did get some outside work done at the store. It had been a long time sense the weeds had been taken care of around the building and sidewalk so I started make that look better. The last thing to day was the fact that Shari & Tex came by and invited us to a dinner of barbecued ribs. What a good dinner it was. It's getting to be almost 11:00 PM so I had better get this machine shut down.

July 13, 1999 Tuesday

Today is one of those days when you weren't sure just what the day would bring. Yesterday I did start to clean up the sidewalk on the front of the store and the north side but didn't finish so I went down there and got that done. I when to Harlowton to get a hair cut and the shop was closed. It wasn't a lost trip because I went to the museum and they wanted four more books. They have sold several and continue to do so, that's what makes it worthwhile.

July 14,1999 Wednesday

We are stating the next leg of our trip this summer. Left Ryegate at 9:00 AM heading for Billings to see Evelyn and AlBurt Kraft my sister and brother - in - law. We arrived in time to get setup before lunchtime. After lunch I went over to a muffler shop had a new exhaust pipe put on the little car that tows behind the Motor home. After getting that fixed, I looked for a carburetor shop and found one just down the street. I got an appointment for 8:30 Monday morning to get the carburetor worked on. I thought I would fix it myself the day before we left home but found out that what I did wasn't all that good. It ran all right but was hard to start in the mornings. We just finished dinner that was very good. If we keep eating that way at every stop we will have go on a diet when we get back home.

July 15,1999 Thursday

We are here at Evelyn's in Billings Montana. Didn't do much today. The first ting we did was sleep in until 8:00 AM and it was about nine when we finished breakfast. After 10:00 o'clock, all four of us went to do some shopping, then at noon, we went to the Country Buffet for lunch. Had a short nap then visited for a while. Well it is shower time so will leave you and return tomorrow night.

July 16, 1999 Friday

This was to be a full day with appointments. The first was an old timer's potluck at a place here in the west side of Billings. This event is held each year for the people that at one time or another had lived in Ryegate, Montana and went to school there. There were some people there that I hadn't seen for 50 years that I went to school with. It was a very pleasant gathering with sixty attending and a lot of food.

This is the one thing that we came to Billing for one of the largest weddings that I think I have ever been to. The Church that the wedding was held was a large Church, I would guess that there where about 400 to 500 people there. It was also a very well organized wedding. After the ceremony, the crowd went to the largest Hotel in Billings for the reception. There was all you wanted to drink and eat. The food table must have been forty feet long. Then after we all had eaten the dancing had began. This is where you could understand that it was a group of young people. When that music came on it had to be the Eastern Swing and it was loud. There were a few of us old people there that did stay for a while. There four of us that had couple of dances when the played the slower type of music then we came home. I was about 12:00 O'clock when we got home.

Good night to all.

July 17, 1999 Saturday

The first thing I did this morning was to wake up telling Winifred to wake up sleepy head a new day is here. As we slowly was getting to move around we went to see my brother, Gerald, that lives in Roundup, Montana so drove over there and visited a short time then came home. After the late hours last night, we are really tired tonight. Matter of fact Winifred is so tired that she has gone to bed with a headache and I am about to follow in just a minute.

July 18, 1999 Sunday

Here we are another week has gone by and we are still in Montana. Now at my sister Evelyn's place. I think we had better move on and not wear out the welcome.

We all four went for another drive to Ryegate to see if Charles and Irene had more thing done at the store. Things are going slow as expected it would. After we visited with them for a while, we went out to Tex and Shari's place south of Ryegate. There we visited for a while then after a while, Wayne, Tex.'s dad, Wayne Carpenter, came in and we had some stores to tell about the old times. I can vouch for some of them because I was there in that period of time. Wayne is married to my youngest sister, Donna. Then we went to the cafe for lunch and a dozen of the relatives came in and I paid the bill. The bill came to $70.00 dollars, I didn't mind because we had been sponging off of them to some degree for the past weeks.

July 19, 1999 Monday

We are here in Billings yet. Had a good day got a lot done. The first on the agenda was to take the little car to the shop and get the carburetor fixed. It took only about hour to get that fixed then I washed the car on the way home. At noon, we had a good dinner of creamed peas and new potatoes. I have never forgotten how we looked for each spring to have the new potatoes, creamed fresh peas what a meal that made. The vegetables were all from the garden. Then after lunch and after I had a good nap, I went to town and got the car washed that we had been using of AlBurt and Evelyn's. Now that they are both blind they are selling their car so that was why we used theirs instead of ours beside our car need some work done on it and it was smaller. Then when suppertime came, AlBurt took us out for the meal. This ends this day and will be moving on in the morning.

July 20, 1999 Tuesday

We got our way this morning heading for North, Dakota the long way to St Louis, Missouri. I was hot close to the 100's and better. After about 50 miles out of Billings the air conditioner in the Motor Home, It is called the dash air, got to doing some funny things. You would be going along and all at once the cold air shut down and the defrost air would come on. The air was always cold but coming from the wrong places. I also noticed that when I was going up hill it would make the switch and when I let up on the throttle the air would come in the right place. This was the clue that the problem was in the vacuum system. That told me I didn't have to have an expensive repair to the compressor
   At 5.00 O'clock in the evening, we stopped for the night at a KOA campground in Bismarck, North Dakota. It was a nice park each space was in the trees so it didn't feel so close to your neighbor.

July 21, 1999 Wednesday

I just knew that I couldn't continue on this trip the way that the air conditioner was working, so the first thing after breakfast I went up the road looking for some one that could fix this. After three stops, I found a very nice clean shop that took me in right away. The young man that did the work was very careful and was clean about what he did. He worked on this trying to run down the leak in the vacuum line that seemed to be the problem. Lunchtime came and he went to lunch and so did we. We were late getting back and they had found the line that was leaking so by one afternoon we were on the road again. The bill was only 140.00 dollars and he had but down only 2.5 hours of labor and a $1.60 for parts. Because we had about a half a day left, we took off down the road. We went South on 83 for about 200 miles and gave up at this small campground. At this time, there is one other trailer and us here for the night.

I have to mention the weather here this afternoon. It has to be over 100 degrees today. This may sound crazy but I have paid for the electric but to cool down the Motor Home I have started the generator and am running both the air conditioner and it has brought the temperature of over 100degrees now to seventy two were in side of the Motor Home. I hope tomorrow brings better weather, a little cooler. My dear wife Winifred doesn't like or can't stand the temperature above about 60 degrees so she is thinking that is the end of the world now.

July 22,1999 Thursday

It seems to be a test of the machine against the human being. Today we got up and started on our way. The temperature was very warm all night and this morning it was 74 degrees at 5:00 AM . It felt like it was 90 at noon. As we go farther east, the temperature was going up. At this time of the evening 8:00 PM it is still 90 degrees here in the park that we took early in the afternoon. We were running the generator and the air conditioner at the same time to keep things cooled down when the rear air stopped. That means that I will have to find some one tomorrow that can fix that.

July 23, 1999 Friday

We drove all day in the heat of 104 and 106 it was so hot that we could not stand to be in the Motor Home. With the rear air conditioner not working the front one couldn't keep the Motor Home cooled down any lower then 95 degrees

With that type of heat we took a motel for the night. When we got into the motel we did have our shower and a good night sleep. We did go from Bismarck, South Dakota to De Moines, Iowa, which was a distance of about 400 miles.

July 24, 1999 Saturday

We woke up at 4:30 AM and by 5:00 I was up, shaved and got dressed then went to the Motor Home that had been park in the parking lot. The early morning was very nice. I got the breakfast as usually. Got started at 7:00 AM to get here at Sharon's, my daughter about 3:30 PM. Oh, was it ever hot, someone said it was 100 this afternoon. It was so hot that we went over to the park that is about 1 1/2 miles from Sharon's. This place is close to the lake and in the trees so if the weather would only come down a little am sure that this place could be very nice. It is a little after my bedtime and I am tired so here goes the shut down for the night.

July 25, 1999 Sunday

We are here in St Jacob, Illinois Where the heat is all most unbearable at the over 100 degrees. We were out at the lake for one night but the next morning the heat got so bad that we went in to Holiday Express Hotel. The rest of the day we just stayed in the cool room here at the Hotel. I am to warm to think of any thing to say for the day. Tomorrow Sharon is going to town so I am gong to ride a long and go the Airstreams dealer to find out if any thing can be done with this bad air conditioner. If I had the two maybe we could stay in the Motor Home.

July 26, 1999 Monday

Sharon and I and her children had to go to St Louis, Missouri, Chelsea had to get a shot for hepatitis B. This is preventive shot. Then we stopped at the Airstream Dealer and got an appointment to have my air conditioner looked at tomorrow morning at 9:00 AM I hope the shop can find the problem so that we can have two conditioners gain. If they can fix it, we will move back to the park on the lake. At these temperatures, I don't think that I would like to be on the road yet. It wouldn't be bad when you are driving and have the dash air on but it is when you ha have to stop over the night.

July 27,1999 Tuesday

Lay awake a lot of last night wondering what might be the problem with this air conditioner. I was up at 5:30 AM and thought it was to early so went back to bed didn't sleep any but did rest. At 7:15, I was on the way to St. Louis where the dealer was. I didn't get lost so arrived a little before the appointment was but they took me right in and found the problem and had it fixed in less then 30 minutes and I was back home checking out of the Hotel before the check out time of 11:00 AM. Now that the air conditioners are working, we have moved back into the campground . I went over to tell Sharon where we were then she stopped by and offered to cook the evening dinner and we would have a picnic here at the Motor Home. I got the chairs out and set up the table thinking that they would come any time. They must have had lots to do at the tavern because they didn't get here until 6:30 PM it was still daylight so it wasn't too bad. Sharon, Chelsea and Trevor were the only ones that came. Jason and Jerry had to work. They don't know what they missed when they could have come here and got away from that smoke and the noise from the tavern.

July 28, 1999 Wednesday

It was nice to be back on the Motor Home then being cooped up a Hotel. We both had a good nights sleep. This park only costs 12.00 dollars a night and it is very quiet so far. Most of the people have their units here just for weekend use. The one next to us hasn't been moved for the past 10 years. I was talking with them and their unit is an old milk delivery truck. It has been rebuilt to make a Motor Home looking RV. I went over to Sharon's and took some laundry over for Chelsea to do. Then after noon Sharon took me out to see Teresa that is about to have triplets. She early has done a great job of fixing up a room in the house. She was thinking three all through the scheme when she did it

July 29, 1999 Thursday

This is the last night that we will be in St Jacob. At this time of the evening it is 8:00 PM the temperature is at 100 degrees. About the only thing we did today was to try to keep cool. We have been in this park for four days with the air conditioners running day and night. I don't think that they are making any money on us when the parking fee is only 12.00 dollars a night.

Winifred had a good idea that we take the family out to dinner a good place in Highland, IL. We had a very good dinner and the cost wasn't that bad for seven people of 102.00 dollars. After the good bye's and thank yours so now we can leave any time we wake up in the morning.

July 30, Friday

Another day on the road, all day in temperatures of around the 100's or better. Our bad luck hasn't left us yet. As I pulled into a State park there was a hose hanging from under the Motor home, it turned out to be the propane supply line. It must have happed a shot time before we stopped. I turned off the fuel and we still had a half tank of fuel so after parking I took the line off and went over to a small town and got some clamps. Installed the clamps and attached the hose, every thing back in order. It was real to all night but we did get some sleep with the air conditioners running al the time. When I got up in the morning, it was still 85 degrees out side.

July 31, 1999 Saturday

We got a rather early start this morning, as the weather was cloudy at this time of day. After we had gone just a few miles the weather seem to be cooling down the farther we went the cooler it got. As a matter a fact, I didn't turn on the air conditioners like I had all three running all day in order to keep the temperature down to make it livable. We quit early today but didn't think it was as early as it was until we checked into a park and it was only 2:30 PM It is now 6:00 PM and the temperature is 68 degrees, I am sure that we will sleep tonight.

August 1, 1999 Sunday

We were in central South Dakota for the night. I had just got set up when it started to rain. It rained most of the night and the best thing about it the weather cooled off so a person could sleep in comfort. Got an early start this morning. The weather was a little rain for about 20 miles and the clouds stayed with us most of the day. It was the first time in a long time that we didn't have the air conditioners all running. We traveled all the way with just the vent on and didn't get to warm. Some of the trip was a hard wind blowing from the North that made driving a little bit of work to keep the Motor Home in the lane at times, other wise it was a good driving conditions. Went about 600 miles that I drove today and I was a little tired, to tired to read when we went to bed. I wanted to get to Billings so I could get the little car in the shop to have the carburetor worked on.

August 2, 1999 Monday

The first thing that I did was take the car down to the shop. They brought me to the Motor Home Evelyn's place herein Billings. They had the car all day and they came and picked me up at 7:00 PM to get the car. The rest of the time today we spent visiting. I was trying to get things done so that we can move on to Ryegate. I have one main thing that I want to check on and that is what as transpired with the property, of Mary Fiske's Estate. I would like to get the two pieces that are in the town of Ryegate. The larger lot that use to be the old blacksmith shop. This shop I had spent a lot of my time as a young boy watching the Blacksmith do his artwork with iron. Several times of the year Dad would let me take a team of horses there to be shod. These were dad's workhorses and they were 2000 pound or 3000-pound type but this man could take one of the horse's legs up and that horse could not take it away from him, that is how strong he was. The other piece of property is the old laundry building that young brother had built. The laundry didn't work out very well so he had abandoned that idea after about 4or 5 years of trying to keep the machines running. The other thing was to help Charles and Irene with what ever they need in the line of work. I am not looking for pay job just some thing to keep busy. It sure is much nicer here then in the mid part of the United States where we were for three weeks as I stated in the earlier dates of our trip. Here it is cloudy today and he temperature is around 85 to 90 degrees We got here at lunch time and had lunch at the restaurant in Ryegate, as we entered there was the kids just getting their lunch so we had lunch together. The best part we were there in time for Irene to buy our lunch. Thank you Irene.

August 3, 1999 Tuesday

After getting in Ryegate there were some changes that had taken place. Charles and Irene had moved to the Ronald place. They had rented an old Motor Home that was on a space for a month the month was up and the house that they thought they were going to move into wasn't empty as was planned so this is why they now are in Ronald's and Marie's place. Ronald had passed away several years ago and Marie has poor health so had to be put in a home in Billings. Tex and Shari now own the property and Charles and Irene are renting from them. Maybe things will settle down soon. So today, I asked Charles if he needed some help and he did need help with that wall removable that did several week ago. Today I spent finishing off some of the messed up places so that he could get his shelving up and the stock on the shelf. A very comfortable weather today. Cloudy most of the day and had temperatures in mid 80"s

August 4, 1999 Wednesday

Cool morning with some more clouds, it was nice for a change went to the store to help Charles and I finished one of the walls so it was ready to put stock by 3:00 PM. Winifred and I went to the senior Citizens for lunch. They had a good lunch for a rather small crowd. After lunch I took Winifred out to the Motor Home so she could be more comfortable and out of the sun and heat.

August 5, 1999 Thursday

Helping at the store here in Ryegate, Montana yet doing some remodeling for Charles. I finished two corners that have to have pegboard put on the walls where the standard shelving won't fit. The weather was nice today it got to 85 degrees this afternoon. As I write this the wind has come up a little and the temperature is 74 at 8:00 PM. Today they had a moving bee going on at noon when Nick and his friend came over to get his items from the house that Charles and Irene have rented. At the same time, they were taking some of Audrey's things from the basement. Then this evening Charles and I got two lawn mowers going ad cut most of the dry grass that surrounds the house. It is a real danger when things are this dry, all it would take would be one lighting strike and all would go up in a flame.

We are parked here at the same place that Ronald had put in so I could have a parking place with full hookup because I use to come and help him some with some of the repairs to the equipment each year after the folks passed away. Before that I would park in town in front of their house

August 6, 1999 Friday

Today I finished at the hardware store. I have been helping so Charles and Irene can open shop and start to bring in some money instead of paying out every day. The first day that I got here, he put to cleaning up the unfinished walls where we had taken the partisans out to open up more space for retail display. When all was said and done we had four corners that the standard shelving wouldn't cover, those were the areas that I had just finished.

It is 6:30 PM and we are getting some thunderstorms coming through the area. With this, there is some rain but not enough to help any crops. The temperature at this hour is 60 degrees. I hear the thunder yet and some wind that could be the end to this big storm. As a young boy growing up in this area , I remember that this could go on all night and still not get any moisture.

One other thing before I close down is that the kids that inherited the Mary Fiske place was having a yard sale all day and there was a large crowd there most of the day. I am sure that they did very well.

August 7, 1999 Saturday

Not much to tell about out today. I have finished the job at the store so I took the day off and the first thing was to show Irene where some of the old places were when I was growing up. The first place was where Grandpa and Grandma had the first farm here in Montana. Freeman and Minnie Fisk had moved here from the Red River Valley in 1909. They had traded their farm there for one section of undeveloped prairie land. Today there isn't any thing standing but I found the location. The present owners have taken out all the fences and are farming over the top of all the old homesteads and farms. I think they are farming a strip one mile wide by five Mlles long. They are doing what ten small farmer use to do on the same ground. I guess that is progress. I have talked to these people and they say that they are farming 100,000 acres that is in all wheat.

August 8, 1999 Sunday

We left Ronald's old place where Charles and Irene have rented the place for a while at 7:45 the AM. We are now heading westward for our home in Olympia, Washington. We are now parked this evening at the silver bar place 435 miles from starting this morning.

August 9, 1999 Monday

We left western Montana this morning and arrived in Olympia, Washington at 4:30 this PM. Weather was nice and the traffic wasn't that bad.
This is when Winifred had a stroke of the eye

October 30, 1999

We are getting ready to move to Tacoma, Washington. Monday is when the truck will arrive. Today I unhooked the desk computer so I was trying to get n E Mail from the laptop but it didn't work and it is getting late in the evening. Also, I have the clocks to turn back to standard time.

October 31, 1999

It is Halloween today and it is Sunday, for us it was a day of work getting the furniture ready for the Moving truck that is scheduled to be here at 8:30 to take the bulky and heavy items. I had a bid from three places and this is the low bid. Now we will see if they do a good job. Some times low bid means cheap work. I think I had better get off to bed.

November 1, 1999

Today has been one of the longest days that we have put in for a long time. We got up at 6:00 AM this morning so that we would be ready for the moving truck to arrive here at 8:30 AM and have us moved to the Franke Tobey Retirement Estates in the morning. You don't have to guess but when 9:00 AM came and no truck I called and they had a mix-up in the dispatcher's office. The did get a truck here by 10: 00 AM so they didn't get loaded until after 12:00 noon. They arrived at Tobey Jones at 1:30 and we right behind them. When they entered the grounds they didn't go to the correct place so that took some time for them to get to the right place then they drove in and had to back out then back in to unload. I judged that took them at least a good half hour, on my time. It was four in the evening before think were unloaded. Then they wanted $ 45.00 more then the bid that I objected to so I paid them the bid price. Now that it had taken so long, we stayed for the home supper, it wasn't a very heavy meal, but I thought it was plenty. After supper we got home at about 7:00 PM. Am I ever tired after this long day, some think I am not use to any more, so I will be going to bed soon.

November 2, 1999 Tuesday

Another election day is coming to an end. We went up to the retirement home to take some things and do some emptying boxes. We worked until dinnertime the Then stayed to get a meal. What a meal it was, all any one could ask for, just like home cooking. Then after dinner we came back Olympia. The day was very nice so Winifred got the windows washed from the out side. Now that is done and would be in the way when the house goes up for sale. We had called the first Auctioneer and they were so filled up that they couldn't do any thing until after the New Year. That would be about some time in the middle of January. We wanted to leave here by the first of the New Year to head south for the winter or some part of the winter. I called another auctioneer and they can do all the work of boxing things up for a sale and haul it all to the auction house. The other things that they will do all of the above for 30% to them. That is the best I could do here in this area. All I have left to do now is pick out what I must have or couldn't get along with out.

November 3, 1999 Wednesday

Today started out rather slow but picked up speed before the day ended. Winifred and I discussed the change of Auctioneers and it was the Thurston Action that we gave the job to mainly because they could do the job by the 17th of November.

This means that we can get house on the market that much earlier. I t would be great if we were able to sell the house before the end of the year. It was about 1:00 this afternoon that we came to an agreement on what day the boxing and hauling will take place. It will be this Friday or the 10th of next week and then the sale will be held November 17, 1999. We have been poking along but now we must have what we want to take along with us out of the way. Once they take the sale items, we cannot get them back. I understand that they, the Auctioneers, won't let us bid on our own merchandise. Now that put a rush on this old couple to get moving. I am sure we can get it done. We have all day tomorrow to do our savings of some of the most sacred items at the same time we only have a small space where we are going. This is plenty for the day so it is time to retire to the bed. I will let you know how we came out tomorrow in getting the task finished.

November 4, 1999 Thursday

I will take just few minutes to give you the run down as to what we did today. We had to get started early because we hadn't had a firm time when the truck from the Auction house was coming to pick up the last of our belongings. Then about 2:00 PM, we had a call from them the date would be November 10, 1999. I think with this my helper Winifred took this as the time to quite for the day, and we did. With the early start, we got in the mood to take out the last before going to the Auction. Just a few things that may need some time in the future. Also, we sorted out for any of the family that wanted some of this collection of up to 85 years. I wonder if this kind of thing could be eliminated. If a lot of this could have a shelf life of some kind that the item would disintegrate and we would never have to see it again. People, after so long, they die and disappear never to be seen again. I must make one more suggestion, the junk or earthly savings should take place a few years before we go. Then the kids or some one wouldn't have to do this dirty job.

November 5, 1999 Friday

Dinner or supper or whatever you want to name it, I have just finished a meal that is in the evening and now going to give you some of the activities that took place today. Yesterday we had taken a lot of this from many of the cabinets that is in the house and garage. Today we are to finish so that, what is left will be picked up by the Action house the 10 of November. Just after getting started Winifred called a neighbor and then before I was aware of what was going on they were here going through the kitchen drawers taking things that they wanted. When I came into the house, they informed me that Winifred had given them permission to go through just some of the drawers, which they were doing. You know that they took a lot of this so that is that much less that we sell. Their gain and our loss. That could have been from a dollar or one hundred dollars who knows, at this point who cares. We didn't get a lot done but several other neighbors also came in and they went home with an armload of goodies. What else can I say but to say good night for this day.

November 6, 1999 Saturday

We got up a little early this morning and got started on the normal duties of sorting out the items that we want ant those that we will always wonder if it was put in the action. At 9:00 this morning we did go to the coffee and rolls that they have every Saturday morning. This is the first for us in many moons. The last time that we went was about two years ago when I had a donut and it was taken away from me in front of everyone, it was done for my own good but I didn't take to that very well. In order to prevent it happening another time it was by far better to not go. Today when they asked for announcements, I got up and told the crowd that we had started to move and our home would be on the market soon. After the close of this I had one person come to me, for some one else, to ask about the price because he had a friend that could be interested, maybe. Then one of the members that live here in the Harbor stopped by to find out what I wanted for the place. I think was for more gossip then to help sell the place. We finished the day with a trip to I-Hop for dinner. This is the first time in a long time that we have gone out to eat. The place we are moving to will feed us three meals a day so when we move from here we will not have to take any food. So, I have tried to eat up all we could so we wouldn't have to give away a goodly stack of food that we had stored ahead that would last us for several months if there ever was an emergency.

November 7, 1999

We are still sorting out some of the, now junk, left over after taking out what we thought was enough but as the old saying goes where do you draw the line? Then you stop and say to your self, do I really need this? I haven't had to use it for many years. I may have had some of this material in the shop for 50 years and still never found a use for it. Day after tomorrow all this kind of thing will go to the action house maybe some one else will hold on this junk until it may come to be an antique some day. There is some of this that if I could hide it some place where the Martians would find it maybe they would be of some use. Getting back to the task at hand. I did get some more work on the little car that we haul behind the Motor Home. The job on this is to fix the back seat area to haul a heavy marble tabletop that has to weigh about 90 to 100 pounds of top that is 42 inches in diameter. I had to build a wooden cradle to keep it from rolling from side to side. Then the next step was to brace that monster from moving forward and backward. It is too large to lay down so it has to be standing on its edge. I took it for a ride and found that what I did was good as there wasn't a bit of movement to it. Tomorrow is another day so I had better take care of the night now.

November 8, 1999 Monday

The move is going along slow but sure. Had a good day not quite so much to go through. I made some repairs on some of the item that we are putting into the auction. These were items that I should have done long time ago, it was some that kind that you put off for a rainy day, It isn't that we didn't have a rainy day. Any way we have the car loaded to take to the new place tomorrow morning after we go to the Clinic and have our annual checkup and then we will have the results of the blood so the Doctor will have that when we go for the physical on the 11th of November. I sure hope that we can see our same Doctors after we move to Tacoma, Washington. The reason that we are going to Tacoma tomorrow is that we had signed up for an Art class.

November 9,1999 Tuesday

We were loaded for the trip to the new place called Franke Tobey Jones, the retirement estates in Tacoma Washington. The weather was a little on the rainy side so we had to work fast when the rain stopped. There were some boxes that went to the room and I had also had the garden tools and chemicals that we put in the garden area tool shed. We got to the Art class at 1:00 and the teacher was a little late but that didn't bother the class at all. I thought that this was a good class and I was very pleased with it. I have missed my painting classes that I had been taking right after Zelda had passed away. Then after I remarried, I was so busy that I didn't have time for painting. This evening we have been picking up loose ends and getting ready for the auction house mover truck.

November 10, 1999 Wednesday

As we got up this morning, I had just finished shaving when the power went out and we were left in the dark. Because we had been packing, the thought went through my mind as to how we would handle this mess if there wasn't any power for a very long time. The day started out with some concern. Then the auction house truck hadn't arrived as we had planned. So, I got on the phone and made contact with his office to find out that the owner was always running late. He did show at about half hour later. It didn't take long before everything got into gear and it went very well. There were four of them and they loaded the large heavy things first. Then they concentrated on the household items. At about four o'clock this afternoon they had almost finished with everything that was in the house, yard, studio, and the garage. To close of with 323 tagged items and boxes. They would have finished but the truck was filled to the tailgate. They are coming back tomorrow for the last.

November 11, 1999 Thursday

Today was a large task, with more sorting and putting things in boxes. It was mainly the big job of starting to clean up the mess that the auction house people left when they loaded the truck with the better of the merchandise then to the truck was full so can't blame them for leaving some of the smaller things. There was a trail of debris as they went through the house and garage.

November 12, 1999 Friday

This is the regular garbage and recycle day, and that is just what I started to do after breakfast. Winifred started in the house one the cleaning of all the wood work and counter, bath rooms, while I started on the studio so that we could have a place to place the items the we will take with us to the new place. Then Smokey came over with his truck and hauled a large load of waste to the landfill. He came back and we loaded him up again with a full load. By the end of the day, we had things in good shape.

Heard from Charles and Irene that the insurance company didn't payoff on the damage that was caused to their place just as the place was sold. We were out there the day after the vandalism was done and met the adjuster and the salesman was there also. This was at about 10:00 am.

November 13, 1999 Saturday

Another day of this moving. Some times I wonder if it was all that it is cracked up to be, but how else can you get the job done. Both of us had lots of keepsakes and a lot pure junk. You hear that things that are old get to be valuable. We will see when the auction is over and we get the money, if there is any, after all he expenses that goes into this kind of a move. Winifred's son came over today and hauled a large load of left over articles to the landfill. This makes four loads in his pickup that has cost $ 40.00 dollars to dump. There were several items that had been left behind when they, the auction house truck, took the first and only load. There wasn't room for any more that is the reason for some not being on the truck. Now the place is almost cleaned out so the carpet cleaner man won't have any thing to keep him from giving the floors a good clean job.

December 3, 2000 Monday

We have been living at the Franke Tobey Jones Retirement Estates. And today is the time that we had planned on heading south for the winter. The first stop will be at The Tate's place to unload the little car of a lot of Winifred's collection of dishes, pictures, and furniture That Connie thought she would like. Also, there are some tools in this load for David, something for Debbie and who knows what for the people in California. We have got as far as the old place here in Lacey for the night. The place hasn't been sold yet but hope it will sell in the spring. We had a rather late lunch today and Winifred and her son RoBurt got to visit over lunch. She was very glad that he could come over because we will be gone for most of two months that she wouldn't get to see him. I hope the weather will hold to rain only not any of that white stuff called snow.

December 4, 2000 Tuesday

Today started out to be a, some what a good day and in all it was if you add up all the pluses and minis We traveled from Olympia Washington to Tillamook, Oregon on highway 101 South. There were times that it rained so hard that you could hardly see the road a one hundred feet in front of you. The there times that the sun was out just like summer time. That didn't last very long then the wind would blow rear hard. We did drive 250 miles and didn't get started until after 9:00 AM. The late start was because we had some more things to load into the motor home, also empty the holding tanks and fill the fresh water tank. It is getting to be 4:00 PM and we saw this good-looking park so pulled in. The office was closed until 5:00 PM. This place is very clean and only 16.00 dollars a night. I think I have said enough for one day and it is time for bed.

January 5, 2000 Wednesday

This was a nice day and we came 295 miles and stopped in Brookings for the night. Winifred wants to play some cards.

January 6, 2000 Thursday

Today we went 350 miles and arrived at Connie and Burt's place at 4:00 PM. We would have been here a little sooner but we went around in circles for a while we couldn't find the street. I got the car unhooked and cleaned before dark. It was so dirty that you couldn't tell that it was a white car. It took me three times over before I got it clean. I am glad that it is a small car. Then we had dinner at about 7:00 PM we hadn't finished when David and his girl friend came to see us, then Debbie came. The young people was sure having a good time and it got to be 9:00 PM when we had to go to bed, We have been going to bed at 7:00 ever since we left on this trip. So this made a long day for us and after driving all day, I was really tired, so tired that I didn't read to Winifred when we did get to bed. I think that I might be getting older now that I am almost 86 years old. The answer; maybe I should slow down and act my age?

January 7, 2000 Friday

The little car is still full of the give away items that we had promised Connie she could have. I the afternoon we did get the car unloaded but not cleaned up. I did get the motor home washed before it got dark. It wasn't as dirty as the little car but I had to wash some places couple of times to get it clean.

We did get it unloaded enough to get the front seat empty and one place in the back seat. Winifred, Connie and I went shopping at Cosco's and Trader Joes. Between the two places we spent over $250.00 dollars and didn't get the car over loaded with that much material or supplies.

January 8, 2000 Saturday

It was a lazy day for us, so we didn't get up very early. It seems like we hadn't had a time like this for the past several months with the moving into our new home and getting things moved and disposed of so that we could take this trip like we have been doing for the past four years. Winifred took some pictures of Connie's and Burt's house and yard then we took them down to have them developed by one of the one-hour places. We thought that we would go to K Mart so that I could get another pair of shoes. Then we came home had some lunch. Connie had made some Gumbo(a fish dish Crab, Shrimp and other things) it was a very good soup.

Then in the afternoon I got the little car unloaded and rearranged some of the boxes from four to one and arranged the last of the load so it has every thing in its place.

January 9, 2000 Sunday

I had to get the tanks emptied so Burt and I took the motor home down the road about five miles where they had dumping facilities as well as gas and propane. After getting the motor home ready for another five days, we went to a lumberyard where Burt wanted another storage cabinet for his garage. He couldn't haul it in his small car so we loaded it the motor home. After getting that home at Burt's place and got it unloaded he went to work putting the cabinet together and I worked on the motor home washing all around each of the widows where the caulking around each window is deteriorating and it runs down the side of the coach leaving several black streaks that has now stained the paint. I will try to buff some of it out but I have my doubts that the streaks will ever come out. It would cost a fortune to have it painted

January 10, 2000 Monday

This was a rather nice day and we moved from Connie's and Burt's place over to another part of town to see Loomis & Nuzums a very good friend of Winifred's where we will be there for the better part of the week.

Sunday night when watching a video I must have been coming down with some thing as I was about to freeze when we went to the motor home, I don't think I got warm all night. After getting set up here at Loomis & Nuzums, I knew that I had a fever and I turned the heat up and took some medicine, that's where I stayed.

January 11, 2000 Tuesday

I am still in the motor home trying to stay warm and some more medicine. Winifred did run down a thermometer and took my temperature and I had a two-degree temperature. So, here I am yet nursing my wounds but all day my fever has been down so I don't feel so cold all the time. If it stays good all night I will be able to go out not that I think it is a good thing to do but the weather is horrible raining off and on and some wind to top it off. Maybe tomorrow will be better.

January 12, 2000 Wednesday

Today I stayed in the motor home all day, thought that I felt better but I was just kidding. The weather was nice and some off and on rain and cloudy all day. I had some chicken soup for dinner. The Loomis's where we are parked wanted to bring some of their dinner out to me but I didn't want any thing very heavy.

All at once Winifred came in so cold she was shaking all over, with a headache. I took several minuets before she could stop the shakes. We turned on the blanket and she went to bed. I could feel for her it is the same way that I came down with this pesky cold. So far it hasn't turned to any thing else but a good old fashion head cold, not an easy one.

January 13, 2000 Thursday

Another day of a sick household in the motor home. This is the first time that we had to hold up for sickness while traveling. This reminds me of the time we went to a rally in Leavenworth, Washington, this was to be a four-day rally. As soon as I got the trailer setup and every thing started like the water heater, refrigerator, electric cable hooked up, I knew that I was coming down with a bad case of fever. I went to bed in the afternoon and that is where I stayed all weekend.

The TV went out so yesterday Winifred called all over town for some one to fix this TV in the motor home. After many referrals, she found a repairman. He was to be here 9:30 AM. He had to put a new fitting into the cable on the roof then we got a fare picture. At 4:30, we turned on the TV and it was working but no programs that were any good so we turned it off. Then at 5:00, I turned on the TV and there wasn't any thing on the tube. I called the service man and he is coming out at about noon tomorrow. This bug that I have is bugging be. I have had enough of this coughing for a spell.

January 14, 2000 Friday

Oh my, oh my with all the sickness here I have neglected doing some writing. It has been three days and that is a long time for my mind to remember. Nevertheless, will give it a try. If you ever went through this thing of not remembering, you will bear with me for a few days of catch-up. It was Winifred's turn to be sick with this bug that is going around and I hear it is everywhere in the country. Some one told me that it was so bad in England that the hospitals were full and they had to close their doors. As I think about it, what if you were the next in the waiting line and you have been there for several hours. The first thing that comes to my mind is what I think the feeling of a convicted criminal feel when he has entered that cell and the gate closed with a clang.

It was 11:30 PM when Winifred got to feeling very sick and wanted to go to the Hospital. She asked that I call her daughter that lives here in town. I did and she and her husband came over and we went to the emergency room. After about hour wait we were taken in and it was 2:00 AM when we were released to go home. They had given her some medication that made her sleepy. The also did some blood work during this time. After getting home and getting her to bed, it was 3:00 AM. I was so tired that I was sure I would go to sleep at once but that didn't happen, it took me three hours before I did get to sleep. All this time I wasn't in the peak of health either. After being up all night it was difficult get much done. Winifred did sleep a good part of the day. All the time we have been here with all our ailments Diane and Fred Loomis have been keeping us in food and a telephone. They are the best.

January 15, 2000 Saturday

We are still here nursing our old bodies. This is not the way to go visiting then get sick when parked in the front yard. It is very nice that we do have every thing with us so it's not so bad that way but I still feel that it is burden on our friends. What can you do? I had this happen to me one time when my boss and his wife came to visit for a weekend and my boss got so sick he wasn't able to get or drive the vehicle with the trailer on so they were in the yard all weekend. Then came morning we got him up and took him to the doctor. The doctor ordered him to bed for three days. I didn't take it an effort or an implosion at all. What happened couldn't be helped or no one could have changed it.

January 16, 2000 Sunday

Today I feel good but had trouble sleeping last night for the cough that wasn't good. My stomach and my chest ached with all the pressure and for so long a time. Winifred wasn't good at all, and not good yet. We did the best we could by helping each other. I tried to get her to eat but she wasn't in any way going to do that. After a while I talked her into taking some Jell-O that I had made that is suppose to be good when you start to dehydrate. Our good friends are continuing to bring out our cooked food, what a help it is for me. Winifred did stay in bed all day. I did a lot of resting on the davenport.

January 17, 2000 Monday

This is a holiday of one of color. I would like to say a lot of things about this thing that our early ancestors did for there pleasure. This country will always suffer for that small mistake that was made.

Last night wasn't the best, I had a lot of coughing and had to get the heating pad to put on my chest to loosen the phlegm After wakening in the early morning we kind of snuggled together as she lay on my shoulder we comforted each other.

Winifred did eat a little breakfast and after words she called her daughter and she came over and checked her mothers vital organs It didn't turn out very bad because we didn't take her to the hospital like we had to do a couple of nights ago. Connie made out a good report as to what to do and when so that we wouldn't have to let thing get out of hand. Connie gave her mother in instructions that she is not to just lie in bed. I know that those instructions have sure helped me to help her mother.

January 18,2000 Tuesday

It wasn't an easy night last night. The both of us had trouble sleeping, Winifred is still having some trouble with her bowels. As for me I was told to sleep sitting up, that didn't set with me very well, sitting up, and sleeping on by back is not one that fills the bill for me. So, I had to cough al night and rolled around trying to get comfortable

Connie came over again this noontime to se us and check up on us and our condition. Connie has a lot of things to do so it is kind of her to make this extra effort. We do appreciate it very much.

I have made several calls just now letting people know that we have been sick and will be on the way home day after tomorrow. We have cut our trip because of illness. I plan on backtracking our route down here. I know that it is abut 745 miles and I hope it will be the same going back. I am sure that it won't be shorter but if we have some detours on the way back, that could change things.

January 19, 2000 Wednesday

Another day we are sitting here trying to get our health back so we can head for home. I think Winifred had a better night and I know that I did. I didn't cough as much and slept very well.

Connie came over and brought one of her rice dishes for lunch. This sickness has put a burden on so many people I am ashamed. All I can say is these friends have to be very diligent and truly a very loving and caring.

The plans are to leave here at about 9:00 AM heading north from Santa Rosa, California and we will be going up Highway 101 that follows the coast. Any other route would be very uncertain as to if it is open so you may end up in some small town in the mountains.

January 20, 2000 Thursday

It was decided between us that it was best that we head for home. We made plans to start north by 9:00 AM and it did work out that we did get away. We followed Connie Tate from where we were parked direct to the highway 101. We made it about 200 miles and we stayed at a KOA park. Good park but very pricey.

January 21,2000 Friday

It was about 8:00 AM when we got started again. Winifred wasn't feeling any good so I decided to drive the balance the trip home today so that we could get Winifred into the Olympia St Peters Hospital. We did get into Olympia at 8:30 and was parked at the Washington Land Yacht Harbor. She didn't want to go to the emergency that night she thought that I had done enough for one day. I agreed that I was very tired

January 21, 2000 Sater4day

After a little sleep, I took Winifred in to the emergency room about 7:30 AM so that she was going to be about the first to be seen by a doctor. We did get a good Doctor that was very though and very complete. After some blood and lung check, she was admitted and given room 1129 that is on the top floor. I had heard that this area was used when there was a full Hospital they put the over load up there. Winifred and I both thought it was the best room in the place. You couldn't beat the view when you look to the East over the top of a lot of trees and the Cascade Mountain range in a distance.

January 22, 23, 24, 25, 26, 2000 Wednesday

Winifred was being treated for, what they called the Flu. Even though we did have our Flu shot this year as we do very year. I guess that we had found a new type of the flu when we got down to Santa Rosa, CA. I checked her out of the Hospital this morning and took her to our new home at Franke Toby Jones. We arrived here just before dinner and they made up two trays and sent them to our room. What a meal it was. This place can't be beat for wanting to help you every time you turn around.

July 7,2000 Friday

This is a new trip now after the last one it has been along time that this motor home sat around gathering dust. This trip we have planed is from Tacoma to Alaska by the highway with the motor home. We left

Tacoma at about 9:30 AM and arrived here in Abbotsford BC Canada at about 3:00 PM. The weather was almost perfect all the way. This was a great park.

July 8, 2000 Saturday

We had considered staying there a day or two but changed our mind when morning came. Had our breakfast and then went out filling the gas tank then heading north for Alaska. Weather was great and so were the roads up to this point.

As we headed up the road and left some hills behind us, we arrived just a short distance north of the town of Cache Creek and we are staying in the Cache Creek Campground. Not a bad camp but not what the other one was. Ran into a little rain but missed the center of it as the road had signs that the storm must have been very heavy just a short time before we got there. We just got back from having a dinner of Sirloin Steak to order, Baked Potato Coleslaw and Garlic Toast for $8.00. I must say that both of us thought that the Steak was very well done. Went to look at the stream that is behind the park to see if there might be a place we could wet a line and maybe get a fish. When I asked the operator about it, the answer was the stream was too high and to fast. The other thing was that they didn't sell a license, which took care of that.

July 9, 2000 Sunday

Today we had a good day of rain and more rain all day long it followed us or was in front of us for the complete day as we traveled the one hundred and ninety miles. There weren't any great hills or steep grades so it wasn't a hard drive. We thought that we saw a nice looking park for the night but we passed it and didn't want to back track so continued down the road. At about 2:30PM we saw a good-looking sign of a park that is called the RoBurt's Roast on a lake. As we drove into the park, Winifred fell in love with it and wanted to stay here and go no farther. This will end our Alaska trip. This evening we tried to call Charles in Montana. From the camp it would go through but they couldn't hear us as I could hear them clear. We did move from this park as it is located down in a low place. I thought that might be the problem. I think it was a great help because we did get through and found out that Charles and Cary did get there and they would be loading the large truck that is scheduled to arrive there July 10, 2000 by 10:00 AM. From what Charles told me he had help all lined up there with the Hutterite that is a neighbor.

July 11,2000 Tuesday

This is our second day in this great park. I am sitting here looking out the window as the sun is setting just crossed the lake from where we are parked. This park has about sixty spaces not counting the tent spaces. There appears to be about half-and-half of the older retired people and the younger working class with children. There is one real bad thing about this park. There are thousands of Geese and Ducks that leave so much waste behind them. It is so bad that you can't get on the water with out walking through all of the mess. Today the camp crew came through and raked up all they could, it made it look better but you still had to watch were you step or you might be carrying it into your RV and making a dirty mess on the carpet.

We got a new Cell phone so that we would have a means of contacting some one there is trouble with the motor home. With our age of 81 and 86, we are not kids that could get out and walk miles to get help. I am just getting started on this cell phone. Right now a I read the instruction they want me to do a thing with the battery .They want you to run down the battery then charge it up again for three times to build up the battery. I understand that this will make the battery last a lot longer. What I started out to say was that I wasn't to get hold f Charles to see if things are going as planned. Just as I started to make the call the battery went dead so I have to wait for tomorrow to see how things are going. It is getting time to shut this machine off and go to bed. The weather has been ideal all day. It got to high of 72 degrees today.

July 12, 2000 Wednesday

This morning started out to be a good day and it has been very good. It is late afternoon now and we are out in the garden surrounded by well-manicured lawn and flowerbeds all around us. There is a cool breeze coming to the gazebo that Winifred is sitting doing some painting with the watercolors. That is one I know nothing about. I dab in some acrylic and some oil. I have painted several pictures in the oil and a few in the acrylic. I like the acrylic the best.

It startled me because it was the first time that it did that and it was Susan that had called some place and got our phone number. That tells you that today you can't get away with anything. Here we are some 800 miles from home and they find you even when you hadn't given out the number. As a matter- of- fact, I don't know the number myself. Anyways it didn't work very well because we were still in the park and it is down in a low area. Susan is married to my grandson, Cary. After that, we went up on the hill about one mile away and I called her. She had said that Charles, Cary and Irene had left Montana heading for Washington she didn't know much more then that. I had better close this off until another day.

July 13,2000 Thursday

Today is the beginning of the great event of the year. Called the Billy Barker days. This man was ht first one to discover gold in this area. Because we have stopped over here not knowing what this is all about. Today we attended the festivities all after noon. This was the Seniors day including a free lunch for all also no charge for the full show. That is what I call a great deal. I That's of this because many of this older group don't get a chance to attend some of these function, not that they couldn't afford them but most programs are after dark that stops a lot of the. Many have trouble getting around as well as some can't see that well after dark.

All in all this was a good day here in Quenelles, BC Canada, where we are now and have been for the last six days, we hate to leave but our plans were to go to Alaska. I think we are about one third of the way to the pint where we turn around and head for home. Every thing has been going very well, feeling well both of us and the equipment have been good. The equipment was in very good condition before we left on this trip.

July 14, 2000 Friday

After the good day yesterday, we had thought we would to one of this area's large gold fields. This was the spot that Billy Barker had hit the first sign that there was gold in the area. It was a 75-mile drive one way. If ever there was a true tourist trap this was one of them. You had to pay an excessive price to get in then the services were minor. Although there was one restaurant there after paying to get in that was open and

I must say our meal was good and service was good. I had only one complaint and that was the roast beef that I ordered was very tough. I mentioned to them that it was as tough as Billy Barkers boots was he best I could think of at the time.

Arrived back at the park about 3:OO PM and had a good nap some thing that has been missed on this trip. Then we went to the top of this hill to see if we could get the grand kids on the cellular phone. I tried and got through but the phone was busy. Wanted to keep them informed as to where we are and find out about how Charles and Irene are and if they are back in Washington. Haven't been able to reach any one from this point in BC Canada. I was trying the regular telephone system and that hasn't been that good when you carry the United States calling cards.

July 15, 2000 Saturday

Started out from the RoBurt's Roast RV Park this morning headed north for Alaska. Checking the speedometer, we ended up with 260 miles for the day and stooped in a campground at 3:00 PM a little early but it is better then not being able to get a park because they would fill up. I have been in that situation a time or two and it is not funny or very safe any more today. At the end of the day, we have ended up at a park that is about 10 miles from the town of Chetwynd BC Canada. Its time to hit the sack for the day.

July 16, 2000 Sunday

This is a new day as we leave the RV Park heading north once again. We left Chetwynd BC Canada to stop at Ft. Nelson 354 miles. This is the most miles that we have driven so far this trip. There is a good reason for this distance. Most of these miles were just a lot of road ahead of us. Left in the rain and had it almost all day some times harder the then others. Also, there was a lot of construction in several different areas. I think that they did a good job handling the traffic with out more then ten minutes delay. Some of those repair strips were several miles long and the speed was controlled by having a pilot car that was on the lead. He set the pace, which was a blessing because some driver would just speed and stir up the dust so bad every one would suffer, not only from the dust but the rocks also would do a lot of damage. This place we got a place to park with out any hook ups. We weren't here very long when the space next to us gave us some power from his Motor home. Isn't it great that there are people in the world that do some good deeds. I thank them for the thoughtfulness. These people are from Minnesota if that would make a difference, I think so as they are of Swedish decent.

July 17, 2000 Monday

Started out from Ft. Nelson at 8:30 AM headed north for Watson Lake, Yukon after putting 315 miles behind us. Today was a few miles less but a lot harder to drive because of the winding road and a lot of raw construction where we had to travel on some detours and some of the time we had to mix with the heavy equipment. The road was so rough and some of the road was soft and muddy with motor home sinking into the mud. Not enough to stop us but it did slow all down to a crawl. Our motor home and the little car that we are pulling is a coat of dust and mud. I knew that we would experience a lot of this type of conditions when you travel to the North Country.

This is the first day that we had seen some wild animals on the side of the road. The first was several young Moose calves but didn't see the older ones anywhere. The next group was mountain Goats with their young kids that were still nursing. When we first saw them, they were on the edge of the road licking the stones to get the salt. The next was the single Bear that was just off the roadside with a motor home stopped and the lady had her camera and was taking some pictures. This lady was unaware that she was to far from that motor home to get there in the event this Bear wanted to attack she would have been a casualty for sure. As I went past them the Bear was interested in some thing else or he could have had his dinner.

We have now settled in at the Camp ground Services here at Watson Lake, Yukon. It's not a bad camp but they sure had large one. The weather was raining and some sunshine this evening and through the night.

July 18, 2000 Tuesday

Left here 9:AM after gassing up with this 81.9 cents per liter. That would be about $ 2.50 a gallon by US standard. In Canada, it would be about 1/3 more by Canadian money. We didn't do very well in distance today. With a lot of rough roads and crooked one added to the delays for construction in several areas. I stopped a little earlier this time in a park that has one of a kind type of parking. It is laid out so when the RV's are stacked it is like sardines in a can. There's no rime or reason as to why they did this. I guess it would be all right if you wanted a change in bed partners. There was so much mud on the little car Winifred did a partial wash but it did help.

July 19, 2000 Wednesday

My son Charles had an appointment with the foot Dr. in the Virginia Mason hospital in Seattle today and I wonder what his condition is now. I wonder because we are about 1500 miles from home. I just now checked the cell phone and there isn't any service yet. It's just too far up in the North Country.

Left Deace Lake RV park at 9:00 AM heading South on highway 37. The day was full of construction and that meant that there was a lot of time waiting for some of the equipment to get out of the way for us to travel. We covered 245 miles today. I feel that this stop was a good one. Fueled up the motor home with one of the largest number units so far on this trip at the cost of $ 79.9 cents per liter $149.00 Canadian money. The attendant said they would wash both vehicles for $40.00 and they had a space for us to park for the night for an additional $22.00 that's spending it all in one place. Then to top it all off we had dinner that cost $13.00.

The weather has been raining all day some times not more then a mist to a good down pour. At the present time, it is a good shower like it is never going to quit. We have seen some beautiful scenery there was a lot of snow in the higher mountains. Tonight it appears to be snowing now in the mountaintops.

July 20, 2000 Thursday

The first thing that we did was go up to Stewart, BC & Hyder, Alaska from the camp we were staying at last night. Now we can say we have been to Alaska by road as well as by water. We drove the small car on this trip and left the motor home in he park. It was a nice drive. First town was Stewart then Hyder was the town we had to go to see the salmon and the bears. It was about four miles out of town where they had a vexing place where people could be some what save to watch the fish going up the river to spawn and the bears know where they can get a meal fish. There were about 50 people there with some very expense camera's that was all set up ready to catch all the action. Winifred and I walked in with my camcorder, as we got to the viewing area a bear came out in good view and I took several feet of pictures of this bear crossing the river but he didn't find a fish or he was already full, he didn't tell us, and we didn't stay any longer.

After getting back from Alaska, we stopped at the camp and picked up the motor home. Then we went 96 miles to the town Kitwanga, BC RV park Cassiar, not a bad camp. We have had a lot of wind where we are parked on a hill, over looking the small valley. The weather has been a little better today with only a small amount of rain. The roads didn't have any gravel or construction that made it easier to drive. Time to leave you now and will see you to morrow.

July 21, 2000 Friday

Early this morning Winifred got sick at 4:00 in the morning, so we stayed here in this camp for the day. I got a chance to do some little things that has to be done as you travel. One of the things was that I wanted to wash the car. Even though it was washed yesterday, we had come through some more bad roads that left the car a mess. Other then that we didn't do very much. We did take time out to go up town here in Kitwanga, as we need some groceries. We drove what we thought was the town and found that we were leaving the town. We stopped one of the town people on the street. They said that you have passed the store so when you go back don't blink you could miss the store again. We ended up getting some of the needs but we can get by until we find a store down the road tomorrow.

July 22, 2000 Saturday

Today is one of the best days we have had for a long time. The roads were very good with two short construction jobs that didn't hold us up at al as we came just as the line was moving. We left Kitwanga by 8:00 AM and ended up at Prince George after 300 miles. Checked in to the Southpark RV Park and Campground. And they had only two spaces left so we took one of them.

I was thinking that we would stay here tonight and then go to RoBurt's Roast where we had stayed on the way headed for Alaska. Well, when we called just now they were booked up for the next week and a half. Now we must change our plans. Well, for one thing, we are going to stop and see Cary and Susan before we head for home. There is about 600 miles left of our trip that started July 7th. I would like to see one of my oldest friends that live in Monroe, Washington.

July 23, 2000 Sunday

Didn't have a good night, was awake most of the time. Although I did do a lot of dreaming, something that I don't normally do. After breakfast, we got things together and down the road we went, heading south and home after some 900 miles yet too go.

We are back in the same park that we stayed at on the way north. I must say this is a nice park so we may stay fore several days again. I do have to do some repair on the motor home, nothing very serious but it should be checked now before some thing else goes wrong. I'm not looking for anything, as we are out of the rough roads, those are behind us now.

On the way down this morning we came up on a wreak on the highway to find out that a large semi truck loaded with fresh crab had hit the abutment of a bridge and ripped thing off of the truck and trailer dumping the load over the edge. I am sure that some of the load had to get in the river below. At the time that I checked in to this camp, they said that it was on radio. It happed at 40:00AM this morning and that the driver must have gone to sleep bur he walked away from the wreck unharmed. Down the road there sat the truck and trailer, a complete and total wreck.

We have been here a few hours and now we have called the kids, Cary and Susan, then called Charles and Irene. It sure was a relief to hear they are doing much better now that they are getting settled in the Ocean Shores home. I think I had better get going for now.

July 24, 2000 Monday

Winifred just came out with some chocolate pudding with ice cream that was our desert after coming home to the motor home from eating out this evening. We are staying at this nice park RoBurt's

Roast here in Quenelles, BC Canada. This park is first class except for the Canada Goose and the Ducks they have almost taken over all of the waters edge and the lawn areas. They are beautiful when they are some place in the wild. These geese are tame and they are now a threat to the business here on the lake. It isn't just this RV Park that has the problem. Many city parks all over North America are being threatened by the number of geese.

Today we spent doing some small repairs to some of the cabinets that got shook up a little on these rough roads. Just a few screws came loose. I don't mean in the driver but in the coach. As I sit here, I am looking across the small bay where the sun is going down, the water is so smooth, and the sparkles are fantastic.

July 25, 2000 Tuesday

We are still here at this very nice park. It's on Dragon Lake here in Quenelles, BC Canada. I think we are leaving tomorrow needing home. There will be one more stop in BC then we will cross the border into Washington. We have been traveling for 26 days. There will be a few more before we get home.

Did some more cleaning and fixing today. The weather has been any thing but good, very little sun and a lot of rain with thunder and lighting. As a result of the clouds, we had slept in this morning, that's not some thing we can do where we live. Their meals are right on time three times a day. This being breakfast 8:00 AM, Dinner 12:00 PM, Supper 5:00 PM. You must be there or there isn't any other time they have food out. They don't believe in any snacks. We sure don't miss them, as we don't feel hungry any time.

As I sit here, doing this typing, I am looking out of the motor home parked with view of the lake. Last night the ducks and the geese were all out on the bank and tonight there are only a couple small ducks. Maybe the stormed has driven them some other area in the park. There is a young man that is fishing from the dock about 200 feet from here. He has some young lady now come to help him. She didn't stay very long. I can see why she left. He is fly-fishing and she didn't want to have that line wrapped around her neck. Winifred is sitting here in a chair listening to her talking book and eating peanuts that need to be cracked before she can chump on them.

July 26, 2000 Wednesday

We had been at RoBurt's Roost for three days this time and we felt that it was time to get on the road again. Left the park at 8:30 and drove 301 miles today. We are now at a nice park here in Spences Bridge, BC Canada. They tell me that this is in the same range as the desert. I understand that the temperature reaches up to 110 degrees this time of the year. Today the temperature has been very nice and reading in the 70's this evening.

We are parked looking out on the Thompson River. The owners say the trout fishing has been good lately so I went and bought a one-day license at the cost of $ 16.00 Canadian money.

July 27, 2000 Thursday

Today was a rather slow day as we had decided that we stay over one more day before heading for the States. We have been out of the country for three weeks will be glad when we get back to the old routine of just eating sleeping and waiting for the next meal.

We stayed over so that I could say I have fished in Canada. I am glad that I got one-day permit, as I didn't have any luck as I had fished in two different places on the Thompson River. It may have been that I hadn't fished for over 10 years. The first thing I am not sure that I had the rigging set up properly. I hadn't forgotten how to cast because I was doing well even against the hard wind.

There is always some thing that has to be done with the vehicle when you travel this way. I cleaned the windshield and rearranged some of the cargo

July 28, 2000 Friday

We left the park in Spences, BC Canada now headed for the US We crossed the boarder ad got to Everett, Washington where we went to Cary and Susan to see them and the great grand children. Har arrived just as Cary got home from work. We had a good visit in the motor home, they love to gather in the motor home and sometimes they like to blow the horn. It sounds like a tugboat. Then in the evening, they took us out for a good meal on the bay here in Everett.

July 29, 2000 Saturday

After leaving the kids there, we came on down south and went straight to Ocean Shores to Charles and Irene's place. Cary had Charlie's computer and it would save them a trip if I took this to them. We got the computer to them and Charles was putting a new computer together. I helped him with that and it was getting past mealtime but hadn't been invited to stay for something to eat so we went home to the motor home and had our own dinner. This was a little upsetting to us. We had made a special trip down here to get this computer to them so Charles would have his computer to play with when the weather got bad. With his bad foot, that he should stay off it a lot of the time so that it would heal.

July 30, 2000 Sunday

This is not a good day for any of us when we had a talk about what had happen last night. There a few words and it softened our stay as we left then and headed for home. I sure didn't want any thing to upset Charles and my close relationship that we have had all of his life. We had worked together a lot. It upset me very much that this had to happen. So on the way home we stopped at a park to rest up and get our senses together. As I finish the writing for the day, it really hurts to have this kind of upset. I have only two children and Sharon is so far away that I never see her very often and don't hear from her very often ether. She is always working so many long hours in her business.

December 10, 2000 Sunday

It has been a long time since I have written and there have been a lot of things going on around here. To review this lost time after getting home. Soon after we got home, we started to look for a retirement home. At this point I felt that we should get ready and downgrade our style of living, as Winifred didn't have all her vision once she had that stroke in the eye. I guess I was a little selfish and didn't want do a little extra when she couldn't do all she normally was doing.

We had looked for retirement place fro Seattle to Olympia and every thing in between. Then it came down to a nice home in Tacoma, Washington called the Franke Tobey Jones. This place was built in the Studier style and was built in 1924. We looked at a nice apartment there that over looked the Commencement Bay. They were in the process remodeling this apartment. After a few months, they had it finished and it was the best in the building 600 square foot of space.

Now we had a big job of getting rid of all of our collection of the standard home furnishings. We gave away a lot of it to family and then the last truckload went to the auction house where we just as well have taken it to the dump. The only thing is that we got a little for this material and it saved us the cost of dumping.

It was in November 14, 1999 that we moved into this nice home and a different live started to take place. Now there wasn't any more cooking or house cleaning to do and then on top of this we got three meals a day. There was a lot of time to go to the different places and volunteer for some of the many jobs that could be done buy the residents of the home. Winifred and I took on the resident's garden and greenhouse that hadn't had any one there for several years. The weeds and grass was waist high. I purchased a weed eater and a tiller to clean the place up. There had been several people that had some very nice flowerbeds and berries in this place. When I started to clean it up with the weed eater, all I could do was start making a pathway through the weeds. When I could see something that looked like it was some good plant I would go around it and watch for the next plant. This was a piece of ground that was about an acre. Winifred had a lot of cleaning up of the green house of some old things that had been stored into it be every one that wanted to move it from their rooms.

In mid summer, we took the motor home for a trip to Canada and the Yukon then to Alaska. After getting back from this trip we had a lot of clean up to do but we did enjoy all of this time there at Franke Tobey Jones Retirement Estate. Now it is over one year that we have been there putting up with a lot of noise form the kitchen, shop, motors, and fans that were vibrating the walls. After these thirteen months, we couldn't put up with any longer. That is when we went back to where we had been living for about five years and purchased another home in the same place we had moved from.

December 4,2000 Monday, we purchased a Mobile home in Olympia, Washington. Then the next day we gave the Retirement Home notice that we were moving out. Then Friday December eighth the carpet was installed. Now things are going along very good. Sunday the tenth we went back to Tacoma, picked up some of my tools, and finished the load with boxes from the locker at the home. We had dinner there at noon and right after that we went shopping for new furniture at " The Old Cannery " in Sumner, Washington. It didn't take very long to find out what we liked and we purchased a bed and mattress, a dinning room table and chairs and a small desk for Winifred for the tune of $ 2,300.00 for all of the order. Because we had service people coming to hook up the telephone and the carpet layers had some more to do, as they didn't get the message from the boss about what we wanted done with the carpet. One of the things was that we didn't want any mettle in the doorways and they missed a bathroom and a small closet. In the morning, I went out to get a small pickup for some of the hauling that I will have to do while I am fixing up this older home that we just purchased. It is an old 1984 black GMC S-15. It sure looks good and will need some work to make it run better then it is doing at this time. I took it to the shop and they couldn't work on it to day so have to take it back tomorrow. In the mean time, we are working on the inside of the house. One of the first things that Winifred wanted was to lower all of the drapes in the dinning room and living room.

I took the truck to Mikel's to get something done to it and find out what good there was in the truck. The report was that the engine is very sick and it should be replaced. The one price was a new engine installed would cost about $ 3000.00 dollars. That kind of a repair cost is out of the question, I went looking for an alliterative to fix this nice looking truck. If only I could find a wrecked vehicle that had a good engine. After stopping at two wrecking yards I found just what I wanted in a clean vehicle so they wanted $ 450.00 for the engine and $ 350.00 to install the new engine. This is what I was looking for, sure hope there isn't some kind of a slip of the hand. If this goes bad, I will have to eat it, as these people do not guarantee anything they sell. I had thought that I would try to buy the wrecked one and do the engine change myself. There was a time when I would think nothing of doing that job. Not today at my age of 87. I have a few stiff joints wouldn't like me putting them to the test.

The above came out very good as the wrecking yard did take the motor back and they gave me what I had paid for this engine. I think it is because the repair shop said they would talk to him about taking this engine back because he had helped this wreaking yard boss get out of some other situations. I didn't ask any questions at this point.

We came down here today, December 13, 2000 a Wednesday with some of the hard to pack items from the retirement home and did a little work on the inside of the house like taking down the old Chandelier and putting up a new one. It isn't up yet but is being put together when dinner was ready. You must leave something to do the next day. This item was put on the back burner today when the weather was very nice, December 15,2000. So we took the truck and went to pickup the furniture that we had purchased earlier form the Old Cannery Furniture Warehouse in Sumner, Washington. The old truck that I had purchased was very sick engine and now sick transmission was doing some funny things. When I checked the fluid, there wasn't any. After putting in some fluid, we made it home with the heavy load for this small pickup. After we got almost home, it started to rain like we have not had a rain and wind that came down with a blast and it is still going at it like it will be doing this all evening.

When we got home, Winifred called her son to come over and give us a hand at getting this load unloaded but also out of the rain. To help this with rain situation was that I had to get out a tarpaulin and put it over the load. It didn't take very along to unload this load as they were all in boxes and heavy plastic. After that we got started to open boxes starting with the small box first. It was a small roll top desk, when that was finished, I started on the bedroom set. It is now out of the boxes and partially assembled. Now that it is getting to be bedtime, we will start again tomorrow.

Tomorrow has come and returned to the retirement home and the last thing we were going to was get the Christmas made, signed and envelopes addressed. We didn't buy any store cards this year. Winifred painted a poinsettia on the front and made up a small verse for the inside. Then I set up the computer to copy all of the fifty cards that were sent this year. There was no way that I could figure out how to both sides at the same time so had to run them all through twice.

Now that this is finished, we start on the big job of packing to make the move to Olympia on December 21st. We were packed in time, thanks to Winifred as she did a lot of the packing while I had to go to Olympia. The engine that I had found was to be out of this wrecked unit so that I could pick it up, when I got there, the engine wasn't out so they said they would have it out the next day. Because of time, I gave them another day and I would pick it up December 21st after we got the moving truck unloaded.

The movers were there to load on time so things went very smooth. The truck was loaded and we arrived in Olympia and unloaded by 2:00 P.M.. I can't believe that we had so many boxes in this little apartment and when we got it into this new house it seem that his place is over loaded and this is new place has 1140 square feet as the apartment had 625 square feet. The boxes hasn't been unloaded yet and put away, it doesn't look like we could store that much in the cupboards.

Being only a few days before Christmas December 22,2000 Winifred was sick yesterday and today she didn't get out of bed but very little until 4:00 PM she got up and got the evening meal. She thawed out a chicken parts that w had in the freezer and baked a couple of potato's. It was a good meal after a year of having someone prepare all our meals, every day. While she was recuperating, I had started to unpack the boxes that were the movers had delivered to our new place in Olympia, Washington. It is sure taking longer to unpack then it did packing. In new place, you have to find a place that it fits so when you need it you would know where to go.

This has been a big day of opening boxes and putting furniture in the right place as we are having Winifred's son and his wife for some thing to eat. This day of December 23, 2000. I have been informed that it will e spaghetti it isn't a Christmas kind of a dinner but each one for them self's I have never known that there is some kind of a rule that you have the same thing. There are still a lot of boxes left to unpack, but I am not going to get all worked up about it and break my neck. After getting settled in, we should have a lot of time. That is what I thought when I retired in 1974, as of this time it hasn't happened that is twenty-six years ago so why should things change?

Now it is Sunday May 20, 2001 , as we get ready to go on an Airstream club caravan called the Columbia Gorge Exploration caravan U-2266. We were to rendezvous at Brookhollow R/V Park Kelso, Washington. We couldn't arrive in this park until 2:00 PM. There were several of us that live in the Washington Unit, Washington Land

Yacht Harbor. Each of us lined up to leave the Harbor at 10-minute intervals, so as not bother the normal high way traffic. At 5:30 PM there was a drivers meeting. This meeting is held each day to keep the group informed as to what is going on from time to time as the leader would call. There are twenty trailers and Motor Homes, these are all Airsteam RV'S. This is the first day of this eleven day caravan the will end May 31, 2001, in the evening at Lewiston, Idaho.

Monday May 20, 2001 at 8:45, we assembled to car pool to the Longview Fiber company. It makes and process wood chips that they use to make the pulp for making cardboard. There are 40 people in this group of Airstream members, and they give us a tour of the plant. This plant must have had many miles that we had walk, know one said just how many miles this tour was and some going up steps and down again. This was the worst part of the trip, for me it almost got to me.

Then in the afternoon, we all went to the Cowlitz County Museum that was just up the road from the park. Nice museum for a small town, well put up and it told a good story of the area. Now it is getting to be time for the Happy hour for the drinks of the group and then they had a drivers meeting to inform everyone what to expect for the next day.

I had taken the new set of croquet with us and we had it out to play a game or two with some new friends that we had meant at this caravan. They were new members and were great company. They were Chuck & Elaine Hurlbut that live in the Duvall, Washington area. Now is the time for this worn-out group to head for the RV's where we will sleep in our own beds not in some strange Hotel room.

May 22, 2001 We are still on the caravan. The first order of the day was to meet and go on another tour, this time it will be to a steel mill in Klama, Washington. We were so worn out from the day before that we passed up this trip as well as the others on this day. The only one we went to was the dinner at JJ North Restaurant and the drivers meeting after dinner.

After returning to the RV park we got out the croquet set and played some more. We had so much fun with this that we didn't remember who won or lost, but who cares when we are having fun.

May 23, 2001 On our own for most of the day and then some looking around the city. Then we got to do some more croquet this evening and get ready to move up the river.

We left the campground this morning, May 24,2001, for Washougal, Washington and go through the Pendleton Woolen Mills tour. This mill was a very interesting operation. The group had to walk about a mile in this plant. They start from the raw material to the finished garment. It is a wonder when you see the large machines that it takes to make these garments. It is no wander that they cost so much..

November 3, 2001 Saturday

It has been a long time that the Motor home has been parked at home while we were rebuilding our new place back at the Land Yacht Harbor.

We are feeling very good, and after we had our physicals, the Doctor said we passed with flying colors. After getting the motor home ready and packed we took off for the south at 8:30 AM. We had scheduled to stop at a great couple in Vancouver, WA and visit them for a short time. We stayed over night there and took off for Coos Bay, OR November 4, 2001 Sunday to see my niece. I had talked to her over the E. Mail and here was a question as to being able to get to their place with this large rig. When we got there was no way that I could get up that road with car in tow so I called and she came down and we went back up   the road to the RV camp ground. Then she took us back to her house and we had a good visit and a very good meal with them. After the World Series baseball game was over, they took us back to the motor home.

After getting the motor home windshield cleaned, we took off today the 5th of November, heading down the coast to see Winifred's daughter that lives in Santa Rosa, CA. We hadn't gotten very far, about 20 miles south of Coos Bay, when the engine gave up and we sat along side the road for over four hours before the tow truck came. After he got there, we discussed the problem and got the engine to run so I followed him to the town of Bandon, OR. The driver led us to an Electric shop right on the highway in town. This shop and parts house didn't find the alternator that w needed so here we are sitting in their yard for the night. They should have the correct alternator and they are sure they will have it ready by 10:00 AM so we can continue down the road.

Every thing went as scheduled this morning November 6, 2001. We had a nice rest with all very quiet al night. Got up at 6:30 AM, had our breakfast and had the dishes washed as the mechanics came to work.

This new alternator was a good one and it took about thirty minutes to install. We were headed down the road at 9:00 AM After going through the great Red Wood forest we were staying at the same place that we had been before. The RV Park is called the Redwood Trails Resort the cost is $ 18.15 for the one night stay. This is better then the last park charged $ 25.00 for a one-night stay. As we drove in here was about a hundred Elk out in the front of the place. After we got the motor home set with all the hookups, we took the camera over there and got some good pictures on the camcorder. There was one old bull with a good rack of horns. There was also a young spike bull in the heard of about 80 to hundred cows.

Got a good start today, November 7, 2001 after emptying the holding tanks and filling up with drinking water we were on the road by nine o'clock. By 3:30 this afternoon, we had arrived at our destination here in Santa Rosa, CA. After driving only 260 miles. We are parked at one of Winifred's friends. Now that we are set for a few days, we went over to see Winifred's daughter, Connie Tate. We are now back at the motor home and settled down for the night.

November 8, 2001, Thursday We are in Santa Rosa now and will be here for several days yet. We were over to Burt & Connie's place for the better part of the day. Winifred and her family had a good visit.

Today November 9, 2001 Friday We went over there and was there most of the daylong out to a Mexican restaurant for there noon meal. I hope those that was with us enjoyed this meal, as for me I didn't feel that it was much good. After getting back from this dinner, we went to the house and Winifred had one of the best visits with Jay and Connie while the other Connie went to take her nap. It is now 6:00 PM and we are back to the motor home for the night.

Not much going on here November 10, 2001 Saturday. Winifred's family was going out for breakfast this morning and we didn't feel up to having that late of a meal. We had our normal breakfast in the motor home. We would have liked to go with the kids but you know that they run on the fast track and we are on the slow track.

I did get to play with the Cell phone, trying to learn how they work. The first thing that I did was to go to the store that sold this to me to seek help with out any satisfaction. After getting back from that trip, I started to call the Cell phone Company. After several tries, I didn't get the information that would help me get my voice mail from the mailbox. It seems that when you go out of your local area there is a problem. Time ran out with my patience so Monday I will get on with is problem.

Monday is here and we are still visiting Winifred's family. It is November 12, 2001. We visit From time to time. When between some of them going ands some coming and then there is the time that Connie(Winifred "s daughter)has to take her nap. She has to have naps during the day a she has trouble sleeping enough all night.

November 13, 14, 15, 2001

Things are about the same yet, we go over to Connie's and Burt's to visit with Connie, as she is home alone to answer the phone and do the bookwork. I did get to put up some shelving in the bedroom after her son Jay and his wife Connie had gone back to their home in Georgia.

November 16, 2001 Friday

We left Santa Rosa, CA this morning at 9:30 and stopped at a place in town that had a place to empty the holding tanks. That was test on any driver to get into this place and out again. I had to line up to empty tanks first, then I had to go around the station in order to get the propane. Then on top of that, it was raining all the time while I was there. Went only 250 miles today and quit at 4:00 PM. We are in the Almond tree RV Park in the Coalinga, CA. They sure don't know that there is a war going on, when they charge $ 25.00 a night just to park the motor home. I see that some of the Hotels are charging about half as much as they were getting before the terrorist highjacked four airplanes and drove them into the two New York trade center buildings destroying both of those buildings with two of the planes. And then there was one that went down in upper Pennsylvania when the passengers took charge of this plane when the highjackers had killed the pilots the plane crashed. Then the fourth highjacked plane hit the pentagon in Washington DC .

November 17, 2001 Saturday

We left the campground at 8:00 AM and got down to Riverside at 3:00 PM. Now we are here Larry and Doris's for a good visit. These are Winifred's Nephew and Aunt. They are great people. They are both handicapped he had an accident on the job and he has lost an arm and a leg when he was electrocuted. Doris has a problem with her feet so she can't walk very far at any time

November 18, 2001 Sunday.

This was laying around time of the week. We did some more rest, which I think we need. This trip may have been a mistake as Winifred is suffering from the heat already and we are just getting started travel for the winter.

November 19, 2001 Monday

Got up with a lot of spunk and going to turn the world around to day. That didn't last very long. At lunchtime we went out for hamburgers and then to Cosco to do some shopping for Thanksgiving. Got home to the motor home after eating and shopping. It was time for all to take a nap so that we will have the strength to have dinner. Isn't that the life for people that are retired?

November 20, 2001 Tuesday

Sitting around doing nothing. This seems to be the job of the day.

November 21, 2001 Wednesday

This was a little busier day, as we were getting ready to go over to Sharon and Elray's for an evening meal. It was a good evening, after the delicious meal where they served, ht e biscuit and then came the mane dish called Gumbo and then the desert of pumpkin cheese cake that we had taken. Every one sure seemed to being enjoying them selves. Then after dinner, the kids and Sharon were prepared to decorate the Christmas tree that had been put up earlier. It was not very long and every one was in the act, including me, by opening some of the boxes. It's 11:45 as we are to be ready to go back to the same place for the Thanksgiving turkey dinner.

Being it's now Thursday November 22, 2001, we didn't do much except sit around and talk and rest. Not for the girls they had to make lunch and get their naps taken. Of course, Larry and I took a nap even though we did a lot of work, we got tired of doing , I guess.

November 23, 2001 Friday

We are still here at Larry and Doris's in Riverside California. I really feel bad about sponging on them for this long a time. It just so happened that their daughter wants us to stay over and be included in their 45th wedding anniversary celebration. We are going to even it up a little by taking them out to eat dinner for the rest of the week, if we can get them to do that. There are people that take in someone and treat them the same as a family, well, this is the way we are treated and it has always been that way for as long as I have known them. Winifred and Larry are blood related so I am glade they have included me as one of the family.

November 24, 2001 Saturday,

This morning it looked like a good day, well it was, the in morning. Then when Larry and I went to do some shopping, we were caught in the rain at our last stop when we were in the grocery store. This rain came down so heavy that it looked like some of the rainstorms that I had seen in Montana when I was a young man. There was water standing and flowing a foot deep in the parking lot. We made it home in good condition. By the end of the day, the weatherman reported that we had .82 inch of rainfall for the day.

November 25, 2001 Sunday

Winifred and I did sleep in and had a late breakfast after all was cleaned up I had a small but nicer thing to do was to empty the holding tanks on the motor home. We are fortunate to have a place to dump here as when he had a motor home he had the city put him in a drop at the curb. It isn't in the right place for me to just hook-up, so I have to go down the street, turn around then pull over to the curb to empty. After that is done, I have to turn around again and get in my place to park where they can get out of their driveway. Because we park on a downgrade, I must block up front of the motor home to be level. Now that is done it is time to take a nap.

November 26, 2001 Monday

Had a big weekend for this old couple, some rest and some going here then some place else. If only I can get the time to keep this writing up to date. Now, I have forgotten just what is going on around here. As you can see, I have put down a few words to make it look like I know what I am doing.

November 27, 2001 Tuesday

This is the day that Winifred has been looking forward to sense before we went on the trip. She had put together some craft items that she had around the house and then she had purchased some more items that would complete job. When we got here, she had made with Sharon Konkel that today they would get the girls together and start this craft. Well, I had better tell you what this project is all about. The items consisted of six Styrofoam angels and then she had several different colored napkins that they would separate the two layer napkins then use the color portion. The next move was to tear up these into small pieces then put some pod or glue on a small part of the angel then stick these small pieces all over the Styrofoam angel.

November 28, 2001

Larry, Winifred and I went out to eat some lunch at a Mexican restaurant as Doris wasn't feeling up to doing any thing so stayed home to rest. After eating, we went to the store to pickup a prescription for Doris. When we got home she was still resting but came down for the dinner time but was not up fixing a meal for us so Winifred and Larry got a bowl of soup while I just sat there doing nothing. You know that too many cooks in the kitchen spoils the porridge. This is what we all need was to cut down on our food intake, I know that it didn't hurt me any to eat lighter.

The weather has been on the cool side for me. Then on top of that, these people have the house cold at all times, as Larry has a bad disorder in his system after he had his accident on the job. He had been electrocuted when he touched a piece of equipment that had hit a high voltage power line. As a result of that, he lost a leg and an arm on the left side. It was miracle that he even survived.

November 29, 20001 Thursday

Doris was feeling so good this morning that she got up earlier then usual and was ready to go shopping as planned. She and her daughter and Winifred went shopping and Larry had to go to his therapy this morning so, guess what, every one went off and left me all by myself. I did some cleaning in the motor home and then vacuumed the floor and I sent some E Mail. Then when noon came, I made myself a raisin sandwich on wheat bread with a side of backed beans then had a cookie that Carol Brown had baked and gave to us when they came from San Diego for thanksgiving. Now what is wrong with that kind of a meal?

November 30, 2001 Friday

It was very cool this morning and we stayed in bed under the electric blanket until the motor home warmed up a little. A little slow around here this morning, the lawn keeper was here and then the housekeeper came, with all of that going on we were unable to do anything for most off the morning.

After lunch we, Larry, Winifred and I went shopping and over to see another one of Winifred's relatives that live in the area. When we were at Jan's she was running a yard sale and I made a good buy there. They had two new battery tools without batteries that I could use as I had one of the same brand and the batteries were the same.

December 1, 2001 Saturday

Starting a new month and we are on the road yet. Today we got up a little early to go do some shopping. Then we were to go to the Cosco store to pickup a 45yh anniversary cake that will be used tomorrow Sunday When Larry & Doris will be celebrating.

After picking up the cake and as we were going to the car, Winifred and I were pushing the shopping cart with a few things in it. Just before we got to the car, another car was parking in a no parking area in front of the store. A short distance from this car the front wheel of the cart hit a sucker stick lying on the pavement, it made a lot of noise when it slid ahead for a little distance then came loose. Just as I got to the van that I was riding in that belonged to Winifred's nephew and niece This foreign girl came up to me and accused me of hitting her car and putting a scratch on the front fender. I had denied that accusation. At that time, she calls the police, we stood around there for about 30 minutes, and no one came so I left the girl and her mother there. I had asked them for some identification and they refused to give me any. The mother did go over and take the license number from Larry's van. They may turn that in to the police. When Larry came over, I asked him to bring a cart so that I could prove to them that a cart didn't make that scratch in that fender. The end of an unhappy event.

December 2, 2001 Sunday

The big party is on now with all of the main family and Winifred and I came along as we had been invited by Sharon Konkel, daughter of the bride and groom that is celebrating their 45th Wedding anniversary, this is an honor for us to be included.

They had reservation at the most expensive place in Riverside, CA and this place was the oldest landmark. It was a huge and was decorated for Christmas, what a site it was. There were trees in every area of the building and lights all around the outer part of the structure. We had a table the farthest away from the food. This being a brunch, you wouldn't be able to find a place you wanted to go that had better variety, and huge amounts. I think we did a good job of reducing some of that great food, even if we did have to tote it that long way back to the table. Some of the items did get a little cold before it was eaten.

After the brunch, we headed back the house for more cake and goodies with a toast by Larry Lee to his parents for all the good things they had taught him to know right from wrong. The party ended when Larry and Doris along with Winifred and me playing some dumb board game that took up the last hour of this party. What a day to remember.

December 3, 2001 Monday

It's time to move on so this morning we got things put together and let the motor home off of the jacks then turned around where we could pull up to the place to empty the holding tanks then also take on some water. I had almost finished this job when the deliveryman showed up with m hearing aid's that I ad been looking for, for three weeks. With all of this, we were ready to move on to San Diego for a few days to visit with Winifred's brother. Arrived here at noon, unhooked the little car and were parked in his driveway.

December 4, 2001 Tuesday

After visiting for the after noon we went out to have dinner then back for some more planning the next day. Winifred had been wanting to go to the world-renowned zoo. After Carroll had made some phone calls that plan hit the dust when they found out that for the two of us the cost would be $ 150.00 for a day or any part there off.

December 5, 2001 Wednesday

Today the girls, Winifred and Carol went by them selves to an art gallery some close to here. They had to be back by noon so that Carol could take her dad Bill to a Doctors appointment that had been scheduled for one PM today. We had planned to leave here this morning but was talked out of that we were to go out for dinner today and then go over to Carol's place for a home cooked meal tomorrow so we have stayed over and will e looking for that meal today. I am sure she will have a good one as we have been to her house before and it was very good and up town style with all the trimmings.

December 6, 2001 Thursday

We didn't do much today as I was waiting for the big party at Carole's house. We   got the full fancy meal that she put up just for the three of us. She had her home all decorated for Christmas. That girl was married once but had been single for many years yet you would be surprised to see how she has kept up this place for about 20 years.

December 7, 2001 Friday

It was a good drive from San Diego to Yuma, AZ today and got a space at the same RV Park that we have stayed in before. That was hard drive yesterday as the wind was blowing very hard. There were times that I felt that I need two lanes to drive in. We made in good order.

December 8, 2001 Saturday

After getting set up here in Yuma, AZ, we had a good nights rest and went to the breakfast that the park people put on for all that want to join them. We were the last to get there and I ate in a hurry thinking that the help would like to get things cleaned up. I ad to go the Radio

Shack to see if they would do any thing for me about this Lap top battery that I think isn't going to be very good. At this time, it will not last over 10 minutes and it shuts down the computer.

December 9, 2001 Sunday

Didn't get up very early, Then we had a good breakfast in the motor home. The day looks like it is going to be a good day with the temperature in the upper 60's with a good amounts of wind that shook the ,motor home a few times. We made a trip to town and on the way we stopped at one of the newer flea markets that started up a short time ago. While going through this place we found the straps and stakes that I was looking for, to tie down the awning when this wind gets up again. I had found a different system that sold for $ 20.00 and up so when I found these that I paid $ 6.00 did just what I had in mind.

We got home just after noontime and while Winifred was making the dinner, I almost had the tie down job done. Now we don't have to worry now that the awning will stay on the motor home.

December 10, 2001 Monday

This is the day that Winifred had done a great job of getting the Christmas card addressed and ready by mid morning. Then we took them down to the post office here in Yuma.

December 11, 2001 Tuesday

Last night I didn't have a good night. Yesterday I had done something to my back and all night I wasn't able to get any way to rest, the pain was always there. After breakfast, I called the chiropractor and was given an appointment almost as soon as I had got in there. They put me on the standard bed and they put some heat on the back then they gave me a message all up and down the back, that was something different then I had ever had when getting the vertebra adjustment.

Just laid around the rest of the day, doing nothing except washing some dishes. I t is feeling much better tonight as I go back Thursday afternoon.

December 12, 2001 Wednesday

Last night was a very bad night. The pain that I have wasn't helped very much if any. The first thing in the morning I called the place to get some help with this back pain.

After the chiropractor did some adjustment and applied some heat the back felt very good. He gave me some homework to help with this problem. The therapy was to put ice and on the spot for 15 minutes then put on the heating pad for the same length of time. That met that ice, heat, ice, heat. I did the first one in the afternoon and then I was to do it gain before bedtime. You know that this did help considerable.

December 13, 2001 Thursday

There was some pain this morning so I had to take this therapy the first thing in the morning. Then I had an appointment for 20:30 PM today and after this adjustment, I have been feeling fairly good. Will see what tomorrow will bring.

December 14, 15, 16, 2001 Friday, Saturday, Sunday

The first two days there wasn't very much going on. Only recovering from my stiff back. Then this Sunday I felt good and wanted to look around the area a little so we asked the neighbors to g with us and they were very pleasant and they hadn't been in very much of the this area that we took them.

December 17, 2001 Monday

This is the day that I shouldn't write anything as there wasn't a thing that I had touched today that worked . The television went bad after I tried to get cable for Winifred. So she would be able to see something besides listening to her books. (Books for the blind). I even had trouble writing tonight.

December 18, 2001 Tuesday

Today we got things in order to move on to Phoenix Arizona to see my cousin and her family also a brother and his wife that live to gather in my cousin's home. Shirley Fiske is a cousin and she is the one that owns this large house. She is Doctor and single so this is a good place to have some relatives around. It is her brother Don and his wife Sally that get along very well. Sally is in a high up job at the hospital and Shirley is a top notch Radiologist for several of the hospitals in the State of Arizona.

December 19, 2001 Wednesday

We left Yuma this mooring and got to Phoenix just a little after the noon hour. Then went looking for the place.

They live in this country club fancy place that has security guards and you have to have a pass to get in to this area. Needless to say, we couldn't get the motor home into their place so we have a place to park in an RV park just down the road five miles. We stay in the motor home at nights and go to visit during the day. This works out very well and we still have our own bed at night.

December 20, 2001 Thursday

Today, we just went to Shirley's place, watched some TV, and laid around doing nothing as all three of them go to work early in the morning. Sally gets home first, in the late afternoon. Then Shirley comes home at suppertime. As for Don, the poor guy has to work 12 hours a day on his job. He works in a custom cabinet shop. He is the late one coming home about 7:30 each evening.

December 21, 2001 Friday

Doing the same thing, going to their house and laying around doing nothing. We had come down to Arizona to get some warm weather but up to now we haven't had any thing but cold winds and colder nights in the mid 30's to the upper 30's at night.

December 22, 2001 Saturday

Same as yesterday maybe doing some shopping or driving around the country. Didn't see much where we went.

December 23, 2001 Sunday

Same as the other days not doing much but waiting for Christmas. We do go to the Shirley's house and then I check my E-mail on her computer.

December 24, 2001 Monday

The day before Christmas , we went over to the shopping mall and did some shopping purchased some things for gifts. That sure didn't take all day so back to the motor home and take a nap.

December 25, 2001 Tuesday

Shirley and Sally were cooking up a storm for a large feed about 2:00 PM and it was a great meal. After the dishes had been washed, we had the gifts that were under the tree divided up for all the people that was there. Richard Fiske, Sally and Don's only boy was there also and he did the Santa Claus job. Every one enjoyed the evening getting a lot of great gifts.

December 26, 2001 Wednesday

This is the day that we were going to leave and start home by the way of Quartzsite, AZ but we were talked out of leaving as I wanted to take the cooks and the total group out for an evening meal on us. It was the only payback that I could do for everything that they had done for us for the past several days. We went to the Anthem country club restaurant and had a nice meal.

December 27, 2001 Thursday

We left at 9:00 AM This morning, checking in at a park here in Quartzsite for the night. After parking, we went up town to see how the Flea Markets were doing. The day was a good day but most of the venders had high prices. We then came back to the motor home and now we have had our evening meal it is time for us to go to bed.

December 28, 2001 Friday

Didn't buy anything at the flea market. The first place there wasn't very many there yet for the season and the prices were up.

We went from Quartzsite to Lake Havasau Where we were to find one of Winifred long time friend that had purchased a new house there and we found them. They didn't have any furniture yet and were sleeping on the floor. This is their winter home as they have a business in Colorado. While there we set up the motor home and then they went to see relatives and folks that had come there for the winter, they had RV's and were setup side by side on the lakefront. A very nice group of people.

December 29, 2001 Saturday

I will have to fill in later when I can get more dates correct.

December 30, 2001 Sunday

December 31, 2001 Monday

We drove all day and ended up at Hi-Way Haven RV Park in Sutherlin, OR. It was a nice park with a lot of spaces. It rained all ay but not very hard so he driving wasn't that bad.

January 1, Tuesday

We left there at Nine o'clock AM and arrived home in Olympia, WA at 3:00 PM

It rained hard all day, Traffic was bad, couldn't hardly see the road at times. There was one big plus, there were hardly any trucks.

September 6, 2002 Friday

It has been a long time sense I have written any thing as we have been busy getting the house fixed up. But today we are not writing, as this is a hurry up trip to go by the car only to a funeral in Santa Rosa, CA. We got the sad news that Winifred's only granddaughter is 30 years old and she had passed away when giving birth. This is real shock to every one and a very sad thing to have to cope with. It is different when it is some old person like our selves

We left Olympia, WA at 9.00 AM and drove 460 miles to day and we are in the Great Western Hotel for the night. We are now in Yreka, CA and it is raining like cats and dogs. We arrived here at 4.30 PM That means that I driven 71/2 hours today. Went out to eat and liked to froze to death. So far, the day has been very good driving weather, no bright sun and a lot of clouds with just a few raindrops once or twice..

September 7, 2002 Saturday

We left Yreka this morning after we had breakfast. Hit the road at 7.30 and arrived in Santa Rosa this after noon at about 2.00PM and Winifred was able to see her grandchildren and her daughter and son in-law here. So it did help her cope with the loss of her granddaughter that had passed away. It has been hard on every one when a young person would have to go when there was so much ahead for a good life. I know it has been hard on us as neither one of us has had a good sleep yet.

September 8, 2002 Sunday

This is going to be a busy day for us. We are going over to Connie's place and all of the family will be there, they will be planning what to, do to get ready for the funeral for Debbie. This being Sunday there isn't much that we can do but to get the feeling of the family would want and what is wanted.

Winifred and I are staying with her very good family as Connie and Burt have a house full that some of them must be sleeping on the floor but hear we have a nice bed. These people are the best. They can't seem to feel that they are doing enough for us. Do we ever appreciate this because we can go and come as we want. I am an outlaw so I don't get into any thing but hang around like an old worn out shoe.

September 9, 2002 Monday

We have had a good rest yesterday and last night so this morning we were up at 6.00AM had breakfast then went over to, Connie's to see what the day would brings. This is the day before the funeral that the family can view the deceased, then later today the friends can come in to see Debbie.

We went to order some flowers then we went over to the funeral chapel. It was open from 10.00 to 12.00 AM for the family. This is one of the hardest things about a funeral. Every one is all upset over what had happened with a lot tears were shed. But when you think about it, it is better to have this time for the family when there isn't a butt of the public is there. I hope it has that effect when the funeral tomorrow will be smooth with every one happier, rather then being sad and do a lot of crying at the service.

Leonard Fiske

Winifred and I didn't think that Debbie looked like herself. Of course, she had gone the nine months of pregnancy and was carry a 9 lb three oz baby. She was a small little girl and very trim all the time. The poor girl had put on a lot of weight and looked as if she was puffed up a lot. I don't mean to be critical of her. She must have gone through hell for this to happen to her. I couldn't help but shed some tears with the others.

September 10, 2002 Tuesday

Today is the day that Debbie is being put to rest. As I write this, my feelings may be a little different then someone else but as a writer I have the right to put down my feelings. It is no different then the artist. It is a blessing that she has been spared the abuse that she would have to go through if she had lived. I have seen so much of this type of a marriage that didn't work out to every ones satisfaction, including the baby. It is a very common thinking that, it is the baby that has to suffer the most. The other one in this, is the twin brother, he must be having a real burden on his shoulders. It is one I sure wouldn't want on me.

The service was to be a morning one at 9:30 so the family was asked to be there a little earlier. A very large number of Debbie's relatives were here from as far away as 1000 miles and her husband's family came at least 3000 miles. Debbie was beautiful a lady of only 32 years old. She always wanted to be loved buy everyone. She would do any thing to help some one out. There was a beautiful service. After that ended there was a large number that went to the grave site and when we got there was a small mix-up as to which place she was to be put in. When her mother got there, she told them that wasn't the right lot. Every had to stand around until the crew moved every thing to the correct lot. After that, we were all invited to lunch at Connie Tate's (Debbie's mother's home) for noon lunch. A group of friends and church members brought enough food for an army.

September 11, 2002 Wednesday

This is the first time in a week that we had somewhat a good sleep. Winifred and I are staying at some long time friends. They live close to Connie Tate's place, Winifred's daughter. These people are the best people in the entire world. They gave us the key to the house as they had planned a trip to Utah to help their daughter. You don't find many like that in these days and times.

Just before lunchtime, we went over to the house to help them eat that food that was left over then we visited the rest of the day. I think it is called winding down time.

September 12, 2002 Thursday

This was a very upsetting day for all of the family as the father of the child that has survived sense birthed she had to have an operation when she was about one hour old. She had to be air lifted to San Francisco, CA to be operated on. She didn't have an esophagus, so they had to build one or she wouldn't have lived very long, she would have suffocated in her saliva. There was no way into her stomach.

There was lot of trouble when the father, who is black, got drunk and started to give the mothers and family a bad time. The mother's brothers were going to kill him that didn't happen after they were talked out of it. I can sympathy for them, IM only an uncle and I would like to have him go through some pain the same as his wife had to go through for most of the nine months. I have a way but IM' not sure that it would be legal or not. I would like for him to be hung by his privet parts for the same length of time that his wife Debbie had to go thorough.

They were to have a family get together to discuss things about how were they going to take care of the many things that the little baby would need.. I didn't go but I heard about it when I did get over there. The father got wild, started calling people names, and used words that can't be printed. They left the house and were putting on a show on the middle of the street yelling. I think he wanted some sympathy or he was out of his mind, if he had a mind.

September 13, 2002 Friday

I put this date up here and now after eight months I cannot remember what was to go in the place. Why don't I leave it alone. It must have not been very important

May 26, 2003

I think that we must have been ready to go on another trip in the motorhome. We have been going with the car only on several trips, only because the weather wasn't the best for the winter conditions. We were planning to leave Olympia the 27th after the memorial traffic was off the roads. As we talked about the traffic, it came to us that we would be leaving town and the main traffic would be coming home. So, we left a day sooner and we were very right. Our trip was to go to Montana to visit and to attend the memorial for my brother that passed away in January. Some of the family wanted to have the memorial at that time and my brother's wife wanted it in the summer, that's the reason for the two memorials.

Today we stayed at Riztville, Washington for the night in a small RV park that costs us $12.50 for full hookups there isn't many of those kind of places today. The average price is 20 to 30 dollars per night.

May 27, 2003

We left Ritzville at 9:00 this morning after breakfast and then we had to clean off the bugs that had committed suicide when they got in our way on the road.

The day had been a nice day a lot of sunshine and the traffic wasn't very bad either. Every thing going fine, drove about 200 miles and have pulled over on a rest area for the night. I hope. This place looked like it was going to be just what the doctor ordered. It was one of the worst places as when the sun went down and it got dark, it seemed that the world changed to something else. The large 18-wheelers started to pull in to this area. We were in bed and they surrounded us with the engines running and the freezer motors were running and there they sat or went to bed for a rest. This place sounded like a racetrack when cars were lined up ready to go, a little pumping of the throttle. The lesson was not to park in those places with an RV or you had something equal or larger so to hold your own.

May 28, 2003 Wednesday

By daylight, most of the trucks were gone. We had our breakfast and then left to never return to this spot again. It was a very nice day and we got to Bozeman, Montana for night. Here we are in a nice large KOA park but very pricey like $ 36.00 dollars for a place to park. Here it may be quiet so we can get a good nights sleep tonight.

May 29, 2003 Thursday

It was a little warm to start but a cool storm of wind and rain came through the park with a bang. It was a little shocking at first then every thing settled for the night. Did I ever sleep from then on until after 6: 00 PM. We had our breakfast then there was the task of getting the bugs from the windshield empty tanks and fill water tank We made our destination in Billings, Montana at my sisters place It sure did get warm today, it made it up to 92 but will be cooler tomorrow.

It is now May 30, 2003 Friday

The temperature was much cooler today and they say it will be cooler for about a week. Thetas what makes Winifred happy and for me I can take it but will be putting on a coat if it gets a little bit cooler.

We visited a lot this day and then we took time out to rest because tomorrow will be the big day. When we got here, we were informed by an invitation that the memorial for my brother was changed. Now it reads that they are going to have a potluck and everyone would bring something to eat. Isn't that what a potluck is? But not for a memorial. After traveling some sixteen hundred miles, the only thing to do was to go. We are staying with my sister and brother-in-law, so the four of us went.

May 31, 2003 Saturday

This party was to be from 2 PM 4 PM, we got there and there wasn't any one there yet. We were told to go ahead and eat, that we did but all the time were there, there was one or two people that came n and they just came to wish every one luck. Just a few minutes before 4:00, we picked up our dishes and went back to Billings.

I must tell you that his was the most unusual Memorial that I had ever been to. I know that my brother did attend the bars a lot but not for his last rights. Here is the setting. This was a small bar that was about 20 ft x 30 foot and they added on just lately for a storeroom on the back of building. That part was about the same size as the bar where we had this party. To say the leased I didn't think much of the whole thing.

June 1, 2003 Sunday

Today should be the day of rest, well I tried that but it seemed that every time I turned around there was something that needed to be taken care of.

We did call one of our good friends that live here in Billings that was our neighbor in Arizona couple of winters ago. The first place we were to meet this couple at one of the best hotels in town for a Sunday dinner. We met there and they were short of help or something else. We were seated and after a little time had passed they came back to the table and wanted us to move to the bar area and sit up to a bar on a stool to have a nice Sunday dinner. I say that does not fill the bill, so we just left there and went another place to eat. We had a nice visit and a good meal.

Our friends had the time so we stopped at my sisters place and introduced them, before long they were talking about this person and that one to the point that they knew so many of the people it was unbelievable.

June 2, 2003 Monday

The weather is very nice, staying around in low seventy took a ride into Wyoming in the town of Cowley, I meet a friend of Winifred's that was at one time a bishop in her Mormon church. He and his family are now in the business of their own making contemporary types of cardboard lamps. They sell them all over the world from this small town, he is also the mayor of the town. One of his son's there, fly for some one that has to inspect petroleum pipelines. He works alone and flies at 200 feet above the ground to check to see if some one is digging close to the lines or there maybe a leak in the line, then he would report that to a ground crew. It was 150 mile round trip so on the way home when we got to Billings at 2:00 PM we had a late lunch or an early dinner. Winifred wanted to go to a place that is called FUDROOKERS or something like that. They advertise the best hamburger in the world. I wasn't impressed

June 3, 2003 Tuesday

Winifred did some laundry and I did some more work on the garage door. The thing wants to come open before it is closed but when

I put a little weight on the door, it works great. I can raise and lower it by hand and there isn't any thing to stop the door from going down. My sister made two pie's, one rhubarb and the other a cherry pie This was done in the morning then for noon lunch we went out to a restaurant for some thing to eat. Got back the house and took a nap, all four of us. About three o'clock when we got up had good visit then the news. Now it is time to test that pie, it seemed that three of us wanted the rhubarb and Winifred had some cake, as she didn't like the pie. As for myself, I ate half of the rhubarb pie and my sister and her husband had the other half. It hadn't made me sick yet.

June 4, 2003 Wednesday

Now it is the next day and still not sick so I must keep going. We had every thing almost ready to move on. That is what we did and got to Ryegate about noon then went out to my brother's place to where we use to park every year until his death. The place is still in the family but has changed a lot. Where we are parked, Winifred can't get over the fantastic view from this place. You can see the animals come in for water and the wild antelope when they come down for water. This year is the fields are all green, this is the first time this has been this way for past six years. The weather hasn't been very good to these farmers. All of the fields would dry out and every one would suffer when there is not a crop. In the past six years, many or most of the farmers and stockmen would have to sell off a lot of the stock to survive. Today we went to the senior club for noon meal that was very good home cooking.

June 5, 2003 Thursday

We have the Motor home all setup and now we can visit around the area where I had grown up. We went to the real-estate broker's office and got the key to my son's Hardware store to make a key for him. This store has been closed now for three years. He has diabetes very bad and may never be able to come back here and open up this place. He has had it on the market for all of this time but no sale. Then we went to Lavina and the store there wanted three of my books, called Homestead Days in Montana. Then went to the restaurant in Ryegate for noon meal. This place use to be a very good place to eat but this time things have changed to the point that it must be the worst place in the State of Montana. Needless to say, I will never go back to that place. We got back to the Motor Home in the afternoon had a nice rest, cuddling up to my wife for a little nap.

June 6, 2003 Friday

We have been invited to the ranch up at the base of the Snowy Mountains. My niece and family is always a good place to go to get a great chicken dinner with all the trimmings. It had rained some in the night so we were going to get into some muddy roads. You should have see Winifred when I started to slip and slide al over the road. On one of the hills, it got so bad that the car stalled from lack of traction. I then had to back up a little way and put the car into a lower grade and then we went like there wasn't any mud. On the return home we went a different road and it was good no mud but a little farther to get home to the Motor Home. Overall, it was a very good day and had good visit.

June 7, 2003 Saturday

This was a day of rest so we didn't get up very early did some going to different places. Some of the places were I had worked or lived. When we got to the Dead Mans Basin, we found that the water level has improved over the last time I was there but it wasn't full by any means. We went up to the small town of Shawmut, Montana They had just opened a small restaurant and it had good food and price.

June 8, 2003 Sunday

It is time that we say good-bye and head for home in Olympia, Washington. We have made it about 200 miles today and now parked at a small RV park in Townsend, Montana. Had a good trip some wind in places that was a little rough.

June 9, 2003 Monday

As I sit here in the town of Haugon, Montana to write, the rain is coming down with thunder and lighting. We have a nice place with free parking at the $ 10,000 dollar Gift shop, restaurant, service station, casino and a hotel. I was in the CCC's in 1933 but this place has changed so much, you would guess it was the same place. We left

Townsend this morning, got here at 2:30 PM, and got this space before it was filled up. This storm is very heavy rain and the thunder was just overhead of us. There must be about 25 RV's here for the night. Let it rain let it thunder we are cozy as a bug in a rug.

June 10, 2003

This is the day that we end this trip. We left Spokane this morning and drove all the way home, over 350 miles.

Here we go again on this day of November 1, 2003. This time we are going south for a short time to see relatives and take a little vacation. This maybe the last time for this old couple, my wife is 85 and I am 89 and will be 90 this coming May the fifth.

We left home in Olympia. Washington on this day at 10:AM arrived at my sister's place in Salem Oregon at 3:PM. I had told her that I would make the dinner for us all and that s what I did. It was the old fashion pot roast that I had learned when I was putting on dinners trying to sell the WHEREVER cooking system. This Pot roast is made on the top of the stove not in the oven and with very little water. It is a total full meal of beef roast, carrots, potato and cabbage.

Today is the second day of November and we are heading south from Salem Oregon. Every thing going good and we made it to Crescent City, California. Stayed in a rather good park that cost us $ 21.00 for the night but we got some of that back as I took on water and emptied the tanks so that saved about $ 10.00. If you were to stop at some of the other places that have dump stations they would have charged extra.

November 3, 2003 We have left the park and heading south. I know that we have about 300 miles to go to Santa Rosa where we are going to stay at one of the best friends that any one would love to have. From here, we can go over to Connie's place to see her and her family. I could feel this is a hard drive but we did make it and did arrive at 3:30 PM. That was just right so that we could get hooked up to the electricity.

Now it is the November 4th and Winifred is wanting to get over to her daughters place to see her, and her little Grandchild. This is the girl that was left behind when her mother died giving birth about a year. As I had said before this could have been prevented if every one in the family would have done what the mother wanted. She had asked to be taken to the hospital on a Monday but her husband said no, it is my day off and she would have to wait. Who knows if that would have saved here life or not?

It is now Sunday the 9th and we have been going over to her place once or twice per day. We spent the whole day there and had a great dinner Mexican stile. It was very good as it was Burt that did most of the preparing the food and then Connie did the clean up. Tomorrow is moving day. We will be going over to one of Winifred's long time friends place to park on the street in front of the house. They have some power so that we don't freeze at night. That is one thing we don't have on the motor home. We can start the generator to give us the correct power.

November 10, 2003 It is the time of this trip that we will be moving from one place to the other place. Today we drive Winifred to Connie's place then in the afternoon we come back home and visit at Ruth's place. Ruth has been bed ridden for some time so Winifred spends some time here then some time with her daughter on the other side of town. This went on for about five days and I put 300 miles on the car for the time that we were there.

It's time to make a move from Santa Rosa to Riverside California. We left this morning at 9:33 and drove 269 miles to this park at the Almond tree RV for the night.. After getting set up at the last place in this park Winifred called her Grandson Charlie and he was over in a minute at no time to have some soup and chips with salsa. The last minute that we were in Santa Rosa, we found out that he was working in Coalinga on a road bridge in the area.

Then the next day we went to Riverside, California to stay at the home of Larry and Doris Ashe's place. These people are Niece and nephew of Winifred's. These are wonderful people so we park the motor home in front of the home, plug into the power and settle in for a nice stay. We were there for six days not doing much as they we having a lot of things all ready to be doing. This didn't bother us as we could get rested up for the next jump. One of the thinks we did was have lunches and snacks with them then have a dinner at 6:30 PM a little late for us but we did enjoy it any way. Now after these dinners we had to play board games, not one of my pastimes in life, the hostess was one of the kind that just loves to play these games. God bless her.

The best part of this was that we went to their daughter's place for a great visit and a dinner out of this world, Prime rib of beef that had been cooked to perfection.

Then today we have traveled to San Diego to visit with Winifred's brother. It is the November the 25th. We were there for three days then took off for Yuma, Arizona where we had planned to stay in the sunshine for about a month recuperating from all the activities of the past month. After about three days of rest we took off for Mexico to get our prescription and pickup some picture frames for the art work that we do when at home. Now it is December 11th and we are still looking for that sunshine. Winifred's brother and his son and daughter came down to be with us for three days. They did that, and left to go home this afternoon, but not until we went over to one of the flee markets that is in the area. Didn't buy much but had the feeling of seeing a lot of stuff. The weather didn't get above 60 degree's and now as I write this it looks like we may have a small amount of rain? Well, hear it is about one hour later and we didn't/t get any rain but a lot of wind and a lot of sand that was starting to rock the motor home so I went out and took down the awning before the wind would make a mess of a lot of things. In the past, I have lost a couple of awning from hard winds.

At one time in life we could have had a lot of fun and bounce back soon but now at the age of 85 and 90 things are not rebuilt as fast as they did when you were younger. We stayed down south for two months. From here, we went to Anthony, Arizona where my cousins live for Christmas. In this area, we can't park at my cousin's place. Because there is a rule against it so, we parked the motor home in a RV park about five miles away. This park is a nice clean park but costly. The second day there I was putting things away and tripped on one of the chair legs and went face down at the edge of the concrete slab and I went into the gravel . My face and my hands took the blunt of it all, the face was bleeding and my wrists were both damaged. The face wasn't bad after a clean up but the wrists were swelling up badly, so I had to go to town and get some ice to put on them. Did they hurt and turned black and blue. I was lucky that they weren't some broken bones but there wasn't any. This could have a real bad situation if I wasn't able to drive as my wife has low vision and couldn't drive

Now is the time to start home. I have healed up very well so we started back, now it is the last day of the old year and we were on he way, the weather was good and so was the drive this first day. New Years Eve we are on the road again. The first part of the day was very nice but about the time we got into Bakersfield Calif., it was raining so we took a Park for the night. After getting set up we discovered that we had no heat in the motor home. So I went to the office and borrowed an electric heater, so now we could keep warm. As I had one heater now we shouldn't have any more problems. Now it is New Years Day and there wasn't anyone open to get to work on the furnace. The next day I got on the cell phone and started to call places, because of the hard rain all night there was a lot of flooding and no one could help me until the next week. As we were thinking about some way of getting this furnace fixed, I took a chance and called the Camping World. They were open and they would fix this furnace, and they gave me a 1:30 appointment. Then we unhooked the little car and went hunting for this shop. When we found it the sign said closed and we have moved to a new location. Here again we used the cell phone to call the company only to find out that we had gone the wrong direction from the camp that we were in.. Just to make sure we drove to the new location and then went back to get checked out of the RV Park and get back to this shop before one thirty, we did make it and had some time to spare. They took our home to the back of the shop and we had only the little car to get around. When I would ask someone if they would get the furnace fixed, they would reply it would be finished before quitting time. Just at quitting time, they had it ready. So, we stayed on their parking lot for the night. There wasn't any power and it did get a little on the chilly side before morning. Without the electric power, there wasn't any way of warming up the coach without running the generator. That I did, but had too much load on the generator so it kicked one of the breakers. It is now seven in the morning and I had to go outside to reset the breaker. Just as I got outside the general foeman was coming to work. When he got there, "he said to me what are you doing out here this early",? When I told him that I had blown a breaker so he reach in and flipped the breaker, we stated up the generator and now all is great. We ran the generator and we had our breakfast

Now it is December 30, 2003 and we are on the road home traveling I-5 freeway. We were watching the weather so that we didn't get into some snowstorm before we got home. It was getting a little late but I wanted to get over the mountain passes today. So, we stopped at a rest area and while I was talking to a State Patrolman, I asked how the passes were and he then asked if I had chains for the rig. I told him I didn't have and he said that if I took off right now he was sure that I could get over before they closed the pass, because of icy conditions. The roads were very good all the way through for this day. Now we took a RV park at Phoenix Oregon for the night.. It was a nice park. Then went out to eat then to bed for us, as we were very tired from the stress of the chances of getting into something that wasn't expected. The worst was behind us now. As we went north there was some more bad roads the farther we went closer to home it was getting bad in spots. Then when we got about 30 miles from home there was a lot of the snow was on the road so that there was trails in the road that you didn't dare move from one lane to the other because of the ice that was under the snow. As we got closer to home, like one mile it was snowing bad and the streets were very slippery and the motor home was doing some sliding when ever I tried to set the brakes When we got into the Park where we live the snow was about six inches deep. The first thing I said was where were the people that should have had the snowplows out and moving this snow off of the streets. I was able to get into the driveway, so I got the motor home plugged into the power source then we went into the house and stayed there for four days before we were able to unload the motor home. After the unloading was done, I put the motor home back into the parking space, which is where it sits.

Now, after all this time we have the nerve to take the motor home from its parking place. It is September 11, 2004 and we are heading to Montana to visit and to check on my sister who as been put in a care center. She is the one that had married a blind man and the some time back my sister lost some of her sight so that it was very difficult for them to be together again. It is ruff on some one to have this situation. There is know way they could read the prescription bottles and get them correct. We left home this morning at 8:00 AM and now we have stopped at

Moses Lake for the night. Now the plan is to sleep in tonight, then go on into Spokane, and stop in to see how Helen Geer is doing. She lost her husband last months, after living a good life for 62 years together and raises a great family. Most of the family turned out to be ministers of faith.

The day has been good, a little fog in the hills but no rain on us today, so far, it rained all night last night and we thought that we would have rain all day, but none. Now it is Sunday morning September 12th 2004 and Winifred is making breakfast as I sit here on the davenport waiting. I am hungry. Today will be an easy drive as we are going only as far as Spokane today. There isn't any rain yet today but the sky is full of clouds. We made it in god time with out any problems, then we got onto the traffic of down town Spokane, Washington The brakes on the Motor Home stared to scream at every I put on the brakes. This meant that there was some think wrong with this new brakes job that I had just had done in Lacey, Washington to the tune of $ 2000.00 dollars. Being it was a Sunday I had to wait for Monday to get some work done. That meant that I would have to get up by six O'clock in them morning so I could get the ball rolling. The first thing that I did was to call the Garage that did the brake job to inform him that I had this trouble. He told me to go ahead and have the work done in Spokane. One thing for sure I wasn't going to go back or continue to travel with this problem. You, know that things worked out very well. My sister-in-law Helen has called this repair shop and asked to put me on the books so that I could get on the road again soon. At 1:00 this after noon and called and said the Motor Home was finished and ready to get on the road.

Today is the 14th of September 2004. We left Spokane with an extra passenger, Helen Geer, she has never ridden is Motor Home. She is going back to Ryegate with us and then she will stay with the DeBuff's. We are now at Haugon, Montana where there is a place that is called the $10,000 silver Dollar Restaurant and a large gift shop. We just got parked and the two women took off for the gift shop. That's what I am going to do right now. See you when I get back. Well, I am back from the little trip to the gift shop but I was too late they had spent a fortune Now its time to get down to something else. We picked up all the loot and got back to the Motor Home. After we were home for short time, we got out a story that I had written or typed from a trip that we had taken to England. This wasn't planed but each of us wrote a journal each day of the days happening. When Helen was reading this story to us, she was laughing so hard, she had a nosebleed. I am glad that the nose was a short time bleeding, as we didn't have to call 9-11.

It is now the next day and we are on the road again. I was out numbered so lost the next move. I wanted to go down the road to get closer to our destination. Now we are 430 miles that we had to do. I had a little help because there was a tale wind and good weather. It took us nine hours to get to our destination. Now that we are here after a short time, we went to bed. After we had breakfast, we drove up to the mountains where my sister and her daughter live. My sister Evelyn who had some bad medical problems and had to be taken from the hospital s she wasn't able to take care of her self and had now that she has low vision and her husband is totally blind. Because of this, her daughter has taken her to a home in Billings, Montana. Her daughter sure did the right thing to give my sister the safe care that she needs. The daughter wasn't able to take care of her as they run a ranch with a lot to do. On an easier note we will travel up to the mountains every day we are here to visit my sister. She will be 89 this October 28, 2004.

Today it is 9/17/04 and we have been up in the mountains so we can visit with my sister. It is 7:00 PM as we are ready to go to bed, I know it is early but when you get old it seem that the days are longer. My sister Evelyn is looking very good.

This is repeat of yesterday, we have been there to see my sister, as she will be gong back to the care home soon.

Now it is Sunday 19th of September. This was a big day, first off, we had to get up early to make it to the Sunday church serves. One of my little two-year-old nieces was to be baptized. You wouldn't believe how well this little girl sat in her Dads arms taking it all in as if she had been put in a school class. After church, we wet to Ryegate, Montana to have a little sweet rolls and coffee as a snake. From there we went back to the mountains for more visiting and a great meal. This was a day of the best for such nice visiting and watching the little one running around doing their thing. It brings us old people back to the time when we were there age. It seems that today the young people know more then ,when I was a child. It is time that this old couple will be going to bed.

The 21st of September we took my sister Evelyn to Billings, Montana so she could rest in this home. It is a nice place for some one that needs some help and can fed her meals. She has been improving in her health sense she got away from the other home and her husband. It isn't known just what was going on that my sister was starving to death or maybe it was that she was getting to much medicine of the right type. When she was taken into the hospital, her blood test did show over medicated. Her husband is totally blind and she has lost a lot of her vision to the point that she cannot read print. While I was at the home, I made her a bookcase so her painted dishes can be put away where she can see them, not in some box. Then I went back to my wife Winifred who was at the Mormon Temple where I had left her off. We then went to eat at a

nice place and she had baked chicken and I had a good beef steak then we went back to where we had the Motor Home that was parked at my younger brother Gerald's place four miles south of Ryegate, Montana. When he was alive, he and I made a place for me to park the trailer that had power, water and septic tank so we could stay longer and not have to move to some place to empty the holding tank on the Motor Home. In those days, Zelda and I would stay for about a month, as I would help my brother with his work on the farm. Sometimes it would be overhauling one of the machines or maybe help put up hay.

Today is a new day and a new place. We are here to help build a SKY WALK as I call it. We have been home for a short time and today we left home in Olympia, Washington at 12:15 this PM and arrived here on Bainbridge Island to help the relatives do this little walk. When I arrived today, they had done a lot of work already. They did the hard part doing cement work. The other people are workers yet so they get a four-day vacation this weekend called Veterans Day. Now it is yesterday and it is November 12th 2004. We were at the Konkel's place where we are helping get their new yard cleaned up for the holidays. They have been very busy moving from California to Washington. We welcome them. They had a small work party of two teenage girls, two older women and three older men, which was the whole crew. The female group did the brush clean up, the men worked on the SKY WALK, and everyone was ready for the evening meal prepared by lady of the house that had all ready been working on the clean up. The weather has been very good, with out any rain so far this week. Things are looking up for getting this built before the guests from California arrive for Christmas.

This is the third day at building this SKY WALK. Now we are missing one of the family members that had done a great job in getting things rolling along with the owner that is doing the master minding of this project. Today the family and I kept right on with the job. The two young ladies were very good workers. There mother, Sharon, and my wife, Winifred, were right in there pitching with the rest of us. One of the girls took on the job of finishing of the heavy part of the job. The other girl took on the job of attaching down the walk way that are 2X 4's that make up the platform of this walk. The walk is 10 feet long and four feet wide above ground for most of the length of project. There won't be much more to do after tomorrow, if the weather will cooperate. I hope the good lord will forgive us for working on Sunday.

Now I sit myself down to write myself a letter. This isn't really what I am going to do. Today is Sunday and we had a little rain but the job went on as if it wasn't raining. The weather was very nice and warm. We didn't get the walk finished as I played out at 3:00 PM. I don't fell bad that I had to give up, the young people went ahead for some time later, I am over 90 years old and the kids were, maybe in their 40's. What we are doing will surely give this place some added value. But then, the taxman will love it. We will be going back home in Lacey, Washington tomorrow to rest up and do some outfitting of the Motor Home as the plan is to come back here next week and sit three dumb dogs while they go back to California, where they came from, for Thanksgiving. They will be back after about three days.

Now it is the next week and we are back on the Island to help these people out by dog sitting while they go back to California for the Thanksgiving weekend. We drove the trip today in a good time, maybe we are getting use to the route. Today we had good weather, no rain until this evening. As the weather was so good, I did get two large flowerbeds tilled before the rain did start. It is the 23rd of November 2004 so you can't bet on the weather. The old saying here is if you wait a couple of minutes, it will change. Today is another day. This day is that the Konkel's have left us to sit the dogs. In the mean time, today I did a little work around the yard until the rain came in about noon so I took the rest of the day off. I did get some thing laid out and went to town to get some supplies to complete the skywalk. Tonight is Thanksgiving eve. So today is the Thanksgiving Day that many families get to gather each year. It is a traditional thing but as the time goes by many families have separated or moved to places to far away for that celebration. There are people that say it is the time of the year to make a pig of ourselves, a good excuse for putting on the unneeded extra pounds. Today we are dog sitting for a relative as they have gone to their faunally in California. I keep busy here to finish the Sky Walk that was left for me to do, I guess. Anyway, the weather was good enough to work in the very light rain. What was left was the ramp to the walk so that a wheelchair can use it with out several people helping. With weather cooperating I am sure that I can get the job done in time for the gusts that are coming in a week or so. With nothing better to do, we had a reservation to have our Turkey day at this restaurant that is only five miles for us to go. It was a very swanky place and the price to go with this kind of a meal. Winifred had salmon and I had prime rib. There wasn't any to much on the plate but very tasty. The bill for two was sixty-four dollars. The people we are sitting dogs for gave us the treat.

The day is the Friday after Thanksgiving, We are here yet, as the people that own this place will be on their trip to California until tomorrow and they will be coming in late in the evening. Just depends on what the weather as to when they can fly or not. Then we will be going home to Olympia again. This makes the third trip to help them get started in their new home in the State of Washington. These people are great people and did not live on large acreage before. They had large homes but not much land. They are middle age with a 13 year and a16 year old. Guess what, the kids want horses and that will be new to them. They have never been on a farm to live. Not like I was born on a homestead in Montana, that was when you learned to take some bumps from time to time as you grow up.

I did get a little done today but had to do some looking around for something that would help the appearance of this Sky Walk. We did go out for lunch today at the Indian casino called the Suquamish Clearwater that is just up the road a short distance. We had the buffet, it was very well cooked, and the place was very clean. The best thing about it the cost for two people was $11.90. We will go back some time, like tomorrow for lunch. Now another day has come to us and we have been making the best out of it all. We went to the casino for lunch, it was a very good meal. We woke up a little later today as things were coming down to being finished and also this old couple did love act this morning that I didn't think we were capable of doing. As a result, she went back to bed to recoup. I made the breakfast as I always do when we are in the Motor Home and Winifred sleep a little while. I had just a small amount left to do on this Sky Walk that was started back several days ago but I put the finish touch to the project. I am crossing it off from any farther need any more work now the people that are using the guesthouse will have a nice way to get to the main house. It will be just what the doctor ordered for any handicapped people specially wheelchairs. We have been here five days doing some of their work while they go south for Thanksgiving. I wanted to keep busy, the time goes faster when you are working.

..Now it is December 23, 2004. Today we are up and ready to get the Motor home for the trip to Bainbridge Island were the folks from California that moved up here some time earlier. Now it is the day before Christmas and the family that was left in California is coming up here to the good old State of Washington. Winifred and I have been going south for the past ten years having the holidays in the south. We are getting older and this traveling has got to be slowing down for this old man that is almost 91 now. I feel good only a few acts and pains from time to time. Then about three weeks ago an odd thing happened to my right knee, it started to give me a pain. I checked in at the Doctors office, he took an x-ray of the knee, and his recommendation was to put some medicine as the old bones is wearing out. I have used them a lot and didn't baby them but mad the work when it was needed.

At this writing, the people here have gone to the airport to pick up some of the family that will be joining us for tomorrow for the big day. Winifred and I had our Christmas before coming up here to this large gathering of her relatives.

Ho, Ho, Ho, it is Christmas of 2004 and we are here on Bainbridge Island of Washington State. There is 14 of us including our self's. This is a great group of relatives, they are so loving and considerate of other people, not just them self's

265

They have put up a large tree in the house and then they had room for all the gifts that Santa had left. I would bet that there had to be a value of at least two thousand dollars worth of gifts under that tree. I cannot over look the food line, this host and hostess at one time had a restaurant and could they put on the display of appetizers that was available all day long. From simple to the most delicious items. Then when time for a meal it wasn't just an old potluck, it was a set table for 14 people. It was served some place between the family type and the buffet type. They served it from the large plate to each of us that were sitting at the table. It didn't seem to make it wrong at the least. I had never seen it done that way before. It worked out very well when you have so many to serve at a time. The main thing was that the table wasn't cluttered up after all the food had been served. I thought it worked out very well. Now the Christmas dinner was served of Prime rib, Lobster and twice-baked potato what a meal, I will never for forget it.

The day after it is now December 26, 2004. All is quiet on the western front. I hope that all is happy with what Santa had left for us. With so much to eat yesterday, Winifred and I took all of the crew down to the Indian Casino for Sunday brunch. After the brunch, some of the group went to town and Winifred and I went home to our Motor home. The day is running down, now it is 5:00 PM. After all of this celebrating over the holidays is all this old man can take so I took the day and went back to Olympia. I left Winifred there to visit with her family. When I got back to Olympia, I went to work in the shop making a steel cabinet for my son to haul his generator under the bed of the truck. He had brought the new generator over to the house just before we were to leave there for Christmas. I did get some of the layout ready and had started to weld things together. When I got home after Christmas, I went right to work and got a lot more of this job together. I finished up with that part and then welded it all together by an electric welder(called a buss box) it had been some forty years since I had used this welder so some of the welds did look like some new kid on the block would do. Then in the afternoon, I went back to the Island. What for, I don't know unless I was homesick for my wife. It takes me two hours to make the trip. I left there at 2: 30 PM and got here on the Island at 4:30 PM. Found all doing well so they didn't miss me much.

Now it is February 27th of 2005 we are heading south again to visit her family that live in Sebastopol, California. We got a little late start this morning because we had to make a couple of stops. Then we got on the road at 10:AM. Even at that, we got over 3000 miles today. Then it was about 4:00 P.M. It sure was a beautiful day sun shining and the traffic was a little lighter then usual. I saw a new sign on the side of the freeway so I took a change and the park turned out to be a nice park and the price was good at twenty-two Dollars. We had a good nights rest and were on the road today by 8:30 A.M. Then quit driving at 4:00 o'clock about 10 miles south of Redding, California. Now it is bedtime Good night for now, will be back.

We are here at Winifred's Daughters home, been there overnight and to day I got to over look the yard to see if I can help them get started on the sprinkler system to keep the flower garden wet. The first thing was to find out if the pump will handle this much area? I may have to put in several zones. This is a private well system so it depend on how much will supply a full water pattern. I did go to town and talk to the party that had put the water system in. This is enough for the day and it is suppertime , I hear the bell ringing

Today it is the first of March 2005 and we are lowing low to get rested up after all we have bin on the road enough to earn a rest.

Now it is time for me to check out the area to see what was needed for this place to get the watering system working. Between scouting out the area I found out that, I could get all I needed at a large hardware store here in Sebastopol. Here where the traffic is bad the closer to home makes the cost of items look good even if they charge a little more.

Today I was ready to go, so went to town and got a starter amount of supplies that cost $ 250.00 I would say that was a good start for this small place. Today I started to put things to gather and found out that I was short some items so I went to town that was only about eight miles away. This wasn't the only time that I had to do the same thing, it seems that I was never going to get the job going.

Now it is March the 8, and we are here yet, Winifred is doing her visiting with her daughter and great Grandchild, I am doing the odd jobs around here. Up to now I have completed my jobs so it is time we move on to the next great friend of Winifred's. Tomorrow I will do some maintenance on the Motor home, checking out things to see if it is falling apart or not.

Getting ready to move on for a few days, today I did some running around. I had a lunch in town and what a horrible lunch it was, I am not sure that I can eat this Greece and Mexican combination or not. This meal sure didn't do me any good.

We, did get to one more stop on this trip for the next week or two then we will heading north to Olympia, Washington. This last stop we had a good time with these people, Florence and Willard Hall. She is from Australia and Willard is from Montana. He was raised in the northern part and he is part Indian. They met during World War II so they had some different stories tell. They are in their 80's, with a large family that has flew the coop and have many grandchildren. One of their boys has nine children. This is a family that knows how to raise their family. That is some thing that is very rare for these times when there is so much drugs that has had a bad impression on all people. It is very sad for this use of drugs and another dope off the time. Many of these young minds are damaged to the point of no return but they do have families and what do they know how things are so bad. Many of the kids die at Burth. This morning we went over to see one more of Winifred's friends , and will stay there about three days and then move on. We go back to her daughters place for couple of days before heading for home. So far, on this trip, we have had good weather. Except for one or two days when it did get a little too hot for comfort. What a meal we had at this place, this is another good family that had good parents. When we got there, the table was set up for 14 people, this I found out was for one of this family and it was his 12th birthday. Grandparents like to give a dinner to all of the grandkids for their birthdays. That's not the end of it they also prepare a dinner they what and this one was cracked crab, my favorite, did I ever have a fill of this crab.

We moved out of that place back to Winifred's daughter's place Wednesday March 16th 2005. I have a little chore while the rest of the family will be going have a family picture taken for they have five generation of the family all in one place. This is rather unique for the family when a little girl was born her mother died giving birth so they are going to have a picture of the mother in place of the real mother that can't be able to be there. This time they had a nice little job for me

268

while they were gone. This time was to hang a screen door on the front door to the house. I hung several doors but his one had me thinking for a little while as I unwrapped this door I put it up to the jam and it was to small until I found out that this was one of the adjustable type. This didn't take long after finding out what goes. I had just finished the owner came home , and you should have seen the look on her face, what a change that this did for the appearance that it made to this house

The next couple of days I took it easy and did almost nothing but rest, as we will be heading for home this next Sunday the 20th of March 2005.

After being home for while, we took off for the Bainbridge Island to sit three no good dogs while they go back to California to some kind of a party and birthday. So here we sit in the Motor home and the rain is coming down all day. I was to fix the lawn mower, as the blades were not cutting correctly. When I took the blades of there Was one that had hit a big rock and bent this blade so bad that it has be replaced so we went hunting up a place to purchase a set. It took us all day and a lot of miles to find some that had them. It was a good time to go shopping because it was raining. it is now the 16th of April, 2005 how time seems to keep on going even if you don't get as much done in the same time as it use to be when you were young. We are here on the Island dog sitting. This to me is one of the dumbest things a person can be doing. Yet a lot of people say that dog is mans best friend. The dog should be, he doesn't have any thing to worry about. It is still raining and maybe it will be better later in the day. I do have a lot of jobs to do yet if weather will corporate.

We are still at the Island and the weather has cooperating that could get a lot of things finished. The first thing was to start on the watering system to locate where the sprinkler heads are and find out what if any will need repairing. That has been done on the front of the property now for the rear system. I got started but didn't get far as time was running out for this day.

Now it is the 29th of July and we are on the road again. Only this time we are heading east from Olympia, Washington. Planned for some time to go to Montana and then on to Illinois to see my family, my daughter and her three kids, two boys and one girl. I haven't seen them for about 5 or 6 years, by this time they sure wouldn't know their granddad. We only traveled 250 miles today but I hope that I can get more miles on tomorrow. The weather has been in the upper 90's all day, with that kind of heat, it drains a person. Stopped hear in Ritzville, Washington and got a park for the night. This park we have stayed in it before, not the best but it is nice.

I won't take much of your time with what we did today. The day is July 30th 2005 and it was the same all day long. I got a few more miles on the speedometer. As we were coming to the end of the day I was on the lookout for some nice park for the night, I pulled into a couple of parks but they didn't look very good, so pulled out and went on down the road. This park that we had pulled into was just what the Gander ordered. I would give the park an AAA.

As I sit here this evening in a park that is run by the city of Harlowton, Montana the trip today went real well wasn't quit as hot as it has been. We didn't go as far as we did yesterday, as we will have a short trip to morrow to our destination at my nieces place up in the snowy mountains that are 30 miles north of Ryegate, Montana. It was this hot weather that we still ran into a shower that came down heavy for a short time. This storm was a long way ahead of us. By the look of the road ahead of us the cloud and storm was10 miles wide. We did get a small amount rain on the windshield, but not enough to turn on the wipers

There hasn't been any one around to collect for the stay to night. The only thing they have here is the power that is needed bad when you have this hot weather. The sun is going down and giving us those long shadows in the evenings. It was very hot this evening that one couldn't sleep with out some air conditioning of some kind. It stayed hot all day but we did get to the ranch where we were heading for. Now that we are here, it is time to do the thing called setting up Motor home, get the power cord out, and find a place to plug in so we could have power to run the air conditioner

My niece is a very good cook and she did a top-notch job of it today. We had old faction fried chicken, corn, potatoes and chicken gravy. That is what I call the best in the food line.

Today it is the 3rd day of August and we are here in the mountain area with things going some good and some not so good. Last night it sure did rain here. Not so good for the farmers and ranchers but good for the land. With all of the rain, the country roads could be some thing better then good. I know that some of these roads can get very nasty. It is what you call gumbo. It is very slick when wet and then as it starts to dry out it is very sky. It is so sticky the wheels of the vehicle can get so big and heavy that you can't move any more

After getting things straightened up here in the motor home, we went to town that is 30 miles from here. It took us two hours to get there because the rainstorm was so hard some times that you didn't travel any faster the 10 miles per hour. The roads are all gravel and now it is somewhat muddy. Some places it looked as if you were driving up the creek or two creeks one in each tire mark. When we left the (motor home), we had planed on going to the senior center in Ryegate for Wednesday noon meal at 12:00 PM we made it bye the skin of our teeth.

Then after lunch, we went over to their place for a short visit. Then we went back to the motor home. There were times that we did get into some more rain, but not near as much as it was on the way to town. It didn't get up over the 70 degree all day what a difference as a couple of days ago when we came here when the temperature was checking out over 100 degree.

We got up today to a temperature 41 degree that is a low for this time of year. As I write, the temperature is reading up 86 degrees at 4PM. I went with Ken to a place that butchered cattle. He gets his winter supply of meat all cut to his liking. Here they use a heavy-duty truck to haul this large stock hauler 5th wheel type.

On Friday we went to Ryegate for the memorial for Audrey Fiske She was my niece that had Alzheimer's and she had been in a home for several years not knowing who she was or knowing any one else, in my mind it was a blessing. After the services, we went on to Billings to check in at the campgrounds.

This morning we got up to go to the family reunion when our Arizona cousins came by and we talked for a while then it was time to go to the Park where all the group was to meet. When we got there were several that had got there to get some things set up .There were

116 that had registered and I think came to the event. I saw many of my cousins that I had never seen, but some of them they were small children the last time I had seen them. I thought that it was a very nice gathering. As I said, it was a Fiske family reunion that was the off spring of the two oldest of Grandfather and Grandmother Freeman and Mini Fisk. My dad was the oldest of my dad's family and I was the oldest of that group

At this reunion, I was the oldest person in the crowed so they took a lot of pictures of me and my three sisters. One of my sisters was in a wheelchair and one with a walker. The other and myself was walking with out supports I thought that it was great that we still had four of seven in our family. That should be enough to confuse the readers.

Now with all of the great party is over and I want to give some of my cousin a big thank you, you did up proud, it will be memorable for a long time. I do know that some of the younger ones were getting in formation to put this in books to remember when some of us have passed on to greener pastures

Now it is Sunday August 7th we are packing up and heading east to see my Doughtier and my three grand children and one step-granddaughter. All the way we were faced with the heavy traffic of Motorcycles. I found out that there was a rally that they are going to for about ten day long. The records say that there will be some 600,000 of these on the roads. My wife and I are traveling by Motor home towing a small car. Well, when nighttime had come we went looking for a park for over the night. I pulled into one park and it was full then I was sure that there wouldn't be the same in another park well that one was so full they had to guide me out to the main road again. It was no way that there would be any openings in the area and the owner of the last park said that it would be Lucky if you could find one within 60 to 70 miles down the road. I didn't see any thing until I , must have gone about 100 miles that we found a park that was all most empty so we stayed there over night.

We are still heading east to get to my daughters place. So far we have had high temperatures in the over 100's and nights in the 80's. Some times, I think, why did I want to pick this time of the year? Well, the distances between us, there is bad weather like snow that I don't like and it is more dangerous then heat.

Another day on the road that is very hot temperature is 103 today. The only thing that likes this heat is the corn crops. We are in Iowa the corn country the scenery is one cornfield after the other. We made another 200 miles today, that should put us a little ahead of schedule, which is good. There was a bad luck for some one. I didn't see the accident but it was soon afterward. It appeared to me that some one had lost his control and went into Median and there was a lot of damage, a lot of twisted RV. I hope that they didn't get hurt.

The weather was real hot last night that I didn't get very much sleep didn't feel like gong on the road so took a short nap and then I was ready to continue on this trip.

Now that it is August 12th 2005 and the weather is still making it a miserable trip to say the least. We arrived at my daughter Sharon Casper's yesterday and the heat was up to 103. You must say that it takes a lot out of you.

It was yesterday that we got to the town of Nauvoo, IL This place has a lot of history when the Mormons were driven out of there homes. A lot of them were killed and the leaders were jailed. My wife being a Mormon wanted to see the place, stay there for a few days of rest, and do nothing. I was to go see my daughter and then pickup her to start back home. It didn't work out that way. We took a motel for the night and we had a great buffet that evening then we had our showers and to bed. The air conditioner running all night and couldn't keep it cool so we tried to get some rest. The plans she had made didn't turn out the way she wanted so she went with me and now we will take a different route home.

We left the motor home parked in the parking lot for the night, well, when we got up and went to the motor home and it wasn't in very good condition. Not that it had been damaged but it goes like this, the little car had a low rear tire and then the refrigerator went off and defrosted some. Then the batteries were dead so the only thing to do was to get the motor home engine started so that it could start charging the batteries. It started right off. I felt that from there we could get on the road as to the tire we stopped at a place where I could get the onboard generator going then I would have air so that I could pump up the low tire. All of the above was corrected and we were on the road again.

It is August 14th today and we got up a little early so that we could get going after Sharon and Jerry could be home to thank them for all they did for us. The main thing was all of the electric we had used trying to keep the motor home when the temperature was staying in 100's daytime and night times in the 90's that wasn't good to try to sleep when it is that warm, or a better word would be hot .

The rest of the day was driving on and on in a short time we ran into rain that lasted all day. About 100 miles down the road we came up on a very bad accident on the inter state that was a 19 car and truck. The pile-up closed both sides of the road. The fist thing was, that they detour that took us about 30 miles out of the way on a rough road. As we got to the freeway now the other side of the road was blocked for over 20 miles with that was just sitting there. The weather may have been a factor in the accident as it has rained all day in this area.

Now it come the time when you don't have much to tell when all that I do is sit up in the drivers seat making sure that I keep out of some ones way. Then I have to be sure that I don't run over any one. If it is like double talk, well it is, when there isn't talk about any body.

Today is the second day out on the return trip home. Today it is the 15th of August, 2005. The morning started out not so good. It was raining and I had some work to do on the windshield wipers as I had some problem with them yesterday when it was raining all day. The wipers started to come apart and we were on that detour that took us on some bad roads as well as some narrow places. And there weren't any places to pull off of the road. I hoped that someone in front of me would have run out of gas or some other thing, which would make for another traffic backup, like the blind leading the blind.

Now it's the 16th and we are going down the road as we have been now the third day. Tomorrow will be the same more miles. Today has been a rather good day nothing special. The weather started out a little cool for a change. Now this evening we are in an RV park and it is hot 86 degree with the wind blowing, thank goodness for the wind. With out the wind it could get very much hotter than it is.

Today is one of the days that starts out like it should, but things start to give out in the afternoon. First of things went bad when the wind started to give me a lot of trouble. The farther we went the wind was getting stronger, I saw one of those air socks and it was out strait, when it is out like that there is a meaning so that the planes know what to do when coming in for a landing. As the driver has to be on the feel that when the gust of wind of this nature you have to react or end up in the ditch. That is why when driving this large motor home with a small car behind it would be a large loss, I estimate that the value of this unit would be in the $ 100,000 or more. If you didn't know, we have awnings on both sides of the motor home. We were heading north and the wind was coming at us broadside making the coach sway and dance around. The wind got under the awning and spun or rolled it and sent it up in the air like a sail of a boat. I stopped along the road and the awning snapped down in its proper place. After we got an RV park for the night I checked the awning by pulling it out all the way and there wasn't any damage at all, what a relive that was. Retired and travelers when they choose this type of travel it a chance that something will go wrong, that's the risk you take. I guess this is enough for today the 17th of August 2005.

(Now today has been much better, no wind and better roads. We did go close to what I normally do when I did 365 miles and got into Billings Montana for the night. The weather was cool and cloudy so that made it better to drive in. Nothing unusual happened today.

August 19th 2005 @ 6:pm. Home again after 64 years. I left Ryegate, Montana after I had lost my job from the State of Montana when the job finished the crew was told that they could go out and get work any time some place else. They also told us that the Boeing Company in Seattle was looking for people to help build airplanes. And didn't take me long to put things together and take off with lock stock and barrel. As they say. I left from here on September 15th 1941 in a home made RV(they called them camp trailers) not a refined calling for the few people that were going that way. The one thing that there a few of these people that needed some place to live. In that day and age there were a lot of people out work, they would do anything to find a job, and that didn't pay very much.

Although, over the years I have made many trips to Montana to friends and relatives. This could be the last time for me, after all when you get to my age you never know when the good lord will call your number. I am 92 now and feel like 80years old. I had always said that I was going to live to be a 100.)

I wanted to make this trip to see my daughter and her family before it was too late. I am still driving a 33-foot motor home and towing a car behind the motor home, mainly in the event that we broke down we would have some transportation to get help.

Today was a slow day, we got started late. We went to the restaurant for hot cakes and met one of my family members just as we were ready to leave so we stayed to watch them eat. That didn't bother me, as we were very full after eating a short stack of hot cakes. Neither one of us cold eat all of that, I think it was 8" diameter. I didn't tell you that today is the 20th of August 2005 we only drove a little over 200 miles today. The weather was very good and it was much earlier driving. Well, we see how many miles we make tomorrow. That day has come and about to close. We put on 365 miles today that is a long ribbon of asphalt that made that roadway.

It as been a hot one today I think that it is 104 to day. You don't notice it while traveling but when you stop for anything then the heat hit you. The time I had a bad fitting on the propane tank that I had to get fixed or loose all of the propane. Then we would loose all the food in the refrigerator. At that time there wasn't any shade because there wasn't any in sight. This was way back in our travel times but I didn't feel that good working in the sun but it had to be done. It is amazing what you can do if you have to.

Zelda's Journal ------She was my first wife of 54 years. I had give the State of Washington my best for the 30 years I retired and was on the go soon after. We had been planning this for several years.

We were on the way to Chicago where we will visit one of Zelda's nieces. It's gong to take some time before we get that far. The first day out we made it to Lake Easton State Park, where we will stay the night, this was about a 150-mile trek. I didn't intend to make a lot of miles in a day, after all this is to be retirement time. We didn't have to get up to the alarm clock as I had been doing for the past 50 years. This type of travel will be some new life for us even though we have been a member of the club for four years we didn't get the time off work for any travel but just for a weekend and then back to work. As I continue this writing, I am going to try to insert what my wife Zelda had written in her journal that she had kept on every trip and mile we traveled. The only thing I will have a hard time reading the writing as she would do a lot of the time would write as we were going down the road. At time that would almost be impossible when some of the roads were very rough, partly because when pulling a trailer you do get somewhat of an extra shake. I am sure that some of those times she didn't write. Then when there was some thing to look at I am sure she took out time again from making any notes.

From her journal-, Sept. 4th left Olympia and camped at Easton State Park in the cascades a lovely place. Sept. 5, 1975 parked at Leo Geer's place in Moses Lake, Washington her brother's place and had dinner with them. Sept. 6 Parked at a KOA Park in Idaho in the mountains. Sept. 7 we were in Boulder, Montana. The next day we went to the school where her little brother Claude Geer was for the handicapped people Sept. 8, we camped at the Bozeman Hot Springs. Walter and Charlotte Cline visited with us that evening Then on September 9, we had Gertrude Cooper from the nursing home to our trailer for noon dinner. In the afternoon, we had some work done on the car and then we had to go in the pool, as she wanted to test a $ 35.00 swimming suit. We left the next day for Ryegate to stay for couple of weeks with my dad Roy Fiske. Then on Saturday we went to Billings to see Mavis & Carl Burg who were visiting Becky her sister also Dana & Warn Holmes were there and we all had dinner with them. The next day we went to have dinner with Evelyn & Floyd's. This is looking good we get a lot of meals as we move around the country. We were resting at Pops (Zelda would call him) in Ryegate. Ronald came in and we had a good visit in the yard. It was a lovely after noon. Pop made a meat loaf and I fried some eggplant that we didn't like. Then Mary & Gerry came to town in the evening. She didn't say how long the evening was but I am sure, when us kids get together, there is much to discuss. From here, we went to Lewistown to see Zelda's sister and family, that farm in the area of Danvers, Montana. When we get in this area there are so many relatives that it will take weeks to go any farther. That is all right with me after all I am retired and no job to go to. Now it is the 16th Of Sept. we arrived at 4:00 PM at Russell and Debbie Sliuka. That was as close to Zelda's sister's place that was up the road about mile but the roads were to rutted and large rocks that were in the way for a low car that I was pulling the trailer with. There was another thing we had to go over a cattle guard that was also built for trucks and tractors. These farmers live 30 miles from any other town and the town of Danvers was just grain elevator and a school. There was a train track that came in the get the grain when it came time to sell or ship out of the area. After we got the trailer set for living in we had the kids and all come out to greet us. Zelda writes that Jennifer was a sweet , loving little girl that is 4 months old. Lucille and Walter and us went into Lewistown had dinner and met Gerard and pug DeBuff(cousins) and waited for the train to come in from Boulder, Montana that was bring Claude our brother for a visit. It is raining tonight and early morning it is now 12:50 AM the 17th of September a good day. The men, Walter and Leonard were unloading material that had come in to build a shop and a storage area. Lucille, Debbie(Russell's wife) Claude and I visited, looking at pictures then getting a chicken dinner and all enjoyed the evening. With the rain, it prevents the outside work so we all went to Winifred, Montana to see the other brother and his family with a new baby and a new farm for them. Crops were all looking good. Sure hope that this holds out so the kids can get on their feet and start to live as good as expected of farmer's life on the farm can be. A farmer is biggest gambler in the world. There is one thing that makes them keep going is that they are working for them selves they are the boss. September 18, It rained all night and we got ready to move to the next place. We left for Ryegate and it stormed all the way to Harlowton, Montana. We had dinner in Ryegate café saw Helen Bettinger Fox. Then she writes that we saw the twins and David Capenters. How cute they were. Had a good chicken and dumpling dinner then talked with Pop for the evening and read some in my book. Just another day September 19, 1975 Zelda did the laundry and baked a bread pudding and then some sweet and sour meatballs. Then after dinner, she and I went to Harlowton to see some of her cousins Emerald Miller at Polly Riggs place. Emerald is in bad health with cancer, hope and faith sustains her. Had dinner with Polly. Then we visited for a while then we left for home. That is to my dads place where the trailer is that we call home now for some time. We didn't get home until 11:00 PM that is late for us to be out running around. Then the next day we went to dinner at the senior citizens in Ryegate had a very good meal and then met a lot of the old people that we hadn't seen in years. Mary Ellen Williams, Myrtle Bartz and Stella Sterling. Marie & Ronald came home with us then Marie cut and set Zelda's hair but had a very nice visit it is 10:30 PM now will study my Bible lesson and read a little before bedtime. The next day we got up and had our breakfast. While traveling we had a rule that we never did have a breakfast with the people that we were staying with. That way I could sleep in when ever I wanted to. Now it is September 21, Went to Evelyn and Floyd's place again. Visited for a while then went out to see Nick, Tex. And Ronald's. Ronald and Marie have done beautiful things to the old home place. We did miss the windmill. Ronald, Marie, Evelyn, Floyd, are such nice people. Of course, there will never be another Pop like our Pop. Zelda had cooked some steaks for Pop's dinner and prepared for the move to Billings tomorrow morning to where Evelyn lives. Evelyn gave Zelda a lovely Montana agate. I will have it set in a ring. Also, a comilla set - pin and ear rings of Mom Fiske's and agates for Leonard. He also got the coffee grinder, Old lantern and old churn. She gave some 15# or 20 pound of hamburger to Evelyn for the Senior Citizen Saturday noon dinner. We have been on the road for 18 days now and we have covered about 800 miles and visited about 50 relatives so far. Now we are leaving Ryegate and going to Billings Where we may find a valve that is needed on the Airstream trailer. We got a place to park at the KOA, RV camp grounds that is located on the Yellowstone River This will be the second time we have had to rent a place for the night. This is the way to go until some one says no we can't have you using our power and water. On the complete trip, we never did have any one turn us away. Every one was more then happy to have us. The one thing that I would do is help them at their farm work and Zelda would help in the kitchen. While here in Billings we had a couple of my cousins that came down to the park to see us. It was nice to see them and we had a great visit. They were Marie Fredrickson and her sister Katherine Schariff. They had welcomed us warmly. We are going on to Gillette, Wyoming tomorrow. My wife is saying she is tired of travel all ready, may be new country will help and get more interesting as we go from one place to the next. September 24, 1975 Will be leaving Billings in the morning and heading for Gillette. On the way, we stopped at the Custer's last stand Of Harden, Montana. She took pictures and sent some historical post cards to Dale, Cary, and Roy. Wyoming proved to be as I had pictured it from Zane Grey's books. Red hills, Mesquite and Cotton wood trees then the Bad Lands are all there. Stayed in the yard of Cleo's mechanic shop. Parked the trailer there and went to there house for dinner then visited for a while then went back trailer for the night but would leave in the morning for Sundance, Wyoming and found there was a KOA so we stayed there to see the Devils tower. If you haven't seen this, it is most spectacular Thing that I have ever seen it was worth the trip up there to see. They have a 11/2 mile walking path that goes all the way around it. One half mile diameter and 500 to 600 feet tall. It is a rock formation that the rocks that have fallen down are all in heptagon shape. On the backside of this rock there is, what is left a ladder that some one had built on the side of this shirr mass of stone. There were a lot of birds, animals and wild life there. Hears is where Zelda wants to go home. We came back to the park after having a good salmon dinner at Matea's restaurant lounge. When we got back to the trailer and found a flat tire. We just unhooked the car and went to the tower, didn't see what was wrong in the trailer if any. We found that the door of the refrigerator had come open on the trip today and things were tossed around pretty bad. Frozen meat fell out and broke the door at the bottom. This is the second time in these few days that she writes that she wanted to go home. I don't think that she told me how she felt. Fixed the flat and left camp in a wild wind wanted to visit some sights but storm too bad. Got just two miles from Wall drug, South Dakota and parked for several hours in a rest area as the wind was blowing so hard it wasn't save to be on the road. We had some thing to eat and then went on only to give up at the next KOA park just down the wind was getting to be rough. Hope the wind calms down by morning want to get to Sioux Falls, South Dakota. It is much like western Montana in scenery lot of farms and huge herds of cattle. She writes that she thinks the people are much friendlier then In Wyoming. Time does fly when you are having fun. It is now September the 27th 1975 and we are now leaving Sioux Falls, South Dakota. Here we parked at another KOA park that was close to the Airstream dealer here and they didn't have the valve that I need. Then the next morning we took out still going east. This day took us through the State of Minnesota We saw a lot of nice farm land with rolling hills, groups of trees. Zelda said it is boring traveling here. Today we camped just before crossing the Mississippi River. We stopped at a rest area and the State Patrol invited us to stay there as there wasn't a camp ground any where close to this area and it was getting late in the day. It was a lovely place with a lot of trees and color being this time of the year. They really had the fall colors, very much like the falls we have in

Washington. Here we could identify some of the trees like the Elm, Maple and Oak. We left Minnesota heading to Sparta, Wisconsin where Zelda had an older relative. We didn't have an address for them so when we got in town she went to find a telephone and that was hard to find. The town was an old town with very few businesses. After that hassle she did find the phone but when she got them on the phone they were both to hard of hearing that we didn't get to see them as we wasn't able to make them understand just what was going on. We got tired of trying to make a connection with her relatives here in Sparta so we went on down to Lafarge, Wisconsin. It was a nice drive down covering the central part of Wisconsin. The roads weren't the best. Heading to my cousin Keith and Madeline place that is about 10 miles north of Lafarge but it was impossible for me to figure out their road system. I will try and give some kind of a way this worked. They used the township and the range with some other numbers to mark where some would get their mail. With all of that, we drove all the way into Lafarge and found out that they were way out in the country. I was able to get close then I called ahead so they would meet me and I would follow them to the house. Then the roads were getting narrower as we got farther south and the bridges also got narrow to the point that they were a one-way traffic on them. They had a very nice place on a hillside and without any place to park the trailer except in the driveway. In order to get the trailer level we had to get a lot of wooden blocks and build up the lower side as I remember it took about a foot and half. After all of that, we had a great dinner with the family and few extra. We meet Don and Sally, Harry and Lynda, Zelda said she thought that Sally, Dons wife was very sweet. Keith's wife Madeline was a great skipping rope person and she was good at it as she was selling them for people to use as an exercise system. She sure took it to heart and she was very thin as it was. Zelda bought one but I don't thing she used it very long as I didn't see it around after we got home. Zelda also give some thought to how she felt about some of my family. Up to now, we were visiting mostly her family and she hadn't seen these people before. Keith and I had a good visit. She thinks that they are very busy with their own affairs however, Keith gave me the impression that he was a big wheel and likes it. I don't know how she came to that thinking. I may have told her about him when we were going to school. You could find Keith in the book and me out in the field. I was no match for him when it came to the books. Mater of fact we were with in a two month apart in age, I was the oldest of the clan. Keith was out of grade school three years before I could make it. Then when we were in High school, I was just coming in and he was going out. She writes that the boy's seemly successful. I will write to Sally and Don they are to me genuine good couple. I also liked Harry and Lynda very much, my kind of people. The family all came to have dinner at Keith's place and Zelda supplied the Washington grown beef roast. The next day we went to AlBurta's to have a dinner. AlBurta is another cousin of mine. And what a cook she was. I think that it was all from the farm to the table. After this big dinner, some of the crew walked off the dinner to climb a large hill that was on the place. It looked like I didn't go it looked too big for me to waste the time. She also wrote that, I wander why our ancestors left this for Dakota's and Montana. We had a short trip to go this time when we were to see one of Dad's sisters that lives in Viroqua, Wisconsin. We did wander around the hills and up and down to get there. We had to have some more directions. At Gathums, a lovely young man who graduated from the St Martins College in Lacey studied the map that Keith had given us and kindly directed us to Aunt Blanche's farm. She was alone now and here son-in-law was using the farm to have a milking dairy. What a dairy it was he had that barn so clean that it was better then a lot of homes. This was a lovely place when my uncle was alive and operating this place, they had a cheese factory for many years. We thought that this was one of the better places in the area even if it was very old. Zelda said that this is so lovely that she could come and stay for a week. Don is so neat the place is beautiful. Lucille his wife is lovely and Aunt Blanche is just like Minnie, Blanche's mother that lives in Montana. I want to go to bed as it is 12:45 and I want to be up in time to see Don do his chores it won't bother him or the cows. We were just about ready to leave and found that there was a flat tire on the trailer. It was a good place to have this flat. I removed the wheel and took it into Spring Green, Wisconsin to get it fixed. After getting it fixed it was late enough that we had lunch with Blanch, and Don and Lucille joined us. They are really very lovely people. Hope to meet them again. We never did get back there again. Now that we have the tire fixed and our lunch, it was time to head for Chicago. Even with the late start, we got to Chicago at 6:00 PM we arrived at Betty and Ron's place. We had some meat and cabbage balls for dinner and after dinner, we had a long visit into the evening. Betty was the daughter of Myrtle & Don Snyder, My brother-in-law and sister-in-law. The next day Betty took us all around Chicago to see the Sears building the largest in Town. Then down along the lake with its many boats. We then stopped at a Chinese restaurant where we were to meet Ron for lunch He was there and he had a couple of his associates with him. After lunch, we walked up State Street. In Chicago It wasn't the best place in town it was very noisy and it was ethnic, disheartening and displeased me. Then we looked at some of the residential areas that Ron was interested in buying. Then in the evening Ron went to his tennis practice so the girls Betty and Zelda had a good visit and talked a lot about Betty's mothers health, Eccentrics maybe this helped Betty to give here a since of mind. Betty is a wonderful girl and she could have been mine. I was wise enough to refuse. The lord works in mysteries ways his wonders to perform. We stayed at their place for several days parked in the driveway. Betty and Ron took us to the Terrace Inn for a dinner. Then again, there was also two of Ron's assistance joined us. I had my first taste of snails. The group at the table informed her they were very good eating. You should have seen her eyes when they brought the dish to her with a small pick to get the snail out of the shell. We were sure pampered and were taken to the nice places in town. After this great dinner, we went over to the dance area. I don't know haw it happened but I got roped into doing the bump with one of Ron's friends because they were good dancers. Zelda didn't say she got sick from eating those snails but she didn't say she was hungry either. Now that is Saturday October 4, 1975. Where is the time going. Here it is a month and we are having fun every bit of the way so far. We arrived at our daughters place in Highland, ILL at 5:00 PM and Sharon was there to greet us with a good welcome and a hug or two. Then the next day we tried to find a sewer line so that we could empty the tanks as need. The need was there just now when we were Chicago the tanks got filled up so when we were getting ready to leave I was checking over the maps and couldn't find any place discharge the tank. Zelda's niece said she would call the city hall they might know of a place. When she got hold of some one, she was informed that there wasn't any place in this area and then went on to inform her that the trailer that was parked in her drive way was illegal. In one of my travel books there was a place to empty that was about have way to where were going so that would work out just find. To get to this place was somewhat out of the way by about 50 miles. When we got to this place, they had trouble with the septic tank and had a machine in there at the time to replace the old one and there wasn't any way that we could have a place to dump the tanks. So when we got to Sharon and Jerry's place I had to do something soon. If you were ever in the area, there aren't any bushes to hide behind so I had to find this sewer line. It didn't take to long to find the line so I cut a hole in that and put in a fitting so that now we have all the services that we needed as we were going to stay with them for a long time but would be living in our trailer. Went to a lake for a picnic lunch. Sharon had taken cold slaw, tossed salad, had some deep fried chicken, and had a keg of beer the host and hostess were tavern owners. We spent the next day getting things set up, tying down the awning, and making a small place to sit under this awning. Then we had a hard time getting the trailer level. That country is almost flat but this area had a lot of slope when it comes to level this small trailer. Sharon and Jerry were both working so by the end of the day were snug as a bug ready to stay for two months. Zelda got up early to work out the colt. Seems that it is useless as there isn't any one really interested in him. She filled the water tank and picked Fly eggs off the colt. By the way, this area has the most bugs and flying insects that I have ever seen anywhere, I have been. The next day we went to Highland to get some service on the car but couldn't find a place. I will have to do some looking around at a later date. First things first. We have tried to find some repair parts for the trailer every place where could find some one that did this kind of work or had any parts so that I could do the job myself. We found that in St. Louis there was a dealer, we went over there, and he had every thing that I needed to make the repairs. As we were down town of St Louis, we went over to Sharon's office, met her boss, and had coffee with them. It was a very nice office and Sharon seems to like the work. Sharon is a good, fast and accurate in here work. On October 9th, Zelda wrapped package for her mother and also mailed a package to Livinda. Then did the usual things, cleaned Sharon's house and worked with the colt. After that, she did her own house then went to St. Jacob to see the place but there wasn't much to see. By October the 10th, she writes that Leonard is getting restless he and Jerry do not have much in common Leonard talked of moving on he feels we are imposing on Sharon & Jerry. Jerry told me I must keep him busy. Then on the eleventh, Jerry and 3 others hauled hay. Leonard, Sharon and Zelda went to town. Zelda said that she didn't spend anything no money, our banks still fouling up our paychecks. At least the statements are slow coming. Then Dottie, Sharon, Leonard and I went to St. Jacob for an auction. Jerry and Joe went fishing. Joe and Dottie are Jerry's aunt and uncle. On Sunday Jerry and Sharon took us to an auction house they were interesting. Had dinner in Trenton restaurant not good but bad. The next day we didn't have much to do so Zelda put up 24 pints of apple jell for Sharon. It is getting warm here now the temperature is reading 92 degree. Made some drapes for Sharon's front room and cleaned up the mess then Jerry fried some stakes for us. The next day I did Sharon's and my laundry, baked some cookies. With all of this going on it got in Jerry's hair, must begin living in our home and let them live in there's. Will start that Monday. Friday we are going to leave for a weekend in Kentucky. Will get the trailer off of the blocks and prepare for this trip we may go and see if there is some sightseeing, we could do. Must also take Sharon's tape recorder in for repair. I must realize there lives are there own and we must always be here when needed I have feeling Sharon wants us to stay. But wants us to stay out of the way. Zelda and I wasn't the kind that hang out in the bars or taverns, we were not drinkers. We always had a lot of work to do. I guess that when we got our first house in Seattle during World War 11. There were repairs to be done in and out of the house and the there was the outside to take care of when weather was good.

At this place there was a lot to do in the yard. When we purchased the place the black berries were coming in the back lean-to where the laundry was. The place was a nice place with a view of lake Washington. It also had three bed rooms, one down and three up stairs. I was working at the Boeing aircraft Company on the night shift so when I got home I would go to work on the floors that had to sand the floors where the dogs had left their marks. These were all oak flooring through the house.

Leonard and I went to see Tammy Wynette also Conway Twitty and Loretta Lynn. I was disappointed in all three including the belly dancing.

I will end this book with a few loughs, when we took a trip to England. Nether of us had been to this country. Each day we would write about what we thought about as we traveled in this country. There was no time that we talked to each other as to what we had thought about this trip, it was after we got back home from the trip that we made up a story that I had put on the computer. I looked into her journal. I decided to put into, each day I had labeled it like this, She Said and he said .

A Horrible trip to England

This is a translation from two dairies
Each writing was done each day

Winifred said DAY one:

October 8, 2000, don't everyone start that way? Left Sea -Tac 6:10 on a 747. At least 400 bodies & four infants that cried continually. We were so crowded. I couldn't reach my shoes to get my shoes off. Len was so good no complaint but I know he hated it.— So the air trip to Hawaii is off, no flights over five hours. It was hectic at Heathrow airport I had to laugh. Miles of dragging two suit cases. We were so tired and hungry and stiff. We finally got to our "Royal Court Room. It's so small we had to take turns standing up. Will take a picture. Stayed in bed for the next 14 hours no lunch, no dinner. Kay Clark had given me small pack of chocolate crackers. We would wake up use the bath room have a glass of water, some energy bars and a cracker and go the sleep again. We finally got to feeling good and went across the street to the basement for a breakfast of toast and coffee. Now we are going out and about.

Leonard said:

October 8, 2000 Today we got ready to take a trip to England. With every thing packed we had to wait for about 30 minutes for the air porter. At last he came and we were the only ones traveling from the Franke Tobey Jones retirement Home so there wasn't any trouble for the driver to get there on time.

The flight was on time and we left Sea-Tac at 5:30 PM starting the 91/2 hour ride to England. Arrived at Heathrow airport on schedule at 11:30 AM, now it is October 9,2000 After embarking we had to walk ,what seem to be miles before going through Customs. We were last getting off of the plane but when we go to the customs line up there was one of the attendants that saw us tugging along, both pulling our luggage, she broke the line and sent us through a separate line with out any delay. We thanked her as we were tired out for sure.

After getting on one of the fast trains we went out to Pattingham Junction where we had reserved a bed and breakfast place from the WEB. I wasn't sure where this place was in the England area or in what type of a neighbor hood or maybe the worst was a ghetto. When we got off of the train, we walked and walked and walked pulling out luggage behind us so decided to take a Cab After finding the cab place the line up was at least 300 feet to the end. I had almost gave up and would walk to the B&B but the line did move very fast. It was only 2 blocks from the train satiation and it was raining a little but it did cost us $2.00 so not bad for a couple of old people. After the cab left us off at the B&B we went to the door and it was closed and locked no one would answer the door. Thinking that we may have gone to the wrong door, I went all round the place and there wasn't any other door but when I got back Winifred had found a small note that directed us across the street to the office. Sure enough they had all our papers and was waiting for us to show. The place was called the Royal Court Apartments We must have looked worn out when the clerk gave us a nice small room but complete.

When we got settled into this place we had snacks of energy bars and went to bed at 2:30 PM getting up couple of times for bath room duties. Then about 2:00 AM we got up and had a little coffee and more snack bars then back to bed for an other session of sleep after 14 hours not to include the 9 1/2 hour flight. As I write this we are feeling good and rested.

Winifred said day four Oct.11:

Big day today. Early rise (8:AM) over to the dungeon for toast and coffee. Nice little walk to Paddington junction train station to catch bus for tours of London. Hopped off at the national gallery to see Van Gogh collection. The sun flowers were pitiful. I could have done better. I better get busy, but now I'm devoted to Sumi style and hope to buy a good brush in England. Back to today- At the gallery on the mezzanine we had a very wonderful lunch with steamed salmon on leek bed with very light sauce and a side of roasted red potato's and Italian assorted lettuce. With small slices of bread and sweat butter then on through the Gallery which is huge. We saw ½ of it.

Next came madame Troussade wax museum. Much cloister phobia and too many people. Could hardly get a clear view of exhibit, which were to real for comfort. The eyes would follow you. Pavarotti was my favorite so took his picture. Hopping on the bus just stayed put and did a sight seeing thing as the fee for the tower of London was really we passed it by. The traffic was really unbelievable buss coming within inch of each other yet all is well saw no accidents or rage. Which is good because no emergency vehicle could have gotten through. Got home in time to nap before dinner which we walked to a lovely place and again some thing special. We had a very tender chicken, sauteed onions, stuffed tomatoes and roasted potatoes. Again assorted lettuce all in meat juices with garlic bread with sweat butter. Policy to serve ½ cup of coffee and no refills and that is $ 4.00 we opted for nice cold water. A light rain started at dusk so we got slightly damp on fast walk back to the hotel. As we were both writing a journal. It's very quiet and peaceful. Early to bed for a good night sleep, so good night.

Leonard Said: October 10,11 2000

It is now the 10th of October. We have been here three nights so we move on to some place else. Then today the 11th of October we went on a buss tour, one of the red double decker, I didn't go on the top deck as the weather wasn't that nice. Then we went to the wax museum, there were so many people it was very difficult to see very much with out getting run over. Then we went into the famous Art museum and had noon lunch there, didn't get over fed but it was good for a good price. Then we got back on the buss and road around until we got to the Bed and breakfast place. Was tired and took a nap before going out to eat.

Winifred Said: October 12, 2000

Day five, Glad to leave and Glad to leave the Royal Court Hotel, it sure was a flea-bag but we lucked out with the Taxi. When we called him we were just going to go over to the train to go back to the airport to get the rental car. This taxi driver said that he had an other passenger going and he would take us to the rental place for $ 30.00. I guess you could call it trouble started right away with those crazy round-a-bouts, then driving on the wrong side of the road. Drivers were very rude and yelling and blowing their horns at every round-a-bout. I was really afraid for our life. About 4:00PM we finely got a terrific B&B food and service out of this world. Old Victorian so nice and clean. Lots of treasures. Dinner was exquisite, Salmon stake for me and trout for Leonard, served with sliced cucumbers, mashed potatoes, slivered carrots, fresh green beans poached cabbage satiated squash and pepper dinner rolls we ate it all. A lot of white and dark. I watched Good Will Hunting with Robin Williams and Mat Dillon, good movie and Leonard slept.

Leonard Said: October 12, 2000

Time seem to get away from you now it is the 12th of October the first day with a rental car. First we got a cab to take us to the train, but ended up making a deal with the cab driver. I had asked the driver what he wanted to take us to the airport were we had to pickup a rental car. The driver had an other person with him that was going to the airport. Then we got the ride for $ 30.00 and was delivered to the rental place. That was a good deal as we didn't have to carry our luggage any where here. Now come the time to check out the rental car, then they had upgraded us to a mid size car a new Ford. Now with the steering wheel on the wrong side and then to drive on the wrong side. We headed out from the airport going West then North East out of London driving until about 3:00PM and thought it time to look for a place to sleep. This is when the fun started. Soon after we left the highway we drove around and around past the Hotel we wanted. We couldn't find the entrance on the first time. What looked like an entrance looked like a dead end of a junk yard. Because of the round-a bouts we could see this Hotel but couldn't get there as we were on the inside and no one would let us out to the outside of the ring. We took the next exit then go lost. But after about three times we were close but not in a position to get on the front street. For about three hours we finely did get to this place. After the first time when I missed the driveway I went around the block thinking we would come back to the same place, but it didn't . We were lost again. The next time we did take a chance and got a nice room on the 2rd floor, had a good dinner and a good rest then in the morning we had a long English breakfast that was included in the price of the room for 55 lbs.(I don't know the exchange)

Winifred said: Friday October 13, 2000

Started off to Farmington & Laxfield. Met a nice couple that were Scottish at breakfast this morning by the name of Wendy & Nick. Found Framingham really typical English picture post card. Lost or left behind the camera so no picture. Ran into an old B&B cold and damp but nice. I have a doze of a cold. Located the Fiske ancestral Manor,. not too impressive but ancient. Beautiful large tile all around, Leonard is now talking to the owner, (Jackie) I am in the car sneezing and Etc. Hope Leonard is impressed with his linage? It is hard to impress him.

Found Framingham a very nice small village with a large school. Couldn't find a B&B and were desperate, saw a terrible - terrible one that, a prison would be better. The proprietor went to a great deal of trouble to find us a better place. She found a wonderful place around the corner, her name was Elizabeth Wright. A typical English town cottage, elegant & sweet and done so English. She fed us tea, later soup and later crumpets. Made us feel like home and we had the sitting room all to our selves. Leonard drank tea and liked it, kinda, bless his heart he read a long time as both of us got a good sleep. We did have a lunch at Crown Head Hotel. Had cheese sandwich and extra good corn soup very thick with corn. Leonard bought crakes, cookies, milk just in case

For breakfast we had a lovely spread in the formal dinning room. Fresh orange juice, fresh grape fruit, poached eggs, toast, ham, strong coffee, sweat butter, three jams and honey, coffee came in a plush pot. We live on the 2nd floor in a very cozy bed room bath too although ran out of hot water last night and my hair is a mess, who cares? We have slept a lot yet now Leonard has caught a mild cold. Walked through the village found a little Pub had soup and buns & ice cream. Visited the church and it's grave yard, has at least four "FISKE'S" Robert and William saved the castle for today and the wind was cold. Had a late tea and biscuits (cookies) Then Linda and John Fiske came for a nice visit, they were about 45 years of age. Their father is into genealogy but never been to the Fiske Manor that is only a short distance from where they live. I don't believe they are closely related. Maybe way back in the 13/ or 1400's very nice kids he is in the roofing and tile business. We had a lovely fire going coal and Elizabeth kept popping in to tend to the fire although two men present Price here is 50lb first night and 40 lb's there after quite a bargain, I'd say.

I would love to get rid of going to Ipswich and go to Bath by train and back to Heathrow. If not Ill just take a pill and go to sleep. I don't think Leonard feels good right now. One thing at the church which looks like a cathedrae. They had a small plot just for peoples ashes. It had 8 full dark green flowage roses. The beds were was about 8" inches higher then the grass. Inside the church had graves under the floor and carpets along the walk, Lovely pews etc. Equities was marvelous. I would have loved to hearlike the choir but forgot Sunday. Left our camera in Ipswitch called and they are to mail it to us. Must buy another today.

Leonard Said: October 13, 2000 Friday

Good old Friday the 13th the day was a good one. Winifred wasn't feeling very well and rode in the back seat of the car. We got to Framington about 10:00AM I started to ask questions about the Laxfield area where my folks were and the name started as it is today FISK(E). I have seen in some literature, that some spelling in year 1600 was ffisk or ffiska. The old place here in Lexfield, I found the place and the sign Stadhaugh Manor Farm that was in the bushes as there hadn't been much work done on the yard grounds. I did have some information as to what to look for and that was a weather vane that was on the top of the house with a cutting in the tail of the vane the numbers 1602, it was assumed to the be the year that the house was built. I had met the owner and she informed me that she was to busy at this time and to come back tomorrow for some more information at 11:00 AM. I talked to the new owner the next day. So we went looking for a place to sleep and found a nice working farm that had chickens. We had nice room but the bath room was down the hall in the opposite end of the house. It was a very nice widow that was trying to help out a little by renting out rooms and made a B&B out of the place.

Winifred said: October 14, 2000 Saturday

We are in framington today. Had a nice breakfast this morning Fresh orange juice, Compote of fresh pink grape fruit, home made bread, three different jams, sweet butter, the best poached eggs and pressure coffee all served beautifully in a formal dining room little cold though. My cold is bad but not so bad, Im not enjoying . Leonard has got it also. Lets pray he doesn't get liquid on his lungs. He is being gracious and kind. I did relieve the situation by taking a tranquilizer and lying in the back seat and keeping quiet. He said it really helped him. I don't know why, all I did was scream and holler all the time.

We are back in Bentley Towers Hotel and got room number one. Here they have excellent Sumi Art work which we will take copies of. They are a little extreme but very interesting. Will take picture for Phil and Andrea. For Dennic almost nothing, the famous English gardens a ill pest nothing spectacular at all He could have stayed home or got videos. As you can't get served after 2 and we weren't Hungary before . Have to wait till 6:30 or 7:00 for dinner. Leonard went out and picked up some nice spread cheese and biscuits crackers), dried apricots prunes lot of goodies like chocolate cookies and a quart of hole milk. He wouldn't admit to it being a picnic as we had no ants or flies or bees or dogs. Just finished another of Simon's wonderful dinners and his secret to a small moist chicken is to cook it on a rotisserie - massage a mix of olive oil, salt, pepper, all herbs and garlic for five minutes and honey , not too much of any thing.

Leonard said: October 14, 2000 Saturday

To start the day we had a great English style breakfast with bacon, ham, eggs, toast and cereals. After that we drove out to the Stadhough Manor farm to check out the place where the FISK(e) name was to start. The information that I got today was that this place was built in the early 1200's. The first size of this property was 115 acres. After about 800 years the land has been sold off, leaving about 2 acres with the building now. The house looks good on the outside and the inside looks as if they have made some resent upgrading as the new owner told me they have worked on bringing it as close to what the original place was like when it was built. The one date we had was 1602 a number that was on the weather vane that is mounted on top of the house. The new owners had to take down the weather vane to do some repairs and found out that the weather vane was built at the time of 1602 not when the house was built. We left, to head for Bath but we stopped in Framlington for lunch and ended up there for the night in a nice B&B but after a long time of trying to get a place to stay over night. The only hotel in town was filled up. Now what are we going to do, didn't what to go on and we didn't what to back track on these narrow roads. Here we are nothing to eat and the hotel was filled. Then Winifred went to clerk and wanted a place to rest her tired head for the night. This young lady was ver nice to send us to a pub. that had rooms above. They hed a room with twin beds. When wq looked at it was cold and damp and all of the others rooms were rented bu a bunch of young noisy boys. The lady was very good she understood and got on the phone and found a B&B just around the corner from the Pub. This place was on Double Street, she didn't just find the place but took us to the place and introduced us to this nice lady. This lady had a nice room with the bath just outside of our room. It seems that these places have cold rooms and baths. This place had a great parlor and a coal fire place. We sat around there the first evening and she brought us out some tea then some soup. She just couldn't do enough for us it seemed

I was reading a book that had been put on the side table in this parlor and there was a name of Fiske so I called them and this lady answered It was Lindy Fiske. I am Leonard Fiske and that we were traveling and wanted to have them come over and we could find out if we were related. They were very interesting but they didn't have any information that I thought would lead to us. They were some what younger then us but they hadn't got into who they were. In fact they hadn't heard of the place where our name started from. We talked for about 2 hours and I came to the conclusion that there was a large gap in our families even though we spell the names the same. There isn't any doubt that we are related then the lady at the breakfast looked up the name in the book Doomsday and found that the name dates back as far as1055 the first year the senses was taken.

Winifred said: October 17, 2000 Tue.

Both sick with colds but in good spirits. Had a nice breakfast, great eggs. Leonard re-read the end of our book, after which he slept and I walked up the hill to get cough medicine. We napped and talked then we both walked up the hill and bought Connie a beautiful cane- Onyx handle(?) And then we found, me a white colac sable cane. We found some darling trinkets for the folks back home. A little fake clock for Bill, a Mr & Mrs mouse for our table. Tiny basket for Betty, ring holder for Kay Clark, Dog for Irene. So far has spent very little money. It's 55lbs here including breakfast, dinner at 6:30 is 8 or 10 or 11 # and never was or is a better food. We talked about taking the train for some thing to do but Leonard didn't want to do that. The same day the train that we were thinking on taking crashed killing 4 and injuring 34 it was a mess. So he saved us from the crash we think. We know that we have been helped a long the horrible, horrible, horrible roads the drivers are simply crazy.

Leonard Said: October 15,2000 No report

Leonard Said: October 16, 2000

At 8:00AM we were served a great breakfast by the lady of the house. There was a large goblet of fresh grape fruit and plenty of toast, coffee and cold cereal. Winifred had two poached eggs with toast topped with jam. After breakfast I went down town to the corner store and purchased a throw-way camera as we had left ours in the room at Ipswich the Bentley Towers Hotel. I had called the to hold the camera for us to pick it up. About noon we arrived here at the Bentley Towers Hotel not only to get the camera but to stay while. By the time I got this far going through all of those crazy roundabouts. Plus getting lost several times.

Winifred Said: October 16 No report

Winifred Said: October 17 No report

Winifred Said: October 18, 2000 Wednesday

The train that we should have taken crashed and killed 4. Leonard wouldn't agree to go and I for once didn't argue we are still shaking. Just loafed around taking it easy. Was able to get a hold of the series "up stairs down stairs" and "My Fair Lady." Maybe I can get Dale to copy and give original for Christmas? (When we got home Winifred went to play these tapes and they were only good in England). I got so pooped Leonard had to rescue me in a Department store, I barley made it walking home as no taxi. We had a little sleep before another wonderful dinner. Half of which I will save for lunch tomorrow. We plan to do the museum. I have booked a 4 star Hotel Hilton for Saturday. Leonard still maintains he will drive. I'll simply take a pill and keep quiet. Weather cold, operating, Rain but not on us. Have secured 2 bulkhead seats for return trip. Looking forward to.

Leonard Said: October 17,2000 Tuesday

Now that I have this straightened out, I can get down to writing some thing with substance. It is about time for dinner or supper , what ever you want to call it here in England? Both of us have come down with a head cold so to day we took out time getting down to breakfast. All night I was doing a lot of coughing, that I didn't get much sleep. At 3:00AM I jabbed Winifred in the ribs so she would help me put up with this coughing. We had given some thought about taking a train to Scotland and return the same day, that would add up to 16 0r 18 hour day. At our age that would be a little to much. Then this after noon we heard that this train had an accident killing four and injuring 80 people. That could have been the same train that we were to be on. Some time it is better to change one's mind.

Walked up town from this B&B and did some resting. Just got back from the dining room where Winifred had Lamb chops and I had Salmon. These people here in England don't have start the evening meal until 7, 8, or 9:00 PM and we are use to 5:00PM supper and to bed by 8:00 PM, well it is after 8:00 PM now and I have take my shower yet, better get going.

Winifred didn't write October 18, 2000

Leonard said: October 18, 2000 Wednesday

I was thinking about how I could write these each day and not make it look like a calender. We took our medicine and went to bed. I must have been tired as I went to sleep soon after I had stopped reading to Winifred. I am sure she went to sleep soon as I started to read because I could tell she wouldn't last very long. We woke up rather early for some one that didn't have any thing to do. I had to wake up at 5:00AM and didn't need to be up until 7:30AM. Had a good breakfast then Winifred got one the phone called all the stores looking for to find some old video. She found what she wanted and we walked up town center about a mile then we looked up the store and got the videos. Then we went to get a bite to eat. We went up the street to where there was a restaurant That was located on the 2rd floor. I turned around to see that Winifred was almost to claps at the counter. She didn't as I got her up the escalator and in the restaurant got her a cup of water then I went around and found a good pizza. After that we went shopping to get a Sumi paint brush. The store we went to didn't know what we wee talking about. We both were getting tired by this time so we headed down the street for the next mile stopping each block to rest. This type of exercise , this old couple didn't need. When we were just getting over a cold. Winifred got to perspiring very much. I am sure this had been because she was a little weak yet from the cold she was just getting over. Also she had been busy calling to find the videos. After she had them in her hands she had a let down that had drained her body. We made it back to the Hotel that were are staying at for a few more days.

Winifred Said: October 19, 2000 Thursday

Had a long walk to Museum and got really tired but had a small gift shop[such great items. Bought nice little replica of Kent Pin also some Roman coins for Fiske. Finally had to take a cab back to Bentley Towers. So stayed and laid around all afternoon. For dinner Winifred had a filet of sole and five veggie. Leonard off his feed.

Leonard Said: October 19, 2000 Thursday

We started this day by sleeping in. I didn't know why a person would have to sleep in when they didn't do anything all day and didn't stay up late. After a late breakfast we started up town walking headed for the museum but before we got there my walking partner gave out but we did make it to the museum where she and I got a chance to rest for a while then took in a small part of the display. Winifred did find a few trinkets to take home. It had to be something from England. Why? Then we called a cab to go home to the Hotel. It only cost us three franks and it took about 5 minutes compared to us walking when it would have taken us an hour at least. After we got back to the Hotel we went right into doing the same thing, doing nothing. Winifred had saved some chicken, left over from dinner that was put into there refrigerator. When we got back it was noon and we aasked them for the chicken with some bread, it turned out to be a good meal but I ate to much as I have been doing. When we first landed in England we had trouble finding places to eat and had to go some times 12 to 16 hours with out eating.

We are counting the time when we can get back on that plane and head for the good old USA. Now we are waiting for the next meal. While we do this we are in our room bored to death. As I write this Winifred is on the bed watching TV a mystery. What else is there after the news keep on rolling the same thing over and over. The news that the train wreck was close to Pattington Station have found over 100 bad rails on the line. It had been found that a rail had broken after the engine and two cars had gone over it. That broken rail had separated the train in several parts and of twisted track was torn out. As I mentioned back on Tuesday there were people killed and injured. We had give a lot of thought about taking that train to Scotland and back. I thank God that for not letting us change out minds.

Today has been a great day sun shining all day with no rain or wind. The sun is going down as I look out the window, the closing of another day or the beginning of the time when people that work and play can take to the streets and the amusement houses of there desire.

Winifred: Said October 20, 2000

We took a cab to the art Gallery met Jack Haste, owner almost blind from WWW II Very personable and I am going to urge him to get his eyes examined not in 29 years has he. Art shop and Haste Gallery 3 great Coleman St. Ipswich, 1p4 2 AD, Suffolk, England UK.

Took a cab home, there sits the Bentley. We bought a apple turn over for Leonard and a cream puff for Winifred ate them as we strolled along the lane. Haven't tried my cane yet. Leonard has read the paper an a snooze then we better walk a bit so we can sleep tonight. Heading out for Hilton Hotel to be ready for Sunday 22 11:AM I will do my thing in he back seat, close my eyes head down and the mouth shut and Pray, pray, pray.

Leonard Said: October 20, 2000 Fri.

We have just got back from a stroll around the block and to see how some of the neighbors kept up their yards. Not much different then we have here, only I think most of are a lot smaller then our average size. We will be having dinner in about an hour and half. This will be our last dinner here in Ipswich England. We are feeling good today but not so good that we would want to gadabout on busses or train or anything else after that train wreck. I am not sure that I would ever go on one of the fast trains. The latest of the accident is , they found, not only 100 bad rails but now it is 150 that could cause an accident It seem that the rail department was saving money by not making all the repairs that they should.

Because of the episode yesterday of Winifred getting worn out, we took a cab from the Hotel to up town to buy a Sumi paint brush. She had called them and they said they had them and they had what she wanted. This time it was three pounds for the ride. The store had several of the kind of brushes she took the larger ones and then she just had to have a set of water colors and a color book. I don't know how much she spent but Winifred had to have something from England. We then took a cab back to the Hotel that cost us 3.80 pounds so what does this add up to, don't ask, All I know is that it adds up that makes the little brushes very expensive. Now she is sitting on the bed testing her new brushes and paints. She seem to be happy and that is what life is all about at our ages 80's. I looked over where it was very quite and saw that she was painting a bird with the new brushes. After getting back we rested for a while and she wrote some more cards to send home. This time we walked to the post office to mail these cards it wasn't that far so se made it without any problem getting back home. On our way back we saw this bakery that mouth watering samples in the window. It is getting to be 1:30 PM and hadn't had any lunch yet so we got one apple turnover and cream filled turn over for Winifred. We munched on these as we went down the street it sure did hit the spot. When we arrived the second trip we took a long nap. When I woke I thought we had to do something as we had rested so much I am sure we wouldn't sleep at night. We left the Hotel again and walked around couple of blocks and back to the Hotel because the streets go in every direction here in town that you had to be very carful you could end up in some other district after a couple of turns. I discovered that the first time that we came to town and was looking for this Hotel but had a hard time getting back to the same point. I went up what I thought was a standard block and it never did come back to this Roundabout. At this point I had been back in the same yard three times so I checked with a service station after following his directions I got in front of the Hotel but I was afraid to turn into this driveway as it looked like it wasn't he entrance any way. It appeared to be like a back yard of some home. I went around to the side street thinking the entrance was there. When I went just a short distance there wasn't any opening on this side street. I was now lost again. I went several blocks and came back to the front of the Hotel but I was on the other side and you couldn't cross over there. I thought I was doing something wrong by passing over the on coming traffic, it wasn't wrong but I parked the car and never used it for 5 days. We walked or took a cab.

Winifred Said October 21, 2000 Saturday

Worst day of my life. Just read Leonard's day, poor guy. But it showed what a great patience and fortitude he has. The roundabouts are simply terrible mainly the other drivers are so impatient and rude.
BUT WE ARE HOME SAFE AND SOMEWHAT SOUND.
NEVER AGAIN.

Leonard Said: October 21, 2000 Saturday

Now it is time for us to get moving to the London airport. We have a reservation at the Hilton Hotel that is close to the airport for the night so we would be close to the Heathrow Airport so we wouldn't miss the flight in the morning.

After breakfast it didn't take long to load the car and get going. We got out of town in a short time and drove about 30 miles to find out that we were going in the wrong direction. I had a feeling some thing wasn't right, when I didn't see any signs that said London on them. I had stopped a truck and they were the ones that had to think for a while before they told me we had to go back to the last roundabout and take a left lane. This roundabout was the one that was just four miles from where we were staying in Ispwich. Now I am headed in the right direction for a long time we stopped in at a petrol station to get more directions. Just as we were stopping we had a large truck pull in behind us. We got to talking with this driver and he offered to give us some help by us following him and he would give us a signal when we came the right turn off. It must have been at lest 10 miles before we got signal. That sure did help a lot as I don't think that I would have been able to see this road other wise. Now we got on the right road # M25 headed for the airport. After several miles I saw a sign that wasn't # 25 it was some small number. I drove around trying to find the correct carriage road # 25. I was given some directions that led me into the residential areas now that isn't right I should be on one of the motor ways not on the city streets. Stopped at a place for directions and went that way but no motor way yet. After several ,or of these stops I would get a different direction. Then I found a store keeper that gave a good direction that put me back on # 25 going the right way. After all of this driving for several hours I am back on the same corner that I started from # 25 going the right way. Now the sign said 30 miles to the airport. I followed the airport sign and took the exit it wasn't very long and I had lost the airport road again. Then I was in the area of the Hotel and we stated to look for this Hotel. When I stopped for more direction now to the Hotel they said that you could see it from here. As I left this place and to get back on the road we had to go around one of those crazy roundabouts then I got lost again. Now the time is getting dark and raining so I stopped in one of the delivery type of a place and they gave me good directions. We got to the Hilton just before dark. We got checked in and had a bite to eat and then went out to find the rental car place. We were told it was just a short ways to the rental place. We drove for an hour and saw a rental car sign return area, just what we needed What a relief that the shuttle took us back to the Hotel. This has got to be the longest day of my life, what is left of it.

When we arrived in Seattle we were last to get off and there was a wheelchair and a pusher to go with it. He took us to a special line to check out of customs. This pusher just brock line and let us go through ahead of a thousand people standing in line. This help isn't over yet, we still had to go through the metal detectors. Then after that we still had to go the claim our luggage so he took us there and watched for our baggage I think that we had some preference and got out of going through all the line time. When you think about it we were the first on the plane so the luggage would be the last to come off. We waited and watched and there wasn't any more baggage on the belts so we were sure that they had misplaced our bags. Then there was an announced that there was more luggage that hadn't been unloaded yet. Sure enough it was on this load. It wasn't over yet. That luggage had to go thorough the check area that was on the next floor where we pushed by the helper that knew just where to go when this happens and he also broke line again for us. Now we are getting closer to getting out of the airport to where can call for the air porter to take us home to Tacoma. We arrived at 6:00 PM worn out, we went right to bed for the next 12 hours after that nine hours of being in the air. I am ending this trip with a positive attitude that the flying should be left to the birds.

LET ME SAY THIS, I DON'T THINK I WILL FLY AGAIN IN MY LIFE TIME I hope that going to heaven isn't by plane.

This was taken 1967 at the club grounds for the Airstream members. Zelda and Leonard Fiske. We were married for 57 years.

Taken 1950 Charles 10 and Sharon 8 months and the dog that took 1st place in play ground dog show

1969 at the beach in Ocean Shores. Zelda Fiske with the dog and her daughter. That was a large log with roots and all that had washed up on the beach.

1990 snow storm here in Orting, Washington

Here is best of the clan, Author and his Son.

Building a garage on the side of the house

Just a little snow, this is hard to build when you have this kind of weather

The first stop was in the State Park, lake Easton. Now we are our way for a long trip. It turned out be six months and 15000 miles.

This is where I worked when I was in the
CCC program for boys 18 to 25 years of age.

We were payed $ 5.00 a month and then our folks
got $ 20.00 for them.
This is the Montana tree nursery That is located in
Hugan, Montana Where were one third of
the boys from the camp worked. I was one of them.

My daughter Sharon with her horse that she was riding
in the four H fair in Centraila, Washington 1966 she took
a red ribbon.

39

This is Charles Fiske when he
was five years old.
He was going to go in and take
the food from the crow, but he
changed his mind, as you can see.

This must be when I first staring to write, it is
so clean.

1962

'Leonard Sandy - Penny

This was taken in 1962, the author was caught sleeping
on the job. Some time you have to get some rest. This
was at the farm in Centralia, Washington

Fiske Ranch 1961

near Centralia Wash.

Leonard & Gilders home. Front

This is the Fiske ranch house, taken 1961 just out of
Centralia, Washington.

Leonard and Zelda Fiske taken in front of our
home in the Washington Land Yacht Harbor.

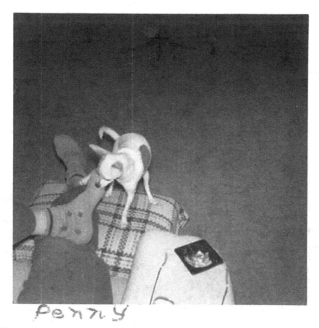

Penny

This is my little dog and she didn't like for me to
take up her space to take a nap.

My daughter three years old all
dressed up with out a place to go.
Isn't she cute as a bug.

Memorial day for my wife Zelda Fiske.
I did what I could with her Roses
from her garden.

This is the mess hall at the camp
Where the three hundred of us ate
And slept in tents.

This was taken 1994 after My wife of 57 years
I now have this new type of traveling. It was lonely
to be alone.

My little darling daughter doing a little dancing.

I am not sure how, I am going to look and say that
this old man is the one that is in the mirror every morning.
This old man, looks better in the bushes, no matter what.

This is the same number that is on the front of the trailer
I got when we joined the airstream trailer club in 1970
4338 that is thirty six years and I still have the same
number.

Had to throw this in to show that I didn't have
white hair all my life. Taken July 1933 when I
in the CCC

This is the clan that is living on the Pacific Not west
From the left is the Author next is my oldest grand son, in back Cary, and his
dad Charles to his right is Irene his wife, front of her is the Roy.

This isn't just a play thing, This is work when
you do this by your self

Just one of the Rallies that we went to. This was 1986
At long beach, Washington.

Part of my hobby, building a three wheel car.

The other picture is the same tree, with the same people that was in picture # 7

Isn't she pretty? That is my Wife Winifred,.
You thought it was the flowers, Didn't you.